The Gilded Edges of Shadow

A Paul Marzeky Mystery

Stefan J. Malecek, Ph.D.

DEDICATION

I want to dedicate this book to all of those who strive to express love, dedication and creativity through artistic pursuits of every sort. As Henry Miller once wrote in *Big Sur and the Oranges of Hieronymus Bosch:* "Whoever uses the spirit that is in him creatively is an artist. To make living itself an art, that is the goal."

And to all those who are working tirelessly to unravel the conundrums of the contemporary world and establish a more attuned and rhythmic relationship with Our True Mother, Earth. Love and generosity in service cannot fail.

ACKNOWLEDGEMENTS

Though I am a reclusive person, this book, like any literary pursuit, was not written in complete isolation.

If I were to name all of the influences that have contributed to my life and my writing, it would be a volume of its own. I would like to acknowledge the enduring friendship and brotherhood of Topher Allan, Harold Dick Junior, Darel Grothaus and Michael Hithe. And the continuing love and support from my dear friends Sharon Curtis and Tanya Stephenson; my spiritual guide Inaiya Ray; and my new friend and fellow author H. J. Samuel, whose recent book Just an Ordinary Girl I had the singular honor of editing and highly recommend.

And, as always, to my dear friend, technical advisor, and editorial assistant Andrea Scholz without whose astute assistance this book would not have reached readable form.

CHAPTER ONE
A Priori

San Francisco   Thursday December 13th, 2001

Paul had never before lost a client to suicide, especially not in such a dramatic fashion.

With lightning speed, Massimo plunged the super-sharp blade of the Cold Steel OSS™ knife into the superior thoracic aperture, the soft "vee" of his throat, the incision a bizarre tracheotomy. A huge gout of arterial blood, a glistening glissando, spurted like a malformed waterfall four feet out from his body, and splashed in a crimson wave breaking on the sidewalk. Massimo crumpled into a sodden heap wearing a strange, preternatural smile on his face, his glazed eyes looking at Paul as the life force forever left him.

"I keep seeing that knife!"

It had taken months of work to begin to repair the impact that reverberated from the ensuing flashbacks, often at inopportune moments, triggered by a wide variety of stimuli: large knives; the sight or smell of blood, that cupric blasphemy; ambulances, and sirens of any sort, Hospitals, he couldn't get near them. He especially repelled people who whined about their victimization, when he intuitively knew they were lying or seeking false-sympathy. Paul'd become withdrawn and reclusive, lost his taste even for his perambulations in Golden Gate Park and Muir Woods.

He had turned to Regina Wentworth, his consultant become therapist, and one of the most brilliant and empathic people he knew. She was five foot ten, proportionally well-built for her size with long legs. She routinely wore her waist-length brunette hair in a pony-tail, and preferred wool or cashmere pants with silk blouses and flat shoes.

"Did you have any sense that he was guilty?"

"No! I totally believed him! I even intervened with Phil McLaren and the cops!"

"He initially had an alibi, right?"

"His partner on the ambulance. He was a paramedic out of San Francisco General Hospital."

"And?"

"After repeated questioning, he remembered that Massimo had been away for about twenty minutes—and the cops proved he could have killed her and been back within the time period."

"Then why did he blame you?"

"He kept saying I was responsible for him being in the mess he was in!"

"What? Why was that?"

"When we first started working together, he told me he had gaps in his memory. He asked me to help him remember!"

"It's all your fault!"

Paul reacted, he had to admit, less-than-therapeutically.

"I'm not responsible for how you feel!"

"Not how I feel, bastardo. For getting me to remember!"

"Massimo, I did the very best I could for you!"

"But now I can't forget! I can't stop remembering!"

"What had gotten triggered in him that freaked him out so much?"

"This all started when he came in complaining of 'pains in his belly.' As we worked to locate the source—you know me, it's never strictly physical—he started complaining about the 'smell of cigar smoke.' We worked on it for two sessions, and he came in the next week after that telling me he had run into an old friend of his Uncle Tomassino's at Geno and Carlo's. He told me that as soon as he smelled the man's cigar smoke, he knew the man had sexually assaulted him twenty-five years ago at the old North Beach Playground. He was completely enraged and wanted to kill the man!"

"That doesn't make any sense!"

"He claimed it opened up his memory!"

"And?"

"I was to blame for helping him remember!"

"Let's get back to that original experience with the cigar smoke. What did you do?"

"I helped him release it therapeutically."

Paul had taken the precaution, when designing his office, of lining it with six inches of soundproofing insulation, enclosed by a false wall. His office was good for up to 10,000 decibels (the equivalent of a massive heavy-metal rock concert or being up close and personal with a Rolls Royce jet engine).

"I walked him through it. I encouraged him to allow his body to have its own way, to simply open his mouth and let his belly speak.

"UUUnnnnggh!"

"Louder, man! Let it go!"

"UUUUNNNNNGGGHHH!"

Massimo gripped his belly in great discomfort, but still restraining himself. Paul could empathically feel the horror of what lay there.

"Let your belly speak! Open it up!"

"AAAAAAAHHHHHHH!!!   FUCK!   GODDAMN! MOTHERFUCKER!"

"That's it! More!"

"YEAAAAAAAAAAH! FUCK! MOTHERFUCKER! FUCK YOU! FUCK YOU! FUCK YOU!"

"Fuck who, Massimo? Fuck who?"

"MY UNCLE'S FRIEND! HE HELD ME DOWN AND MASTURBATED ME!!"

"Go on! Tell him what you think!"

"LEAVE ME ALONE!! LEAVE ME ALONE! FUCK YOU! FUCK YOU! FUCK YOU!"

"More!"

"I WILL FUCKING KILL YOU!! DON'T FUCKING TOUCH ME!!"

"Now you got it! Give it to him!"

"FUCK YOUUUUUUUUUUUUUUU! FUCK YOU!"

With this last outburst, Massimo collapsed onto the floor sobbing, drool leaking from the corner of his mouth like a hydrophobic baby.

"Wow! You really trust yourself, don't you?" asked Regina.

"This is the kind of work that has freed me from the imprisonment of my childhood. It's the best way I know to help my clients get release."

"You don't use that technique with all of them, do you?"

"No, of course not. Different forms of it, depending on when the client is ready."

"Go on."

"I put a box of tissues and a glass of water near his right hand, and sat down to allow him as much time as he needed. The integration back into the present is one of the most important aspects of the work."

A few minutes, maybe ten, went by, before Massimo got up from the floor, and took a seat in the leather chair next to Paul's.

"I told my mother about it, and she didn't believe me." His voice was both sad and angry.

Paul nodded his head and gestured for the young man to continue. Massimo took a deep drink of water, and blew his nose several times, and then wiped his face.

"She told me to not 'to make waves.' Then she slapped me really hard when I started crying!"

Paul allowed the silence to speak for itself, then asked what had happened next.

"I remember deciding I could never trust her again."
"And?"

"I never trusted another woman...until Veronica."

Paul looked at him quietly and asked him how his body felt.

"My belly is tender, but I'm not cramping anymore. I...I've been so afraid she doesn't love me anymore!"

"Why?'

The younger man started sobbing again, then reached for another tissue, wiped his eyes, and looked imploringly at Paul.

"I don't know."

"I think you do. Come on. Tell me. I see it in your eyes."

"Veronica...reminds me of my mother!"

"Ah!"

"I've been freaking out ever since I ran into that asshole! I wanted to kill him!"

"And?"

"I wanted to kill Veronica too!"

"OK."

"I'm just so goddamn ashamed!"

"Of what happened?"

"No! I let the fucker get away with it!"

Paul could see that there was more and decided to wait patiently for it to tumble out.

"But when I saw him, he was just this bent-over old man with a three-toed walker!"

"So, what did you do with your shame and rage?"

"What do you mean?"

"It doesn't just go away. What happened to how you were feeling?"

"I'm not sure what you mean."

"OK. Did you go out and scream? Beat up a tree? Drive a hundred miles an hour?"

"No. I just...sort of kept it to myself."

"Did you share it with Veronica?"

"No. I was too ashamed!"

"And now?"

Massimo looked perplexed, the fine features of his face drawn as he looked distractedly up at the corner of the office ceiling.

"I wanted to tell her, but I'm afraid she won't believe me!"

"Like your Mom?"

"That sounds crazy!"

"I'm not saying you're crazy. Do you feel angry with her because she reminds you of your mother?"

"What'd you mean?"

"You had a sudden confrontation with someone from your past who harmed you. It brought up all of these feelings, and you couldn't follow through—you couldn't kill him, right?"

"Yeah."

"And your Mother shamed you further, right, when you told her?"

"Yeah. OK."

"Is there any connection? Between the past and the present?"

"OK! OK! What? You think I'm turning Veronica into my mother?"

"You said you were too embarrassed to tell Veronica. Just like with your mother!"

"I don't know. Maybe."

"When did things start going sour with the two of you?"

"Shit! Right about the same time!"

"It might help if you tell her, clearly and honestly."

"I want to go home and tell her everything!"

"How does your belly feel?"

He rubbed his stomach tenderly, and said, *"It's sore but it wants my sweetie to know all about me!"*

"Then that's exactly what you should do, if you feel complete for today."

"Thanks, Doc."

"No, congratulations! You had the courage to go into that deep, dark place, and recover yourself. Good job! Leave me a message tomorrow, tell me how you're feeling. OK?"

Regina took a deep breath as Paul said, "And now?"

"I'm cured, Regina!"

"Oh, stop!"

"No, seriously, I feel better. I'm so glad we talked. You've always been here for me when I've needed you."

"You're most welcome, Paul. Stay in touch."

CHAPTER TWO
Transition

San Francisco Wednesday January 2nd, 2002

Paul decided to coordinate his return organically with the start of the New Year. He was doing better. He had sorted through all of the new referrals and scheduled them during the next two weeks. Three previous clients had patiently awaited his return, and one of those he had referred to another therapist had decided to return. He had temporarily increased his daily workload to three two-hour appointments (from the usual two), but it would still leave him plenty time to write and contemplate—his first priority. He was feeling pretty proud of himself.

Until he met Henry Cameron Mortenson Junior.

It all started with him playing phone tag with Roxy Christianson, a woman therapist friend of Regina's in Los Altos. The two of them had been cross-referring clients with her for years. Roxy was retiring, closing her practice, and moving to Montana. One of her clients had requested a male therapist in The City. After exchanging phone pleasantries, she started immediately to present him.

"Whoa! Whoa! We've never talked, though I know your name from Regina! And you seem really intent on referring this case to me. Why now and why so fast?"

"Like I said, I'm retiring and want to make sure my clients all land with good therapists."

"And?"

"'And' what?"

"Why me? Why is there such a hurry? Why didn't you just fax me the info?"

"Regina tells me you're a really excellent therapist." He definitely heard her hedging.

"Is there something...strange about this client?"

"Not really 'strange' per se. This is just an unusual case, and I think you might find it intriguing. Plus, I figured you might turn me down. I am a little anxious."

"'Anxious?' You? Why?"

"I know you don't usually take clients who are on psych meds—"

"No! I never take clients on psych meds unless they are willing to titrate off under a physician's supervision."

"Henry, that's his name, Henry Mortenson Junior, takes a light dose of Trifluoperazine..."

"No way! Stelazine! How much?"

"Currently he is stable on 10 mg BID."

"When I worked the units, I always found Stelazine to be pretty effective for delusions. So, he's psychotic?"

"Not blatantly. Or dangerously. But he has a very

complex delusional system. I thought if you'd let me explain it a little, you might be intrigued."

"I just don't take anybody who is on psych drugs."

"I know, but I thought you might find this fellow interesting."

His every instinct was urging him to get off the phone ASAP, but she was a friend of Regina's so he asked the next logical questions.

"How long have you been seeing him?

"Just about a year."

"Does he have other psych history?"

"I have all of his records."

"How many times has he been hospitalized?"

"Three."

"When was the last time?"

"Two years ago. He really is very stable on Stelazine."

"And?"

"'And' what?"

"Why me?"

"To be totally honest with you, Paul, I've heard that you 'rant' about the government and conspiracy theories."

"And?"

"Henry has conspiracy theory on steroids."

"What does that mean?"

"Well to begin with, he believes the US Government has been interacting with alien races since Roswell in 1947, trading for advanced technology."

"Oh Jesus!"

"Don't bail on me yet!"

"What? There's more?"

"Oh, much more!"

"And because I happen to believe that there are incestuous ties between the 'G' and Big Business, you think I might like a delusional client? Thanks a lot!"

"Don't be offended. I just thought you might be intrigued!"

"Roxie, I think I'm going to have to pass."

"At least let me tell you the upside about this guy."

"Oh, this is going to be good!"

"He's private pay. He has beaucoup bucks."

CHAPTER THREE
Into the Fray

San Francisco Friday January 4th, 2002

Paul wasn't mercenary, padding his bills or adding a few extra minutes to push the session to the next fifteen-minute billing increment. (He remembered working in a Community Mental Health Agency and being reminded that he could always bill the next fifteen-minute segment if he went seven and a half minutes overtime). Neither was he what some people called a "Pollyanna" therapist, the type (often newly-minted) of therapist who takes on clients with no eye to how or whether they are able to pay, or their ability to enter into agreement with treatment goals, or how inappropriate they might be in terms of current mental health symptoms and/or drug and alcohol use. He never took an A & D client until he or she were at least a year clean and/or sober.

The potential client candidate was twenty-nine, lived at home with his father who traveled extensively. He had no driver's license so he was transported everywhere by a live-in chauffeur/bodyguard. He was purportedly "highly intelligent," but had limped through high school and was not working.

Hearing that the new "intriguing" client had a rich family that was willing to pay for his treatment was a substantial incentive for Paul to listen further (despite the fact that the man was taking psych meds). Paul had to admit too, that he was kind of fascinated by the fellow's delusional system. It seemed, in some ways, that he had stepped over that imaginary line between tortured disbelief and frank psychosis. Paul believed in the possibility of his own healing powers, and decided he might like to take a shot at this case.

"Tell me something. Actually, two things. What precipitated his getting hospitalized the last two times? And what's he like when he's not on meds? I assume that might be what led him to being psychiatrically incarcerated."

"You're right. He stops his meds because he says they make him feel 'Heavy, leaden' and he can't 'Think straight.' Claims they affect his vision, too. They 'Make everything foggy and off-center.'"

"From what I know of psychotropics, all of those things are considered to be 'side effects.' Which is bullshit. They are actual effects, but painted and sold as if it is natural that the client should have to suffer these weird brain symptoms so that he, or she, can look and act more 'acceptable,' or be more 'appropriate,' or whatever the psychiatric masters would have you believe!"

"Wow! You are just as advertised!"

"I always say that nothing ever really changes, it just gets more intense!"

"You certainly seem to have—gotten more intense!"

"We're not here to do my mental status! When was the last time he was off meds? For how long? And what symptoms did he exhibit when he was unmedicated?"

"You are intrigued!"

"Just asking the routine questions any clinician would when considering taking on a client."

"He gets manic when he stops his meds, almost frenzied. Tries to randomly proselytize people. He's been known to confront strangers loudly proclaiming his 'special understanding,' telling them that they are being 'mined by the aliens for their emotions!'"

"Two years ago, you said?"

"Yes."

"And his presentation?"

"As I described."

"Any history of violence?"

"Not really."

"What does that mean?"

"The first time he was hospitalized was age five, soon after his mother died. He was depressed and withdrawn; didn't speak for three months. Then ten years ago (age nineteen), he became...animated in his speechifying. Grabbed a woman's arm when she wouldn't listen. Claimed he was 'Trying to save her life.'"

"So, they put him on a hold for 72 hours. Then what?"

"Fourteen-day hold followed by a 180-day commitment

as danger to others. Eventually a civil commitment for two years, followed by the father getting a conservatorship."

"So, what exactly does he do these days?"

"Walks in Golden Gate Park a lot, mumbling to himself. Feeds the squirrels and pigeons. But he's clean and well-dressed, well fed. The police know him and don't bother him

too much. Plus, he has this… "bodyguard, Andrew is his name, follows him around, keeps him out of trouble."

"And the course of his treatment with you?"

"We made a contract that he would take his meds faithfully and see me once a week without fail."

"And? What direction have you taken with him? What techniques have you used? How well has he responded? Do you think he's making progress?"

"I usually do reality reorientation quite a bit. He's very delusional. He doesn't respond very well to CBT (Cognitive Behavioral Therapy) or to Motivational Interviewing (MI). He has trouble staying focused."

"Is he ADHD (Attention Deficit Hyperactivity Disorder)?"

"No. He's just manifestly delusional. He does not respond to any traditional treatment modalities."

"So, you, in effect, have spent the last year denying his perceived reality?"

Roxie was quiet for a moment, and sounded like if she had just witnessed a car wreck when she answered rather stiffly, "I guess you think I've been wasting my time?"

"And his! You can't get anywhere with a client who has a fixed delusional system by telling them that they're wrong!"

In Paul's estimation, it was perfectly in tune with the entire premise of corporate psychiatry. A bunch of highly educated White men long ago established parameters of health and illness. They used their power and privilege to impose their own standards, modeled on themselves as paragons of mental health, on the entire population through legal and government intervention!

"I did the best I could!"

"Why didn't you reach out to someone with more training?"

"It's...difficult. His father is his conservator. He's quite...testy!"

"So, you stayed within the accepted guidelines!"

He related to her a brief history of the rise of corporate psychiatry, the psychopharmaceutical industry that started when Menninger and Rockefeller approached Kennedy in 1962 to increase mental health funding for a more wide-spread use of neuroleptic chemicals.

In 1962, President Kennedy, influenced particularly by psychiatrist William Menninger, decided upon a new policy that "Relied primarily upon the new knowledge and new drugs...Which make it possible for most of the mentally ill to be successfully and quickly treated in their own communities." The great renegade psychiatrist Thomas Szasz observed that what followed was "The transfer of funding for psychiatric services from the states to the federal government, and the shift in legal-psychiatric fashions from long-term hospitalization to long-term drugging."

The massive expansion in government spending to underwrite the Community Mental Health Centers translated into a 6,800% increase in the cost of running them during the next 25 years. According to US Department of Health accounting, from $140 Million dollars in 1969 to $9.75 Billion in 1994. The national mental health budget during the same years rose from $3.2 Billion dollars to 33.1 Billion dollars—a 934% increase. Within the next five years, it rose to $80 Billion.

"Please Paul, I'm not ready for any of your rants right now! I'm trying to close my practice so I can be on my way to some peace and quiet in Montana!"

"It's not a 'rant,' Roxie. It's fact and public information."

"I don't really care. I've been a therapist for forty plus years, and I'm done. Burned out if you want the truth." Compassion burnout was a real diagnosis, applied to healthcare and social service workers when they have exceeded the limits of their ability to extend empathy to their clients.

Paul immediately felt empathetic. He decided he wouldn't mention the point he had been about to make about not denying a client's delusions and using the extended trust to get "underneath," as it were, the symptomatology to start the real healing work with the underlying traumatic materials.

"So, I guess I'm the perfect choice! Fresh and ready to go!"

Roxie sounded shocked.

"You mean you'll take him?"

"With two provisos. One is I get to meet him first, chat with him for...fifteen minutes in your office. You can introduce us."

"OK. And?"

"I want him to sign a Release of Information so I can talk with his MD prescriber openly and frankly about his meds and 'side effects.'"

"I'll set it up. How's next Monday morning at ten? That's his next scheduled appointment."

"Great! I don't have anybody until twelve."

CHAPTER FOUR
Burrowing In

San Francisco Monday January 7th, 2002

Paul was introduced to Henry and his presence was explained.

"Oh good! I was hoping to have a male therapist!"

They smiled at each other and shook hands. His eyes provoked an almost alien, sense, as if Paul were staring into the deepest of space.

At first glance, Henry looked like an ordinary well-to-do young man. His hair was cut long and well, reaching his shoulders. He was wearing a turquoise silk shirt with the sleeves rolled to his elbows, a pair of grey gabardine slacks with black Bruno Magli's on his feet. His energy felt strange too, as if the warp and woof of him were a piece of cloth that was being altered moment-by-moment. Paul made a note to himself to have him checked for neuromuscular disorders, as he exhibited a few facial tics and he had a small tremor in his left hand that Paul thought should be examined.

Paul unobtrusively sat through the entire of Henry's session with Roxie and made small notes about treatment approaches that he might most effectively use, questions that he wanted to ask (and didn't), and other observations of the client himself.

Henry was twenty-nine and lived in St. Francis Wood, an exclusive enclave in one of what were called The San Francisco Residence Parks, located in the westernmost neighborhoods. Inspired by the lofty ideals of the City Beautiful, and the Garden City movements, starting in 1905 with Presidio Terrace, there soon followed: St. Francis Wood, Sea Cliff, Lincoln Manor, West Clay Park, Forest Hill, Balboa Terrace, Ingleside Terraces, and Jordan Park. They all featured landscaped plots intended to replicate suburban living close to downtown. They had curving boulevards and lush landscaping, and neoclassical ornamentation such as pillars, gateways, public stairways, and sundials. There was no commercial activity allowed, and originally included racial covenants. These neighborhoods became especially popular after the '06 earthquake.

Paul imagined Henry as a cartooned version of himself, age-regressed to an emotional age of about five, almost like Tom Hanks in the film *Big*. Paul almost grinned at his own imagining, but kept as straight a face as possible and managed as friendly a look as possible. Roxie's entire approach seemed to be that of a doting auntie rather than a competent therapist—or perhaps he had given too much credit to her purported level of skill. Henry, for his part, acted very much like a distracted five-year old. Paul mused that Henry's expensive clothing looked as if a more mature adult had picked the items out for him to wear, as if he were masquerading or playing dress-up. Paul resisted saying anything, or intervening in any way. He had given his word he would not interfere, and he wouldn't, but still...

"Are you one of them?" he said looking at Paul with more curious eyes, taking Paul by surprise.

"I don't know who 'they' are."

"Oh, come on! They sent you to infiltrate my network!"

I looked at Roxie and shrugged my shoulders.

Clearly fighting her irritation as she smoothed the purse from her lips and the heat from her eyes, Roxie looked at me and said "Henry believes he is part of a network of those sent to Earth to resist the continuing trade of technology with aliens."

"You know it's true! I've been researching this for years! I have proof!"

She assumed a stern mien, her facial features subtly tightening as she admonished him.

"Henry, we've talked about this so many times! I know you believe what you are saying, but there is just no real objective evidence to support your opinions!"

The young man looked stricken, face twisted into a rictus. Then suddenly, he jumped up off the couch and took two threatening steps toward Roxie. Paul had jumped up as if he might have to intervene, but Henry stopped in his tracks, and spoke to her.

"You always tell me I'm wrong! Goddamn it! Can't I just be right once in a fucking while?"

Then he turned toward Paul.

"Do you think I'm crazy too?"

Paul took a deep breath and met Henry's eyes.

"I am not really sure what you mean by 'crazy,' but it does sound like you've got some pretty far out ideas. I'd like to explore them with you, if you want to do that."

A sudden confusion melted the younger man's face, as he staggered back to the couch, and sat down. He put his right hand to his face, and started to cry.

Paul got up, grabbed a box of tissues, and set them down near the young man's left hand, and then returned to his seat without a word.

Henry reached down and took a couple of the tissues without looking up. A few moments later he started to speak into the air, still refusing eye contact. Then he drew a deep breath, and made eye contact, addressing Paul

"I suppose you have a business card" he said in an affronted voice as Paul obligingly handed one over.

Henry held out his hand to shake, and then, in a very clear voice said, "I'd really like you to help me. Please."

Then he looked at Roxie very icily and said, "You never really did get me," and walked toward the door.

As he got there, he glanced over his shoulder.

"One of these days I'll be proven right, you know."

CHAPTER FIVE
The Next Round

San Francisco Tuesday January 8th, 2002

Shortly after his twelve o'clock client had left his office, his service called and told him that they had a "Henry Compton Mortenson, Senior" on the line, insisting to "talk to him immediately"—and what should she do?

Paul sighed. He'd been anticipating this. After all, the man was his client's conservator and one of the Bay Area's richest men. The only part of the equation that was missing was whether he would come at Paul with threats (implied or otherwise), or with money.

"Put him through please."

"Doctor Marzeky? Henry Compton Mortenson Senior here."

"Yes sir. How may I help you?"

"Henry Junior, well actually he's Henry the Third, had your card when he got home yesterday."

"Yes sir. I'm scheduled to see him this afternoon. He verbalized his wish."

"The thing of it is, I am Henry's conservator. Ever since his last hospitalization."

"Yes sir."

"Well, I just thought you should know."

"Yes sir."

"That's all you have to say? 'Yes sir?'"

"I'm simply affirming your information, sir."

"You could have at least called me before allowing that, that woman..."

"Roxie happens to be a highly regarded therapist, sir."

"She did not have the right to transfer Henry's care to you without my permission! I'm his conservator!"

"Respectfully, sir, Henry has the right to choose his own therapist."

"Well, dammit, why did you not call me first?"

"Sir, your son has a right to choose his own medical and psychiatric providers—even if you are conservator both of his person and his estate."

There was a long silence, punctuated only by the older man's heavy breathing.

"Are you really that smart, or did you research probate law?"

"Actually, I did a little investigation last night. I anticipated your calling."

"You did, did you?"

"Yes sir, I did."

"In that case, I'll just cut to the chase. How much?"

"How much what, sir?"

"How much is it going to take for you to drop my son from your caseload?"

"That sounds suspiciously like an attempt at bribery."

"No not at all. Simply a father's offer to allow his son to get the very best care possible."

"The very best money can buy?"

"If you must put it that way. How much?"

"You are not my client. Henry is. And until he tells me face-to-face that he wants to change treatment providers, I have an ethical obligation to stand by his decision."

"Oh please! 'Ethical obligation!'"

"That's correct, sir."

"How much are your ethics worth? Twenty thousand? Fifty?"

"My ethics are inviolate. No amount of money can change that."

"Oh, come on! Everyone has a price!"

"You may not understand this, sir, but I gave my word to Henry to try to help him."

"He's had dozens of therapists, psychiatrists,

psychologists. Not a goddamn one of them ever did a damn thing for him except bill me exorbitant amounts of money!"

"Perhaps if you'd have allowed him to stay in treatment with any one of them long enough, he might have gotten better, sir."

"The longer he stays, the more money it costs!"

"Excuse the presumption, sir, but I do believe that all of Henry's 'reasonable expenses,' including his therapy sessions, are reimbursable. At least that's what the court says."

"What do you mean?"

"Simply that my understanding is that whatever is spent in his favor is refunded to you from his estate, sir."

"I control his estate!"

"Yes sir, I understand that. I also understand that, though the exact number is not available through public records, Henry has a considerable estate that should easily be paying all of his bills and pays you a 'reasonable recompense' for doing so, sir."

"Whom have you been talking to? I'll feed his balls to my dogs!"

"The broad outlines are available in the public records. You just have to know where to look, sir."

"That's unethical!"

"No sir, just due diligence."

There was another long silence, followed by a smacking sound from Henry Senior, a sound Paul attributed to the older man's lips and throat having become dry secondary to the vitriolic bombast he had been broadcasting.

"So, you won't take my money. I don't suppose a call to the Psychology Board with an ethics complaint would scare you away either. Or a word with my friend, the Mayor."

"I don't scare easily, sir. One Hundred and First Airborne, Vietnam, 1968-1969."

"Why are you so damn determined to work with my son?"

"Because he asked me to help him, sir. And I gave my word that I would."

Stefan J. Malecek, Ph. D.

CHAPTER SIX
The Beat Goes On

San Francisco Tuesday January 8th, 2002

Henry arrived five minutes early for his two o'clock appointment. He was neatly dressed again, but seemed to have shaved rather hurriedly as there were small patches of bristles on his face that gave him the appearance of a Dalmatian. He was nervously chewing his fingernails and kept pulling his sleeves down as if he were unable to keep them in place and worried about his wrists being exposed.

"Henry, come on in."

His "chauffeur," a swarthy, well-dressed man in his early thirties by the name of Andrew, stood with Henry. When I very purposely asked him just to sit in the waiting room, he seemed as if he were going to disagree, but then he simply nodded and took a chair.

After Henry had seated himself in one of the two extremely comfortable leather-bound office chairs, Paul took the chair across from him on the other side of a small mahogany coffee table and waited. He had found it to be a very effective strategy, allowing the client to break the silence when he or she got uncomfortable enough to do so.

The quiet lasted but a few seconds before Henry, looking as if he might burst, explosively asked, "What are you doing? What do you want?"

"Henry, I volunteered to be your therapist because I thought I could help you. And you told me yesterday that you wanted me to be your therapist. Is that still true?"

Henry twitched, then progressed into full-blown shaking, his head moving anxiously from side to side. Then he stopped and blurted out, "You told me you weren't one of them. Is that true?"

"Who is 'them?'"

"You know. The ones working for what Eisenhower called the 'military industrial complex.' The ones trading technology with the aliens."

"Wow, Henry! You give me a lot to answer in one sentence. Let me break it down just a little bit."

"OK."

"First of all, I do not work for anyone else. I have a consultation therapist I work with once a week. She shares our confidentiality. I am a psychotherapist. This is my private practice. Everything that happens here stays here. OK?"

"OK," answered his client, more quietly and less agitated.

"I work for and with you. Only you. Total confidentiality. Unless you freely give permission in writing, I am neither allowed nor willing to share anything at all with anyone—including, even especially your father. Nothing at all."

"He's very powerful. He always gets what he wants!"

"I've had a conversation with him. And I repeat, I will not share anything we talk about unless you give me permission, of your own free will, in writing. I will absolutely tell him nothing. OK?"

"OK. I guess. You think I should give permission?"

"That is completely your choice."

"I don't want to! I don't want him to know what we talk about! He always tells me I'm 'full of shit,' and never wants to talk about anything that matters to me!"

"I know you really crave feedback. We all do, Henry."

"No one listens to me!"

"I imagine you can be kind of passionate about your beliefs!"

"Well, of course. Aren't you?"

"Of course. But it's often how ideas are presented."

"But people don't listen!"

"I'll be honest with you, Henry. I cannot say I believe what you're talking about, but I am willing to listen to you. I am willing to talk about anything you're experiencing, anything at all. But we have to make a deal."

"A deal? What kind of deal?"

"I will listen to anything you have to say. In return you

will listen to what I have to say, and you have to promise not to yell or scream at me when we are just talking. If, when we are in process, feelings come up, I will encourage you to express them in a safe and appropriate way. Can you agree to that?"

"I don't know! I'm so scared all the time! I'm always afraid somebody is going to..."

"What?"

"Are you sure you're not...one of them?"

"Absolutely."

"I never know who to trust."

"I'm not asking you to trust me with everything. Right now, I'm only asking that you believe I'm telling you the truth."

"OK. I can do that."

"And agree, as far as is possible right now, not to routinely start yelling and screaming."

Reluctantly, Henry agreed.

"No matter what your father wants, I will always do my very best for you. You're my client, not him."

"I want to try. I'm tired of being afraid all the time."

"OK."

"OK. I'll try it."

"And no violence, no matter how angry you get. You

can always tell me what you're feeling, any time. We can work through anything until you feel better."

"This is so different than Roxie. She was always trying to," here he made air quotes, "'reframe' what I wanted to talk about. She...I never really got to talk about what I really felt. She kept trying to put me in a box!"

"No boxes, though I might occasionally 'reframe' something you say. But I will always explain everything. And, I will never lie to you."

Henry's face mirrored a mix of depression with flashes of hope and fear. He looked up and replied, "I've had so many therapists! I... I'll... try to trust you!"

Paul just looked on and waited.

"But I just have these feelings! They're so strong!"

"Listen Henry, I promised to help you, and I will. It may take some time, but you just have to have a little faith in me right now—even if you don't have any faith in you. We'll get there."

CHAPTER SEVEN
Further Considerations

San Francisco Still Tuesday January 8th, 2002

Immediately after his session with Henry, Paul called Regina to discuss his initial session and affirm a regular consultation once a week.

"If it works for you, we could chat after his Friday sessions, say 5 PM."

Regina replied, "That would work for me, if we meet at my office."

Paul said, "OK. Excellent. Thanks!"

Regina considered, and then asked "How about today? Do have time or inclination to talk?"

"I must admit I'm concerned about the meds thing."

"I figured as much."

"I know we've talked about this before, but I don't consider so-called modern treatment to be much better than the methods of what I call the 'Dark Ages of Psychiatry'—confinement, isolation, chains and shackles, straightjackets, fire hoses, cold sheets, and insulin shock. All of these were supposed to be more barbarous than lobotomy and shock therapy."

"And now we've got brain damage, tardive dyskinesia, and Neuroleptic Malignant Syndrome." Regina was quite aware of all of the so-called "side effects."

"That's right!'"

"You probably saw a lot of that when you were working the units, I bet."

"And such a list it is! Akathisia; phenothiazine-induced Parkinsonism; acute extrapyramidal symptoms; oculogyric crisis; tardive dyskinesia; akinesia; anergia; daytime sedation; insomnia; excessive salivation; constipation; weight gain; all kinds of sexual difficulties; amenorrhea; even galactorrhea in men and women!"

Regina laughed. "Jesus! You're like a Bible of side-effects!"

"That's how they're sold, but they're actually real effects of the goddamn drugs!"

"I know. But what else?"

Paul knew he had been fed the perfect introduction, so he launched into one of his patented rants.

"Two other really good reasons. The industry standard for any psychotic condition has always been drugs first, and therapy next, if at all, and usually "medication management groups." I believe that approach really sucks. It is not designed to assist clients. The other thing is, very few therapists have ever attempted long term 'talk therapy' with delusional individuals. Insurance companies who don't want to pay for the very best and most humane treatment.

They've denounced it as 'heretical.' Then there's what I call the 'quasi-religious' approach some therapists take, who use religious doctrines or other pseudo-scientific dogma, to attempt to dissuade clients of their symptoms. It's just another twisted aspect of grandiosity."

"OK. I'm following you. But are you thinking of using that kind of approach?"

"There's a fellow named Bert Karon who wrote a book called *Psychotherapy: Treatment of Choice for Schizophrenia.* Bert was convinced that the therapeutic bond was the strongest asset anyone could create in therapy, even with someone immersed in the tangled garden of psychosis."

"What's the downside?"

"The client has to be able to pay for treatment. It's necessarily very intensive and expensive. Karon recommended at least twice a week, every week. But he achieved incredible results, even though his sample size was small. He was one of the few therapists who experimented with such a path. He participated in documented studies in Michigan and Illinois. Most insurance companies would not pay for what they would consider to be exorbitant fees."

"But if it works..."

"It's far more expedient to just give a client a prescription once a month during his or her fifteen minute "medication management session" than to slog through the traumatic artifacts of an individual's life, especially in our so called 'modern civilization.'"

"This is all so fascinating! Let's meet again on Friday!"

CHAPTER EIGHT
Mac

San Francisco Wednesday January 9th, 2002

Paul had initially been intimidated by Mcallan Dabesh, a tall, lanky Chiricahua fellow with sinewy muscles and a sardonic outlook. He was also the most wry and skeptical vet he had ever known, who was the most honest man he had ever known, brooking no bullshit from anyone—he had even refused to work the lights for the Rolling Stones in London because he did not like Mick Jagger!

Mac was a Marine—never an ex-Marine. Such a thing did not exist! He was destined to be a genuine cross-border, blackest of black ops, Force Recon raider. He was an indefatigable warrior. Mac had experienced that rare expanded Universe of combat very, very few had ever had, wherein unimaginable experiences were common and the surreal normative. He was the man with more combat experience than anyone Paul d ever known.

He was the only man to whom Paul had felt he could unburden his long-troubled heart of some of his own traumatic shit and grit from the 'Nam.

Paul had always severely underrated the value of his work in-country, counseling hundreds of combat vets in tents, bunkers, on berms, in jeeps, and deuce-and-a-halfs, and APCs, in bars, cars and cathouses, in the chaotic jangle of Battalion Aid. He had held them as they cried, screamed, and raged; as they spewed, lamented or repudiated their lives, the fucking gooks, their erstwhile commanders, the fucking government that had sent them there and betrayed them, that killed and maimed their friends and brothers, and just did not fucking care. He helped them reconcile their time in the bush, their presence in the fucking 'Nam, and even discussed the twisted essence of a forlorn and violent God.

Mac assured Paul that he might always carry vivid pictures stored in his hippocampus but that eventually the intense edge of brutal vibrancy would fade—until at some future point the gruesome pictures would have faded like old photographs. He'd comforted Paul by adding that except in rare or extreme circumstances, they would no longer trigger him.

Despite the vast experiential gulf that existed between them, "Mac" always treated Paul as an equal, as a brother and saluted Paul's heart from the very moment of their first meeting.

"Are you fucking crazy? You were there every single fucking day, listening to guys like me puke on you! And you don't think you're a combat vet?"

"I am so grateful!"

"Fuck that shit! We're brothers-in-arms—even if you are a fucking leg!" Mac frequently verbally jabbed at Paul for not having been airborne.

Paul's intuition prompted him, out of this tremendous reservoir of love and trust, that, after the trying day he'd had, he needed good company, a long walk, and a stiff drink. So, he called Mac, who immediately agreed and told Paul he would meet him with a pair of visiting Norwegian twin sisters at the venerable Spec's in North Beach.

Jesus! Mac was definitely a magnet for wild and exciting women, sisters, twins and exotic visitors! This was going to be fun!

Jennie and Jorrie were bright blonde-haired young women who spoke very little English. But they were vibrant, bubbly, blatantly alive—and genuinely excited to be meeting two handsome Americans!

Paul was immediately smitten, couldn't stop smiling at their exuberant faces and joyous laughter, even though he could only understand by inference a word here and there of what they were saying. Paul and Mac hugged and bumped fists as they took seats.

Both men fell into their usual banter and then, pretty much as per usual, started discussing the philosophy of war. It was a topic with which they were both only too well acquainted, one of the perennial topics they never bored of exploring.

Paul mentioned one of his favorite citation, though it was likely to have been apocryphal. "I read the other day that we've had 9000 wars in the last 3000 years!"

"Most of them unreported! Never will be!"

The two women seemed to be enjoying their own company, speaking in the native tongue. Paul and Mac continued their dialogue after ordering more drinks and having a moment of very-limited-English small talk with them.

"It's like your being in Laos. Your service is generally ignored, certainly not even recognized!"

Mac huffed. "I certainly do. But I don't really care. I didn't go for recognition."

"I know. I know."

Mac continued. "I went to keep my word. When my ancestors gave their word to defend this country, they meant it. It didn't matter if the U.S. Government never kept their word!"

"God, man! I don't know how you do it. I'd be so fucking pissed!"

"At this point, it really don't mean nothing!"

Paul laughed and they dapped. Then Paul continued.

"Most people expect wars to recur on a regular basis. They're so important for the predatory economy. If Big Business didn't own the government, we'd have a hell of a lot healthier country!"

"We had a healthy country until you fucking White people showed up!"

"The worst of it for me is that the system needs people to be emotionally crippled because they're more easily manipulated and coerced. It's better for business that has to be suppressed or denied in favor of business. Charlie Tart spoke to that. He said it is in the best interests of the cultural elites that one's 'normal' mind be not shadowed by too much introspection or insight. Rather, one is early conditioned by the media and governments to embrace what Gold called this traumatogenic, and dissociogenic model." Paul was always quick to point to the trauma-generating nature of societies that always led to the creation of a less than aware populace.

"Say more."

"It leaves most people as wounded children, either attempting to salve old wounds and only acting like real adults garnering status symbols or to become the "walking wounded," spending their lives struggling with poverty, substance abuse, or 'mental illness.'"

Both of the ladies' finger-waved as they got up to go to the bathroom.

"I know you and I are on different pages about these topics."

They'd been having this type of discussion for years, with Mac always standing for self-determinism and a Marine Corps "drive on" philosophy, whereas Paul was ever the therapist wanting to create strategies for healing and ameliorating the past, especially his own.

"One of the biggest differences is that your people always took great care of children from the moment of birth, even the Sunrise Ceremony to introduce the new child to Creator."

"No shit! The system always puts children second. That's why White society is so fucked up! Children end up taking care of their parents' needs, and they're currying the favor of politicians and government like Big Mommy and Daddy!"

"Amen, brother!"

When the two women returned, they were both wearing bright smiles, and seemed to be sharing some kind of private moment as they shared a deep look and sat down.

"It always involves triangulating children in unhealthy emotional bondage."

"It's what Demosthenes said two thousand years ago. "Nothing is easier than self-deceit. For what a man wishes, he also believes to be true."

"The whole advertising industry feeds off of that. Most people feel a lack of what I call "enoughness" and trying to get their needs met through external means. It aids and abets all of the desire-provoking, addictive mechanisms of this predatory society!"

After laughing their way through a couple of rounds, and joining in the raucous mix of conversation in Spec's (Paul noted at least half a dozen languages), they decided to go back to Mac's flat and continuing the party. Then Paul's cell phone rang. He checked the number and decided to ignore it.

"My service! Screw it! I deserve a day off!"

Moments later it rang again, and Paul decided to answer.

"If I don't answer, they won't stop calling. It might be urgent!"

"Paul Marzeky here!"

"Dr. Marzeky, it's Marcella at your service!"

"Hi, Marcella! What's up?"

"I have a Mr. Henry Compton Mortenson Senior on the phone. He insists on talking to you immediately."

Paul turned back to Mac and the ladies.

"Go on back to your place. I'll catch up. I have to take this."

"Dr. Marzeky."

Henry Compton Mortenson Senior here."

"Yes, sir."

"I wanted to apologize if I seemed too brusque or rude to you last time we spoke."

"No need to apologize, sir. I understand you're a man who is used to getting your own way."

"Thank you. I don't want to seem too...intrusive, but I'd like you to reconsider dropping my son as a client."

"Has he requested it?"

"No, he hasn't."

"Then why are you calling?"

Paul knew that, as his conservator, Senior had certain rights when acting in his son's interests. But Henry was not under an LPS Conservatorship (Lanterman-Petris-Short), an aspect of which was that he could be forced to take meds against his will. But in either case, his father as conservator could neither choose whom his therapist might be nor abjure the client's choice.

The Lanterman-Petris-Short Act of 1972 was passed to clarify involuntary psychiatric admissions. Briefly, it is a civil commitment in which an individual (who has legal representation) is committed involuntarily because of being a danger to self or others or is deemed grossly disabled and unable to provide for his or her well-being. It is an evidence-based, court-ordered commitment versus a privately requested placement.

A mental health conservatorship expires at the end of one year but may be renewed year-by-year if the treating medical team makes a formal request to the Probate Court to continue the conservatorship and the Judge determines it is necessary. The conservatee is entitled to a full evidentiary hearing and legal representation on the renewal petition as well.

"I was hoping you might have reconsidered. I am very good friends with Doctor Ronald Oakes Whitney. Do you know who he is?"

"Yes sir. He's Professor Emeritus of Psychiatry at UCSF

Medical Center."

"I was hoping you might be willing to refer Henry to him. He is a man of vast experience, far broader than your own. No offense meant."

"Sir, I know that Dr. Whitney is a psychiatrist, and he's deeply immersed in the medical model. As such he believes implicitly in using psychiatric medications. Henry has expressed a distinct aversion to such meds, both to me personally and exhibited by his stopping them every chance he gets."

"I'm his conservator! I think Dr. Whitney would be a far more appropriate treatment provider!"

"I must respectfully disagree, sir. In advocating for my client, and in keeping with his expressed wishes, I respectfully refuse to accept your recommendation."

"I'm really sorry to hear that. I'm his conservator, not you. I have a legal right to make certain decisions for him."

"Yes sir. But Henry has a right to choose his own therapist."

"We'll see about that."

By the time he got to Mac's place, events had proceeded without him, though they all quickly made him welcome as soon as he slid out of his clothes.

CHAPTER NINE
Rolling Along

San Francisco Friday, January 18th, 2002

"Henry, I'll tell you again. I will not report anything we say to your father unless you tell me you are planning to murder someone, or commit child or elder abuse. Is that clear?"

"Yes. Thank you."

"So, we're going to take some time to set up a treatment plan for you."

"Why?"

"Well, for one thing, I need it to be legal. But mainly because I use it to keep both of us on track, make sure we're working what is meaningful to you and to make sure you get what you want from our work."

"No one has ever asked me that before."

"Seriously?"

"Yes! Usually they just tell me what they have in mind, what they want me to do."

"Well, I really mean it. I'm pledged to help you. I can't do that unless we're on the same page. We need to talk about what you want."

"I want to expose the relationship between the U.S. Government and the alien visitors!"

"OK. OK. I've got that. But it's beyond my pay grade. Maybe we can concentrate on some goals that we can accomplish together."

"Like what? That's my main desire right now."

"How about relationships? Those with your father, others or friends?"

"Father and I do not get along too well. Actually, that's an understatement. I fucking hate him."

"That's pretty strong."

"He's an asshole!"

"OK. So, no hope there. How about getting off the conservatorship? Would that be a goal worth pursuing?"

"Are you serious? Hell yes!"

"OK. We'll make that the first goal. How do you think we might accomplish it?"

"Isn't that your job?"

"I can't do it without your help."

"What do I have to do?"

"We can talk about that. What do you think it would take to convince a judge? What do you think he might require?"

"I guess he'd have to think I wasn't crazy."

"OK. And what is the main impediment to that?"

"Mainly that I'm convinced that the 'G' is doing business with aliens—trading high technology materials and weaponry!"

"And what are we, they getting in return?"

"Are you sure you want to know?"

"Of course!"

"OK, let me give you a little history background."

"OK."

"Have you read *The Day After Roswell* by Colonel Phillip Corso?"

"No, but I've heard of it."

"OK. I'll make it easy for you. After the Roswell crash in 1947, there has been an enormous increase in inventions and innovations. More than 50% of all technology that exists now has been 'discovered' in the last fifty years."

"OK."

"Corso worked at the Foreign Materials Desk at the Pentagon for 21 years, in essence reverse engineering artifacts from the crash by giving them to private companies who then release them without anyone mentioning their provenance.

"OK."

"I've made a partial list. Are you interested?"

"Of course!"

He reached into the pocket of his jacket and produced a couple of tri-folded pages.

1947—Transistor: first general-purpose computer; Defibrillator; Supersonic aircraft; Acrylic paint; Magnetic particle clutch

1948—Cable television; Flying disc

1949 Radiocarbon dating; Atomic Clock

1951— Wetsuit; Stellarator (earliest controlled fusion device, containing and harnessing nuclear fusion of hydrogen at temperatures exceeding those at the Sun's surface)

1952—Barcode; Artificial heart

1953—WD-40; MASER; Crossed-Field Amplifier; Heart-lung machine

1954—Active noise control; Radar gun

1955—Nuclear submarine; Hard disk drive; TV Remote Control, Microwave Oven; Polio Vaccine; VELCRO

1956—Pacemaker (first successfully implanted in a human 1961); Industrial robot; Operating system (batch processing) Videotape; Fiberoptic cable

1957—Birth Control Pill; Laser; Gamma camera; Cryotron (using superconductivity)

1958—Commercial Jet Airliner; Laser Beam; Super Glue; Carbon fiber; Integrated circuit

1959—Float Glass; Fuel Cell Vehicle; Fusor; Weather satellite; Spandex

1960—Magnetic stripe card; Global navigation satellite system

1961—Cordless Tools; Industrial Robot; Carbon-Fiber Composites; Wearable computer; Biofeedback Machine

1962—Communications Satellite (Telstar); LEDs; Video Games; Computer Mouse; Communications satellite; Jet injector (of meds without needles)

1963—Geosynchronous satellite

1964—Unmanned Aerial Vehicles; Moog Synthesizer (a crucial step in developing audio technology for computers, cellphones and stereos); Plasma display; SQUID (Superconducting Quantum Interference Devices to measure extremely small magnetic fields based on superconducting loops)

1965—KEVLAR; Automatic Adaptive Equalizer (used on all computers); Cordless telephone; Compact Disc

1966—High-Yield Rice; Dynamic RAM; Thermo-sonic bonding

1967—Coronary Bypass Surgery; Calculator (hand-held)

1968—Virtual reality

1969—ARPANET; Smoke Detector; Charge-Coupled

Device (ultimately leading to the development of digital camera); ATMs; Lunar Module; Electromagnetic lock; Taser

1970—Wireless local area network

1971—Personal computer; Microprocessor; Floppy disk

1972—GPS; PET scanner; MRI

1973—Mobile phone; Recombinant DNA (allowing cloning and other genetic experiments)

1974—UPC; Scanning acoustic microscope (uses sound to measure)

1975 Digital camera; Ethernet

1976—Gore-Tex

1977—Human-powered aircraft; Personal Computer

1978—In-Vitro Fertilization; GPS; Genetic Engineering: (produce insulin, create vaccines, clone sheep, increase shelf life of tomatoes, manipulate human cells to prevent disease)

1979—Sony Walkman; Polar fleece

1981—Scanning Tunneling Microscope (launched the emerging era of nanotechnology); Space shuttle; Total internal reflection fluorescence microscope; Graphic User Interface

1983—Internet

1984—LCD projector; Pointing stick; Polymerase Chain Reaction (PCR), used as a template for replication; DNA Fingerprinting

1985—Polymerase Chain Reaction (makes millions of copies of a tiny scrap of DNA quickly and cheaply to do DNA fingerprinting, searching for trace amounts of HIV genetic code to diagnose infection)

1986—Atomic force microscope (to image, measure, and manipulate matter at the nanoscale); Stereolithography (leading to 3-D printers)

1987—Digital Micromirror Device: (silicon chip of up to two million hinged microscopic aluminum mirrors under digital control that tilt thousands of times per second in order to create an image by directing digital pulses through a projection lens and onto a television or movie theatre screen)

1988—Electron beam ion trap

1989—ZIP file format; Selective laser sintering (uses a high-power laser to fuse small particles of plastic, metal, ceramic, or glass powders into a mass representing a desired 3-dimensional object); Hypertext markup language" (HTML) to make Web pages and the "Uniform Resource Locator"

(URL) to identify where information is stored, leading to the creation of the World Wide Web

1991—Ant robotics (A special case of swarm robotics, utilizing simple and cheap robots with limited sensing and computational capabilities deployed in teams to take advantage of the resulting fault tolerance and parallelism)

1995—The first of a class of drugs called HIV Protease Inhibitors

1997—Hybrid-Electric Car

1998—Genetic Sequencing (leading to the Human Genome Project in 2001); MP3 Player

2002—IEEE 802.16 (a wireless metropolitan area network standard that functions like Wi-Fi on steroids).

Paul was overwhelmed, stupefied. He had no idea that Henry was so immersed in what he would call his "work."

"Henry, I am amazed!"

Though he did not speak, Henry's face reflected an admixture of fear, concern and humor.

"I have never seen this kind of...'evidence' before. It seems substantial, but isn't it possible that at least some of these were just discovered organically?"

"That's what they want you to think," Henry said with a half-smile.

"I just cannot figure out where you got all of this?"

Now there was concern.

"Father rarely leaves me any unguarded time except when I am on the Internet. He only freaks out if it's porn sites!"

Paul laughed, then sat up straighter in his chair.

"This is quite a list."

"I've been saying it for years: the U.S. Government is in

league with aliens. They're trading technology for mind-controlling the population. And the bloody-ass G-20 is nothing more than an opportunity for the so-called world leaders to discuss strategies for spreading their disease! Haven't you noticed the incredible increase in so called 'mental illness' since WWII? The Cold War was a perfect opportunity to create even more anxiety and worry."

"So?"

"They feed on it, negative energy. The more we create the better they like it."

CHAPTER TEN
Delving Deeper

San Francisco
Tuesday January 22nd, and Friday, January 25th, 2002

Henry showed up for his next appointment. His father had called again with more veiled (and less opaque) threats. Paul knew that what was most important was to establish himself as an anchor holding space for his potential sanity against the relentless tides of his father's constant carping and criticism.

Building trust was a delicate proposition, especially with an individual who was as damaged as Henry. Paul had to constantly reinforce what was good and right in him (called "joining") while at the same time carefully walking the line around his delusions (his own conspiracy theories having to take a back seat to Henry's, and never be mentioned) though Paul used them as deep background for better understanding the process.

Paul decided to start mapping Henry's symptoms as an outgrowth of trauma. It was not formal, but he had a design in his mind with lines and arrows connecting various aspects of Henry's presentation with events (remembered or otherwise) as they were presented—sometimes in a long rambling monologue, sometimes in a tearful breakdown that left him looking quiet and peaceful for just a moment.

Though his father was the conservator of Henry's estate, he could not plunder it at will, much as Paul suspected he might like to do. He was responsible for reporting, and having receipts for, any and all financial activities related to Henry's care. One positive aspect of this was that his bills (sent out faithfully every Friday afternoon) were paid by direct deposit to his account within three days. So far, his father was cooperating.

"Wow, Henry. I must admit that there may be more here than I can comprehend easily. Why don't you take me through this step-by-step?"

"You really mean it?"

"Of course. Why else might I have asked?"

"I guess there's always the possibility that you might be helping my father."

"But why, Henry? Why?"

"He has a lot of money. He's bought off my therapists before. Well, of course, he picked them."

Paul sighed and sat back in his chair for a moment then took a deep breath and made eye contact.

"That may be, but he's not buying me."

"I think I'm beginning to trust you...a little bit."

"It seems maybe that you have been neglected, maybe even abused, for many years. I have no doubt about how intelligent you are. Have you ever taken an IQ test?"

"No. Father thinks I'm a dumb shit!"

"Would you like to get tested?" Paul believed that it could strongly influence some positive self-feeling in the young man.

"I don't know. Maybe. I get nervous when I take tests."

"We'll make it easy. You can do the test here, and although I won't be able to help you with it, I'll be here in case you get too 'nervous.'"

"I don't know. Maybe. Can I think about it until next time when we meet?"

"Absolutely."

"So. Have you been practicing your homework?"

Paul had taught him a simple breathing exercise that was actually a shortened version of a technique he would hopefully get to share with Henry later on down the road to use any time he got anxious. It was one of his treatment goals.

"It takes maybe three seconds, but it does require that you concentrate."

"OK."

"If you're alone or feel safe to do so, close your eyes. Then breathe in through your nose, pushing your belly out. Then breathe out as if you were breathing out the bottoms of your feet, releasing all of your fear and anxiety into Mother Earth."

"That's it?"

"It's a start."

"Then what?"

"Do another one. Breathe until you feel more relaxed and comfortable."

"I did it a couple of times. It felt weird."

"'Weird' how?"

"I don't know. I guess I'm just not used to being quiet."

"Got it."

The only other burning desire he had was to get off his conservatorship. He agreed it should go on his Treatment Plan, as long as Paul agreed to keep it confidential (password protected on his computer). Henry Senior could legitimately request a copy as proof of work done in his son's name, but he had not yet done so.

Henry started to babble, manically filling the atmosphere with his fear and anxiety. It seemed that this was his first line of defense. It both alienated others and to defended his fragile self (especially useful when he got floridly paranoid and delusional).

Paul reached out and placed his hand lightly on Henry's forearm. The touch was sufficient to stop the mildly pressured speech, and Henry looked into Paul's eyes.

"It's me, Henry. You don't have to be afraid. We can practice here today. OK?"

The younger man looked uncomprehending at first, then flashed a wisp of a smile and nodded.

"So, do you need me to run through the instructions again or tell you why it is important, or both?"

"Please." Paul was surprised. He was expecting a somewhat less appropriate response.

"OK. Here goes."

"Practice makes perfect," Paul explained. "Henry, you build success by creating success. You never really learned self-soothing as a child. So, you have to learn now. Once you can do that, I'll teach you how to go deeper, get quieter. It will help you to be more comfortable in the world. It'll really help when you talk to the judge."

Henry's eyes cleared momentarily, a phenomenon that had happened occasionally during their sessions. Paul did the exercise himself, held his breath for just the slightest moment then breathed out slowly and completely through his nose. He felt instant delight, briefly immersed in the enveloping silence. Then he opened his eyes.

Henry was staring at him, transfixed.

"See? I can go there with just one breath because I've had a lot of practice. Let's try it together, OK?"

Paul could feel Henry's apprehension radiating off of him, but he closed his eyes again. Paul proceeded to breathe again, ignoring Henry. He knew he had to model for the young man. No other way would work. Building trust with him and modeling safety for him were the primary keys that could eventually build to developing real healing and changing his life forever.

Paul took several additional deep breaths and then opened his eyes to a fading golden glow. Henry was staring at him in wonder.

"So, how do you feel?"

"I...I'm not sure. Feels weird. But...nice."

"Good! Excellent! Now this next week I want you to practice taking just one breath every single time you feel angry or upset. You can keep your eyes open if it's too embarrassing, OK?"

Henry simply nodded his head.

"We'll do this again at the end of the session, too. OK?"

"OK."

Henry had brought in a list of triggers, anything that had a negative effect on him, troubled or set him off. It was pretty extensive. Henry had indicated that some of them "made him" feel small, intimidated, or gave rise to his wanting to push others away. The list included:

> Barking dogs, screaming children, spider webs, angry voices, loud voices, intrusive people, yelling, bad breath, cloying perfumes, body odor, ammonia, stale beer breath, bubble gum on shoes, rotting fish, crying children, telemarketers, constipation, people touching him, being on the bus, closets, small elevators, confinement, old people smells, women,

people blocking him, smell of excrement and caves.

The list grew every week the more Henry trusted him, even though Henry still had bursts of rage about the world-at-large and his father in particular. Paul always listened respectfully and encouraged him to express himself freely during his sessions. Henry grew less and less intimidated and afraid of his father's finding out. Paul reassured him frequently of client-therapist confidentiality, a privilege only Henry could break, if he chose; and that Paul would only do that if served a court order (not a subpoena) or with Henry's expressed written permission.

When Henry mentioned how 'confined' he felt living in his father's house, Paul decided to step into that particular minefield.

"This is really serious. I...he...could make it really bad for me, if he found out I told."

"Who is 'he'?"

"Father."

"Ah. OK. I do not tell him anything we talk about."

Paul didn't tell Henry about his father's twice, even thrice, weekly phone calls, demanding information or continuing to dissuade him from being Henry Junior's therapist.

"He...I...don't really get a lot of freedom."

"What does that mean?"

"He always tells me that everything he does is for my

own good."

Paul shook his head and waved the fingers of his left hand in a "tell me more" gesture.

"I...never get to go anywhere by myself."

"What about Golden Gate Park? I was told you take walks there almost every day."

"I don't get to go alone."

"What do you mean?"

"Anthony is there with me the whole time."

"He walks with you?"

"Usually five feet behind. And one of the other guys drives one of the house cars along the road not too far away."

"Have you asked your father to stop it?"

"He says I might hurt myself or get mugged; that it's for my own protection."

Paul sat quietly digesting this, and then asked, "How does that feel?"

Henry's face froze, a mask of fear and uncertainty. Then he slammed his right hand hard onto the arm of his chair, and then half-rose, face showing a depth of emotion Paul had never seen.

"I fucking hate it!"

Paul jerked back slightly and to his right, surprised but

not shocked. Then just as suddenly as the heart of the man appeared about to open, his face slammed shut. Paul knew that he had just seen one of the hidden masks Henry had worn to endure the life he'd lived. He wanted to offer advice, but steeled himself to be professionally proper.

"Wow! I can see that!"

Henry relaxed further when he was not censured or rebuked, and smiled wanly. Then he opened another, safer, line of monologue.

"Of course, he's just doing his job as a part of the global hierarchy. He's not supposed to allow anyone to feel any sense of autonomy. Their job is to farm human emotion. They only want shit and fear and chaos."

Paul shifted mentally to get in step with the new dance his client had decided to orchestrate. Or rather, the old one he usually hid. But he decided to push a little and see if he could elicit more of the hidden affect.

"Henry, would you be willing to tell me about being 'confined'? It seems to be a really hot topic."

Henry looked into his eyes deeply, searching for something Paul couldn't name. Then he answered.

"It's...way more than just that. Father insists that Andrew pick out my clothes and make sure I take a shower every day, even if I don't want to. And I never get to go to any parties...at least not anymore."

"'Anymore?'"

Now he cast his eyes downward, and Paul felt as if he

were about to cry.

"I had a girlfriend once. A long time ago."

"And?"

"I was really happy with her. We met in the hospital and decided to stay in touch when we got out."

"And?"

"That was before Father decided I need to be 'monitored' all the time...when he was in New York a lot."

"What happened?"

"We ran away together. Went to Europe—to Paris and then to Florence. She was an artist. We were happy."

Henry sat in his disconsolate position, face clouded and downcast, lost in reverie.

Paul sat quietly and allowed the silence to serve him.

"I...we...spent a lot of money. I bought her clothes and jewelry. We went to the theater and five-star restaurants. We were in love."

"And?"

"It's my money! Grandfather left it for me! And Father won't let me spend it!"

"Tell me more."

"Father hired detectives. They found us. Her parents flew in and took her away. I never saw her again."

'And?"

"After that Father took me to court. Now I can't access my money any more. I have to do anything he says, including having 'protection' all the time!"

Having said this, he looked up sharply, and asked in a voice fraught with fear and tension.

"Why is Father allowing me to come here? Is he paying you to report to him?"

"Yes, Henry, he is paying my fees. I am your therapist and will be as long as you say so. I do not tell anybody, especially not your father, anything about our sessions. That's called confidentiality. It is my obligation. I cannot reveal what you tell me here unless you agree in writing, or unless your father gets a court order. But he has to have a very good reason, and there is a legal proceeding."

"Oh. OK. Sorry. You told me that before, didn't you?"

"You have what is called 'privilege' which gives you the right to exclude anything you have told me in sessions from a legal proceeding. These two rights hold even if we were not actively working together."

"Sorry. Sorry. I'm just...kind of dumb sometimes."

"Nothing to be 'sorry' about. You can ask me about anything, any time. I just want you to feel safe. You have sanctuary here that you don't have anywhere else."

"OK. Thanks."

"Really good work today! I am proud of you for

opening up. I know it was hard for you."

Henry's face lit with the first real smile Paul had seen.

"Let's try seven breaths together before we close for today. I'll count and then make a little 'Om' sound at the end."

CHAPTER ELEVEN
The Continuing Unfoldment

San Francisco Late Afternoon January 25th, 2002

He truly enjoyed Regina's company, even though their relationship was professional and he paid for it. Or ultimately, Henry did. It was a legitimate business expense. Besides, it was worth it.

"I probably shouldn't have accepted him in the first place because of the meds."

"I know. You're always so adamant about symptoms being trauma-driven and not the result of organic injury or the "chemical imbalance" so widely-touted by the psychopharmaceutical industry. It encourages lazy thinking. It's really no more than official brainwashing mediated through the media, a kind of mind control shaping 'public opinion' and selling the disinformation, using the advertising industry to promote it just to make more money."

"You're beginning to sound like me!" Paul laughed.

"I probably shouldn't have accepted his diagnosis at first blush."

"The paperwork certainly seemed to be in order," she

said, glancing through the packet he had brought. "I probably wouldn't have questioned it either."

"He seemed so preoccupied. His theories, his delusions about the alien interchange. It's sort of logical."

"Isn't that one of the prime characteristics of a delusional system—logically consistent, but with a flawed premise?"

"But having accepted the diagnosis, even provisionally, I allowed myself to accept him, even with the meds."

"But why?"

"I thought of him as kind of a challenge."

"That's all?"

"No. I must admit that a guarantee of two sessions a week, plus our supervision, looked really good."

"And?"

"I admit that I harbor hopes of getting him off meds and see what he looks like without them."

"OK."

"I mean, when was the last time anyone had ever examined him when he wasn't under the influence? I'm going to review Henry's medical records again and see for myself how 'they' arrived at his diagnosis."

"He does seem delusional, at least superficially."

"I may end up not disputing the fact that he's

delusional. I just don't believe he 'needs to be on meds the rest of his life.'"

"I hate that kind of death sentence, too."

"I'm considering the possibility that he might be a Paranoid Personality more than a Delusional Disorder NOS (Not Otherwise Specified). There's a significant element of social anxiety, maybe even Generalized Anxiety Disorder (GAS)—especially living with his father's incredible rigidity. He's so authoritarian, even fascist. I cannot understand how he's managed it."

"I notice that you've included a provision in the Treatment Plan that he intends to get off the conservatorship."

"That's right. It's what Henry wants and I want to support him. But that's a very long-term goal. He's nowhere near ready to tackle life on his own."

"Are you seriously considering taking on his father in court?"

"At some point, perhaps. Any competent practitioner would shred him on the stand."

Paul knew it would be tough getting him off meds, especially with his father actively encouraging Henry to keep religiously taking the toxic chemicals.

Regina asked, "Does he really believe that access to his money will fix his life?"

Then she laughed. "Oh my God! He is delusional!"

Regina responded as her most cynical self. "Just like most of the population. Most people think that the only thing wrong with their lives is a lack of financial resources."

"That's true. I remember the first psychiatrist I worked with. He used to say that he thought most people were psychotic. It took me twenty years to understand that."

"'Psychotic' in the sense of delusional?" she asked.

"Exactly! The obsessive greed and the need for acquisition are at the very heart of out warped society."

"So, you're saying that the entire society is delusional?"

"Absolutely! No question!"

"I would be remiss if I didn't ask. What about your own obsessions with government machination and the conspiracy between the 'G' and Big Business?"

"You've heard me rant about it enough times. Regina, do you really think I qualify as 'delusional?'"

"I think the real difference is in intensity."

"Are delusions more intense in content and presentation than obsessions?"

"They're both fixed belief systems. Who's to decide where one crosses the line between obsession and delusion?" Paul asked with a slight undertone of disrespect for the "Fathers of Modern Psychiatry."

"Is obsession psychotic because of the intensity? You know the phrase 'the psychotic intensity of childhood?'"

"I don't know the origin of the quote. But it surely makes a lot of sense. The influx of energy and sensation in infancy is extraordinary! To manage it with a still-developing nervous system—whew! I can hardly imagine it!"

Regina looked a little incredulous. "And you're saying what exactly?"

"There is definitely an intensity to the driven-ness of obsession, but compared to the drive of infants to stay alive and develop their brains, it's relatively minor!"

"So, we're all born psychotic?"

"It's an interesting idea, isn't it?"

Regina smiled at him. "I always like your thinking. And, yes, it is. It would make sense then, that the more the brain matures, the more the in-dwelling spirit takes possession of the body and allows the brain a more full and intricate ownership."

"It sounds like the intensity would lessen the older one gets."

"There is some level on which I believe that the search for intensity is an artifact of that earliest imprinting. One seeks intensity in various forms throughout one's lifetime. Addictions are simply an example of one such artifact, very likely an attempt to blackmail the brain into feeling whole despite whatever deficits it is experiencing—by artificially overamping on serotonin, dopamine, opioid peptides, and/or oxytocin."

"I hadn't really thought of it that way."

Paul smiled and said "I have been known to be wrong once in a while, but in this case, I don't think so."

"So, answer my original question: Is your intensity psychotic in nature? Are you driven by ideas and images that are either super-human or even psychotic?"

"We really should define 'psychotic,' don't you think?"

"Next you'll want to define 'reality'!" she laughed.

They both laughed at the conundrum, that of defining "psychosis" despite whatever the symptomatology as being out of touch with "reality;" and, according to psychoanalysis, the "reality principle" is concerned with mediating control between "conditions imposed by external reality" and what Freud called "the pleasure principle" that seeks gratification of one's personal needs and the avoidance or discharge of unpleasurable notions." This last definition implies that that there is always conflict between the inner worlds and the outer. The entire idea, therefore, postulates an eternal duality, and therefore does not embrace any form of organic wholeness. Thus, the very nature and formation of understanding and conversation about the nature of essence is tainted from the very beginning.

"I mean, we could get very weird and define it as "that which is real," but that leads nowhere either. If we were to delve into the philosophical dictionary a bit, we could come up with 'something that exists independently of all other things and from which all other things derive...as distinguished from something that is merely apparent.'"

"OK, I see your critique of Freud. It's very clear. But

the term is usually used to criticize opinions that disagree or oppose one's own. Most people use it to refer to their own reality—naïve reality."

"That is so true! Very few people go beyond surface definitions."

"So, how does one decide what is real and what is not?" Regina asked, riposting.

"It goes back to epistemology. How do we know that we know? Or more properly, the origin, nature, methods and limits of human knowledge."

"But it's not just a matter of semantics."

"No, of course not!"

"Especially not when you consider the 'real world' consequences. Millions of people are psychiatrically incarcerated every year because they have ideas or attitudes that differ with the entrenched authorities, the psychiatric establishment."

"Whoa! Let's backtrack a little," said Regina, being ever cautious.

"No! I do not consider myself to be psychotic—despite my obvious intensity!"

"Do you consider yourself to be sane?"

"You know as well as me that 'sanity' and 'insanity' are legal terms, not clinical ones! They apply only to the ability to tell right from wrong vis a vis being able to stand trial."

"OK! OK! How do you define yourself in terms of orientation?"

"I consider myself to be a transcendentalist. One creates 'reality' by what one believes, which in turn, is conditioned by how one translates or interprets life experience, whether one perceives events to be beneficial or damaging. Even when one has made such an assessment—and this is where therapy comes in—one has a chance to reassess and better integrate experiences that one might have originally seen as negative."

"And?"

"Thereinafter, it is a constant process, a daily process, always unfolding and growing. One either gets better or worse. As Bob Dylan said, "He that isn't busy bein' born is busy dying."

"How does that apply exactly?"

"One is always growing, swimming like a shark, or one starts dying, degrading mentally and gets worse."

"So, back to Henry. How are you going to approach dismantling his twisted mental structure?"

"Symptomatology is like an investment. I have this theory that psychic weight is like physical weight. The more one carries, the more it affects one's behavior, physically or mentally. Symptoms are created to hide or suppress traumatic affect. It takes a lot of energy that could otherwise be used for other creative purposes. The more one sheds of the traumatic material, the lighter one becomes emotionally."

"Or the more agile one may become physically."

"Exactly! And the more weight one carries, the more one has to adapt to the extra weight. It takes extra energy to adapt. So then, one is carrying psychic weight plus energy to adapt to it—and that results in what we call 'symptoms' that are the outgrowth of the adaptation, just as physical disease is a result of the malfunctioning and adaptation of the physical."

"OK."

"So, I believe that I can help Henry the best by making him an ally for himself, getting him to be on his own side by reducing the internalized negativity he carries."

"Isn't that what Freud called the 'sadistic superego?'"

"That's right! He ends up continuously perpetrating against himself! He's his own oppressor!"

CHAPTER TWELVE
Another Step Along the Road

San Francisco Friday March 1st, 2002

Henry seemed increasingly lucid, more emotionally open and confident. During the weeks we had been working together, Henry had become more animated, at least in the office. He admitted that he had "caved in" twice to what he called his father's "grilling" him after sessions. He said his father had seemed especially interested in what questions Paul had asked about him. Henry reported that he told him he was not going to talk to him at all about his "personal business." After all, it was his therapy.

Henry also told Paul that it helped him to know that Paul 'believed' him; that he did not constantly question or critique him and was always willing to talk to him about anything he was feeling. It was totally anomalous for him. He had never been allowed any privacy by his father. Henry said, "Father picked out every single one of my previous therapists!"

"Seriously?"

"Yes. And he would pay them extra, on top of their fees, to tell him everything we talked about!"

Paul considered the fact that Henry was taking 10 mg of Stelazine BID, so the depth of his thought processes might be somewhat suspect. Still Henry seemed to be benefitting from therapy. He seemed less stiff, less withdrawn-appearing.

"I'm wondering about Andrew."

"What about him?"

"You call him your 'chauffeur,' sometimes your 'bodyguard.' What is he really?"

"I don't know exactly. More like 'Father's spy!' I guess."

"'Spy?'"

"He tells Father everything!"

"Do you have any idea why?"

Henry snorted.

"Money obviously!"

"Do you go places together?"

"He takes me to the movies sometimes. Also, to the aquarium, planetarium and the library."

"Do have any kind of relationship with him otherwise?"

"No! Why would I?"

"You told me he took you to gay clubs!"

"For money!"

"Where'd you get the money?"

"Internet! Father doesn't know shit about it! He thinks I'm on porn sites!"

"How is that making you money?"

"I...do some day trading. I have an untraceable bank account in the Canary Islands."

"And you draw cash from it?"

"Yeah. I use it to party, go to clubs."

"Have you thought any more about taking an IQ test, Henry?"

"I think I'd like to wait. I hope you're not too disappointed."

"It's not about me, Henry. Since your father has such a low opinion of your intelligence, I thought you might like to have an objective measure of your intelligence. You're way smarter than he thinks, just not in ways he appreciates."

Henry gave me one of the shy, sheepish smiles that always made him appear to be about five years old.

Paul continued. "I know you really believe what you've told me about the alien-government conspiracy. That's why they," he made air quotes around the word, "all think you are 'crazy' and need to be on meds."

"And you don't?"

Paul looked at him for a long moment then took a deep breath.

"That's a complex question. I always tell you the truth. I don't believe in any of that 'for your own good' bullshit!"

"OK. I believe you."

"I agree with a lot of what you believe—especially about the nefarious relationship between Big Business and the 'G.' It's obvious that the Big Banks and Big Businesses run the government since Reagan and the Rich White Man's Club are in control? 'Trickle down economics' was a huge bust! What a joke, like the ultra-rich were going to let go of billions to help the poor, to enrich the economy. But it all went into numbered off-shore accounts!"

Henry simply listened, having grown acquainted with these little mini-rants.

"So, he cut taxes and social programs, even government bureaucracy. Big fucking deal! Then the little puppet spent us deeper into debt with his insane military budget, as if building an outer space defense could ever make him feel safe! We went from $74 Billion in debt in 1980 to $221 billion in 1986! And they have the nerve to call him a financial genius!"

By now, Henry was smirking.

"That all makes sense. There is a kind of logic to it, even though it lacks any element of ethics. But that's ostensibly the essence of capitalism. Any corporation just has is to make a profit, with no considerations for environmental damage or healthy communities."

"And?"

"I just have some difficulty extending that particular line of thought to include aliens."

Henry retorted "Why? What about Hermes Trismegistus?"

"'As above, so below?'"

"Precisely."

Paul responded quickly. "By extension that means that because there are predatory corporations on Earth, there must be predatory aliens willing to conspire with human counterparts to rape the Earth and its population?"

Henry shrugged.

"I guess."

"I've read The Kybalion, written by 'Three Initiates,' alleged to be Hermes' philosophy" Paul said, to keep the topic moving. He had always loved smart clients.

This was one of Henry's favorite topics. "It only makes sense that if scientists on this planet are experimenting with genetic manipulation, then alien scientists, with potentially hundreds of thousands of years of life in which to experiment, would even have gone much further. They certainly would have the advanced technology to travel multiple light years to trade what for them might be common ordinary tools and procedures."

"Again, very logical. But I question the premise—the unproven presence of aliens and their contact with human beings, especially for nefarious purposes."

"But look at the level of technology that has developed in the last fifty years? Half of all technology that's ever existed! Is that a coincidence?"

"I... there has been an explosion of technology since WWII."

"And they all call it a 'coincidence?'"

"Just as likely as an alien connection."

"But there's so much more to the story!"

"Henry, I'm willing to be convinced of the propriety of your position, but..."

"You need 'evidence,' right?"

"Well yes! In a word."

"I have all of the links in my computer."

Paul took another deep breath, and sighed.

"OK, Henry. Can you spell it out a little more for me? Link it up."

"How much? Where do I start?"

"Start at the start."

CHAPTER THIRTEEN
The Story Continues

San Francisco Friday March 8th, 2002

"As near as I can figure, it all started with the Roswell Crash in New Mexico that was first reported in July of 1947. Maj. Jesse A. Marcel was the official investigator from the Intelligence Office of the 509th Bomb Group. He verified the first-hand testimony of area ranchers. They all testified that they had seen 'a disc'—though it was later repudiated by the Army Air force who called it a 'weather balloon.'"

"And?"

"And the Army Air Force's sold the weather balloon bullshit to the radio and newspapers, pretended it never happened."

"And covered it up until 1978."

Henry jumped up out of his chair with a huge grin.

"That's right! You do know something about this!"

"I've done some reading."

"Then you know!"

"I'm not a believer, Henry."

"And Project Blue Book?"

"What about it?"

"One of the biggest deceptions ever!"

"Say more."

"All of those sightings, many by extremely credible sources like pilots, and they dismissed them all as 'anomalies of the light,' 'ball lightning and other such bullshit!"

"And you're saying that some, if not most, of those sightings were genuine?"

"Absolutely! Roswell was an anomaly because they recovered bodies as well as the craft and other artifacts."

"None of that has ever been proven!"

"Because it's always been covered up! The 'G' doesn't want anybody to know! Think about what would happen if people knew we were having extraterrestrial contact! Who in their right mind would go to work every day or pay taxes or obey any of the laws when people find out that the so-called authority of government is a total fucking sham?"

"That does make a kind of sense. But what is the ultimate point?"

"Trading technology with the aliens is only part of the twisted bargain."

"What do you mean?"

"Do you really think they're altruistic?"

"Truman made a deal to create as much chaos and upset as he could, using all of the resources at his command. The Cold War! All of the racial and political tension during those years! They were all payments!"

Now Paul was starting to think Henry was really flipped out.

"Don't you get it? They're highly advanced technologically, but they have no emotions, no empathy no soul! The aliens feed on negative human emotion!

CHAPTER FOURTEEN
Deeper Still

San Francisco Tuesday March 19th, 2002

Paul was really in a quandary after the previous week's sessions, and couldn't wait to talk with Regina. Now that Henry had revealed the center core of his delusional system, Paul realized that his beliefs were not nearly as radical as Henry's. This, in turn, led him to more deeply consider what might have been the quality and nature of Henry's earliest injuries.

He was enjoying a long, lingering breakfast—chicken apple sausages and eggs over a blueberry pancake with plenty of butter and fresh syrup, along with five cups of dark, rich coffee. He mused about the Hermes Trismegistus' maxim and the relationship between injury and manifestation as traumatic symptoms. It always seemed to him that "mental illness" had been treated in the cruelest ways imaginable out of shame and denial by those whose ostensible duty was to serve and protect their charges. From their perspective, silencing the patients was "perfect" treatment. Those suffering wouldn't be listened to if they complained, and that silence, malicious though it was, quieted the critics and further marginalized the oppressed. Their traumatic re-enactments were considered to be brain anomalies, completely divorced from the savagery and cruelty inflicted upon them as children by the rapacious society—denying culpability and responsibility for the true heinous crimes such as racism, sexism and homophobia.

Freud early on discounted his father's abusive behavior, calling even the possibility "Too indicative of perversion," and blithely dismissed it as "Improbable." He wrote in an 1897 letter, "I found in myself a constant love for my mother and jealousy of my father. I now consider this to be a universal event in early childhood."

As a neurologist, Freud had been avidly seeking a physiological basis for "mental illness" before he became famous for his development of psychoanalysis. His first private patients were referred to him for "hysterical symptoms," aspects of what is now called Posttraumatic Stress Disorder. They were displaying bursts of rage, sleep disturbance, depression, suicidal thoughts, nightmares, social withdrawal, anorexia and periods of uncontrolled and inconsolable weeping. When they reported sexual abuse (many by the very people, his colleagues, who had referred them), he was at first both skeptical to believe them and reluctant to report his findings.

When he finally published these rather astounding findings (especially for 1895) in a book entitled *Toward the Aetiology of Hysteria*, his work was universally panned. In 1899, having been roundly repudiated both personally and professionally, he published the *Interpretation of Dreams*, based on the play *Oedipus Rex* by Sophocles. He introduced both the positive Oedipus complex—highlighting a child's unconscious sexual desire for the opposite-sex parent and hatred for the same-sex parent; and the negative Oedipus complex that referred to a child's unconscious sexual desire for the same-sex parent and hatred for the opposite-sex parent. He also declared that the child's identification with the same-sex parent resolves the complex and that the unsuccessful resolution led to all manner of what he called "neurosis, pedophilia and homosexuality."

Though much of Freud's groundbreaking knowledge and information was now considered outdated, "modern psychiatry" still continued to seek solutions attempting to chemically rearrange the electrical signals of the brain. This approach has proven to be very profitable for the pharmaceutical practitioners and simultaneously shielded society from the brutal truth of its delusions. Masson had stated that "Such a criticism of existing society would have been too profound and the implications for society too disquieting. By blaming the victim, Freud was effectively able to unburden the society of any need to reform or [for] deep reflection... [that would have been] threatening, dangerous and true."

Paul had often reflected on these words that materialized fleeting fantasies of another world like a flock of snowy egrets frightened into flight while feeding. How different the world might have been if bisexual Sigmund Freud had had the courage to act on the information provided him by the hapless children of his nefarious *confrères*. Or, if he'd had parents who had not used him, attempting to get their own twisted, unmet needs met.

This line of thought led him to re-consider Henry's conspiracy process. Paul could not, in all good conscience, refute the possibility that everything he espoused was true, especially since he believed that everything was in accord

with what Ken Wilber had called the "already always perfect."

As he mentally chewed on the concept, he realized that everything in the Universe fit together neatly and perfectly. There was a kind of perfect logic to it that was not at odds with Henry's jigsaw puzzle.

Paul sat back in his padded leather office chair and reflected upon something David Bohm, the eminent quantum physicist, had said about "The Implicate Order." It "exists as an ultimate physical substrate that underlies our present perception of reality. Although the parts appear to be distinct from the whole, in fact, because they 'enfold' or include the whole, they are identical with the whole. If we could invoke the precedent of quantum mechanical indefinability, we could leap to the idea of a united entity encompassing all space and time in which each part contains the whole and is identical to it."

It set Paul off probing as to why he was having such a hard time wrapping his head around Henry's delusions and how to unwind them to Henry's benefit. Whenever he cleared barriers and blockages within himself, he found that the Universe had changed. And there it was again—that connection to wholeness.

He had always followed his inner dictates, intuitively believed that everything he wanted to know, even could know, was contained within himself; and his true, and perhaps only task was to discover that hidden mystery of Self; to fully and indisputably prove to himself that he truly belonged to the living vibrant heart of the Universe; that simply by virtue of his being alive, he too was star-seed material. It was the only thing that could ever satisfy the ache in his heart of hearts—though he conversely had serious doubts about his strength and capacity.

Perhaps that was the problem. One had to be in the desired "place" to adequately describe, not even "IT" itself, but perhaps a "condition" (too ephemeral), or a "way" (too limiting), even "path" was too discriminatory—it seemed that one had to embrace "IT" totally, perhaps even let "IT" become one's very Self (maybe "IT" already was), the higher order of beingness, finding itself winding up an infinite number of steps from the virtual tail from where "normal" (whatever that was) consciousness reigned.

He couldn't help but wonder if perhaps the terminology or the syntax in which humans attempted to describe "IT" were the very factors that limited one's being able to embrace "IT." One had to live "IT," whatever the hell "IT" was, because "IT" was all there was, and one could no more define "IT" than a bird could describe a worm. "IT" just was.

He realized anew that Providence provided everything in a way that required no real personal power or authority per se—always a matter of letting go and receiving rather than asserting and taking. One could describe one's arm or leg as an appendage, a part of one's body, but one could not adequately describe the relative wholeness of one's body without reference to something greater, the next level of wholeness. Wilber referred to this as "nests of beingness," an infinite set of concentric circles, with each senior "holon" being contained in and by, and having all of the powers and qualities of, the next previous junior "holon." Each "holon," each autonomous self-reliant unit, was always whole and complete within its own boundaries—center everywhere, circumference nowhere.

Getting immersed in the "God process," often left his head spinning and his heart aching that he had somehow "missed the boat" in this life. He always felt there was an enormous weight of knowledge and esoteric wisdom hovering just beyond his grasp but tantalizingly near enough as to almost touch it. It was related to his feeling that the presence of the bulk of humanity, as if suspended around his neck like a giant albatross, though compassion always reminded him of Plato's long-ago dictum: "Be kind. Everyone is fighting a hard battle." It inevitably led him to Wilber's words:

> And comes to rest that Godless search, tormented and tormenting...gone the madness of a life committed to uncare, and gone the tears and terror of the brutal days and endless nights where time alone would rule. And I—I rise to taste the dawn and find that love alone will shine today. And the Shining says: to love it all, and love it madly, and always endlessly, and ever fiercely, to love without choice and thus enter the All, embracing the only and radiant Divine: now as Emptiness, now as Form, together and forever, the Godless search undone, and love alone will shine today.

CHAPTER FIFTEEN
Further into the Fray

San Francisco Tuesday April 2nd, 2002

"Paul, I have a question for you: What makes your conspiracy theories 'sane' and mine a 'symptom' of 'mental illness?'"

"It's all a matter of functioning. You're pretty withdrawn and non-functional."

"What's that famous quote you're always throwing around? The one from Krishnamurti?"

"Oh, you mean, 'It is no measure of good health to be well adjusted to a profoundly sick society?'"

"That's the one! I've started writing down some of the quotes you use."

"Well, I think it's true."

"Does that put my situation in a different perspective?"

"I'm not saying I agree with the definitions of the DSM, but I do have to use it in order to have sessions with you—and get paid!"

"So, you're functioning inside of a 'profoundly sick society.' Does that mean you're sick or well?"

Paul laughed.

"That may be a question that we could debate for a long time!"

Now Henry laughed, too.

"So. What do you want to explore today?"

"You've never mentioned you mother, just that she died when you were six."

"I was hospitalized for the first time when I was six. When I got out, Father said 'She's gone now. We just have to go on without her.'"

"Nothing else?"

A small moue marked Henry's face, then a wave of shame and pain splashed across his features. Before he could muster his defenses to hide or retreat into dissociation, a tear ran down his left cheek, and his eyes took on the color of storm clouds.

"Just go ahead and feel it, Henry." As suddenly as the storm had appeared, the clouds broke and copious tears began to fall. In the months they had worked together, Paul had never seen Henry express this level of emotion.

"I have never felt like I belonged. I've always felt alienated...because I'm an alien!"

CHAPTER SIXTEEN
The Long-Awaited Opening

San Francisco Tuesday April 2nd, 2002
(Same Session)

What had started as a trail of tears quickly became a deluge as Henry went from sitting to slumping to sliding, finally falling onto the floor in a pseudo-downward dog position and then onto his side into a fetal position where he sobbed in gouts and bursts that lasted for several minutes, finally subsiding into ripples of sniffles and snorts before settling into an uneasy quiet.

Paul sat in silence and let the quiet reign. A timeless time later (actually twelve minutes by the clock), Henry started to shiver as if the tiny tremors passing through his body were on a journey to infinitude.

When Henry came back to a fuller consciousness, he fluttered his eyes, which then went wide, and he ran to the bathroom. The sound of gastric eruptions pierced the air from behind the door. Then the toilet flushed, and then again. Paul heard the heard the "pffft" of the bathroom spray and a pale-faced Henry emerged.

Paul kept silently breathing as his client became more cognizant and aware of his surroundings, made eye contact and spoke.

"I...I'm not...ready to go yet. Can I...can I ...may I have another session now?"

"I have the time, but I'll need a bio-break first."

"Thank you. Thank you."

Henry's eyes looked as if they were in a pinball machine. Paul handed him a glass of filtered water, Henry drank it down and then gestured for a refill.

Henry started reconstituting as if he had been melted and then allowed to re-harden without a form. He eventually began to look more recognizably human and made an attempt to speak to Paul. What came out was a garbled gumbo that did not resemble any known language.

"I'veneverreallyallowedmyselftofeelthismuch.Thisiskindo fweird.I'mscared."

"Wow, man! Slow down a little! Please!"

"Idon'tknowifIcanrightnow.Mybrainisspinningsofast!"

Paul listened, translated and then responded.

"OK, got it. Let's breathe together a little bit. OK?"

Paul gave him the instructions again, closed his eyes and started breathing rhythmically. He took several breaths as a model for Henry. When Paul finished his final breath, he fluttered his eyes before he opened them.

Henry was sitting quietly, gazing at him.

Paul smiled and asked how he was doing.

"I...I'm not...sure."

"Your speech sounds a little clearer."

"But my brain! My brain is revving...so fast! Yet I feel like my brain has been emptied out!"

"That sounds trippy!"

Henry nodded.

"You don't have to talk until you're ready."

Henry nodded again.

Paul's mind started pursuing alternative pathways for explanations for Henry's behaviors. He was far more convinced of Henry's early trauma. His father's bad attitude was so evident. It was only a question of how much violence and what kind.

Henry got up and made his way unsteadily to the bathroom. He emerged with his glass filled and drank it dry before sitting down again.

"Wow!"

Paul laughed and echoed him.

"I'll say! That was quite a reaction!"

Henry sat quietly and Paul jumped into the gap.

"The way you reacted leads me to think that you have some dark history. Are you interested in looking into it right now? If it gets too heavy, we can stop. OK?"

"OK." Tentatively.

"May we talk a little more about your mother?"

Shrug.

"You maybe don't know much about her, but it feels to me that you might need to grieve her."

"Maybe. I...really have never..."

"That's kind of what I figured. I believe that all 'problems' are the direct result of old pain. But it doesn't just sit there. It grows stronger. When the body lets go of it, it comes out as dis-ease, lack of ease."

"But why is it so important? I always try to not think about it too much. Forget it if I can."

"So, how is that working?"

Henry sniggered, not quite a laugh or a giggle.

"Not too good, huh?"

Paul laughed and continued.

"We'll add a little twist to the breathing method I taught you. Once we get our breathing synched, all you have to do is keep breathing steadily. This will allow you to feel what you're feeling and think what you are thinking. Remember, your father is not here. OK?"

"OOOO-K!" Speculatively.

"Is this too fast? Do you need a little more time?"

"No. Maybe. I don't know?"

"Maybe you're too raw right now. Maybe we should wait."

"Let's try it."

"You're sure?"

"Yes."

"Good. I've found that diving in when a breakthrough happens, like now, can open an individual for healing."

"OK. Let me get another water first."

After he settled, Henry still seemed edgy.

"So, your mother."

"OK."

"Close your eyes and get into your steady breathing, same rhythm."

Henry nodded and Paul joined him.

Paul's first breath took him immediately into a deepening silence whilst simultaneously expanding his awareness of the force field of energy around him, like the rings of Saturn or Jupiter. With the next breath his escalating awareness opened, and he was able to maintain enough of his autonomy to stand apart to allow his professional experience full sway. He read Henry's much more raggedy energy like a distinct signature blipping on his internal radar screen. He locked onto it, observing. With the next breath, he synched his breathing more deeply with the younger man's, and opened the gates of his empathy even further. He then went on a kind of automatic pilot that allowed him to continue to monitor Henry, broadcasting a more radiant and incorporative energy toward him.

"OK, Henry, just keep breathing and watch whatever comes as if it were on a large television screen. No matter what, you are just watching, and you're able to report to me anything you are experiencing, exactly as it is. OK?"

Henry nodded his head.

"So, Henry, you agreed earlier that we could talk a little about your mother. Is that still OK?"

Another nod.

"So, tell me about your mother."

Henry's face took on a form of animation that Paul had never seen before, though his voice remained calm and reportorial as he began to recite some of the biographical facts of his life.

"My mother. She was...wonderful. She was always nice to me."

Paul remained silent until Henry continued.

"She...always kept Father... kept Father..."

Henry's face seemed to implode slightly, and a tear ran down his right cheek.

"Father...got angry with me sometimes, called me names, yelled at me."

"And?"

"Sometimes..." he said and then took another deep breath, though it was quite raggedy.

"He always told me how 'worthless' I was, how 'disappointed' he was with me."

"And?"

As if the simple word was a trigger, Henry exploded as if booby-trapped. He emitted a loud yell following which he appeared to collapse onto the floor, buried his face in his hands, and started sobbing.

"That fucker! I fucking hate him!"

Taken somewhat aback by this sudden expurgation, Paul jerked back involuntarily. Then he took another deep breath, acutely aware that he had stepped into a very tender arena. He simply waited as Henry snuffed his nose once, twice, then reached for the tissue box, pulled out two and blew his nose.

"Whatthefuckwasthat?" he asked, as if his brain had shifted into a higher gear.

"Just take a deep breath, Henry. Be quiet for a minute."

Henry took a breath and angrily spoke.

"He took my mother away! My only real comfort! Said she was 'babying' me!"

Paul just continued to listen.

"She was always...kind to me...gentle," he said, and burst into tears again.

Paul waited. He knew he was right, but so what?

"I didn't...I never..." and relapsed into silence.

Then he looked up, as if startled by his own thoughts, and said, "My God, I just remembered! That bastard used to hit her too!"

"Your mother?"

"Yes! The bastard! And then he would tell me it was "My fault!"

"Your 'fault?' Why?"

"He used to say that if I wasn't such a 'baby,' and if I didn't 'make him' so 'mad,' he would 'never have to hit her!'"

"Why do you think you didn't remember?"

"I was just so scared!"

"And now?"

"I...feel like I can breathe again."

"And how's that?"

"Better. Confusing. I don't know."

"It's OK, Henry. We can close early today. Go home. Drink lots of water. Take a nap. I'll see you Friday. Call me if you need to talk."

CHAPTER SEVENTEEN
A Directionless Jaunt

San Francisco Wednesday April 3rd, 2002

The next day Paul decided to air out his head, as it were, and started out walking from his place on Tuscany Alley, off upper Lombard in North Beach, with a vague thought of walking to Golden Gate Park, perhaps even Ocean Beach. He started his journey with a hearty breakfast at the Café Roma on Columbus—a waffle with extra butter, a pair of sausage patties, and a brace of eggs poached, accompanied by a gallon of coffee. He continued down Columbus to Stockton and then up over the Broadway Tunnel (officially the James C. Levy Tunnel) through the unique neighborhood situated above it like a small rural village, then down the Hyde Street extension over the top of the tunnel, where the underground portion ran beneath Leavenworth, Jones, Taylor, and Mason Streets.

The day was warming though not yet the consistently warmer, clearer days that would come during the so-called "Indian Summer" with which San Franciscans anticipated every year during September and October. The sky was clearing of overnight fog, and the air was freshening with onshore winds off the Pacific. He was wearing his jean jacket over a t-shirt and a chambray shirt, and carrying his small backpack with some dried meat sticks, raisins, a mango, chips, a few biscotti, a quart of water and another of coffee in a thermos and an extra pair of socks. He couldn't stand having wet feet and usually changed socks before the return journey from any jaunt.

He considered taking Broadway all the way to the Presidio, or alternatively, down to the Argüello Gate into Golden Gate Park and through the amazing eucalypti. He loved their aromatic presence opening his lungs. Paul breathed even more deeply in rhythm with his pace, contemplating Henry's latest breakthrough.

The day was gorgeous, and his skin thirstily drank in the vitamin D. Today he marveled anew at the incredible variety of women who peopled the streets of his city. Every neighborhood had a different flavor, like a living palette of beauty and culture. San Francisco always had a particular flair, a distinctive style, of its own that was unmatched anywhere else he had ever been. There was a kind of *joie de vivre* and vivacity in their way of dressing, walking, talking, laughing and even breathing. It was always uplifting and inspiring, no matter his mood.

Aspects of the Corso book ran through his head as he walked. He had read Corso's book over the course of the last two night's running, immersed in the gripping narrative as if it were being recited into his ears by an ancient haruspex reading a goat's innards. The author had spelled it out in plain and easy-to-read English, enunciating the hidden strategies of the government-within-a-government that Paul had always believed existed, though for different reasons than he had originally thought.

He had always felt that the conspiracy was informed by the business-as-usual ethic of the ultra-rich coercing public life for their own perpetual gain (which was true), though not in order to protect the American people (the world-at-large actually) from attack and invasion by extraterrestrials (which he'd not considered), It had only been in a *War of the Worlds* paranoid fantasy sense of the 1940's.

Their thinking was actually logically consistent with typical authoritarian interference, with the government acting *in loco parentis,* treating the citizenry as if they were all untutored children to be herded and manipulated like a bunch of addled sheep. It fed in with the multi-generational emotional incest that poisoned millions, billions, through the course of time, passing on the stain of self-invalidation and subservience to authority.

He was having an almost otherworldly experience of being to too deeply apply his own long history of trauma and recovery to his work with Henry, and therefore had had to develop considerations about how quickly and deeply to proceed with peeling back Henry's well-constructed (albeit obscurative) façade. Due to the severity of his symptoms, and to the clarity he was exhibiting now that he had broken through his emotional armor, though there was still so much more to be accomplished, who knew how long the vaporous results might last. Paul knew that he had techniques in his therapeutic armamentarium with which to uncover Henry's hidden materials, and help him integrate more easily.

Of course, willingness was the key element in the algorithm of healing. That was certainly obvious on the client's part, and training was added in on the therapist's side. It was ultimately a matter of rebuilding the broken bridge of trust, to which Bradshaw had long ago spoken, and then building a new cognitive framework within which to frame living and expressing his or her re-awakened humanity and sense of self.

Of course, such a process of reconstitution requires learning resilience and malleability that, in turn, can only emerge from the fertile ground of heart-felt forgiveness. It is only this latter that restores the missed sense of equilibrium and internal orientation that is the birthright of every human being.

The process could be foreshortened by a sensitive and carefully orchestrated plan of care. This, in turn, relied upon the best of the art upon which the best of psychotherapy was based and practiced. True healing work always embodied the practitioner's assiduously working on him or herself to keep the sharp edge of acute perception available to feed awareness to the suffering client from what, it was hoped, was the encyclopedic compendium of education, training and experience that any viable therapist builds and has available to apply. It was the single greatest gift any healer could bring.

Of course, there are as many specialties and sub-specialties in psychology as there are in medicine. Paul had purposefully chosen to work with trauma clients and in crisis care. Just as purposely he had chosen not to work with children, geriatrics or families (though he did do some couples' work on occasion). His intensive experience working with combat soldiers in Vietnam with the 101st Airborne still held him in good stead. Even though he had been home over thirty years, he was still in the process of trauma recovery and almost twenty years clean from the ravages of cocaine addiction.

He stopped to sit on one of the benches on the top of the hill and admired the magnificent 360° view that encompassed the Bay Bridge, the East Bay hills, south through the Mission District toward the Peninsula, west to the reaches of the mighty Pacific Ocean.

Breathing deeply the refreshed and refreshing air, he drifted into a reverie in which he envisioned the most salubrious possible outcomes for Henry. Fresh air and sunshine were so invigorating. He felt positively positive!

He decided to walk down the other side of Russian Hill, the neighborhood drawing its name from a time when Gold Rushers found seven Cyrillic-inscribed gravestones at the top of the hill, though the status of the Russian men has never been confirmed. The gravestones disappeared in the late 1800's.

He walked down to Hyde Street and took the cable car (hanging on to one of the brass rails, of course!) all the way to the end of the line, and dropped in to have fish and chips, perhaps even one of the famous Irish Coffees at The Buena Vista. After all, it was his day off. He would return to his practice renewed and uplifted. Vista. After all, it was his day off. He would return to his practice renewed and uplifted. What a joy!

CHAPTER EIGHTEEN
Approaching the Morass

San Francisco Friday April 12th, 2002

Henry arrived late for his next appointment. It was the first time this had happened and Paul asked about it. His face looked drawn, even a bit haggard, and his clothing, though clean, was nowhere near his usual level of sartorial correctness.

"I haven't been sleeping very well. Ever since last time, I've been waking up a lot at night."

"Are you remembering any dreams?"

Henry's eyes bugged.

"Oh God!" he said and teared up.

Paul waited.

"I...I've been dreaming...every night."

"Is that unusual?"

"I've...I usually don't. But lately..."

"'Lately?'"

"The last two nights!"

"And?"

"I...I've been...having bad dreams!"

"What kind of 'bad dreams?'"

"Nightmares!"

"About?"

"My...Father."

"What about him?"

"He...keeps showing up...in my dreams!"

"Are you in the dreams too?"

"I'm...just a little kid."

"And?"

"I'm scared. He's giant!"

Paul waited as Henry's tears fell.

"I...never remembered."

"'Remembered?'"

"He...he's always mean."

"And?"

"Is this real?"

"Go on."

"I didn't...remember this before."

"'Remember' what?"

Henry started sobbing into his hands. Paul pushed the tissue box closer to his left hand and waited.

"He's always hated me!"

"Why?"

"I...Is this real? The dreams?"

"I don't know. They may be stress-related dreams, or they could be flashbacks of actual experiences."

Henry's tear-stained face looked at him hopeful and expectant.

"I dreamed I chopped him up with a machete!"

Paul pondered for a moment, then continued.

"Tell me what else you remember."

"I was...three, maybe four. I remember...Father yelling at me, standing over me, yelling."

"What was he saying? Can you remember?"

"Same...kind of thing he always says."

Paul waited, looking at Henry.

"I'm dumb...I'm worthless..."

"And I'll...never amount to anything."

Paul sat quietly and waited as Henry started sobbing again and spoke through his tear-filled face.

"I'm just so...fucking sad! So... fucking sad!"

"Why do you think you're remembering now?" Paul asked disingenuously, wanting his client to connect the dots on his own.

"It...it was the other day! It shook up my memory."

"Is there more coming back?"

"I'm...just not sure what's real."

Paul stayed quiet, observing.

"I...used to think...I knew everything."

"And now?"

"Now...I'm confused... But not about Father."

"'Father?'"

"He...he's always been...cruel...to me."

"Has he ever been more than verbally abusive?"

Henry looked down and refused to meet Paul's eyes.

"Henry?"

"I'm afraid."

"Of your father?"

"No! No! I'm afraid...of getting him...in trouble."

"'In trouble' for what?"

"I'm afraid to talk about him. He's one of the Controllers."

"'Controllers?'"

"They run the planet!"

"They run the planet?'"

"Of course! I've been telling you all along!"

"What are you not telling me?"

"I can't talk about it! He has too much power over me!"

"You've given him power."

"No! I'm weak! He's strong!"

"I want you to think carefully about this. Do you want to take back some of your power?"

"I can't!"

"Henry, the biggest part of your recovery is your willingness to do the work."

"I can't!"

"Henry, do you trust me? The work we've been doing?"

After a long pause, Henry answered sheepishly. "Yes."

"Our work will just be an extension of what we have already done. I'll walk you through it."

"You will?

"Yes, of course."

"We don't have to talk about Father?"

"That might really benefit you."

"I don't want to talk about him."

"OK, I'll explain the work to you, and you can decide if you want to go forward."

"OK."

Paul then started describing a process he had used with hundreds of clients in the past fifteen years called "Sovereignty Ceremony." He explained it as being similar to what in criminology was referred to as "Locard's exchange principle," in which there is an exchange of material between the perpetrator and victim of every crime.

"Sovereignty" uses a light trance state and guided visualization to energetically return energy that has been projected upon the client by others and take back energy that the client has projected onto others. There is an exchange, and the net effect is to create a greater relative wholeness through integrating of such lost or projected energies—thus more deeply empowering the individual and allowing greater freedom to the self.

"At the end we do a kind of closure ritual. Does that make sense?"

"Do you think it will really work?"

"I've used it with hundreds of others. And I've had tremendous results."

"But how? How can it possibly work?"

"It works with the emotional energy contained in the pain and shame."

Henry looked at him for a long time and then slowly nodded.

"OK, we'll work on someone who's harmed you or you have harmed. Your homework is to make a list."

Henry nodded and asked if they could start with the next session.

Paul knew that this was a very key juncture in their therapeutic relationship, and that it would deepen their alliance, so he nodded, and then said, "Of course. My job is to hold space for you. I do think it's important for us to discuss your father at some point."

For the very first time, Henry held out his hand to shake, and then took Paul's hand in both of his—and smiled.

CHAPTER NINETEEN
Questions, Questions, Questions

San Francisco Sunday April 14th, 2002

Paul had told Henry that he was taking some extra time to review the relevant information needed to administer the Wechsler Adult Intelligence Scale (WAIS) to him, which Paul hadn't used since graduate school.

Henry had become one of the most interesting cases Paul had ever worked with, yet it was baffling because there was so much information to which he did not have access. Partly it was due to Henry's severe withdrawal and dissociation and partly due to the many years of really poor therapy. Then there was Senior and his continuing attempts to interfere and intrude. Paul looked at Henry as an unfolding puzzle, an intriguing human being—and yet another lesson in his own ongoing education in traumatic adaptation. Henry's father, on the other hand, was a case study in what was called "Cluster B" personality type. Essentially, he incorporated all of the traits of the Narcissistic, Borderline, and Histrionic categories. It was not really ethical for Paul to diagnose at a distance, but he could extrapolate from the all-too-frequent contacts he had with him. He continued to call two or three times a week, making veiled threats and trying to weasel confidential information out of Paul.

"Sir, why don't you just ask him? He's your son. He's actually quite bright, probably a lot smarter that you give him credit for."

"So, you're buying all this alien horseshit? I've been in the vanguard of business for over forty years, and I have never seen a trace of any kind of alien interaction!"

"Sir, I am not saying I 'buy into' Henry's ideas, but being a wealthy man has always bought you insulation from the daily *sturm und drang*. That's part of what money does, sir."

"It also pays your bills!"

"I do not deny it for a moment. But you, on the other hand, own a large number of multinational corporations and have very little to do in the way of day-to-day operations. So, we are clearly in different realms as far as human interaction is concerned. Your focus is bottom-line expediency. You may not have been paying as much attention to Henry's thoughts and dreams."

"Are you saying I should have been endorsing his beliefs in alien technology?"

"Not at all, sir. I'm just mentioning the possibility that you may have ignored him in favor of decisions more related to increased production and profit."

"That's bullshit! I... how is any of that relevant to my son's treatment?"

"What I am saying, sir, is that Henry may have been having symptoms that appeared odd or strange to you, and you, therefore, may not have equated them with what Henry tells me you refer to his being 'stupid,' 'worthless,' and an 'idiot." Just because he espouses 'conspiracy theories' does not automatically make him psychotic or delusional."

"What do you mean? I've had him to some of the top facilities here, the Mayo Clinic, Menninger's. They tell me he is! That's why he takes medication! Every time he has stopped it, he's ended up in the hospital!"

"Sir, some of the latest research has drawn a very definitive line between 'conspiracy theory' and true paranoia."

"They're the same goddamn thing!"

"No sir. Generally, conspiracy beliefs are more socio-politically-oriented and associated with decreased trust in government and other authorities. Those who hold such beliefs tend to assign blame to the very few powerful people controlling laws and politics, so as to control and manipulate everyone. People who develop paranoia, on the other hand, even subclinical paranoia, tend to assign blame to humanity at large and believe that everyone is after them specifically."

"That sounds like psychobabble bullshit!"

"Sir, you are certainly entitled to your opinion. I am just relating some of the latest research. The thrust of it is that conspiracy theorists are considered to have a political view that is contrary to the 'mainstream,' and that that *per se* is not psychopathological."

"If you're doing some kind of woo-woo bullshit off-the-wall therapy, I'm going to file complaint against you, and stop paying your bills. I've a mind to do so anyway!"

"Sir, while I may not ethically share information from my sessions with Henry, I am trying to keep you informed in a general way about what I am discovering and how that is guiding my approach with him. He asked for a copy of the Treatment Plan. Has he shown it to you yet?"

"No, goddamn it!"

"Sir, I asked his permission to talk to you about this one issue and he agreed, but he did not consent to my discussing anything else. So, sir, I suggest you might ask him yourself, if you're interested. And, that you actually ask, not demand."

"What the fuck do you mean by that?"

"Just that you, sir, have a very powerful voice, and I assume you can be quite forceful in getting your needs met. Ergo, I am suggesting you ask Henry in the gentlest voice you can muster. You, sir...frighten him."

"He told you that?"

"No sir, but it's evident in the way he refers to you, and always calls you 'Father.'"

"Nothing wrong with that! I called my own father 'Father' until the day he died!"

"But perhaps you were a stronger child, a stronger man, than Henry is."

"I always told his mother he needed toughening up! And she always refused to send him to military school!"

"I don't think it would have made any difference. According to what I have read in his medical records—and, by the way, thanks for sending me copies—Henry seems to have had congenital, inborn, tendencies, a certain 'softness' one doctor noted. Another said that he seemed to 'shun close contact with others' even as a young child. Do you remember any of that?"

"I don't. He was always a strange child, hiding behind his mother's skirts! He was never interested in playing sports or being in Nature. He's just always been odd."

"You say that in a very judgmental way."

"Don't use your psychology bullshit on me!"

"Sir, I'm sharing as much as I ethically can, within the scope of Henry's permission."

"Fuck his 'permission'! I'm paying the fucking bills!"

"Yes sir, you are his conservator, and hence responsible for seeing that he gets the best care possible. But technically, it's his money."

Paul continued.

"And I understand you always refused to send him to therapy until after he was hospitalized!"

"It's not what he needed!"

"You say! What about what he wanted?"

"He was a child!"

"And he ended up in the hospital!"

"Are you implying that that was because I didn't listen?"

Paul was tempted to answer completely honestly, but doing so was close to breaching confidentiality, as Henry had given permission to discuss a very narrow range of topics.

"Sir, I'm not saying anything of the sort. My understanding is that he had asked for therapy, wanted to have somebody to talk to privately, at an early age."

"I tried many times!"

"Sir, you've told me repeatedly that you didn't value him or his opinions; that you frequently disparaged him, and yelled at him instead of listening."

Paul felt the older man's rage like a volcanic blast through the telephone line. He imagined the Senior's face turning beet-red, then draining of all color as it seemed as if he might implode. Then he started wildly sputtering, the sound of spittle flying from his lips like helicopter blades cutting the air.

"You are fucking impossible! How fucking dare you?"

"I dare, sir, because my first concern is your son's well-being, not for your image, public or private!"

"You're fired! You are fucking fired!"

"Sir, you are NOT my client!"

"I won't pay you another penny!"

"Then we'll get involved in a legal dispute, one that might become very public. I <u>will</u> take you to court. I <u>will</u> file a complaint against you for failing to fulfill the terms of your contract! I repeat, sir: Henry is my client, NOT you! I am concerned with his mental health. I am not here to assist you to contaminate my relationship with him! Our relationship is sacred!"

"Then what, exactly, are you allowed to talk with me about? Goddamn it!"

"Sir, I don't want this to get any more oppositional!

"That's it! You really <u>are</u> fired!"

At just that moment, there was a click on the telephone line, and Paul could hear his client yelling in an uncharacteristically loud voice.

"You can't fire him! He listens to me! More than you ever have!"

The older man bellowed, "Henry, have you been listening to this private phone call?"

"Yes, Father. I know a lot more about what is going on than you think. And I will not allow you to fire Doctor Paul. He is helping me!"

The multimillionaire started sputtering, completely at a loss for words, unable even to try to mount any kind of belligerent response.

"Thank you, Henry, for the vote of confidence. I'm quite sure your father and I have much more to discuss. You and I can talk about this more at our next session."

"If you try to fire him, I will testify against you, Father!" Henry said and hung up.

"Did you put him up to this?" roared the older man, his voice echoing down the phone line. "If you did, I will file a complaint for collusion and manipulation!"

"I assure you, sir, I did not. Henry is simply learning to express his feelings."

"This seems so sudden! What are you doing with him?"

"In broad general terms, I am allowing him the opportunity to feel what he really feels and think what he really thinks—and speak his own truth."

"That sounds radical! Everybody has to lie sometimes. There's no way society could function if everybody told the truth."

"Sir, I have to respectfully disagree. I live and work amongst a group of people who live by what is called The Sun Dancer's Code: 'I do not lie. I do not cheat. I do not steal.'" Paul paused, and then continued. "Furthermore, Henry is my client. I <u>will</u> honor his wishes even if you don't want to."

Still sputtering, the older man could only reply, "This is preposterous! Ridiculous! Impossible!"

"Not only is it real, sir, it <u>is</u> really happening."

CHAPTER TWENTY
A New Direction

San Francisco Friday April 19th, 2002

"Are you still having heavy dreams?"

"Yes! And I'm remembering them better!"

"Are you in them?"

"Yes. And Father, too, usually."

"Tell me more."

"Father's been less...scary. He used to be a very large monster. Now he's more human. I'm not as afraid of him now."

"Does that feel better?"

"Yes! And scarier."

"How's that?"

"I'm beginning to believe that I can maybe talk to him."

"What would you talk about?"

"I'd tell him how much I've always wanted him to love me. How much I've always wanted him to be 'Dad,' not 'Father.'"

"That sounds big."

"It is! I've always been so afraid."

"And now?"

"Now I want to go further!"

"'Further?'"

"You know, that process, the visualization process we talked about."

"Yes. Did you bring your list?"

"I did," he answered somewhat sheepishly.

Paul just looked at him, as in *What?*

"Well, it's just that 'Father' is the top three names on the list."

"I know he's big for you. We'll just do some breathing first and go into the Sovereignty slowly. I don't want to push you too hard." Paul paused for a moment, then continued. "Did I tell you that I've had another conversation with you father?"

"No! Really?"

"I don't have to keep confidentiality with him. He continues to want to know what we are talking about. I continue to tell him 'No!'"

"I... have been trying to talk with him more too. I'm still really afraid of him, but I'm telling him more of what I feel and what I think. He still thinks I'm weird!"

"Probably always will. He's got his mind made up, and he isn't going to change. It's his way of believing he's in charge of the Universe—so he doesn't have to acknowledge his old pain."

"Isn't that a bit like me? I...do you think that my beliefs are connected to my pain?"

"I do."

"But you still believe me, right?"

"I can still believe you without necessarily buying in to your beliefs."

"That's kind of...fucked up!"

"What matters is helping you get more comfortable in your own skin so you can navigate your own world better."

Henry paused and scrunched up his face in thought. Then he brightened, snapped his fingers, and said "Indubitably."

Paul laughed. He didn't feel that it was appropriate for him to tell Henry that he was enjoying the shift in him.

"Thanks. You're the only one I can talk to like this."

"Can we talk Anthony a little more?"

"I used to talk to him all the time until I found out he was telling my father everything."

"And now?"

"Father insists that he drive me around. He won't let me have a car, but I can drive."

"You don't have a license though."

"No, he won't allow it."

Paul waited, comfortable with Henry's discomfort.

"I used to score my weed from Anthony too."

"What?"

"I don't anymore."

"What? You never told me you smoked marijuana."

"You never asked."

"Wow! When did you stop?"

"I quit after my last...time in the hospital."

"Why?"

"It was probably the weed that...got me hospitalized."

"What do you mean?"

"Usually when I smoked weed, especially the really good stuff that Anthony used to score from this guy in the upper Castro, I used to get...really crazy."

"What do you mean 'really crazy?'"

"I...it made me...I used to hear things, voices...voices whispering in my ears."

"'Whispering?'"

"Telling me things.

"Like what?"

"About...aliens and... the government."

"What exactly?"

"Just...stuff about how things are...arranged here."

"'Arranged?'"

Henry jumped up from his chair and said angrily, "Of course! How the fuck do you think they run things?" He started pacing the room, angrily smashing his right fist into his left palm. "There's key people in business and government who get direct information from...them."

"How?"

"Usually through government agents, intermediates...the fucking CIA, DARPA...they're all connected! The fuckers!"

"How long has this been going on?"

"At least since Roswell!"

"And now?"

"They're everywhere! They own the media—control and manipulate films, books, TV, radio! Did you know six multinational corporations own 95% of all media?"

"Six?"

"Yes. National Amusements, Disney, Time Warner,

Comcast, Newscorp and Sony."

"And you can substantiate this?"

"Of course. I'm not a total nutcase!"

"Never said you were."

"I've done my research!"

"I don't doubt it for a moment."

"That's how they use coercion. It's what Chomsky and Hermann called 'manufacturing consent.'"

"What's that?"

"A way to convince people that the government's decisions are in the best interests of the people; that topics that are being withheld from discussion are 'national security issues.'"

"And you don't buy that?"

"Not for a moment! Do you?"

"I agree that governments have always manipulated populations. Why is this any different?"

"They're doing this with a purpose! To cover up the fact that they're trading with the aliens!"

"But why?"

"They do not want anybody to interfere with their business! I thought you believed me!"

"I admit that your list was impressive. And my research

shows you are probably...right."

"So, you agree with me?" he asked incredulously.

"I agree that there has been an incredible increase in technology in the last fifty years."

"And?"

"But I just have a difficult time connecting it all to alien influence."

"But that's the key point! That's the crux of the entire equation!"

"Say more."

"It's like what John Trudell says about slavery. We're still slaves but we're supposed to be happy because we're wage slaves. They count on us, they need us to make money for them."

"And?"

"They want everybody to be unhappy, unfulfilled and angry. They're farming us!"

"'Farming us?' For what?"

"I fucking told you! They want our emotional energy!"

"Why?"

"Because they're technologically evolved, but they don't feel love or have empathy!"

"How do you know all this?"

"I read a lot."

"Like who?"

"Oh my God! Where do I start?"

"I've read a lot of metaphysics. Just give me a few names."

"Most on topic...Jeremiah Sitchin, especially *Genesis Revisited* and *The Twelfth Planet; Chariots of the Gods* by von Daniken; *Mothman Prophecies* by Keel; *Bringers of the Dawn* by Barbara Marciniak. There are so many! But that's a good start."

"Wow! And I bet there's a lot more."

"Certainly! If you look deeply enough, there is at least provisional evidence that we have been visited by extraterrestrials for thousands of years, perhaps longer!"

"Based on...?"

"Read *Genesis Revisited*. He's included both drawings and photographs, especially some Sumerian and Akadian ones."

"Of?"

"What could very easily be spacecraft from as long ago as three thousand years. But there is so much more."

"I'll certainly look into that."

CHAPTER TWENTY-ONE
Reconsideration

San Francisco Friday April 19th, 2002

After the intensity of the prolonged session with Henry, Paul was more than anxious to have a session with Regina. He realized that he was beginning coming to count on her. She always provided valid counterpoint to his theorizing and practice. She enriched him.

He had been reconsidering his diagnosis and his plan to move forward into deeper work. The last session had certainly been a breakthrough, and Henry was clearly improving, though it could also be argued that he might also be getting more delusional. He had not been aware of the depth of Henry's abuse, and might really have just begun to crack the deep wells of Henry's anguish and rage.

Regina looked fresh and sparkling in a canary yellow sundress and low flat sandals. Though it was chilly outside, it was warm and toasty in her large flat, as the last rays of afternoon sun filtered through large bay windows in her comfortable consulting room.

"Regina, tell me honestly. Do you ever think about the nature and development of what has become of our art?"

"What do you mean?"

"Even though Hippocrates proposed that physiological abnormalities may be the root of all mental disorders in the Fourth Century BCE, you've got to remember that the very basis of the 'organic orientation' started when they discovered that Salvarsan, the 'magic bullet' arsenic compound, eliminated the delusions of grandeur and disturbances of intellect and memory associated with general paresis. They assumed at the time that these 'symptoms of 'mental illness' were 'cured' by the drug. It wasn't until much later that they figured out that it killed the dreaded protozoan *Spirochaeta pallida* that caused syphilis. But it led to the seeming revolution in the treatment of 'mental disturbance.'"

"But that wasn't the real beginning! What about Descartes and *cogito ergo sum,* and the birth of the reductionist method?"

"It wasn't until a century later that it got applied to the idea of *specific etiology* that the fire really got lit to identify the microorganisms that caused 'mental disturbance.'"

"The real problem is that it got applied to the emerging world of psychiatry. Kraepelin was the first in modern times to theorize that the different mental disorders are all biological in nature. This, in turn, evolved into the new concept of "nerves," and psychiatry became a rough approximation of neurology and neuropsychiatry. Freud was a neurologist. But Bleuler was a psychiatrist and a eugenicist."

"But weren't they just products of their times? Weren't they upholding principles that were current?"

"Plato suggested selective breeding as far back as 400 BCE, 'breeding' humans for race, intelligence and social status. But modern eugenics didn't get started until Darwin's cousin, Francis Galton, started promoting it in 1883. It was actually most strongly promoted in Britain and the U.S. Then the Nazis took it up, and everybody wants to believe that they started it all."

"OK. OK. But what does any of this have to do with 'mental illness?'"

"The psychopharmaceutical industry always wants to tout how 'modern' their approaches are, how 'innovative' they are when all they're really doing is putting band aids on the mental equivalent of surgical wounds!"

"But they are more modern than putting people in chains and straightjackets!"

"India had psych hospitals in the Third Century BCE utilizing compassionate care. The first one in Europe wasn't until almost a millennium later, and it was started at a time when so-called religious leaders used versions of exorcism and other barbaric practices such as trepanning, to 'let the demons out.'"

"But there was no literature to document their work."

The Persian physician known as Rhazes was the head of an extensive series of psychiatric care facilities in the Eighth Century CE and wrote textbooks about proper care. Another Persian physician known to us as Avicenna delineated what we call 'neuroses' and actually created the basis of cognitive therapy a thousand years ago!"

"OK. OK. Stop! I know you are a resource for ancient psychiatric lore. You're almost an antiquarian!"

"Thank you. I started out angry with the abuses I saw working on psych units, and that got me to researching the field. The most serious problem we face is that of labeling as 'schizophrenic' people who are often overwhelmed by the insensitive and uncaring atmosphere of our world today. Another common misconception is those folks are brain damaged in some way because they are usually metaphysical in some manner."

"What do you mean?"

"Symptoms that get labeled 'schizophrenia' require higher mental function and therefore a relatively intact brain. In most Western countries, however, the diagnosis is determined more by one's lack of personal power and self-determination. As Breggin said, 'The combination of psychospiritual passion and overwhelming helplessness is characteristic of almost all of the people we label 'mad.'''

"Wow. That is excellent!"

"So, if one is born with a sensitive awareness into a world culture that treats children as commodities—and somehow that person is able to retain an awareness of the rift between what is taught as 'proper and correct' and what one's perceptions tell one is accurate—that person might readily turn his or her focus to ontological concerns. Without some grounding in a relatively solid sense of self reinforced through nurturing and support, it is impossible to focus on more mundane matters such as earning money."

"I've always known you were extremely sensitive. I feel honored that you share your openness with me."

"I think it was Grof who said, 'It is somehow implicit in the current psychiatric system of thought that mental health is associated with atheism, materialism and the worldview of mechanistic science. Thus, spiritual experiences, religious beliefs and involvement in spiritual practices would generally support a psychopathological diagnosis.'"

"Wow! That is excellent! I can see you as a member of the Network Against Psychiatric Assault (NAPA) when you were working the units!"

"I actually was in 1976."

"The use and abuse of children is so widespread that it is thought to be 'normal.' It's almost completely ignored in the brain-dead media. Child related crime is just another commodity!"

"I so completely agree! And the media has promoted the idea that there is nothing spiritual about 'mental illness.' Especially since anyone may be afflicted by bouts of anxiety and depression, periods of isolation, tics, quivers or kleptomania.

"Right, and anyone who falls afoul of society's watchdogs may be prescribed psychiatry's 'wonder drugs' to ameliorate 'symptoms' by interfering with the brain's ability to function."

"It's a contemporary world example of the failure of care much akin to Freud's betrayal of children in 1898. It's all considered 'normal' today (as it was then)."

"So, what does this have to do with Henry?"

"I'm not using any kind of standard treatment with him. I disavow the contemporary standard that simply subjugates individuals to camouflage societal complicity. It simply reinforces the seeming correctness of highly paid 'experts' who parrot the party line."

"Hello? Earth to Paul!"

"Oh! Sorry! I'm just trying to get a handle on whether to go deeper right now, or encourage the plateauing."

"Is he more or less psychotic sounding? Expressing more or less delusional material?"

"He's reporting less delusional stuff, even though I don't think I've gotten to the bottom of his secrets."

"I see."

"His mood seems to have improved, though he continues to take his 'meds.' I've agreed with Henry that I will help him titrate his way off of them at some point."

"Who's your medical backup?"

"You know Tommy O'Connell? We worked together at Mt. Zion."

"Oh. Yeah. Just making sure you had backup."

"I feel like I'm just seeing the first wave of lava coming out from under the sea!"

"You know this is going to be dramatic. The hardest part is going to be keeping him on track. Not letting him get too radical all at once when he feels 'liberated!'"

"I wonder whether I should consult with Henry some more about his father before diving more deeply into the relational dynamics."

"Will he want to?"

"I don't know. I just want to make sure he's safe."

"I understand."

"Maybe I'll just broach the topic of scheduling an exploratory appointment with the both of them."

"Might not be a bad idea."

CHAPTER TWENTY-TWO
Plunging In

San Francisco Tuesday, April 23rd, 2002

"Fuck no! Not in a million years!"

"But..."

"No! And I remind you of your duty not to share anything we talk about, especially not with him!"

"Please, Henry. I do know my duty!"

"I... I'm sorry! I know. It's just that this is the first time in my life that I have had anything that was really my own, alone."

"So, what's next?"

"I... feel better since we started talking about Father. Maybe we need to do more."

"We never really got into the material about your father. In fact, we barely mentioned it before you blew up."

"But it helped...talking about him, I mean."

"I agree."

"So...?"

"I believe we should attempt that process you originally proposed."

"When?"

"Now, today, if you feel up to it. Do you need a bio-break first?"

"No. I'm good."

"OK. Do you want to work on your energy to him, or his energy to you first?"

"I'm not sure I can work on his energy to me right now. How about mine to him?

"Then let's start with breathing together. I'll walk you through it."

They both settled into their respective chairs, and Paul listened to his client's ragged breathing settle and become more measured. As his own first breath filled his lungs and expanded, he felt his innate sensitivities open out as if he had been squeezed through a pinhole and become re-animated in a different dimension in which all of his gifts shone resplendent.

By the seventh breath, he felt acutely aware, not only of his own perceptions and sensations and the highly charged, extremely sensitive clairsentient world, but the exquisite parameters of his client as well, outlined as if on an inner screen that brooked no misunderstanding. He could read his every emanation and see each one as if they were his own.

"Henry, I want you to bring up an image of your father. Doesn't matter what age he is. Have him stand in front of you."

"OK."

"Can you see him?"

"Yes."

"I want you to do a quick scan from the top of his head to his feet and then up the back—what I call a 'get acquainted' scan."

After several moments, Henry nodded.

"This time I want you to scan him again like an MRI in micro-thin slices so that you can examine each of them closely. Pay attention to where you notice your energy lodged in him. When you find something, I want you to stop and tell me."

Another nod, and his breathing deepened even further.

"Tell me as soon as you feel any energy."

Henry's breath caught, and a small choke escaped his throat.

"Between his eyes."

"Can you see it? Does it have a color or shape?"

"It looks like a bunch of black grapes."

"I want you to reach out—you can use your hands or just with your mind—and take that energy back. This is your energy projected onto him. You gave it to him. Now take it back."

Henry made reaching motions and pulled his hands towards his chest.

"Is that where it belongs?"

"Yes. It was energy...from my heart."

"Is there more?"

"Just a little," he said and made another gesture to his chest.

"Good. Go ahead and continue."

Momentarily, he stopped again with a pained look on his face.

"His mouth."

"Does it have a color or shape?"

"It looks like a bunch of green-and-purple snakes."

"Where does it go in your body?"

"He stole it from my brain."

"Can you pull it back?"

"He doesn't want me to take it."

"I want you to hold your right-hand palm open toward him and say, 'You may not resist. It is <u>my</u> energy!'"

Henry did so, and the wrinkles in his forehead disappeared.

"He did it! He didn't even try to stop me!"

"Good! Is there any more there?"

"No."

"Continue scanning."

The young man halted his motion, a small rictus frozen on his face.

"His belly."

"What about 'his belly?'"

"Yellow...looks like spaghetti."

"Take it back into your body. Where does it go?"

"It feels like he...took my power!"

"Just take it back. Where does it want to go?"

He tapped his solar plexus.

"You know what to do."

His client rubbed his solar plexus in a clockwise motion and then patted it three times, gently.

"I got it."

"Just continue."

Henry grabbed his scrotum.

"There?"

"Yes. He took my balls! That fucker!"

"Where is the energy stored?"

"In his balls, that fucker!"

"Go ahead and take it back."

They continued with Henry taking back energy from his father's knees (flexibility), ankles (mobility), back of the thighs (strength and endurance) and the back of the heart (shadow emotions). At that point Henry straightened up and said, "I think I'm complete."

Paul could see that there was some missed energy and hesitated before speaking.

"Henry, can you scan the neighborhood of his left shoulder blade?"

"Oh shit! I didn't see it!"

"It looks like a little pile of red arrowheads to me."

"How did you know?"

"I just felt it. Am I right?"

"Yes. He was...it belongs to me. In my neck."

"That's how it feels to me."

Paul then walked his client through the process of filling in all of the holes in his father's aura with blue-white light. Paul then asked if he felt prepared to remove all of his father's energy from his own body. Henry hesitated, scrunched up his face, and then nodded.

For the next forty-five minutes, they scrupulously worked the length of the front and back of Henry's body, and he systematically gave back to his father what he called "steaming heaps of crap" and other scatological references to demonstrate how he felt he had been infected by his father's energy in a variety of areas of his body, especially his penis. After filling in all of the virtual holes in his own aura, as he completed the process, he collapsed onto the floor.

When Paul rose to check on him, Henry raised his head and shook it, gesturing him away. Paul sat down again and contemplated the intensity of the movement of energy that had occurred that day. He felt exhausted himself but got up to drink a glass of filtered water. He then grabbed another glass full for Henry, who drank it down quickly. Paul asked if Henry was ready to resume his seat. When he did, Paul began to speak, asking Henry to repeat after him:

"I, the being known as (state your name) in this particular embodiment, do hereby state to the Universe, the entire Mind and Heart of God/Goddess/All That Is Source, that I choose this moment of NOW to be free and sovereign from (state the name of the other being). I state that NOW I am released and healed, released and healed, released and healed. I am NOW free and sovereign, free and sovereign, free and sovereign, in this lifetime, past lifetimes, future lifetimes, simultaneous lifetimes in all dimensions and in all time frames. I state that I am released and healed, free and sovereign, in this moment. And I ask that it be written in the Book of Life. Let it be done. Thank you. Aho. Amen."

CHAPTER TWENTY-THREE
A New Day

San Francisco Friday, April 26th, 2002

Major breakthrough! Paul was elated. Henry had responded extremely well to the process, paid close attention and neither boiled over with rage nor fulminated from overlong emotional suppression.

He reminded himself of the distinct possibility that Henry could easily regress to some greater or less extent. Paul had seen the phenomena many times, both with clients and himself. For every step forward, he had many times found that individuals might develop some form or influenza, even pneumonia. He had seen individuals develop horrible rashes, eczema, urinary difficulties, all manner of physical impairments following an emotional breakthrough, as if the body needed down-time to recover in relative quiet, integrate a higher level of awareness with often different skills or a higher level of skills that had pre-existed.

He was still thinking about catharsis when he called Regina. In ancient Rome, theatrical performances were staged in order to provoke the letting-go process in the audience, based on the understanding that people would feel better having had a chance to do so, and this would in turn rebound into greater health for their circles of relationship and the Empire as a whole. They had actually taken the word from the Greeks, and it meant "purification" or "cleansing."

"Regina, Paul Marzeky here."

"Good to hear from you, Paul"

"Good to hear your voice."

"I'm in the office today, even though many people seem to have taken a four-day holiday."

"Astute as ever," Paul said, and then told her the details of the Sovereignty Ceremony and Henry's reactions both with him and toward his father.

"I'm not acquainted with that exact process. It sounds like shamanism, based on the work on guided imagery. Do you know Jean Achterberg's work?"

"She chaired my Dissertation Committee at Saybrook."

"How amazing!"

"Listen, let's chat some more when I get there."

"How long?"

"Depends. Do you want me to pick something up? Chinese? Thai? Bar-B-Que?"

"Q sounds awesome! Leon's?"

"You bet! What do you want?"

"Half a slab of ribs, coleslaw and a corn muffin."

"Sounds good. I'll call it in. See you in probably forty-five."

"Good!"

By the time Paul had traversed The City (He in North Beach, she in Ashbury Heights) and stopped at Leon's famous BBQ on Fillmore, he was still immersed in thinking about emotional release work. He continued the conversation they had been having in his mind. It was one of the things he admired the most about her—she was a heavyweight intellect and could hold conversational threads in her mind for a long period.

When he had settled in her consultation room with a cup of fresh coffee, he continued as if she had been in his mind the whole time.

"The method was originally a metaphor for the homeopathic process in which pity and fear create a catharsis of emotions like themselves, through art or any extreme change. Aristotle originally used it in the *Poetics*, comparing the effects of tragedy on the mind of a spectator to the effect of a cathartic on the body—though some people believe that Aristotle may have been responding to Plato's negative view of artistic mimesis on an audience.

"OK, Mr. Smarty Pants, I've got a more modern reference!"

"OK."

"Josef Breuer developed a cathartic method using hypnosis to assist patients to recall traumatic experiences and express suppressed emotions that then relieved them of their symptoms. Then Freud replaced hypnosis with free association and became a star."

"I'll call your Breuer and raise you an Émile Durkheim! He reinforced the original purpose, stating that after the emotional release emotions get shared, which leads to a deeper emotional communion, and hopefully further social integration, and renewed trust in life, strength and self-confidence."

"So, what? You think the government should start putting on emotionally-releasing stage plays and movies for people to go to for emotional release?"

"I hadn't really thought of that, but it's a damn fine idea!"

"Especially as so much money is misspent on treatments that don't really work, or that actually cause harm!"

"Don't get me started on the Hippocratic Oath!"

"I promise. But what?"

"For me, it's related to unexpurgated grief."

"Say more."

"I mean in the really large sense. For example, I was thinking about the American People as a whole having never been allowed to mourn the many, many losses associated with Vietnam. There ought to have been a daylong (I actually think at least a month) day of mourning after we pulled out of Saigon—with pay!"

"That will never happen!"

"No, it's not expedient from the superficial financial perspective. But no one really considers how many lost sick days and other time off from jobs people take, related to drugs and alcohol, which in turn is related, on some level, to carrying around unexpressed emotions and a broken grief process."

"I see where you are coming from. But where would it ever end?"

"It's really an organic process that takes as long as it takes. If we spent the entire military budget on emotional healing and well-being, we'd have a lot healthier country!"

"But what about the Indians? We've never mourned our behaviors killing off, some people say, a hundred million Native people to steal their land!"

"God! Now you sound like me!"

"Thank you!"

"But you're right on point there! We really never mourn any of our losses, so we keep recreating traumatic circumstances by default!"

"Do you mind if we shift a little here? Talk about guided imagery?"

"Sure. After all, this is Henry's hour!'

"So, you really worked with Jeanne Achterberg?"

"Yeah. At Saybrook."

"Tell me some more about this process."

"The central idea actually goes back to the notion of a 'mind's eye,' to Cicero's reference to *mentis oculi* during his discussion of the orator's appropriate use of simile. He referred to allusions to 'the Syrtis of his patrimony' and 'the Charybdis of his possessions' as being 'too far-fetched;' and instead he advised the orator to just speak of 'the rock' and 'the gulf;' because 'the eyes of the mind are more easily directed to those objects which we have seen, than to those which we have only heard.'"

"Wow! You've done your research!"

"I have. I really believe in my work."

"But that was an old reference!"

"The concept of 'the mind's eye' first appeared in English in Chaucer in 1387 when he published *Man of Law's Tale* in his *Canterbury Tales.* He tells us that one of the three men dwelling in a castle was blind and could only see with 'the eyes of his mind,' the ones 'with which all men see after they have become blind.'"

"Really Paul? Chaucer?"

"Well, you asked."

"All you've given me so far is mostly apocryphal. Are there any more modern references? You certainly cannot say it was peer-reviewed evidence."

"No, but I can send you citations as soon as I get home. There's longstanding evidence that mental imagery plays a key role in contributing to, exacerbating or intensifying the experience and symptoms of posttraumatic stress disorder (PTSD); compulsive cravings; eating disorders such as anorexia nervosa and bulimia nervosa; spastic hemiplegia; incapacitation following a stroke or cerebrovascular accident (CVA); and restricted cognitive function and motor control due to multiple sclerosis. It has been shown to be effective with social anxiety, phobias, bipolar disorder, schizophrenia, ADHD and, of course, depression."

"Let's say for the moment that I agree with your basic premise, and maybe I'd like to experience it myself some time."

"I'd love to give you a session!"

"Oh, thank you so much! You are such a warrior!"

"It may sound a little arcane compared to 'traditional' approaches, especially any that 'require treatment' with psycho-chemicals. There's a long and very reputable history of using such methods for alleviating emotional pain. Psychiatry's been trying to find a 'physical basis for mental illness' for a hundred and fifty years. This approach has generated trillions, maybe quadrillions, of dollars in profit, but only for practitioners who have blindly followed the 'authorized' path of what Kuhn called 'normal science' in 1962."

"You sound a little defensive to me. Any idea why?"

"I just get really tired of so-called colleagues arguing in favor of the 'accepted methods of practice,' especially drugging clients. They're always trying to refute my approach—which, by the way, I have successfully used to help hundreds of people."

"Still..."

"OK. I get your point. It is probably related to my never being a part of the 'establishment,' or belonged to any august organization."

"I think you're missing the point."

"I did not come here for personal analysis!"

"Don't you think your beliefs and choice of treatment methods are sort of indissolubly connected?"

"Of course, but I do not want to sit here and pay you $125 an hour to dissect my psyche!"

"Point taken. But I find it intriguing anyway."

"The topic or my psyche?"

"Hardy har har!"

"That's material for another time. This is Henry's hour. I want to discuss his... 'awakening,' and get your perspective. I'm concerned about precipitating an episode."

"Is it really a real concern?"

"I have to consider the possibility. According to his records, he has been hospitalized previously with 'severe anxiety and agitated delusional states.'"

"We've talked about his delusional content a bit, but I understand that you're questioning the etiology of them."

"I don't believe they arose out of some kind of convoluted Freudian scheme involving their arising out of an Oedipal conflict!"

They both laughed, having long ago discussed their mutual dismissal of one of the main tenets of Freudian architecture—especially since Freud had been bi-sexual for many decades, and was decidedly misogynistic—a point that feminist psychology had emphasized for years.

"There must be some kind of as-yet-revealed trauma that gave rise to them. I do not believe in the 'organic orientation.'"

Regina laughed again and said, "I agree with your position! Why else would anybody adopt such obviously bizarre adaptations?"

"Yes! Exactly! Thank you."

"And...?"

"I feel like there's a lot of unexplored material here. He's finally admitted that his father is abusive."

"And?"

"Two things. First, I'm concerned about approaching that too deeply, too quickly."

"And?"

"I believe Henry might have been sexually abused too."

"Hoo boy! That's a big one!"

"I know. I know."

"What the latest with the father?"

"He keeps pressing me to 'share' information about Henry, which of course I cannot and will not do. I do have some thoughts about opening up the dialogue more with Henry."

"Have you spoken to Henry about your concerns?"

"Only in response to either his manifest fear of his Father or his emerging anger and the tremendous relief he's feeling."

"So, what you've done so far is having good results. Have you attempted to get Henry's approval to talk to his father, at least about specific topics?"

"He gave permission within a very narrow frame for a one-time contact, but otherwise, he adamantly refuses."

"I don't see a lot of options without your client's permission. For the moment, I suggest you continue, cautiously, and that we meet again next week, same Bat time, same Bat station."

CHAPTER TWENTY-FOUR
The Work Continues

San Francisco Tuesday May 7th, 2002

Henry appeared early for his appointment and simultaneously expressed both eagerness and fear.

"How do we start? I feel like I'm...really benefitting."

"Good! Excellent!"

"But I...am not totally sure...I can...that I am ready to keep working on...Father."

"Totally understandable."

"It feels like...if we don't, maybe I won't be able to keep...making progress. But I do feel better."

"We can discuss other possibilities."

"But what'ya think? Can we work on somebody else?"

"Sure! Tell me who you want to work on?"

"I don't know," he said. Then his face turned livid and he sobbed briefly before he looked back up at Paul.

"Help me! Please help me!"

"How, Henry? Tell me!"

"I... just want get free...of this prison I've been in... my whole life!"

Paul felt such a strong wave of connection with the younger man; in fact, teared up momentary in an excess of empathy with him. It seemed like a doorway to new territory to be explored.

"Henry, why don't we explore your father a little more, but more slowly?"

Henry hesitated for a moment and then nodded.

"I really believe it might be helpful if we could decide on a list of topics I can discuss with your father."

Henry jumped up out of his chair and screamed.

"No! No fucking way!"

He started pacing the room, mumbling. Then his voice got louder.

"I. DO. NOT. WANT. YOU. TO. TALK. TO. HIM!"

"OK, Henry!"

"I. FORBID. IT!"

"Fine. It's your call."

"I am proud of being angry! Fuck him! He does not deserve to really know me!"

"'Deserve?'"

"He doesn't know me, never has!"

"And?"

"I will not allow him to see my...inner life. I will not let him in!"

"It's obvious that he's harmed you deeply!"

"I won't give him another chance!"

"Our work here is about giving you a second chance!"

"Why does that have to have anything to do with Father?"

"Because he has harmed you so much! Not only the original injury, but also all of the energy you have to use to keep him out. It prevents your healing. It keeps the wound open and alive!"

"And?"

"The only way to heal it is to feel it, as they say."

"I feel better now. Maybe...maybe I can handle another session...another Sovereignty."

"With whom?"

I still feel a little raw about Father."

"And?"

Maybe we can just talk a bit...before we do a Ceremony."

"OK."

"I can tell you more now."

"OK."

"Where do I start?"

"Start with wherever you feel to start."

Henry sat quietly, head down and then looked up and into Paul's eyes before he spoke softly.

"I... suppose you must...have already figured out...that Father is a brute."

Paul simply nodded. Then Henry spoke more forcefully.

"I fucking hate him! I want to be free!"

"Excellent."

Henry pounded the arms of his chair, and then loudly spoke again.

"He has controlled my whole life, ever since I was a child. He never...I never had a chance."

"'A chance?'"

"I've never had the opportunity to...grow up."

"'Grow up?'"

"There's something...wrong with me. Something is missing."

"'Missing?'"

"Yeah. Like part of my brain never had a chance to develop."

"And what part might that be?"

"Sometimes I can't...make decisions...like most people can."

"Give me an example."

Again, the anger, and he pounded on his left chair arm.

"Look at my fucking life! He fucking owns me!"

"You feel controlled?"

"Absolutely! I've never had any joy!"

"I understand. You've had very little choice."

"'Choice?' What the fuck is that? He even has Andrew pick out my goddamn clothes!"

"Wow! That's radical!"

"Every single day! And he goes with me everywhere, except the fucking bathroom!"

"What do you want to do?"

"I don't know!"

"I meant about Andrew. Have you talked to your father about him?"

"I can't talk to him about anything!"

"Have you approached Andrew?"

"He's only 'following orders!'"

"Tell me some more about your father."

"You're not going to like this, but he's...he's one of the controllers!"

"Controllers?'"

"He works with the aliens! He's gotten rich!"

"Can you prove that? Do you have any proof?"

"There is no way to prove it! He's keeps everything hidden!"

"Then how can you be sure?"

"My grandfather..."

"Who set up your trust fund."

"Yes. Did you know that he only left him a single dollar when he died?"

"What?"

"Yes. A dollar so he couldn't contest the will!

"And he left all of his money to you?"

"In trust. Yes."

"How does that relate to...your father?"

"When Grandfather cut him off, I was just a child. Father didn't have any money, just the administrator of my trust fund. He wanted to get a hold of it, use it as he saw fit. He told me he would use it 'for my own good,' Fortunately, Grandfather set me up with good lawyers to keep him from doing that."

"And?"

"He's always wanted my money!"

"But what does that have to do with... 'aliens?'"

"I've researched him. He...I know he...he did have some money when I was young. Not a lot...but then he started investing. But I found out..."

"What?"

"He always seemed...to get really lucky...with his investments."

"'Lucky?'"

"He bought Bell Labs, Xerox, Texas Instruments, even Apple. He's deeply invested in 'defense related industries'—he's friends with lots of scientists and generals."

"So?"

"I think he's one of the insiders."

"What 'insiders?'"

"He's...a conduit to the government!"

"And?"

"He wanted money so badly! He didn't really have any money until I was older. Then suddenly, when I was a teenager, he got extremely rich, traveling all the time. Europe, New York, Japan. Buying companies, airlines, everything."

"So, what?"

"Colonel Corso named so many of the same companies...the same ones Father invested in."

"And?"

"He gets insider information! He's part of the cabal!"

"Why is that so important to you?"

"Around the same time that he started...raping me!"

CHAPTER TWENTY-FIVE
More Clearly the Focus

San Francisco Friday, May 17th, 2002

Paul wanted so badly to talk to someone, and ethically, the only one he could talk to about Henry was Regina.

"We on for today?"

"Friday afternoon 5 PM. It's in the book."

"What'll it be today?"

"How about Chinese?"

"You're on! Choices?"

"Moo goo gai pan. Get some extra pancakes please. How about you?"

"I'm thinking Shrimp and Pork in Garlic Black Bean Sauce!"

"Oh divine! Share?"

"Of course!"

He called in the order to the Golden Palace and picked it up on his way across town.

When they were seated at her kitchen table, enjoying the view of her back garden, he told her about Henry's

revelations and how edgy the energy had gotten just before Henry told him."

"You were really right to not push too hard, though I'm glad this finally came out."

"I still think there's more. He claims it started when he was thirteen. But he's been beating him since he was a kid. Why does he start the sexual abuse when he's a teenager? Doesn't make sense.

"I see your point. You obviously think there's still more."

"I do, though I can't imagine what it might be."

"Me either. Unless his father was having sex with the aliens!"

"Oh Jesus!"

"You pay me for my unique perspective!"

"Thanks a lot!"

"Just doing my job!"

"I know it's more than that, but thanks anyway."

"Tell me again: 'The check is in the mail!'"

They both laughed as they thought of the other two lies of the trio: "I promise I will respect you in the morning" and "I promise I won't come in your mouth!"

"You are such a character! I am so glad to know you. I must admit I have come to really admire you. It's not something I usually consider with women."

"But you do with guys?"

"Yeah, yeah. I know it's really sexist, but it's taken me a long time to learn that women are just human beings, too."

"Kind of like Allison Armstrong. Something she said at a workshop: Men have to learn that women aren't just men with tits!"

"She really said that?"

"Yeah, the audience was like 90% women. The guys who came were very fem-friendly and open to learning."

"Sounds interesting. Will you invite me next time she's in town? I would like to hear more. I know I have had some measure of a shitty attitude toward women for a long time."

"Never with me!"

"No. I have always respected you. Lately I've started really admiring you. Liking you as a person as well as a colleague."

"Why, thank you, kind sir," she drawled in the West Texas accent that was both a vestige of her childhood and one that she took on from time to time.

He laughed. "I really do appreciate you."

"I know. So, to Henry?" she said, deflecting a moment

that had grown a little too personal for the timing.

"I have a kind of theory."

"So, tell me."

"It's a little off the wall, but here goes. He didn't start the sexual abuse until Henry started looking more like a young man."

". Why?"

"When he was a kid, Senior could just throw him around, punch and beat him easily."

"And?"

"When he got older, Senior maybe saw him as a challenge. Or he wanted to punish him in newer, deeper ways!"

"Jesus! What a perv!"

"That's what I think."

"Gross!"

"So, you don't think it's sexual per se?"

"Rape never is. It's always having power over!"

"The guy is even sicker and weirder that we thought!"

CHAPTER TWENTY-SIX
It Keeps Flowing

San Francisco Tuesday May 21st, 2002

Henry entered the office looking what Paul called "flittery," like a butterfly on methamphetamine. He seemed anxious and unable to settle, fidgeting even when he finally did settle down.

He reported that he had been having bouts of diarrhea (no matter what he ate or even if he didn't), intense but relatively transient headaches, general malaise and intermittent spiking temperatures.

"Do you want to cancel today, Henry?"

"No. I... I think...I'm afraid I'm losing my mind!"

Paul decided to tread very carefully.

"What does that mean, Henry?"

"'I thought I had a handle on everything, even though almost everybody thought I was crazy."

"Tell me more."

"I've always been alone. I've...gotten used to living in my own mind. And as long as I didn't ask for too much,

Father pretty much let me be. I mean, he always beat me, especially when he was drunk, but otherwise...he was gone a lot, left me alone."

"And then?"

"I don't know what happened, but one time when he came home from some high-level meeting...in Washington, I think, DC...and he came home, beat me, and then...then..."

"It's all right, Henry, go slow."

Henry buried his head in his hands and sobbed for several minutes.

He looked up with the most pained expression Paul had ever seen and then spoke.

"I didn't know what he was going to do. He beat me like usual, and I thought that's all he was going to do. Then he started taking my clothes off. He'd beat me like that before. But then...then...he put his...dick in my mouth!"

Paul didn't say anything, just allowed Henry to re-gather his wits.

"From that point on, I don't know why, it was always the beating before...the...sex!"

"Have you told anyone else about this?"

"No! Never!"

"Did Andrew know?"

"No! I don't think so! Maybe!"

"He seems to have a lot of power over you—even though you say he's just following your father's orders."

"Father...won't let me make any decisions for myself. The only place I ever have any choices is on the Internet. I have all kinds of hidden files that he doesn't know about!"

"You seem rather proud of that!"

"I... I am. It's the place where I feel alive."

"You were shut down for a lot of years. Now you're waking up."

"I want to work on Father some more. I'm not complete... with him."

"It might be too soon. You just said you were having some physical issues since the last session."

Henry jumped up out of his chair, arms wide, fists curled, and started toward him. Paul pushed back and almost fell out of his chair.

"GODDAMN IT! I AM SO FUCKING SICK OF THIS SHIT!!"

Paul scrambled to his feet and put some distance between himself and his suddenly fulminating client.

Henry stood in place, arms flapping like a large, awkward bird and continued shouting as foam appeared at the edges of his mouth.

"I'VE HAD A LIFETIME OF THIS SHIT! I AM FUCKING

TIRED OF IT!"

Paul held out his hands palms facing to Henry, feet apart, and made eye contact.

"Henry, we can talk about running the process, if that's what you want."

"YOU DON'T BELIEVE ME EITHER! YOU'RE JUST ANOTHER FUCKING LIAR," he said, voice still loud but diminishing in volume.

"I believe you're genuinely experiencing exactly what you're experiencing. And I know that it causes you great pain."

"That's not the same!" Quieter, calming slightly.

"No, it's not! I won't lie to you and tell you I feel what you're feeling."

"SEE? YOU'RE JUST LIKE THEM!" His voice reignited as if from the smoldering coals.

Paul stood his ground, and lowered his hands, still palms out, to his sides.

"Can we...are you...can we sit, maybe talk about this a little more?"

"'TALK?' FUCK TALK! I... I'M SO FUCKING SICK OF TALKING!"

"I feel your frustration, Henry. I know you've lived with this all your life."

A perplexed look crossed Henry's face, and he dropped

his hands as if their weight had suddenly grown impossible to bear any longer.

"We've made progress, haven't we?" Henry spoke in a weak, small voice and Paul wondered, not for the first time, if his client might in fact be suffering from Dissociative Identity Disorder (the old name for Multiple Personality Disorder). He certainly sounded like a very young boy in the moment.

"Yes, Henry, I think we have. At least now you're able to tell me the truth and not feel rejected."

"I... that's...true," Henry said, sounding like a perplexed adolescent.

Paul considered that conversely, he might have slipped spontaneously into what Stone and Winkleman had originally called "subpersonalities," not actual fractured states of separate identity, but nonetheless carrying out specific energies and duties with the larger personality structure.

Having opened himself so acutely, Paul wanted now to explore how much this age-regressed version of Henry was willing to divulge. He was torn between calming the man down and exploring the gaping wound he had revealed. Contrary to conventional "wisdom," Paul elected to go ahead and give Henry choices, rather than ploughing ahead on his own tack or avoiding the eruption altogether. He strongly believed in telling the truth to clients and empowering them, no matter how small the way.

"Tell you what. Let's sit for a few minutes, do some breathing and maybe we'll try another process, one that's not as intense. Or, if you'd rather, we can stay with what you are feeling right now."

Henry sat quietly for the longest minute Paul had ever experienced and then looked up mournfully as his tears started to fall.

Henry spoke in this weak, quavery voice, like a young child. Paul immediately named his 'four-year-old voice.'

"I just...don't know what...to do."

"About what?"

"Anything."

"How old do you feel?"

I don't know. Four. Five."

"Are you Little Henry?"

After a long pause, as if measuring the question and his potential answers with all their implications, the young man nodded.

"What do you feel right now, Little Henry?"

"Scared... Vulnerable."

"That makes perfect sense. After all, you're just a little boy right now."

Another nod followed by an open trusting stare.

"Can you tell me more of what you're feeling right now, Little Henry?"

"I'm afraid. Father always yells at me."

"Why do you think he does that?"

"I don't know."

"What does he say?"

"'Worthless. Useless. Idiot.'"

"Are you? Do you believe him?"

Panic crossed the planes of his face, as tears streamed down.

"Maybe. I don't know."

"Do you feel that you are worthless?"

"Sometimes. Sometimes he...makes me feel bad."

"Any reason why?"

"I'm not...smart enough. I... can't do what he wants."

"Like what?"

"Puzzles. Math. Chess."

"Because?"

"I'm not as good as...him."

"You're just a little boy."

Henry slumped to the floor, crying copiously. His left thumb moved toward his mouth, he didn't quite insert it.

Paul waited. As suddenly as he'd regressed, he roused

himself, standing quickly and shouting in a loud gruff voice.

"That fucker! He fucking hurt me!"

The flood of tears resumed and his shoulders shook as he tried to articulate words that seemed not to want to come out of the shelter of his mouth.

He gawped several times before hawking up a huge wad of phlegm that had lodged in his throat. Paul handed him the tissue box. He quickly spat into a pair of tissues and deposited them in the trashcan and then spoke in an almost inaudible croak.

"He. Hit. Me."

"When?"

"All the time."

"When?"

"Ever since I was a kid."

"Recently?"

"Not so much since we...since I've been... working with you."

"Have you ever told him how you feel?"

"No. Never. I... I'm afraid."

"That he will hit you again?"

"Yes. And worse!"

"Have you ever told anybody about this before?"

"I told...one of my doctors...a long time ago."

"Did he talk to your father about it?"

"I don't know. I think so. After I told him, I never saw him again."

"'Never?'"

"No. My father fired him and got me a new doctor."

"And no one said a word about it? No one tried to protect you?"

"No. No one."

"We can stop for now, Henry. We don't have to do anything else."

Henry got up slowly with a very odd look in his eyes, and a far-away smile on his face. Paul sat up straighter in his chair and just watched.

As Henry got closer, he extended his right hand out toward Paul.

"Paul, I want to kiss you."

CHAPTER TWENTY-SEVEN
Revelations Galore

San Francisco (late) May 24th, 2002

Paul sat back in the deep, comfortable leather chair in her office and sipped another cup of her dark-brewed coffee.

"I think we need another hour today. Are you open to that?"

"Oh, thank God, Regina! You are such a gift!"

"Up to that point, I didn't know what to make of him. He was all over the place emotionally, and I was all over the place diagnostically!"

"But you elected not to say anything and simply see what Henry chose, even though you had at least three different avenues to pursue."

"Isn't psychotherapy invigorating sometimes?" she asked rhetorically.

Then Paul told her about the close of the session.

"Jesus! What did you do?"

"I immediately stood, stepped back and shook his hand before reminding him of our next appointment."

Regina laughed.

"I would have liked to have seen that!"

"It wasn't pretty! I was embarrassed, but I covered it pretty well."

"Are you going to discuss it with him next week?"

"I almost have to, don't you think?"

"I would think so. How you handle the erotic transference will certainly determine the quality and nature of the continuing therapeutic alliance."

"That's for sure! I must admit that I was not prepared for his sexual projection!"

"I understand."

"I froze! Even though I understand the process, with the amygdala generating all kinds of hormones and the parasympathetic decelerating the heart rate, I still locked up!"

She fingered her hair and gave him a deep, radiant smile then spoke.

"Freezing is the universal fear reaction, mediated by acetylcholine that stimulates the HPA (hypothalamus–pituitary–adrenal) axis, that triggers a whole flood of corticotrophin-releasing hormone (CRH) that mediates fear reactions, ACTH, and cortisol, at least in humans. In primates and rodents, it is basal and stress-induced cortisol."

"Wait a minute! Wait a minute! You just happened to

know all of that off the top of your head?"

She smiled again.

"You're always telling me that you recognize my intelligence!"

"But I had no idea you had such depth in psychoneuroanatomy!"

"I am intrigued by science, but I recognize that it's not the essence of healing."

"I am seriously impressed!"

Then Regina took him deeper into a mystical territory. "Healing is more like alchemy. Malouin called it 'the chemistry of the subtlest kind,' that creates extraordinary chemical reactions at a pace faster than Nature and allows the development of profound powers. But only if one is working on oneself. Then it's possible to transmute the dross into the gold of higher emotions."

Paul responded, "That's what I want for Henry. He's been working against himself for so long. He learned all these negative ways of seeing himself. I want to get him to the point where he can genuinely reflect on his own experience, not filtering his perceptions through his delusions."

"Do you think he tried to approach you because he was attracted to you or was it because he was feeling such a strong release—feeling that he could be so honest with you? Or maybe because he revealed so much of himself to you he felt impelled to follow his awakened sexual feelings?"

"I don't know. It's confusing. I didn't even pick up on the energetic shift. I was too busy tracking the transference and the shift of his affect."

"That makes sense. How are you going to approach him about it?"

"My inclination is to be direct but that depends on how dissociated he is."

"Have you formalized his diagnosis yet?"

"No, I'm still vacillating. I've considered DID, (Dissociative Identity Disorder, that they both still thought of a Multiple Personality Disorder), but mostly I think it is more trauma-induced, Delusional Disorder NOS. I'm still holding out the possibility of PTSD because of the depressive episodes. I'm hoping to get some clarity with you today."

"You've really delineated his symptomatology quite well."

"Thank you. For me, a proper diagnosis facilitates treatment."

"I agree with you. These regressive episodes are intriguing. They certainly support the possibility of DID. Does he have any other supporting symptoms?"

"Evidently not. No discrete periods of time loss, no fugues, though he does report some memory lapses. His mood shifts seem to be ego syntonic (appropriate to emotional tone), even though the complete mélange that he presents is both confusing and intriguing. I haven't seen any shifts to alter personalities. He has a kind of shadow life on the Internet. He apparently spends many hours—I'm not sure how many—every day investigating conspiracy theories."

"Let's talk some more about guided imagery."

"What else do you want to know?"

"Guided imagery involves all the senses, and is experienced throughout the body, not just mentally. It catalyzes a naturally immersive altered state and is really a form of meditation. The light trance state I induce through the breathing mobilizes unconscious processes to assist with conscious goals."

"Is there any clinical evidence, studies and citations, to support this?"

"At least forty years' worth! The effectiveness of guided imagery has been validated by research. It has a positive impact on health, wellness, attitude, behavioral change, even peak performance."

"Oh, come on! 'Forty years?'"

"True! It's been shown to lowers anxiety and reduce pain and stress, blood pressure, cholesterol, even hemoglobin A1C levels."

"How does that help your therapeutic approach?"

"By reducing anxiety and reorienting the client to pay attention to his or her inner world, it allows heightened access to emotional depth, memory recall, responsiveness to spirituality, intuition, abstract thinking and empathy."

"Would you call it 'shamanic?'"

"Only in the sense that I often use trance states in my healing. Mostly I use a simple breathing technique to sharpen focus and attention. Also, I totally believe that all of what are called 'problems'—physical, emotional or mental—are rooted in what I call the 'withheld energy,' any emotional energy that is suppressed or hidden. And it builds in power and influence, and eventually manifests in what we call 'symptoms.'"

"And you heal these 'energies' by having your client visualize them?"

"By releasing all of the accompanying pain and shame and the often-traumatically induced affect."

"I know we talked about this before, and I know you are a big believer in catharsis and abreaction, but does it really have long-term benefits?"

"Nothing can 'fix' someone forever, but this process really facilitates creating more room for a person to move within themselves. I think it really deepens rapport."

"Certainly, a complex case."

"Indeed. Listen Regina, if I hadn't experienced this myself many times, I wouldn't be such an ardent supporter of it."

"I'm pleased to be working with you."

CHAPTER TWENTY-EIGHT
A Challenging Episode

San Francisco Tuesday May 28th, 2002

Henry showed up right on time for his session. Henry seemed more distracted than usual. After a perfunctory handshake, he took his usual seat, with eyes cast downward. Paul too was feeling uncomfortable, but was aware he had to take the lead and keep the door open to Henry's inner worlds.

"Last session was quite intense. How are you feeling today?"

Henry sat quietly and did not meet Paul's eyes.

"We really need to talk about the end of the last session, Henry."

Now Henry met his eyes but still did not speak.

"I know this might be frightening, Henry, but I think you can trust me by now."

His client looked up with sad, mournful eyes, stared for a long moment and then spoke.

"Sometimes...everything hurts."

"Tell me more."

As Henry started to speak, his face took on a configuration somewhere between a rictus and a moue and then seemed to implode as tears cascaded down his sallow cheeks. Paul always marveled at how such a rich and influential man as his father could allow his offspring to go about well-dressed but physically emaciated and emotionally bankrupt.

His tears dried in relatively short order, and he looked up directly into Paul's face.

"Sometimes...my life just hurts."

Paul rolled his left hand in a come-on gesture.

"I'm very...confused right now. I'm not sure what to believe."

"About?"

"Anything. Everything."

"Say more."

"Sometimes I... just feel...so much. It's kind of overwhelming."

Paul waited, allowing the momentum of the moment to carry.

I... sometimes I don't think I'm human. I mean...in the sense...I don't seem to fit in with other people. I feel...like an alien."

"Give me a little more detail."

"I... get hurt so much...so easily. I just feel so much...more than most people do!"

"Why do you think that is?"

"It's like I have extra nerves all over my body! It's like...I feel everything, everything, good and bad! Like I can't...ignore things that most people...don't seem to mind."

"Like what?"

"The ordinary daily bullshit!"

"Such as?"

"I don't know! Insults! Being ignored! People treating me like shit! It happens every day!"

"To you?"

"To me, to everybody! But I just don't seem to be able to stand it like most people! Everything hurts!"

"Is that part of why you're here?"

"Ever since...I told you about Father, I don't seem to be able to stop all of these feelings from...coming up."

"Have you been...getting angry with him?"

"Angry and sad too. I... I've been crying a lot. Every day."

"About what?"

"There's so much...so much I didn't remember...before."

"'Remember?'"

"He's such a mean bastard! Always insulting me! Treating me like shit!"

"And this has been going on for a long time? Is that what you are remembering?" Paul asked as he remembered a quote from Jung: "Everyone carries a shadow, and the less it is embodied in the individual's conscious life, the blacker and denser it is."

"There's still so much from my childhood...But no, more like I feel really, really sad...about my life, the way things are. There's so much more I want to do...that I've never done."
"Like what?"
"Sometimes I... would like to go to a club...by myself, without Andrew always tailing along. To dance and..."
"And?"
Henry took a deep breath, then another.
"If I tell you something, do you swear not to tell Father I told you?"
"Of course, Henry. You have absolute confidentiality with me, unless..."
"I 'plan to kill myself or someone else; or if I am abusing children or elders.'"
Paul laughed, surprised that Henry had retained the four proscriptions he had pronounced so many months ago.
"Correct! Very good!"
"Father has always...rented people to be with me."
"'Rented?'"
Henry sighed and then resumed.

"He has...since I was fourteen, Father has paid some agency or other to send...people to...keep me company."

"'Keep you company?'"

"Yeah. You know."

"I probably do, but it will help you to spell it out for me."

Again, Henry looked down and avoided eye contact.

"He paid for...women to come see me."

"'See' you?"

"Yes. For sex."

"And?"

"When I was about sixteen, I realized...I liked..."

"'Liked?'"

"Boys. Better."

"OK. And...?"

"Father wouldn't rent them for me."

"And?"

Another long silence ensued, and Paul sat quietly.

"And... Andrew..."

"'Andrew?'"

"He...sometimes he takes me to clubs...in the Castro and on Polk Street."

"And?"

"And he knew...people who could...help me."

"And?"

"He never told Father."

"Ahhh!"

"But I want something real. A real boyfriend. Someone to love!"

"Is that why you tried to kiss me?"

"I... I am attracted to you."

"Do you always try to kiss people to whom you are attracted?"

"No! It's not like that! You...you've helped me so much! With you, I can be honest! For the first time in my life!"

"So, you felt this impulse and decided to try it on with me?"

"No! I just...I... You've helped me so much. I just felt..."

Paul let the time pass with an open, non-judgmental face.

"I... you...I felt...feel...attracted to you."

Paul realized the import of his statements, and also that he had to approach responding with a certain restraint and gentleness. He realized he had to be firm without being harsh.

"Henry. I'm your doctor, your therapist. There are both legal and ethical restraints that I must practice."

"I know." Sullen.

"And if I am going to help you, we cannot have any other kind of relationship. The American Psychological Association calls it a 'dual relationship'—mixing sexual, business, or financial relationships with professional services."

"I know." Still sullen, still no eye contact.

"So, we have to make some decisions, right here, right now, today."

Henry made eye contact finally.

"I will adhere to the Code of Ethical Conduct. So, that means I will not encourage or participate in any kind of sexual activity with you. We can work on your feelings, but I can and will never indulge them, except to help you clarify them."

"What about how I feel?"

"It is not unusual for clients to develop feelings for their therapists. We call it 'transference.' I hold space for you to release your feelings but not participate in them. I can be aware of them, but never, ever participate in them."

"But why? That's not fair!"

"Mostly because my distance allows you to freely experience whatever is in you to release freely, sometimes for the first time. You get to let go of these old, negative emotions. You get to have a new freedom to experience your own feelings. I'm what we call 'proximal' to your experience of yourself, I'm nearby."

"But still..."

"The other choice, Henry, is I refer you to another therapist."

"No! No! I don't want that!"

"Then you'll have to agree not to act out your feelings in that way. We can talk about them all you want, but I will never cross the line. I want to suggest from my training and experience that the feelings you are having, that you feel attracted to me, are related to your feelings of being released for the first time. I genuinely listen to you. Perhaps no one else ever has."

Silence and a brooding energy met this statement.

"We can talk about your attraction to men, or your desire to have a steady relationship, or even your loneliness, but I want you to give me your word that you will talk to me about these feeling, not try to act on them with me."

Another long silence greeted Paul who did some maintenance breathing while he waited.

Henry looked up with tears in his eyes and gave Paul a look that was composed half of sadness, and half of relief.

"I agree, Paul. As long as you don't drop me! Please! Just don't drop me!"

"I will not abandon you, Henry. I promise."

They spent the next part of the session re-hashing Henry's objections, and Paul guided him into expressing his fears and concerns about being abandoned, which seemed to be, in Henry's mind, exactly what Paul was doing—not allowing him to have deeper access to, and acting on, his feelings for Paul.

"OK, Henry. Let me frame it another way. There is a power differential between us. We did not meet on even ground. You came to me wanting my professional assistance in attaining life goals you did not otherwise feel capable of achieving. Right?"

"Yeah, I get it."

"And, using my skills, education and training, I've helped you work toward them, right?"

"Yes."

"That is because, in a certain sense, you are my client. You are my business. While I may like you, I do not do what I do for personal reasons. OK?"

"I guess."

"No! For real: Yes or no?"

"No. I... got it."

"One of the major tenets of this arrangement we have is that I vow not to take advantage of your vulnerability. Not to exploit your weaknesses. Right?"

"Yes."

"Therefore, when you have these awakening experiences, the energy is there for you to explore within the context of your own life—outside of this office. Our work is sacred. The benefits are yours alone."

"So, will you help me...figure out appropriate ways to express myself, with men, I mean?"

"We can talk about your feelings, Henry, but what you do with them and how you find expression for them is not my job. You're going to have to start using this new energy to build a community for yourself. My job is to help you get free enough to do that."

"Will you still help me with the conservatorship stuff?"

"Of course."

"I know this is better, but it's still confusing."

"It may take a while, Henry, but we are making progress."

CHAPTER TWENTY-NINE
Therapeutic Ping-Pong

San Francisco Friday May 31st, 2002

Paul was fortunate in being able to bill Henry's estate for the consultations he was having with Regina. After all, it was in service of Henry's well-being—especially since the work had become even more complex and variegated. Fortunately, Regina had a low census at the time and was able to accommodate his need. Paul was beginning to feel as if he were the ping-pong ball being batted back-and-forth between Henry and Regina.

Since most of the traffic was flowing out of The City, his trek from North Beach was relatively easy. Today he had come down Montgomery to Pine and followed it all the way out and connected with Masonic through the Panhandle of the Park and then up Ashbury to Belvedere. His parking karma was as good as usual in a city where historically there had been fistfights, even gunshots exchanged over territorial possession of a parking spot.

"So, Paul, the plot thickens as it were," Regina remarked after Paul had spun her the latest tale of his adventures with Henry.

"It certainly does."

"And you talked to him about the inappropriateness of his wanting to kiss you?"

"Not in those terms, but I required his word that it would never happen again. It was important to reinforce his autonomy, give him a deeper sense that he could make a decision and keep his word. I also told him I was open to discussing his needs and feelings, but not participating in them. And I explained the ethical restraints and considerations."

"And he agreed?"

"Especially when I mentioned the possibility of having to refer him to another therapist."

"I assume you're going to add a 'Rule Out' for Erotomania to his diagnosis?"

"Possibly."

"How did he seem after?"

"Subdued. Sad. Resigned. And strangely peaceful."

"When do you see him next?"

"Tuesday. That's why I'm really glad we have our regular session today."

"I probably should have asked how you're feeling."

"Thanks. No apology necessary. I am feeling stronger, more confident in moving forward."

"Still sure of the approach you're taking?"

"I believe we're making serious progress. Henry is really responding well."

"It is a bit of a delicate balance, allowing him to release while at the same time keeping enough connection that he doesn't just blow up or have a psychotic break."

"My concern exactly!"

"What are you doing to simultaneously promote and restrain him?"

"I've been tremendously influenced by Zerbe's work. She worked with children a lot and did a bunch of work on child development and the attendant pathology related to mothers."

"I'm not acquainted with her work."

"She speaks to dysfunctional parenting, usually the mother's, that indicts what she called 'Environmental failure [that] triggers traumatic memory which evokes traumatic affect which leads to the need for some kind of addictive activity.'"

"Interesting progression."

"It's way more than that! She says that a sort of addictive experience develops between the baby and the mother, who she said must 'Remain fused in a highly pathological nexus, with the baby fulfilling many of the mother's needs for care, warmth and attachment'"

"And?"

"Then any attempt of the child to separate or individuate is considered to be a 'grave psychological threat to the mother, who addictively uses the child to fulfill the function of an addictive object.'"

"You always amaze me with how you can remember citations!"

"Thanks. When I taught in Community College, I used to blow the students mind when I would cite an author and then add the year of publication and the page number!"

"Encyclopedic mind!"

"And she says there is a dissociative aspect, what she refers to as 'That which one dares not experience.' It's all part of the inverse relationship in which the child effectively become a quasi-parent to the adult's needs."

"And how is any of this relevant to your client?"

"According to his medical records, he has had a long history of medical problems that are sometimes considered to be psychosomatic, even autoimmune, such as chronic bronchitis, inflammatory bowel disease, and bouts of asthma. His ER record is quite impressive."

"And your supposition is...?"

"It only makes sense to me! The child's immune system is suppressed to meet the overwhelming needs of the mother. It also makes sense of his introjected erotomania severe and chronic need to be nurtured that he never got. And, his paranoid symptoms are related to his early, and continuing abuse by his father."

"When did his mother die?"

"When he was five. I'm investigating the possibility that

he may have exhibited symptoms of early childhood schizophrenia, or, schizophreniform disorder."

"Are you really leaning toward schizophrenia as a diagnosis?"

"No. I'm much more inclined to call it PTSD and Delusional Disorder. It seems to fit better."

"And?"

"It's obvious that some significant traumatic damage occurred very early in his life."

"Go on."

"It's been clearly shown that early abuse creates dysfunctional and distorted relationships that, in turn, create a kind of template upon which further distorted relationships build."

"You've gotten quite far afield in terms of current treatment."

"This work is affirming some of my longstanding theories! I admit I am excited!"

"Does that serve your client?"

"Of course."

"Please forgive my being blunt, but are you having some kind of reaction to Henry's attempt at being seductive?"

Paul sat back, initially torn between shock and insult. Then he took a deep breath and acknowledged to Regina the possibility that she was right.

"But it isn't homophobic! I was just shocked! Not expecting it! I still have a heightened startle reflex reaction. I still have serious reactions to intrusion into my personal space. It's the most intense symptoms of my PTSD!"

"I actually tend to forget that you have war trauma, too."

"I've been in therapy since 1967, so I'm in pretty good shape overall."

"So, do you think you can continue with this case?"

"Absolutely! I think we have made great progress! And so, does my client! In fact, he's told me he's argued with his father's none-to-subtle 'requests' to get a different treatment professional, one who the father could more easily manipulate."

"So, back to my original question: 'What are you doing to simultaneously promote and restrain him?'"

Paul laughed, and sat back on the paisley-print covered love seat, took another sip of his coffee and then sighed.

"Always the astute questions!"

"That's why you pay me the big bucks!"

"It's really a delicate balance. I have to constantly pay attention to my own feelings and needs to reduce the countertransference. I also have to pay good enough attention to his energy so that I can synch-in with him to give my best guidance and help him uncover the hidden material, to heal himself, in effect."

"I've been meaning to ask you if he is reporting any dreams. You know the 'Royal Road to the Unconscious?'"

"Great idea! I almost always ask."

"Are you addressing his associations and their meanings? Making interpretations?"

"Not too deeply, yet. He's still too immersed in his delusions. But I'm laying the groundwork for it, building a deeper trust."

"It seems you've been pretty successful."

"Thank you."

"Have you talked to the father yet?"

"Outside of telling him I won't tell him anything? No."

"Have you talked to Henry about an information-gathering foray?

"Henry has not given permission. He has a relatively extreme reaction every time I've asked."

"It's a rich possibility."

"I agree. Anything else?"

"Do you think you can be vulnerable, that might be the proper word, or sensitive maybe is better, enough with him without violating your own boundaries?"

"Sometimes it's really difficult to maintain firm but

flexible boundaries."

"I know. It's always a dance."

"I always use the word 'tango.'"

"Indeed."

"Other than that, in the famous words of the despicable Ronald Reagan, it's just a matter of 'staying the course.'"

CHAPTER THIRTY
Moving Forward

San Francisco Tuesday May 28th, 2002

Henry's mood seemed slightly askew. He also looked disheveled. It wasn't unexpected, and Paul wasn't surprised. It seemed that the more Henry opened up emotionally, the less attention he paid to the minutiae of his personal appearance, as if the disordering was working its way through from the inside out.

Nonetheless, he had to ask the perfunctory question.

"How are you, Henry?"

The young man stirred himself, as if from a deep torpor, then lifted his eyes to meet Paul's.

"I... I'm OK, I guess."

"Can you be a little more specific?"

"I feel a little...scared. Broken."

"'Broken' in what way?"

"I feel like I'm falling apart. Ever since... I started letting out my truth...I can't contain...my feelings."

"Would it be fair to say that your feelings are leaking?"

Henry's face became suddenly animated, lit up from within.

"That's it! And what's weird is that I feel better."

"So, you're 'leaking' feelings, and you 'feel better?'"

"Yes."

"So, 'leaking' is a good thing?"

"Yes, but it scares me too!"

"Because?"

"There's so much...I've been feeling. I'm afraid... it might all just...rush out."

"And that would be a bad thing?"

"Sometimes... I'm afraid I might hurt somebody!"

"Anybody in particular?" said Paul, thinking that a Tarasoff warning might need to be made.

"No! But sometimes I feel so...angry, so powerless."

"And?"

"I'm afraid it might just...gush out!"

"And you might hurt someone?"

"I... I'm not sure it's safe...to tell you."

"Why not? You know you have confidentiality with me."

"But if I told you about..."

"What exactly?"

"Killing people."

"What about it?"

"Sometimes I have this fantasy about...walking down Market Street and... killing everyone!"

"How would you propose to do that?"

"'How?'"

"Yes. 'How?'"

Henry's face flushed immediately from bright red hyper-excitement to ash gray pallor.

"I....don't really know."

"No?"

"Sometimes...I see myself...I get these pictures of... walking down Market Street slashing people with a machete," he said as his face tightened in a clench after the words gushed out.

Paul jumped internally but showed no reaction to Henry. Then, after a beat, he asked, "Does this happen very often?"

Having not seen Paul register a reaction, Henry's face relaxed and he replied, "Just when I get really angry."

"When was the first time?"

Henry closed his eyes to ponder and then opened them again.

"I don't know. Maybe when I was fifteen."

"How often has it happened since?"

"Just when I get really angry."

"I mean how many times?"

"Oh. I don't...know. I usually don't get that angry...just usually at the government."

"You imagine slashing up politicians?"

"Sometimes. They're all dupes and puppets."

"Then who?"

"Father."

"So, you've imagined slashing up your father."

"Him and other Big Business tycoons. They're the ones...they're the ones who are most to blame."

" For what?"

"ALL THE INSANITY!" shouted the younger man.

Paul extended his hands, palms out, toward his client.

"It's fine Henry. I just need to know."

"It's their fault! They create more damage so they can make more money!"

"Why does that make you so angry?"

"It's the same fucking way Father treats me!"

Paul made a mental note of the increasing frequency with which Henry used the word "fuck" in some form or other.

"How?"

"I'm just another pawn! Nobody really gives a damn about me!"

"Your father..."

"Father! He only takes care of me because of the money! He fucking owns me!"

"'Owns' you?"

"The fucking conservatorship! It fucking pisses me off!"

"I know you don't agree, but you must admit..."

"Just because my ideas don't fit with the 'mainstream' (he made air quotes), doesn't mean I'm 'insane!'" (Again, the air quotes).

"'Insane?'"

"You think I'm not intelligent? That I don't know the difference between being considered crazy and insane?"

Henry sat up in his chair, spine straight and rigid, closed his eyes and spoke in a resonating tone.

"It is a legal term that refers to 'unsoundness of mind or lack of the ability to understand that prevents one from having the mental capacity required by law to enter into a particular relationship, status, or transaction, or that releases one from criminal or civil responsibility.'"

Paul was taken aback a bit at this display of erudition, and pondered for a moment whether or not his client might be exhibiting savantism or even signs of Asperger's.

"That was pretty amazing, Henry."

"I used to have a good memory. It was stronger...when I was young...before...""

"'Before?'"

"'Before' the goddamn hospital and the fucking 'medications!'"

Paul thought wryly that his client was becoming a master of the air quotes.

"They've made your memory worse?"

"Much, much worse!"

"And?"

"They use them as one of the ways to control humans!"

"Who is 'they?'"

"The alien bastards and their human collaborators...like Father!"

"The meds 'control' you?"

"Of course! What the fuck else do you think brain damage is for?"

"I agree that psych meds can and do cause brain damage. But I've never thought of brain damage as a means of social control."

"Why else do you think alcohol and tobacco are legal and marijuana is listed in the same category as heroin?"

"I don't see the relationship."

"Oh, come on! You're smart! Drugs that cause human harm are encouraged, made legal and advertised and promoted and sold broadly!"

"And they are being used to 'control' humans?"

"Most certainly! The more human minds can be channeled into creating negativity, even just passivity, the more the fuckers win!"

"What 'fuckers?'"

"You're not listening! People like Father and the aliens who run them are in charge! The whole fucking system is set up to harvest human emotions!"

"But why?"

"I already told you! Where the fuck do you think the fucking government has been getting all of the high-tech toys for the last fifty years?"

"Are you referring to Colonel Corso again?"

"Of course! The man was brilliant!"

"Some people say 'delusional?'"

"To try to discredit him! To hide the fucking truth!"

"Toward what end, Henry?"

"Total domination! To take over of the planet!"

"And you believe that having people take psych drugs is part of the plan?"

"Absolutely! They kill your will! They ruin your imagination!"

"What about you?"

"What do you mean? I am a perfect example!"

"How so?"

"Father controls my trust fund. Thank God my grandfather provided for me to have a good firm of attorneys for oversight. Otherwise he'd have stolen the whole thing by now. Probably killed me into the bargain."

"Because?"

"He keeps me 'medicated for my own good,' he says. Won't ever let me get out of the goddamn conservatorship!"

"What does he want to stop you from doing?'"

"Telling the truth!"

"But don't you do that anyway?"

"Only with you."

"And?"

"I'm pissed off! I want to be with other people who believe!"

"Does he prevent you?"

"Hell yes!"

"How exactly?"

"That fucking Anthony tells him everything I say and do. I'm pretty sure he has the telephone tapped. The only place I'm free is on the Internet."

"Why does Anthony do that?"

"Father pays him a lot of money, of course!"

Paul had a strong sense that this wasn't all of the truth.

"You're hiding something. What else about Anthony?"

Henry looked stricken. He did not reply.

"What else, Henry?"

"Anthony...you can't tell Father if I tell you."

"I promise."

"Anthony takes me to clubs...sometimes. He...I get together...with other men."

"'Get together?'"

"Yes. You know."

"Perhaps I do, but you have to spell it out for me, please."

"I... I'm gay!"

"And?"

"Father would never approve. I... pay Anthony to keep quiet!"

"What else does Anthony do for you?"

"He...he gets me the best weed there is!"

"Marijuana?"

"Yes. I usually buy half a pound at a time. Picked buds."

"What does that run these days?"

"Around two grand."

"Wow! Things have changed! I remember a line from a Jefferson Airplane song: 'Sometimes it climbs to sixty-five dollars, prices like that make a grown man holler!'"

"It helps me cope with those fucking pills!"

"You seem to have been doing pretty good with me."

"Only because I stopped taking the goddamn things three weeks ago!"

CHAPTER THIRTY-ONE
Yet Another Turning

San Francisco Friday June 7th, 2002

Paul welcomed the opportunity to sit comfortably in one of Regina's leather chairs and sip a cup of her rich, aromatic coffee as he unwound the latest adventures of the on-going tale of Henry Mortenson Junior.

"He just quit taking his Stelazine? Quit altogether?"

"Yes. He says three weeks ago, which was shortly after he had that huge breakthrough in that session with me."

"Have any of his other behaviors changed since then?"

"I didn't really see anything dramatic at the time, but I have been witnessing an increasing, not quite aggression, but forthrightness and, anger. I was going to say belligerence, but it's been more primary."

"With you?"

"No, but he's allowing his anger, especially with his father, to surface."

"Is the father still calling you, wanting confidential information?"

"Two or three times a week!"

"And, of course, you are refusing?"

"Of course!"

"How are Henry's delusional symptoms?"

"They've actually gotten stronger, but not in the disorganized sort of way you might expect from someone getting off meds. He's become stronger, more certain and assertive."

"As if he were more convinced than ever?"

"Exactly! He would be so convincing if I didn't know better."

"As in?"

"He speaks clearly and in a totally ungarbled manner about his delusional material. It's one of the few times when he doesn't thought block."

"Interesting that he has seemingly gotten clearer. One would have expected that he would have decompensated without the meds."

"He acts as if he were one of the few sane ones, and the rest of us were delusional!"

"It sounds like you admire him!"

"I admire his honesty, and his willingness to do the work."

"And?"

"As I have told him any number of times, up to a certain point, I can follow his logic, but I just cannot see the profit motive he keeps holding up as essential to, or even the crux of, his entire formulation."

"Delusional systems are renowned for their impeccable logic and falter because the original false premise is distorted."

"Remarkable! Very poetic! And perfectly put!"

"So, what is your overall assessment?"

"Now that he has had some weird kind of quasi-spontaneous remission, he's still delusional. I await further developments. This is probably the wackiest case I have ever had!"

"Are you considering referring him to someone else?"

"Hell no! He trusts me. We've made great progress. If I were to refer him to someone else, it might take years for him to get back on track. And he would rightly feel abandoned. No. I just need to keep adjusting my approach while maintaining the firmest boundaries I can, so he knows I am holding space for him to unwind himself."

"I can see that. But you have to be very careful because I sense that your empathy for his position vis a vis his conspiracy theories is very high."

"That's true. But I am always watching for the counter-transference. I maintain a sort of dual space in my head, like two television monitors."

"Interesting concept."

"Thank you. This is a very taxing case. I have had to let the rest of my caseload drop. I'm not taking more new referrals either."

"Probably wise. What is your prognosis?"

"Given this latest twist, I have absolutely no idea."

"Are you going to report to his prescriber about his stopping the meds?"

"First of all, he has every right to choose not to take them. And secondly, I do not believe I am required to do so—especially since he told me in session and therefore under the seal of confidentiality."

"Since he's not LPS conserved, and has retained the right to refuse medications, I believe he is the holder of the privilege of confidentiality."

"So, what's next?"

"That's what I want to talk to you about today. I just need to discuss it with you, to get a little better traction, so I can go forward more confidently."

"Are you still considering giving him the WAIS?"

"I don't know. I may. It just doesn't seem all that relevant right now to do intelligence testing. I'm not sure about his ability to concentrate either. It would really distort the results."

"And there are clearly other areas on which you need

to focus? Any further push-back about his attempt to kiss you?"

"No, he was good with it, especially when I agreed to listen to his desire for romance and a bonded relationship.

It's clearly an arena where he has some very confused ideas."

"Are you going to explore them?"

"Not right away. We have deeper things to work through right now. I may do some more visual imagery work with him, but more gently this time and let him set the pace a little more."

"That sounds wise."

"Oh, hey, did I tell you about Anthony, his chauffeur/companion?"

"No. What's up with that?"

Paul filled her in succinctly and revealed the information about Henry's secret bank account. Since this was officially a consultation, he knew he could count on her keeping confidentiality.

"He's beginning to sound more and more competent. Is he going to challenge his conservatorship next time it's up for renewal?"

"It may be a little soon for that, though he definitely wants out from under his father's thumb. I'm not sure I would want to trust him with access to half a billion dollars with his current mindset."

"It would be all too easy for him to get swindled or ripped off."

"Too true. And he's still very unstable. I want him to get a lot clearer and more stable before he decides to confront the court."

"He needs to confront his father in real time first."

"I agree. He's just started to be able to be angry during sessions. He's not yet ready for prime time."

"So, what are you going to do?"

"I feel like I need to probe him some more. Get him to express some more of his latent anger in my office. I believe it's the only way, but it weirds me out a bit that the more anger he expresses, the more lucid he seems—and he's still holding onto his delusions."

"It is a bit of a conundrum, isn't it?"

"It certainly is. He has an odd mix of symptoms. Delusional Disorder NOS just doesn't encapsulate it all."

"What if you took away his delusions, what might be your diagnosis?"

"That's hardly possible!"

"I know. It's just a vagrant thought."

"He is so convinced about the wide range and degree of connections in this conspiracy theory of his. It's so real for him that I wonder what he might be like without them."

"When one's delusions are uncovered and integrated,

there are always residual emotions that can be retrieved and rehabilitated. The client should have more relative access to all, or at least a significant portion, of the previously distorted energy that fed the delusions. Especially since it is the suppressed rage and memories of abuse that seem to feed it."

Paul smacked his hand onto the left-hand arm of the chair and expressed his frustration.

"I guess there's not a lot I can do about it now, other than keep going with what has been working, and wait to see what else surfaces."

"What about his machete fantasies? Especially related to his father? Any clear and present danger there? Possible Tarasoff?"

Paul pondered for a moment; mentally summing up all of the hemming and hawing he had been doing the past couple of days.

"Not currently, but I think it has the possibility of being so."

"Because of the rage that is uncovering as he opens up his delusional system?"

"Exactly!"

"What are you looking for? What might be an indicator of a breakthrough?

"I'm really anticipating the day when I see a crack in

his very rigid and detailed belief system. He frequently accuses me of 'not believing him!'"

"How do you handle that?"

"I tell him I can follow his logic but don't agree with the conclusions he's drawn."

"Good! That's good."

"I'm going to suggest we undertake another Sovereignty Ceremony with his father. It wouldn't be unusual for there to be need of more than one session with a person with whom there is really deep energy involved. Hell, I've done Sovereignty with my father a dozen times!"

"Sounds like a working plan. Next week?"

"Same Bat station, same Bat channel."

CHAPTER THIRTY-TWO
Another Deeper Pass

San Francisco Friday June 7th, 2002

Henry was late for one of the few times ever, and Paul noticed a faint, but distinct aroma of high-grade marijuana. Paul decided not to say anything but continue to observe and catalogue his perceptions.

"How are you today, Henry?"

"I'm...doing quite well thank you."

"Glad to hear it. How was your week?"

"Excellent. Father's in New York. Always good for me."

"Glad to hear it. How do you feel about doing some more work today?"

"I might actually be ready!"

"We don't have to go as deep as last time."

Henry smiled one of his rare smiles.

"No! I think I'm ready to plunge in!"

Paul hesitated, somewhat taken aback by the

seemingly rejuvenated new Henry, and wondered fleetingly

whether this might be an effect of the weed he had obviously smoked.

"Let's start breathing together. I brought this little bell from Tibet with me today. It's called a *dorje*. I will ring it when our breaths are synched and we can start."

Paul then reiterated the standard instructions and settled into his own breathing. Henry fell into an easy rhythm as Paul took his own first breath deep into his belly. His awareness shifted immediately into the kind of a split-screen television monitor he always experienced when working with clients that allowed him to go very deeply into his self and simultaneously be aware of what his clients were experiencing, including counting the number of breaths and an awareness of when the "click" came that signaled to him that they were in synch.

When he felt connected with Henry's energy, he rang the bell. In the Tibetan tradition, the sound represents the "thunderbolt of enlightenment"— that abrupt change in human consciousness that all great religions recognize as the pivotal episode in the lives of mystics and saints.

As the tones reverberated into an infinite silence, Paul asked Henry with whom he wanted to work that day.

"Father! It's always Father!"

"Just continue breathing, bring up his image, and we'll start to work. His energy to you, or yours to him first?"

"His to me."

"Good. I want to remind you that we can stop at any time. I don't want you to get too stressed out?"

"I'm good. I feel strong today."

"Good. So, let's start the scan of your body, head to toe, and then up the back of the body. Let me know when you're complete."

Paul kept his breath synchronized with Henry's, becoming aware of various areas of Henry's body where he could see/feel pockets of his father's energy gathered and secreted.

Henry nodded and showed a small crinkled grin.

"Now do the scan in little slices like an MRI and stop wherever you perceive energy from your father lodged in your body. Let me know when you can see it."

The response was immediate.

"Here," he said, patting the top of his head, the crown chakra.

"Got it. Does it have a color or shape?"

"It's just this massive dark gray storm cloud, like a huge hurricane!"

"Are you sure you can handle this right now?"

"Hell yes!" he said emphatically. "It's him but it's also those fucking awful meds!"

"Both?"

"Yeah, they seem to be related. They...they're feeding each other! That's why it's so huge!"

"Can you handle this right now?"

"Yeah. I need to use two hands."

"Remember he cannot refuse to take it back."

"No! He's eating it like cotton candy. Can't seem to get enough!"

"Just keep going until all of it has been returned to where it belongs in his body."

"He's smiling. Cooperating. This is weird!"

"Got it! Just keep going until it feels complete."

"Oh my God! This is like taking a big giant shit!"

Paul laughed in spite of himself. He felt empathically that that was exactly what Henry was feeling. The awareness flooded through his body as he watched through the separate window.

The process at the crown continued for a timeless minute, then Henry continued downward, only to stop almost immediately at the pineal gland, the Third Eye in the middle of the forehead between the eyebrows.

"Oh my God! Another hurricane! No! This is more like a huge thunderstorm with lightning bolts shooting out around the edges!"

Paul concluded that, no matter what else, Henry's smoking weed had undoubtedly psychedelically enhanced this session.

Again, he used two hands and started reaching out to pull the threads of energy out of the middle of his forehead and then, rather forcefully, send them back to his envisioned father. Henry's body seemed to become more substantial, more defined in shape and less translucent. A marked golden glow, faint at first and growing stronger with each heartbeat, emanated from around him.

"He's eating this shit up!"

"Of course, it's his own energy!"

Paul watched silently as Henry's evident concentration showed, as his face tightened slightly and his inner journey accelerated.

"My heart!" said Henry, his left hand covering his chest as a low moan escaped his pursed lips.

"My heart!" he repeated, eyes still closed, his energy seeming to go further away, as if on a different tangent or to another dimension.

Then suddenly, violently, Henry started flinging his left hand with great energy away from his body, shaking his hand vigorously as if to remove a sticky invisible residue.

He progressed down the front and then up the back of his body, stopping at his penis, his knees and then the backs of his knees and his liver then finally at the medulla oblongata. At each juncture, he encountered concentrated accumulations of energy that ranged from pale yellow grape clusters to black, sharp-pointed arrowheads. He removed each in turn and sent the envisioned, but energy-filled forms winging swiftly back to the ethereal form of his father.

At the end of this epic voyage, he fell back into his chair, arms and legs akimbo, perspiring profusely face wan and drawn, breathing shallowly. Paul brought him a glass of filtered water and set the tissue box near his right hand on the small table nearby.

Paul continued his own deep breathing with his eyes open as he watched Henry's body gradually assume a healthier mien, though he did not speak for several minutes.

Henry sat up and took a long drink of water, and weakly looked over at Paul.

"That was intense."

"Looked like it!"

"I feel...different. Changed. Transposed almost."

"You've released a great deal of energy."

"I'm not ready to continue yet."

"You can rest for a minute or so. Take some deep breaths. Drink some more water. Use the bathroom if you need to do so."

"Thanks. I will," he said and did so.

When he returned, Paul said," We can talk more later. Let's continue the ceremony. Let's go back into your trance stance to complete the first stage."

Henry said, "Okay," and immediately started breathing

very deeply into his belly.

"Fill all of the holes in your aura where you released the energy, with the blue-white light of the sword of Michael the Archangel. When you are complete, let me know."

They carried, following the protocol to take back from his father all of the longing, the soul hunger, the pleas and prayers that had always been denied, all of the unmet needs that had wounded him so sharply on his journey through life, riven by strident aching throughout his entire being.

"He's...he's getting smaller. He...he's changing colors!" Henry remarked at one point.

"Keep going Henry! It's all your own energy!"

They worked the energy more, releasing all of Henry's trapped feeling needs. Henry cried several times during the process, and once moaned "Oh Daddy!" in a mournful tone that mimicked a dirge.

When they completed the second half of the ceremonial process, Henry seemed again to grow more substantial. At the end of the process, Paul directed him to fill all of the holes in his father's aura. As he released him, Henry called out that he was, at last, released and healed, whole and sovereign.

CHAPTER THIRTY-THREE
Out of the Trough, and onto the Crest

San Francisco Friday June 7th, 2002

Paul had called Regina and asked if they could meet an hour later as he was yet unable to drive. He had been deeply altered by Henry's work, and, after seeing him out of the office, simply had to sit by himself for some minutes before he could regain his own equilibrium. She readily agreed.

He stopped by an excellent chicken carry out place on Columbus called "Il Pollo," and picked up two half-chicken dinners with fries and coleslaw. He was still altered when he arrived at Regina's, but very hungry and anxious to share the latest with her.

"I'm starved! Let's eat while we talk."

"You bet!"

They started in on their respective dinners (that Regina had insisted they eat off china plates, not out of the box like a bunch of "scrubbers").

"I can see from how you look that today must have been massive!"

"It was! There is so much to tell!"

"So, give!"

"Backdrop for the session: Henry was stoned! I could smell the weed on him when he arrived!"

"Did you talk about it?"

"No, not really."

"Why not?"

"Because he seemed so much more relaxed and told me he was ready to work."

"Was he?"

"Oh God, you have no idea!"

"Say more," she said biting into a chicken thigh with great gusto.

"He was less anxious than I have ever seen him. He seemed very available."

"And it showed up in the work?"

"Absolutely!"

"Tell me more," she gestured impatiently as Paul applied himself to his delicious meal.

"Just a minute," Paul said as he ate another scoop of coleslaw and several crispy fries.

"He was able to get into the work more fully—I'm tempted to use the word embody—he cried a number of times; and he kind of pseudo-collapsed to the floor once when it looked like he was just unable to carry the energy any longer. He seemed to have a number of huge releases."

"Excellent! I know you love that stuff!"

"I do! It's the only sign I get that the client is really feeling their stuff."

"Did he tell you any more about his father?"

"Just peripherally. He had already told me his father beat him, but it came out that he used fists and belts and sticks too!"

"Asshole!"

"He was probably repeating what happened with his father!"

"Yeah. No doubt!"

"But you say he used a 'mild tone' when he was describing these horrors?"

"Again, it might have been the weed, but he sounded more dissociated than stoned. The net effect is often the same."

"Too true. Whatever happened, I was expecting a loud voice, screaming even. His mild tone might be progress."

"Or it could simply be a side-slip?"

"I'm not sure, but either way I feel better about his jig saw puzzle."

"I've suspected for a long time—right from the beginning actually when you told me about it—that his father had been abusive. Now that I know, everything makes more sense."

"The guy is such an arrogant, demanding asshole—in my clinical opinion!"

"I must say, Paul, I had some reservations about this approach, but it sounds like you had another real breakthrough. Congratulations! Good job!"

Paul looked at Regina' s smiling face and flushed slightly. Though they had been professionally acquainted for a long time, there had been a few occasions when she had expressed what felt like a personal compliment as well. He thought for just a moment that their relationship might be developing another dimension.

He laughed and said, "Thank you! I really appreciate it."

"You deserve it. You've proved yourself correct in your assessment and approach—at least so far."

Typical Regina. She kept his feet on the ground all the time; never let him get too full of himself, even in a moment of triumph.

"If this is a real awakening, I may need to help firm up his new foundation."

"Yes! Exactly! How poetic!"

"I love how you understand my work!"

"It does make a certain amount of sense that if he has had all of these psychic disturbances and he's finally getting released from them, that he would be feeling a new kind of power that might even be confusing for him."

"Well put! I do remain both cognizant of and concerned about some falloff related to his stopping his meds."

"I agree. You should just keep monitoring him." Regina was always mindful of the process.

"I will."

"So, tell me more!

Paul said "He told me that for the longest time his father thought he was 'retarded.' And called him that too!"

"Jesus! What a creep, especially since Henry is really smart. I suspect he might be a certifiable genius!"

Paul the decided to talk to her more about the session materials. "He had a kind of odd thing was that he described these huge hurricane-like forms several times. I can only deduce that these implied tremendous energy and power."

"So, what's next?"

"Keep working with him to reduce his fear and terror, hold space for him to release more and more of his fury; hopefully get more and more sane. Give him understanding, acceptance, time and reassurance. I will continue to be as non-judgmental, empathic and patient as I am able."

"That sounds like the time-honored prescription."

Paul then told her about a classic text he had been reading. "It is part of my general approach, but with him I am treating him along the lines of Bert Karon's *Psychotherapy of Schizophrenia*. I've gotten a lot of great info from there, even though it was written thirty years ago."

"I've read parts of it."

"It's helped me round out my perspective, and bolstered my belief in the human aspect, the utter necessity of the human contact, of person-to-person healing in psychotherapy. It's the only thing that really works."

"You really are anti-psychiatry!" said Regina, only-half seriously.

"Only in terms of the so-called modern trends. By the way, the word is out of vogue these days."

"So? You're older than me." Regina loved it that he had ten years on her. "Were you part of the movement back in the '70s?"

"I almost got fired once when I was working a psych unit here in The City. Another Tech and I—we were the med nurses on days and PMs— figured out that we not only had the right but a duty to inform the patients of what they were taking, and all of the possible side effects. We got written up and almost fired until we threatened to go to the media."

"That's what started your crusade?"

"I wouldn't call it a 'crusade' per se. It's just that I have done a tremendous amount of research on psych meds, so I don't buy the usual hype, especially not the shit promoted by the psychopharmaceutical industry and their tame dogs, the bloody 'med manager' psychiatrists!"

"Wow! You really do mean it!"

"You bet! And I'll never change!"

CHAPTER THIRTY-FOUR
Excelsior!

San Francisco Saturday June 8th, 2002

Paul was extremely involved in a very sensual, very sexual dream with this amazing tall brunette woman he had only seen twice in his life in passing—once at the Marina Safeway, having made passing eye contact as she disappeared forever into the morning fog, the other one of those indescribable moments as she was boarding a plane in New York for Paris and he was debarking at that same gate on a plane that had just brought him in from the Maldives via Barcelona. Not that she was that exact same woman, but they both had almost exactly the same face and physical features, but even more, carried an energetic signature that was so riveting, so embracing, that those brief glances of her imprinted him in a way that he had never forgotten.

So, when the phone rang at an hour that he considered barbarous (it was 0530!), he answered the phone on the eighth ring in a way that he would never have considered under other circumstances; in a way that was reminiscent of the bad old days of the cocaine flow when he had a hundred-foot telephone cord so he could drag it around with him everywhere he went, including the bathroom, and keep it handy even during the amazing plunges he took into the rare and delicious sleep crashes at the end of a five day runs.

"WHAT??"

He snapped into the receiver, the roar of his voice reverberating into the huge empty emotional space left behind by the swiftly vanishing dream and the gorgeous, scintillating woman in it.

"I'm sorry to bother you, Dr. Marzeky. There's a man on the line who insists on talking to you right now."

"AND WHO IS IT THAT EMPLOYS YOUR SERVICE?" he asked still quite gruffly.

"You do, Doctor."

"THEN WHY ARE YOU DISREGARDING MY EXPLICIT ORDERS NEVER, EVER TO CALL BEFORE TEN O'CLOCK, UNLESS IT IS A TRUE MEDICAL EMERGENCY?"

The receptionist started crying into the phone, blubbering as she tried to find words, clearly in some form of cognitive shock.

"I...I... He...he's been yelling at me too!"

Paul felt immediately ashamed to the roots of his hairline and found himself almost stammering, as he repeatedly apologized and tried to calm her down.

Once he had inelegantly done so, he found enough sediment left in his soul to ask.

"Well, who the hell is it? Who is it that thinks he's so bloody important that he can badger you and violate my demands?"

"He...he says he's Henry Mortenson."

"Junior or Senior?"

"I don't know. I didn't ask."

"Why not?"

"I... he...I'm sorry."

"Oh, the hell with it! Put him through."

"Yes, Doctor."

"What the fuck is this, Henry? Yelling at my answering service? And at this fucking hour of the morning?"

"Dr. Marzeky? Henry Mortenson Senior here."

Taken aback, yet not at all mollified, he harshly spoke into the phone.

"I repeat, why are you 'yelling at my answering service?' And at this fucking hour of the morning?'"

"I resent your tone, sir!"

"And I resent your arrogance, sir!"

"I remind you, sir, I pay your bills!"

"And I remind you, sir, that your son is my client, not you!"

"I can and will file a complaint against you with the Psychology Board!"

"Why don't you just go the fuck ahead? Do it now and leave me the fuck alone! I am not now nor will I ever be intimidated by your bully bullshit!"

There was a long silence on the line that crackled and hissed intermittently.

Next came a reply in a very different tone and timbre, so dissimilar that it might have been another person altogether.

"I...," said the almost disconnected voice, "I... we seem to have gotten off on the wrong foot. I'm calling from London."

Paul, not appeased, paused for a moment before replying, "So?"

"I was...not paying attention to the time zone difference."

"Obviously! If I remember correctly, it's ten hours."

"Yes. I... I apologize. I should have checked first."

Paul was shocked that this arrogant, pompous multi-multi-millionaire who had harassed him repeatedly and demanded information to which he had no right, had actually apologized!

"Accepted. Now then, how can I help you?"

"I'm not exactly sure...how to say this, but I... want to thank you."

"'Thank' me?"

"Yes."

"Why?"

"I... Henry called me this morning...earlier."

"He did? Good. I guess."

"It was... the best conversation I've ever had with him."

"Do say."

"Yes. He...he wasn't negative, in any way."

"Is that unusual?"

"It's...it was the best talk we ever had! Ever!"

"Well, that's wonderful!"

"Yes. It was remarkable!"

"Good. That's very good."

"And I called because...I want to thank you."

"'Thank' me?'"

"Yes. And I... appreciate what you have done for him."

"That's something I thought I would never hear from you, sir."

"I'm just...it's been an amazing afternoon. I... I never really knew...how vulnerable he...my son, is."

"I'm so glad. You could be such great support for him, sir."

"I wouldn't know how."

"I can help you, though it would have to be informal. Having you as a client would be a breach of ethics and confidentiality, but I could make general suggestions without specific reference to Henry. And I would have to let him know that I was doing so. We could set up some sessions. Separate from Henry's, of course."

"I travel a lot."

"We could do phone sessions, if you're really serious."

"I... can we talk about this more...when I'm back in the States?"

"Absolutely!"

Paul hung up feeling a broad admixture of emotions, and smiling as he hung up. It was yet another breakthrough, one that he would not have anticipated in his wildest imaginings. Now he was really looking forward to his next session with Henry!

CHAPTER THIRTY-FIVE
A New Level of Connection

San Francisco Tuesday June 11th, 2002

When Henry appeared for his next appointment, Paul temporarily concealed knowledge of the surprisingly honest call from Senior, and allowed his client to settle into his chair. Paul sat breathing and waited. Henry didn't appear to be stoned. In fact, he seemed almost poised, much more balanced than Paul had ever seen him looking.

His appearance had changed too. He looked as if he had not slept, probably not eaten either. His eyes looked bright though his overall appearance seemed muted. Today he had the slightly smudged look of a wounded angel, as if the Finnish symbolist painter Hugo Simberg had painted him.

Henry sat quietly for a brief period, but then started squirming in his chair, looking around the room distractedly, as if he wanted to leave. Finally, after several moments, he settled his eyes on Paul, and attempted a wan smile.

"I... I'm not sure...exactly what to say."

"Whatever comes to mind. Bring me up to speed. It seems like a lot has happened since we last talked."

"I... had a real...conversation with Father."

"'Real conversation?'"

"We...talked."

"'Talked?'"

"We usually don't...talk."

"How was that?"

"Pretty...uncomfortable."

"In what way?"

"He...we never really talk. Usually he yells at me...puts me down."

"And this time?"

"Father... tried to...find out what...I was doing."

"That's really different, isn't it?"

"I didn't...know how to act."

"Did you talk?"

"I was scared."

"'Scared?'"

"He's never...tried, not really...before."

"What did he have to say?"

"It was confusing."

"What was?"

"I didn't expect...did not know what to think."

"Because?"

"He's never talked to me...before."

"'Never?'"

"Not like he cared. Never!"

"What did he say?"

"He asked me...how I was doing."

"And?"

"He sounded interested."

"That wasn't like him, huh?"

"No. Not at all!"

"Did you answer?"

"I was scared."

"At first?"

"Yes."

"And then?"

"He...I took a chance."

"A chance?'"

"Yes. I told him about... our work."

"And?"

"He seemed...interested."

"'Interested?'"

"Like he really cared!"

"What did he say?"

"He seemed to care. He asked me about my health."

"Did you tell him?"

"I...it was hard."

"'Hard?'"

"I was afraid."

"And?"

"I told him I... was feeling better."

"'Better?'"

"I told him...how angry I've been...for a long time."

"What did he say?"

"He started yelling...telling me...all he had done for me."

"That didn't help, did it?"

"No! He scared me."

"What happened then?"

"He...heard."

"'Heard?'"

"That I was...upset."

"And what did he do?"

"He stopped yelling."

"And then?"

"His voice changed."

"'Changed?'"

"He was...quieter."

"And?"

"He really wanted to know."

"And?"

"I told him...I was scared."

"Then?"

"He was...kind! For the first time!"

Henry started crying, tears running down his cheeks. He put his hands to his face and started sobbing, shoulders hunching and relaxing and then he sobbed some more.

"It was the first time! The only time... ever!"

Paul breathed deeply and focused the wealth of his attention on Henry and extended his hands palm out toward him, and flowed the full strength of his empathy toward him.

Henry kept sobbing and Paul put the tissue box by his

right hand, sat back and waited in silence. Henry stopped for a moment, coughed, took a deep breath, blew his nose and then started sobbing again.

When he finally looked up, Henry's eyes were as clear and innocent as the five-year-old analog child Paul knew lived within him. He had worked with thousands of clients and had never seen more clear validation of his belief that abused people carry the weight of emotional injury much as a food addicts carry excess adipose tissue.

"He...I... he never...ever said..."

"'Never said...'"

Henry started crying again and then started gasping for breath.

"He...was nice to me! The only time ever in my life!" Henry continued sobbing.

Paul again extended his hands palm out toward his client and breathed deeply as he felt hot healing energy pour out of his hands. He clairvoyantly saw the threads of golden-white light emanating from him.

At length, Henry looked up again, took a pair of tissues from the box and blew his nose vigorously.

"I feel like...everything I have ever believed in has been wrong."

Paul immediately flashed on the literary concept of peripeteia in which the protagonist realizes that everything he ever believed in was a lie. He instantly converted his insight into action and asked the next logical question.

"'Everything?'"

"I always thought he was...such a corrupt asshole! A bastard!"

"And now?"

"Now I'm just not...sure...about anything!" Henry started crying again, then uttered, "Oh fuck!"

After a few moments Paul spoke, "Please say more."

"I'm...confused. I just don't...hate him so much anymore."

"That's very sudden."

"I think he...might actually...care!"

"That would be a good thing, no?"

"It's just confusing."

"Tell me more."

"I've hated him for so long!"

"And now?"

"Maybe I... I've been wrong!"

"You seem sad."

"I feel...happy too!"

"Happy sad?"

"Yeah, kind of both. Confused."

"And?"

"I don't know what to do next."

"We can start working on that when you're ready."

Henry looked up incredulously.

"Really? You'd be willing to do that?"

"Of course, Henry. My entire purpose here is to help you have a better life."

"No one's ever...really tried to help me."

"Maybe it's time for a change."

"But if I change..."

"Yes?"

"I... I don't know...what might happen to me."

"Say more."

"I don't know who I might be."

"What does that mean?"

"I... might have to change...everything."

"'Everything?'"

"Who I am... everything."

"And your father?"

"Maybe I've been wrong about him too?"

"In what ways?"

"I don't know."

"Let's take a little break.

"OK."

They both had a bio break, and Paul made a coffee for the both of them.

"Great Henry. Let's have a review."

"All right."

"Your father has always treated you badly. Yelled at you. Called you names?"

"Yes."

"And now, suddenly, he treats you nicely for the first time."

"Yes."

"And you are inclined to believe it might be...permanent?"

"Yes. No. I don't know."

"I want to suggest that we wait and see if he continues this new behavior."

"I... maybe...I want him to...really be my...Dad."

It was the first time he had ever called him anything

other than 'Father.' Paul made a note in his head and waited a beat.

"If that's what you want, it may be a bit of a journey yet."

"OK. So, what do I do?"

"If you're OK with it, we'll keep working like we have. Maybe you can make that list we talked about, a list of topics I can legitimately talk to your father about. Maybe then in a while you and your father and I can all meet together sometime."

"I... maybe."

"You've made great progress, Henry. We don't have to hurry any of this. But it's important that we keep moving forward. Does that sound good?"

"But what do I do? With Father? In the meantime? What if he turns mean again?"

"You have my phone number. You can call me 24/7."

CHAPTER THIRTY-SIX
Deeper into the Mystery

San Francisco Friday June 14th, 2002

"Really good work, Paul," said Regina, sitting back in her leather manager's chair.

"Thank you. I was surprised he didn't mention the alien thing at all. He was completely focused on his father."

"Did he agree to create a list of topics you could talk to his father about?"

"He agreed to discuss creating a list!"

They both laughed, acknowledging how incredibly slow and potentially frustrating it could be to attempt methodical psychotherapy with psychotic individuals. Many "therapists" don't even attempt it. Usually cited was the naïve and incorrect contention propagated for years in the media and exponentialized with the rise of corporate psychiatry, was that schizophrenic clients are especially untreatable with psychotherapy.

Those few therapists who, through the decades, have attempted it have often lacked adequate training, proper support and supervision, a solid block of their own inner work, stamina, ability, deep-seated interest and intention, solidity of heart and soul, willingness to read beyond the propaganda, choicefulness, the willingness to risk, to be open and vulnerable and to be empathic to the deep and often twisted neural pathways of their clients. The net result is that those most in need of professional soulful support and guidance end up being those who are most marginalized and neglected by the very ones to whom they might most appropriately expect to look for these life-saving qualities and nutrients.

"Have you ever shared any of your rants about your own conspiracy thinking, with Henry?"

"I've thought about it. I use it as a personal backdrop for understanding the power and dynamics of his delusions."

"And?"

"There are some parallels between our childhoods. I have often wondered how it is that I did not turn out more psychotic," he laughed, "than I am!"

"I have often thought about your journey, around this very topic."

"And?"

"You told me about your uncle, the philosopher."

"He was also a Jesuit."

She waved her hand through the air in a dismissive gesture.

"Whatever."

"And your point about my uncle?"

"You remember Alice Miller? I can't remember which book, but she talks about a 'sympathetic witness' who makes the difference for a traumatized person becoming psychotic or just developing serious mental problems."

"I can't remember exactly. Tell me more."

"Here's an example. When Picasso was three, there was a huge earthquake off the coast of Spain that affected the small island on which he lived. He and his father got separated from his mother for three days, and little Pablo walked around on his father's shoulders through the desolation, asking probing, intelligent questions about dead bloated horses, headless women, and eviscerated children— to which his father answered in such a calm and honest voice affirming Picasso's perceptions in such a way that 35 years later when the Luftwaffe bombed Guernica at the behest of the fascist forces of Spain, Picasso was able to paint his famous painting because he had integrated and stored the memories of that early experience with such clarity and lack of emotional dissonance, that he could, all of those years later, reproduce the images in such startling, grim and horrifying detail."

"Wow! That's amazing!"

"Thanks."

"My uncle really saved my life in many ways."

"How's that?"

"He was the only one who really listened to me, encouraged me."

"In what ways?"

"He turned me on to philosophers when I was eight, mostly Christian, but he gave me so much more than my father who disparaged my uncle. He always discouraged me from knowing him better. He was very jealous of him."

"And Henry never had anyone like that? No 'sympathetic witness?'"

"No, I seriously doubt it."

"Do you see that as part of your role with Henry?"

"No! I hold space for him to allow him to grow; to give him space to decide what he really wants for himself."

"So, you're not actively directing him somewhere?"

"Only in a very general way."

"What about his delusions?"

"What about them?"

"They don't seem so far off from your own ideas about politics and government."

"Not to sound too dismissive, but there is fairly concrete evidence that Big Business runs the government, not the other way around."

"And?"

"One does not have to look too very deeply to see the massive collusion between them based on profit motive and separatist paradigm."

"'Separatist paradigm?'"

"Only those who feel disconnected from the environment and don't feel a connection to others can blithely destroy the environment and want only to ruin other peoples' lives."

"I understand."

"Normal 'socialization' breeds empathy out of most people from the moment of the first breath."

"Toward what goal?"

"Most people are so conditioned to behave, to obey 'authorities,' that they teach their children to 'fit in.' All those unexamined principles get passed on blindly from generation to generation, re-creating the slimy drudge of the past. Hitler said, 'Give me a child when he is three, and he will be mine for life!'"

"So, you're saying that the process of socialization is responsible?"

"Of course! We want good little robots built in our own image! We want 'obedient' children whom we praise when they 'obey.' No one cares what children really want! Very few parents ever ask. They tell their children what to do, how to think, how to be! To paraphrase Descartes, 'Peredo ergo sum!'"

"Translation please."

"I consume, therefore I am!"

"Apt phrasing for contemporary society!"

"I agree. You just reminded me of something David Bohm said about inclusion, what he called the Implicate Order. Let me see if I can remember this."

Paul was silent for a moment, then scrunching up his forehead, quoted from memory:

> "The Implicate Order exists as an ultimate physical substrate that underlies our present perception of reality. Although the parts appear to be distinct from the whole, in fact, because they 'enfold' or include the whole, they are identical with the whole. If we could invoke the precedent of quantum mechanical indefinability, we could leap to the idea of a united entity encompassing all space and time in which each part contains the whole and is identical to it."

Regina looked at Paul with an admixture of awe and incredulity.

"How do you do that? You have such an incredible memory!"

"Anyone who is not demented or doesn't have brain-damage can develop a better memory. My memory has improved because I keep clearing my memory banks of useless or outdated information and traumatic affect."

"Is that why you work the way you do?"

"Absolutely!"

"So, you didn't just decide it would sound good to call yourself a shamanic therapist?"

"I don't call myself a 'shamanic therapist!' I work with energy as it presents itself through the client, and apply techniques from my storehouse of training and experience. Most therapists are trained to funnel their clients' symptoms into the 'approved' theories taught by their instructors—whether they fit situations or not, whether they actually help or not."

"I'm sorry. I was baiting you a little bit."

"I know. It's just a little bit tender for me, all of the different names so called therapists use, especially the ones who are essentially selling snake oil."

"When you have the professional chops, you don't have to create elaborate ceremonies or quasi-esoteric job titles."

"The word 'shaman' has been so overused. It does have legitimacy for various peoples all over Asia where certain healing practices have been used for thousands of years. Native American medicine people have never used that word. They have practiced forms of healing using trance and rituals wherein they act as intermediaries between the visible and invisible worlds."

"You are encyclopedic!"

"Only on certain topics."

"Why this one?"

"Because my Indian friends have strong objections to anyone outside of the traditional cultures adopting the nomenclature, practices, and rituals—specially to justify taking entheogens like peyote, psilocybin, and ayahuasca without the accompanying prayers and rituals. It's cultural exploitation, a form of neo-colonialism."

"God! Another hot topic! But how does it relate to Henry?"

"I don't pretend I'm a miracle worker. I just try to be totally real. I don't contradict his delusions. He's not ready right now to incorporate a different value system."

"I still think you should be prepared for a relapse."

"I am kind of expecting it. After all of these months, it will suck if I have to take a step back."

"I hope it is just one step."

"Do you think he might totally regress? Even require hospitalization?"

"I hope not. You'll just have to wait and see."

CHAPTER THIRTY-SEVEN
Yet Another Twist

San Francisco June 18th, 2002

Paul sat in his office, sipping a dark-brewed coffee, preoccupied with the thoughts, fears, and concerns that had followed on the tail of his consultation with Regina. The previous evening, he had continued considering what direction Henry might next take in terms of symptoms and behaviors.

Paul was pleased when Henry appeared at his office exactly on time. He was unaccompanied by Andrew, who had finally acceded to repeated requests to remain in the limousine. Henry was dressed as expensively as always, but much more casually in jeans and a comfortable-looking shirt with Mexican huarache sandals on his feet. He looked directly at Paul with a measuring glance as if seeking a comment from him.

Paul rose from his chair and shook his outstretched hand.

"You look different."

"I feel different, too," said Henry as he made his way to the chair in which he usually sat.

"Have you been smoking again?"

"No! I don't...really feel the need to."

"Why not?"

"I feel like there's this ...door that's opened in my mind."

"'Door?'"

"I feel like I've been asleep...for a long time."

"And?"

"And now, I want to...see more."

"'See more?'"

"Be more alive. It's like...I've been living underground for years."

"That all really sounds really good. But I still need to ask you a few questions?"

"OK."

"Have you had any diarrhea or stomach upsets since we last met? Fever? Elevated temperature? Discomfort of any kind?"

"No. I've been feeling... better."

After his extensive discussion with Regina, he was positively relieved.

"I am glad to hear it. Can we talk about that?"

"OK."

"Tell me about 'better.'"

"I haven't...changed my mind about...the aliens."

"OK."

Paul waved his hand, motioning for him to continue.

"What has shifted?"

"I just don't feel so alone anymore."

"'Alone?'"

"I can talk to you. I'm not alone in my world anymore."

"Communication is very important."

"It's more than that. You do listen."

"And that's a big change!"

"I've always lived...like I was all alone inside a bubble!"

"Can you tell me a little more?"

"I know I'm not...completely alone anymore."

"Ah."

Paul recognizing that Henry was referring to his relief from the excruciating isolation in which he had lived most of his life.

"We had a pretty powerful session last time."

"Yes, we did!" said Henry with emphasis, and jumped up out of his chair to take a turn around the room.

"It was a... huge relief. It was like what I want when I... touch other people."

Paul remained silent, waiting for Henry to express his own conclusions.

"Only...better. I feel better...longer."

"Longer than when you have sex?"

Henry looked down at his feet and mumbled.

"Yes."

"Sex is a totally normal human function, Henry. Even if it is embarrassing to talk about sometimes."

"But I... like men."

"Statistically four percent of the U.S. population is gay or lesbian. I think it's a lot higher than that."

Henry looked up finally, face aflame, and blurted.

"But it's illegal!"

"That's a very large topic, and we could spend the session talking about it, if you want."

"No! There's something more important...to talk about today!"

"OK."

"It's embarrassing!"

"That's a huge topic too, but it might be more relevant."

"I have these feelings and I don't know what to do with them!"

"Totally normal."

"And Father doesn't know!"

"Ah!"

"And... I want...more from him."

"'More?'"

"I want him to be my...Dad, not just Father!"

"OK. How would that look?"

"I don't know. I've always wanted... a real Dad!"

"What does that mean to you?"

"I will be loved...wanted."

Paul kept a neutral expression on his face and groaned inwardly. He had heard this desire expressed many times by clients. He had expressed it himself in the early days of his own therapy. It contained an atavistic hunger yearning to be sated, an early loss that suddenly felt as if it could be redeemed. It hinged on the fragile hope that, despite all of the suffering one might have suffered, it was going to be possible to magically develop the loving, nurturing relationship that one might have originally missed; and one that would satisfy that archaic, almost antediluvian desire.

The wish behind the wish was, of course, that such a magical solution would or could completely change one's life in such a way as to redeem whatever deep and awful suffering one had endured; as if such an event might change the long and disturbed history one had already experienced. The deep desire is to reframe it in such a way as if it had never happened; and through these fantasized pseudo-healing machinations, one could reconstitute one's life as having always been whole and complete, such that one could pretend or contend that one had never been damaged.

A parallel and equally hoped-for result could only come about through continuous, assiduous work on one's self, learning to uplift and support one's nascent self in the kind of health and well-being for which one has always longed—that guiding light for which one's own work on these issues would be/could be/was the only process that could bring about the desired-for results.

Toward this end, there were a number of techniques that Paul used—among them John Bradshaw's "Championing the Child" from his book *Homecoming*—that could assist an individual in creating and maintaining an analog champion in the place of the one he or she had never had. A requirement for this work meant eschewing any and all hope that one could ever sculpt such a figure out of one's birth parents.

When he was working in the Youth Authority, Paul had had rare and wonderful opportunities to re-unite families, but he was only able to do so because all of the parties were willing to commit themselves to the work. Once a young man who had served eighteen months for methamphetamine was united with his father (whom he had never met) who had served eighteen years in Federal prison for the same reason. Paul had worked with them, separately and together, over a period of six weeks before all of the parties agreed. They had both made Herculean efforts to re-assemble their broken lives creating genuine forgiveness all the way around, that led to deep grief work and the mourning of their tremendous losses—making more room psychically to embody a more healed consciousness, and therefore far more improved (and "sane") behaviors.

All of this ran through his mind in the brief moment before he replied to Henry's multi-leveled wishes/dreams/desires/fantasies/unhealed delusions.

"That's quite a big wish, Henry."

"You don't believe it, do you?" said Henry as he immediately flared into a persecuted anger.

"I didn't say that. I just know how much work goes into such a repair."

"'Repair?'"

"Yes. Your work is allowing you to 'fix,' as it were, your old hurts, and therefore, allow you to better interact with others."

"OK. But what can I...do about...what I feel?"

"That's the crux of the issue. Healing yourself is all you can do. Whether your father will ever be ready is a whole other issue. If he ever expresses an interest, I would have to refer him to another therapist. Otherwise it would be a conflict of interest."

"Is there...do you think...there's any way to convert

him?"

"'Convert?'"

"Yes. Get him to...come around."

"Do you?"

Paul knew that Henry's answer would be a good litmus test for the level of progress he'd actually made—and the extent to which what might be his greatest, yet most hidden, delusion still be lurking in shadow—the desire to be redeemed and found lovable by another in lieu of himself.

"I believe it! I do!" he said vaulting out of his chair.

Paul invisibly rolled his eyes, taken aback a bit by the vehemence in Henry's voice, reflecting his belief in the impossible-to-produce reality for which he so mightily craved. Paul took a counter-tack with him.

"How do you think you might 'convert' him?"

Henry stopped and glared at Paul.

"If he could just see how...lovable I am, he'd have to love me."

Paul immediately suspected that Henry might be doing the mental equivalent of trading addictions, like a junkie quitting heroin and becoming an alcoholic.

"Henry, I have to ask, is there anything that has led you to believe your father is ready?"

"He actually listened to me! For the first time!"

"And you believe he's changed?"

Henry started crying and covered face with his tear-stained fingers.

"It has to be true!" said Henry, conflating his longstanding desire with a transient experience.

"I understand, Henry. I really do. But you may have jumped on this experience as proof that your father has really changed."

Henry looked up and said, "You don't think so?"

"I had a recent conversation with your father. He was less demanding than ever before. I saw it as a potential opening, but not that he had permanently changed."

"Why not?"

"His years of mistreating you is pretty strong evidence."

"Why?"

"People just don't really change overnight."

"But...I want him to...change!"

"You've wanted that for a long time."

"I'm just so...tired of waiting!" Henry replied, pounding the arm of his chair.

"Henry, do you believe we've made progress?"

"Yes."

"Do you trust me?"

"Yes," said Henry, more slowly, though emphatically.

Paul made a leap then, asking the intuitive question that had occurred to him. This was the third time it had recurred, his signal that it was a correct notion.

"Henry, what would you say to your father that would convince him to love you?"

Henry looked astonished, eyes bugging.

"How...how did you know?"

"Just a feeling, Henry."

"I... I would talk to him...like my Dad."

"What does that mean?"

"Tell him...the truth."

"'The truth?'"

"'The truth' about me."

"What truth would that be?"

"That I'm in love for the first time!"

CHAPTER THIRTY-EIGHT
Another Perspective

San Francisco Friday, June 21ˢᵗ, 2002

"What did you say then?" asked Regina, eyes sparkling, clearly amused.

"I was flabbergasted! I was totally not expecting that."

"And?"

"As soon as I recovered— just a few moments, Henry didn't even notice—I pursued the topic, of course."

"And what did you say?"

"'Wow! That's giant!'"

Regina laughed and said, "Very therapeutic!"

"It was a genuine human reaction!"

"OK. I got that. Then what?"

"'It seems pretty sudden, Henry!'"

"'Not for me. I've been waiting my whole life!'" he said.

"And you said?"

"'This is the first I've heard of this.'"

"Then he said, 'You're the first person I've told.'"

"So, I knew I had to handle it delicately."

"I guess!"

"So," I said, "Who is this person?"

"And?"

"He said, 'Someone I met at a club?'"

"And?"

"'We danced all night long.'"

"I said, 'Tell me more.'"

"He said, 'He's twenty-one and really good looking.'"

"'When did you meet him?'"

"'Last week.'"

"'And you're in love?'"

"'Yes! It's wonderful!'"

"Oh shit!"

"Exactly my sentiments!"

"Oh Jesus! What did you do then?"

"I kept asking him questions. It turns out that his 'friend' is new to San Francisco, from Kansas!"

"Oh no!"

"And it gets worse."

"OK."

"His new 'friend's' been out of the closet for six years. He's encouraging Henry to come out too!"

"What? That sounds completely nuts!"

"I think so too!"

"What did you say?"

"I used my calmest, most reasoned 'therapist voice' even though I was really worried."

"And?"

"I suggested to him that maybe things were 'moving too fast.'"

"And he said?"

"They 'hadn't had sex yet even though they both wanted to really badly.'"

"What's this guy doing for money?"

"Very good, grasshopper," Paul said, referring to the old television show *Kung Fu* from 1972 that made a star out of David Carradine.

"Come on! You're withholding!"

"He's 'working at a couple of gay bars, cleaning up after hours.'"

"Yeah, right!"

"I don't believe it either."

"Is he hustling?"

"I think so. Of course, Henry is oblivious."

"Do you think Henry been giving him money?"

"I suspect. He did mention 'hanging out' at Ferdy's place. So, maybe 'to help with the rent.'"

"Oh please!"

"I know. I'm really worried."

"I don't blame you."

"And it gets worse."

"Oh no!"

"Oh yes! Henry wants me to meet him!"

"Professionally?"

"I think he thinks I'm an audition."

"'Audition?'"

"Yeah. He wants to introduce me to 'the man he loves'—before he comes out to his father!"

CHAPTER THIRTY-NINE
Into the Fray

San Francisco Tuesday June 25th, 2002

Henry looked very comfortable and well dressed. Henry smiled, one of his rare happy facial expressions. Then he offered to shake hands and took a seat.

"Henry, I must admit you are looking well today."

"I am well. Thanks. It's the power of love!"

Paul was taken aback a bit, then responded.

"Good. That's exactly what I wanted to talk about today anyway."

Henry settled comfortably in his chair, looser and more relaxed than Paul had ever seen him. Paul hesitated to broach the topics he needed to discuss; hated to shatter his client's ebullient mood, no matter the underpinnings; and yet knew he had to do so in today's session, even if it sent his client off the rails. He decided to proceed cautiously so that he could contain whatever untoward reactions he might invoke.

"I am so fucking happy!"

"Tell me more."

"I... I guess it's because...I've never really...connected with anybody before, not like this."

"And this fellow you've been seeing—what's his name anyway?"

"Ferdinand. I call him Ferdy."

"And you met him at a dance club?"

"I was sort of standing on the sidelines and he was...God, the man can dance!"

"And?"

"He danced by me a couple of times, and then he...came by and held out his hand."

"OK."

"And I didn't feel...afraid of him."

"I understand."

"Do you really?"

"He broke through your fear."

"Exactly! I mean I was...attracted to him anyway, but..."

"So, you accepted his invitation to dance?"

"Yes. Not anything formal, just kind of moving around...together."

"Would you say it was a sexual dance?"

"Oh yes! Almost instantaneously!"

"Wait one. 'Instantaneously?'"

"I fell in love!"

"That's a huge leap!"

"Haven't you ever just 'known' immediately?"

"Well, yes, even though it never seemed to last. But wait a minute. Who is this fellow?"

"He's twenty-one, from Kansas. He works at a bunch of clubs doing night clean up."

"And where does he live?"

"Right now, in the Tenderloin. In an SRO."

"'Right now?'"

"We...we've talked about getting a place...together."

"That sounds pretty radical."

"I know. But I love him."

"Does he feel the same way?"

"Yes."

Oh Jesus Christ! It was worse than he suspected. If, as Henry claimed, they had not yet had sex (which seemed dubious at best), they're deciding to live together on such short acquaintance seemed ludicrous.

"You don't know anything about him!"

"He's always been gay. He told me he knew when he was four."

"'Four?'"

"What I really like...is he's so free!"

"'Free?'"

"He doesn't worry too much about normal stuff."

"'Normal stuff?'"

"You know, like money and stuff."

"Does he know about your trust fund?"

Henry looked at him with a totally blank expression that slowly turned angry as his face turned bright red.

"You sound like Father!"

"You've told your father?!"

"Not yet. But I'm going to."

"Why?"

"Because I'm happy!"

"And?"

"I want him to meet Ferdy!"

"Why?"

"He's the man I love! I'm going to get off this conservatorship...get access to my money!"

"You've told Ferdy about your money? About why you're on a conservatorship?"

"Kind of," he said, lowering his eyes.

"Henry, don't turn your face away! It's important that we talk about this."

"He wants to meet you."

"Who?"

"Ferdy! I told him about you!"

"Have you told him about why you come here?"

"I... was kind of hoping you could...help me with that. Explain it a little bit!"

Oh, Jesus Christ Christmas Tree! It was even worse again than he thought!

"What do you mean? How much have you told him?"

"We haven't...talked about it a lot. He knows I'm in therapy."

"He only knows you're 'in therapy,' but he knows all about your money?"

"Well, yes," Henry answered, looking very sheepish.

"I don't understand, Henry. I really don't. Why did you tell a relative stranger all about your money?"

"I wanted...him to like me!"

"To 'like you' because of your money?"

"I wanted to...impress him."

"'Impress him?' Why?"

"Because he's beautiful! And he loves me!"

Jesus! It keeps getting worse!

"And what does he know about your psych history?"

"Just about you."

"And how much about me and your therapy?"

"Just that I come twice a week."

"That's it?"

"Well, yeah."

"You didn't tell him why you come here?"

"Well, no."

"What did you tell him about your belief system?"

"'Belief system?'"

"Come on, Henry! You know what I am talking about! The government and the aliens?"

"Oh. That."

"Yes! 'That.'"

"I told him...a little about it."

"'A little?' What is 'a little?'"

"We've talked about it...but he gets upset when I get angry. He doesn't like me to be angry. He says it 'scares' him."

Jesus, Universe! Just pile it on deeper and deeper!

"So, what do you talk about with him?"

"We...laugh a lot. I... he thinks I'm silly!"

"'Silly?' What does that mean?"

"He...doesn't think there's anything wrong with me! He thinks it's silly that I come here twice a week."

"And what? What do you talk about with him?"

"We're going to get a boat and sail far away from here, away from all of the cities, all of the people."

"Just the two of you?"

"We'll be really happy. I just <u>know</u> it!"

Oh, my fucking God! If ever he had wanted to immediately terminate a client, it was now. But he knew he would do it just for himself, not in the best interests of his client. It would be unethical and extremely unfair. After all, Henry had made excellent progress, and the fact that his point of view was obscured at this point by an inrush of oxytocin, dopamine and the famous "love drug" phenylethylalanine that also is the effect of chocolate. The infusion of all these hormones was either obviating Henry's delusions, or he was just ignoring them.

When the potent mix of chemicals wore off, Paul feared that Henry would be dashed to the ground like Icarus flying too close to the Sun, having had his waxed wings melt. Henry might become severely depressed, even suicidal; maybe have a psychotic break. It was truly a sticky situation. Paul was especially concerned that this Ferdy was just a low-life hustler. So, he decided that he wanted an irrefutable witness present.

"So, Henry, if Ferdy comes to an appointment, I want to have my friend, the consultant I told you about, present also. OK?"

"Why?"

"For professional reasons. Sometimes, when I work with couples, it's helpful for me to have some support too."

Henry thought it over for a moment and then nodded his head.

"OK. That sounds reasonable."

"Let me call her, and we'll set it up at our next session. OK?"

"Thanks, Paul. I appreciate your work with me."

CHAPTER FORTY
Anxiety and Transformation

San Francisco Friday June 28th, 2002

Paul arrived at Regina's office wrung out and anxious. He recounted all of the fear and negative reactions he had had during the session and shared his misgivings about seeing his client along with his newfound boyfriend.

"Apparently he's told him very little about the true nature of his condition, or why he's coming to see me."

"What do they talk about?"

"Money. Having fun. Buying a boat and sailing away."

"That's it?"

"He claims they're not having sex, but I don't buy it."

"Neither do I. Especially when you're young and 'in love.' I doubt very much that they're spending any time talking about the weather!"

Paul laughed and said, "How very true!"

"Are you seriously considering inviting this Ferdy to a session? With the both of them?"

"I'm considering it. Henry seems keen."

"I understand, but it seems like a huge distraction from proper treatment."

"Yeah, I know this might be way off track. I'm really concerned about his 'being in love.' It bothers me that this Ferdy might be just a street hustler out to use Henry. Henry is so naïve, so hungry for attention. He's not ready for this."

"Is that why you want me to be there?"

"I need the support, and I want a witness—just in case this Ferdy tries to pull something or talks Henry into suing me, or threatening to file a complaint. Maybe I should just say 'No.'"

"I really don't get a good vibe on this."

"Neither do I, but the genie is already out of the bottle."

"Wait a minute. Maybe, just maybe, Ferdy is the real deal. Maybe he really cares for Henry."

"But what kind of relationship could they possibly be having?"

"You think Ferdy might be 'mentally ill' too?"

"What? Maybe they're having a folie à deux?" referring to the psychiatric term for a delusional system shared between two people.

"That would mean that Ferdy is sharing Henry's delusions—unless he's even crazier than Henry, but that's a situation I can't even begin to contemplate!"

"Oh God! Me either!" she laughed.

"So, what direction are you going to take?"

"I'm having some anxiety around this. I'm really feeling out of my element."

"And there's no way to prepare for it either."

"No. I've been over it and over it in my head. I could probably trace the progress of the case in my sleep."

"Can you pinpoint the source of your anxiety?"

"Ultimately it comes down to possible outcomes. How is Henry going to act? What if it is positive? He's already told me he's not only coming out to his father, but wants to introduce Ferdy as 'the man he loves!'"

"Oh Jesus!"

"I know. A disaster!"

"There is absolutely no way his father is going to react positively."

"I agree."

"And he's basing this on the only decent conversation he's ever had with him? God, he must be starved!"

"Yeah, and now he has this 'relationship' with a totally unknown person!"

"If I had the resources, I'd love to see a background report on this Ferdy."

"Henry's father could do it so easily!"

"Senior would freak out meeting his only son's male inamorata!"

"Don't even go there! I dread to think how he's going to react when Henry comes out!""

"What's with that anyway?"

"Henry believes he can 'convert' his father into being the 'good Dad' he never had!"

"Are you serious?"

"He seems to be."

"And have you discussed the potential ramifications of his actions?"

"To the extent that he'll listen. He's as fixed about this as he is about his other delusions."

"Any further mention of aliens?"

"It's gone into the background. I've also talked to him about his possible motivations."

"And?"

"He's convinced that he's doing the right thing!"

"Oh my God!"

"So, Regina, are you willing to come to a meeting?"

She sighed deeply, and replied, "Let's check our books and pick a day and a time."

"Friday during Henry's regular session would work well for me."

"We could have your regular Friday with the two of them, then have our regular Friday after that."

"Excellent!"

CHAPTER FORTY-ONE
Deeper into the Mire

San Francisco Friday July 5th, 2002

Regina arrived thirty minutes early. She smiled as she looked around his office space and complimented him on the quality of his furnishings and the ambiance he had created.

"The energy is very strong here. It feels...very conducive for work, the atmosphere you've created. I can feel it! Your clients must feel safe here."

"Thanks. I appreciate that. I've worked hard to get it this way."

"You learned a lot working all those years on psych units!"

"It's a failing for most therapists that they don't have the first-hand experience of working with hospitalized patients. I had to do so many things when I was a Licensed Psychiatric Technician."

"Like?"

"Safety was a big one. It's one thing to sit in an office and provide safety for a client. It's a totally other level to walk around an open ward with seriously disturbed patients."

"Say more."

"You have to have a 360° awareness all the time, not only for yourself but the patients. You have to make sure that no one gets hurt, even if they attack you."

"How do you do that?"

"I learned a lot of ways to keep from getting hurt while using 'the minimum amount of force necessary' to protect the patient and myself."

"And it always worked?" she asked sarcastically.

"In seventeen and a half years on the units—I'm talking about high profile units like SF General and the old 2 South at Santa Clara County Medical Center, plus Mount Zion Crisis Clinic—no one ever got hurt on my shift!"

"Never? How did you manage that?"

"Awareness at all times. I used to go in early every shift to walk around and check out all of the patients' vibes. I could always tell when someone was going to go off."

"You never made a mistake?"

"Not on my own."

"Never?"

"OK, once, when I was working at University of California Davis Sacramento Medical Center. The Acute Psych Unit was on the seventh floor of all things!"

"Jesus!"

"But they had enough wisdom to install rubberized glass in place of regular glass. And these 300# bean-bag chairs that the patients were supposedly not able to lift. They called it 'safe furniture.'"

"And?"

"We had this 350# patient who called herself 'a bull dagger lesbian.' She was really crazy! I mean seriously crazy, and suicidal."

"OK. Then what?"

"One day she decided she's going to kill herself. She picked up one of these giant bean-bags and ran right at the rubberized window. She bounced off of it with the chair right on top of her! Dazed her!"

"Jesus! What happened next?"

"The Charge Nurse warned everybody to stay back. She'd pushed the Panic Button calling for the Sheriffs' deputies. The intercom was blaring 'Mr. Strong to the Crisis Unit!' This one Psych Tech (she later became a psychologist) pushed the Charge Nurse aside. She was really tall and hefty. She pumped up her chest and tapped herself twice."

"Oh my God!"

"She says, 'I'm a lesbian too! The sister will talk to me!' And pushes out the door."

"Oh no!"

"Oh yes!"

"And?"

"She walked up to the patient and bent down to talk to her." She said, 'I'm your sister! Let me help you!'"

"Then what?"

"The patient shook her head, then pulled back her right fist and smacked the Tech right in the face! Broke her cheekbone!"

"Oh Jesus!"

"But that was the one and only time anybody ever got hurt on my shift!"

"So, your training really does make a difference."

"Sure. It's also why I disagree with most of the 'traditional cognitive approaches' in psychotherapy. They just don't work as primary approaches. They're most useful only after the affective cathartic work has been done—to help reorganize the newly cleared brain."

"OK. OK. I've heard this rant before!"

"Still true!"

"OK. We've got about five minutes. Feel more prepared?"

"Yeah. Thanks."

CHAPTER FORTY-TWO
Geronimo!

San Francisco Later the Same Afternoon

Paul took deep breaths into his belly and tried to dispel as much of his anxiety as he could. Regina sat quietly composed in the identical leather chair next to him. Moments later, there was a knock on the door to his therapy office. Paul got up and answered immediately, still preoccupied with his thoughts (and prejudices).

He was pleasantly surprised (even almost shocked) to see a casually dressed Henry, smiling and holding hands with a slightly chunky mixed race-looking-Asian-something man (he assumed Latino due to his first name) wearing neat clean clothing and wire-framed glasses. He was not at all what Paul had been expecting—a greasy, slimy, disheveled, odiferous sneering psychopathic street hustler.

Henry stammered a little as he introduced them. Ferdy made eye contact when they all shook hands.

"Ferdinand Okisaki, sir."

"Nice to meet you. Thanks for coming with Henry."

He turned and smiled into Henry's face and squeezed his hand.

"I'm grateful you invited me, sir."

The two young men shook hands in turn with Regina, and then took places on the love seat, again holding hands.

"Wow!" said Paul, having a resurgence of anxiety.

Regina jumped right in and asked, "Henry tells me you're from Kansas."

Making only a quick, brief eye contact, Ferdy spoke, mostly looking to Henry.

"My mother was Spanish and my father Japanese. They were both scholarship students who met at K-State University in Manhattan."

"Both scholarship students?"

"My mother was a chemist and ran track. My father was in Engineering."

"And now you're in San Francisco?"

"I always hated the Midwest!"

"OK."

"When did you get here?"

"Two months ago."

"What led you here?"

"My father beat me up when I refused to 'stop being homosexual!' I told him I really didn't have a choice; that I've known since I was four! Then he threw me off the front porch! Told me to never come back!"

There was a sudden uncomfortable silence that surrounded the group.

Several mood shifts had moved across Henry's face as he listened but had not spoken. But now he did.

"Why are you asking Ferdy all these questions?"

"You wanted him to come, Henry. We don't know him at all. It's a natural process, Henry, when you meet somebody for the first time" said Paul.

"It's OK, Henry," said Ferdy. "I don't mind."

"Henry, you said you want to introduce Ferdy to your father."

"Yes, we talked about it," he said looking at his friend.

Then Paul asked, "Do you know about why Henry comes to see me? Do you know anything about his father?"

"Henry's a great dancer...when I get him loosened up," replied Ferdy, and giggled.

Regina replied, "That was a serious question, young man. This is no time for jokes!"

"Well, you're his therapist. And I know he and his father don't get along very well."

"That's it?" asked Paul.

"Well, he's cute! And I... really like him."

Paul and Regina exchanged a look and then Paul

sighed.

"Henry, you signed the Release so I can speak freely. Ferdy, there's a whole lot more to Henry than that."

"I know there must be, but I don't care!"

"You might when you hear the truth."

"Paul!" yelled Henry, an admixture of fear and anger dancing across his face. "Don't! Be nice!"

"Henry, you signed a Release of Information so I could talk to Ferdy! You wanted me to!"

"I... thought you might...help me...to tell Father..."

"Is that all you want me to do?"

"Yes. I... want to tell him...I want to come out to him!"

"Why?"

"Ferdy has helped me feel...stronger!"

"And you think your father will be happy knowing?!"

"I want him to.... really love me."

"And you really believe that'll work?"

"It has to! It just has to!"

"Personally, I believe it will make it worse!"

"GODDAMN IT! CAN'T YOU LET ME BE RIGHT JUST ONCE?!"

Everyone in the room seemed genuinely shocked by his

response, especially Ferdy.

"I ask again: Do you really believe your father is going to be happy for you?"

"He...he has to be...I want him to be my...Dad!"

"And he's going to be very pleased that you're gay?"

"He has to! He just has to!"

"Tell me why, Henry."

Regina watched, entranced. Ferdinand sat gape-mouthed, unbelieving.

Henry's face screwed up as if twisted by a giant screwdriver. Then it burst open like an overripe papaya and he started sobbing.

"I JUST WANT TO BE HAPPY FOR ONCE IN MY FUCKING LIFE!"

"I want you to be too, Henry. But I don't think your father will be very pleased!

"But I just want to be real!"

"You can be 'real' without telling him right now."

"When? When will it ever be the right time?"

"I don't know, Henry."

Henry hid his face in his hands and just sobbed. Ferdy looked completely uncomprehending as he rubbed Henry's back in a soothing manner.

Regina continually took the temperature of the whole room as she breathed easily and deeply. Henry continued to sob, then eventually blew his nose, wiped his cheeks and looked wanly at the gathered group. Ferdy was perspiring copiously and vacillated between rubbing Henry's shoulders and looking longingly at his face. Paul was running rapid crisis responses through his internal library, attempting to find the most perfect response. Then, he abandoned that, and decided to be guided by his never-failing intuition.

"Henry!" He didn't move, seemingly frozen.

"Henry! Look at me!"

His client looked up slowly and met Paul's gaze. Henry's eyes were filled with tremendous despair.

"Henry, this was not the best time for all of us to meet, even though we all agreed to be here. But my mandate is to provide you my best work. I have never lied to you and I won't now. OK?"

Henry nodded, looking slightly less forlorn.

"The truth is, I think it's a bad idea to be too open with your father right now. He would probably see it as a confrontation."

Henry started to object, rising slightly off the couch.

Paul continued. "I know. I know. You have a total right to live your life your way. But right now, you have legal constraints that effectively prevent you from doing so. So, I am strongly suggesting that you hold off on coming out to your father."

Henry again started to object, but Paul patted the air in front of him, and sent mercy and compassion with his eyes to Henry.

"What kind of legal considerations does Henry have? Is he under arrest? Or indictment?" asked Ferdy.

Paul and Regina wove the tale of the conservatorship for Ferdy, with Henry casting anxious glances his way.

"OK. But what does that have to do with Henry declaring himself as a gay man?"

Paul touched on Henry Senior's decidedly "conservative" leanings that, if it were a cocktail, would certainly have a fascist float.

"I further suggest that maybe we all meet with Ferdy at your next session, and sit down to further hash out today's topics."

A prolonged silence ensued, as they all waited to see if this suggestion might take root in Henry's mind.

Henry just kept looking at Paul, and then nodded, as if his face were being slowly reassembled from mosaic tiles.

"I... really..." he said, and then looked at Ferdy in a very loving way, before asking, "Are you OK with this?"

Ferdy looked into Henry's eyes and said, "I trust you."

Henry then looked back to Paul and gave the biggest smile Paul had ever seen from him.

"OK, Paul. You're on. We'll see you on Friday."

CHAPTER FORTY-THREE
A Small Respite

San Francisco That Same Evening

Paul and Regina had decided to go to the Rosé Pistola on Columbus. They shared a whole fish (today it was pompano) with shallots and fennel, accompanied by saffron rice and fresh asparagus. They each had a glass of a 1994 Pinot Grigio from Barefoot that both of them thought was just really right.

"So, what do you think?"

"I really thought his boyfriend would have been...oh, I don't know, call me prejudiced, but sleazier, more manipulative, grubby."

"I understand. I was thinking along the same lines. I'm glad we were wrong."

"Me too. But there's still a hard row to hoe. There's so much that Henry hasn't revealed. And he seemed really withdrawn, even a little regressed today. And then that outburst, his magical desire to get validation from his father for being a real man by coming out gay!

"How fucking ridiculous!"

"Truly delusional!"

"How do you plan on managing that?"

"Just keep rolling with my plan, though his relationship with Ferdy is going to complicate that."

"It could potentially help."

"OK. That's a possibility. But I just don't see it. I wish I had never allowed him to come."

"Henry's going to keep seeing him anyway."

"True, but having him in even one more session will be distracting to Henry, likely keep him from his own work."

"So, are you going to cancel Ferdy's invitation?"

"I don't know. I might."

"But you've worked with couples, even families, before."

"Yeah but they're all more or less on the same page. Henry hasn't really told Ferdy anything. They've gone off half-cocked into some fantasyland based on the hope of Henry getting his trust fund."

"What a disaster that would be!"

"I agree. I had a client who did that one time. She went through a million and a half dollars in a manic month! Spent it all, gave it away. Then she tried suicide with a bottle of pills and a bottle of Dom Perignon!"

Paul couldn't help but laugh.

"How perfectly ironic!"

"Indeed. But what is next for Henry?"

"I'm almost a little afraid to guess. You saw him today. He thinks he's 'cured'!"

"Oh, that word!"

"As if anything were ever truly cured except meat!"

"But he believes it!"

"Of course! That's the nature of delusion!"

"But you've been doing so well unwinding his beliefs."

"I fear that I have gotten him well enough that he's willing to chuck it all away for 'love.'"

"He's so hungry!"

"Too true. That basic unending ache created by unfulfilled attachment needs!"

"Common to most of humanity, unfortunately. No one ever really gets their needs met."

"No, but the more virulent the symptoms, the more likely the depth of injury."

"And therefore, the deeper and more consistent must be the treatment."

"Exactly! But I am beginning to feel that I may not have the wherewithal to sustain holding space for him."

"Why not?"

"The only times I've used cathartic techniques, he's had amazing results. But the aftereffects have been pretty powerful too. I'd really prefer he were somewhere safe enough that I could do abreactive work with him every day and know that he was protected when he left my presence."

"Like a hospital or some kind of more sheltered environment?"

"Precisely. I always feel that he leaves me after doing good work and goes back into an environment that is not conducive to maintaining it."

"What do you mean?"

"His father is extremely toxic and Andrew fellow is a conundrum; ostensibly his chauffeur and body guard. That, and, I am prejudiced, the men he meets in the gay dance clubs cannot be that healthy!"

"I repeat: What next?"

"I think I'm going to ask Henry not to bring Ferdy to the next session so we can hash out what's happening with him a little more. Then, we can take up the issues with Ferdy and his fantasies about sailing away."

CHAPTER FORTY-FOUR
The Writer's Vortex

San Francisco Saturday July 6th, 2002

Paul really needed to spend some time today purely in a hands-off manner, especially since Ferdy had turned out to be against type. He appreciated the fact that his bank account was swelling appreciably, but his work and his social life had suffered proportionately. As John Lennon had once said, "Life is what happens to you while you're busy making other plans."

The day following his dinner with Regina, Paul decided to give himself the morning off to simply lie in bed and contemplate the further course of treatment with Henry. He liked Henry and felt committed to their work. He admitted that he was looking forward to his further progress, especially to being able to look back and see what great work he had facilitated! Termination would be cowardly and self-serving, not even to speak of the ethical issues involved. Besides, this was the most challenging and interesting case he had ever had.

He knew it was beyond his remit to hope to facilitate both Henry and his father in some kind of family integration. (Paul chided himself for his own unresolved redemption fantasies.) The family dynamic was so convoluted it would take years to unwind. Besides, a healthy Henry would never stick around long enough for that level of in-depth work.

After a brief nap, he promised himself the rest of the afternoon and evening would be a "writing day." He always left the manuscript in a good place, such that all he had to do was re-read the last paragraph or two before he synched-in with his flow and the direction the book wanted him to take. He could then very quickly pick up the narrative of his intrepid protagonist. Today, he worked through the day in variegated patches, stopping only occasionally as his energy waned—a cup of coffee here, a rib-eye and French fries there, even reading a couple of chapters of a C.J. Box novel—and in such fashion, managed to amass a fair number of completed pages.

All day long, he had been subliminally considering a parallel line of concern about Henry and his continuing treatment when, in a moment of complete abandon sitting back in his chair, he was struck by a piercing bolt of intuition. In retrospect, it seemed almost like a "Duh!" moment, one he should have seen more clearly more immediately, but he realized he was at a distinct crux point in his treatment scheme—and had either to intensify his course of action, or simply terminate treatment. He understood in that moment that he had been the guiding light of the work with Henry for a long time. Now that Ferdy was on the scene, and, it appeared that Henry was set on making him a more permanent fixture, there needed to be some sort of shift. It was a weird kind of triangulation.

His primary commitment to Henry was to help him get healthy enough to challenge his conservatorship and have a real life of his own. What he did with his life after that was totally up to him—even if he decided to squander his half-billion-dollar trust fund. It was, after all, his life and his birthright, even if twisted or distorted, shaped by forces unknown and unseen, no matter what anyone else felt or thought or wished to do with it or about it. Ultimately, he had the right to pursue whatever path he thought desirable, even if the entire Universe thought him wrong or arrogant, even "mentally ill." Autonomy was the birthright obscured and denied him as it was to everyone in a machine-culture that inundated and infused everyone with propaganda and double-speak (thank you George Orwell!).

He flashed on a passage he had recently written, attempting to further suss out the intricacies of family dynamics.

> *An individual will typically adopt a set of values similar to their culture and family of origin. As individuals mature, they begin to consciously assert their beliefs and values as "correct." One might even begin to take a certain amount of pride in specific values without necessarily questioning them.*

> *Those who embrace the ruthless, unfeeling ethos of contemporary times are usually superbly rewarded because they support the extant power system. They are hailed as heroes and heroines. They are featured in newspapers and magazines. They are the saviors featured in popular books. Everyone is encouraged to aspire to be like them. Global media embraces and lionizes them, this seemingly immense popularity obscuring the fact that 95% of all media is*

owned by six multinational corporations, reinforcing the economic and social imbalance culturally sanctioned as just "the way it is," reinforcing the myth that one must feed the existing system and allow it to flourish (Social Darwinism).

Reading that passage reminded him of the empty, hungry unfulfilled black hole that lived inside of them that directly precursed all addictions to vaingloriously try to fill with food, cocaine, cars, alcohol, houses, sex, boats and/or fur coats. It was the same toxic mix of memories of horrors and abuse that infused what was called "mental illness," that twisted the jelly roll of the mind, aching to be redeemed and integrated.

It was such a convenience for the cultural elites who for centuries, millennia maybe, successfully promoted denial to divert attention and suspicion away from the virulent hidden societal virus that drove the focus on making money.

Freud's greatest crime in ignoring the blatant sexual abuse committed by his colleagues and confrères simply contributed to avoiding a much-needed emotional and ideological cleansing. No single individual had neither the strength nor the courage to confront the warped aftereffects of the whole of society devoted to Mammon and its seductions.

His always agile mind kept flitting around the edges of the central problem like a manic pinball bouncing furiously off rails, bumpers, posts and pop bumpers, frenetically attempting to avoid a drop down the hole. He couldn't keep his mind off the pending meeting with Henry, especially since he had told him of his decision to exclude Ferdy.

CHAPTER FORTY-FIVE
Chasing the Dream

San Francisco Tuesday July 9th, 2002

Henry appeared at the doorway, a slight smile on his face and a fearful look in his eyes. There was a definite dissonance to his presentation. Paul filed the information away for later discussion, held out his hand and they shook and took their seats.

"So, Henry, I finally got to meet your new friend."

Now the smile became radiant, filling his face and his eyes.

"Isn't he wonderful? Isn't he awesome?"

"I didn't get much time to talk to him, but he seemed like a nice enough fellow."

"Nice? God, he's wonderful!"

"I'm glad you're happy."

"Oh God! Yes!"

"Have you told him any more about yourself?"

"Just that you're my therapist; that I've been seeing you for almost a year."

"And?"

"'And' what?"

"How much have you told him about why you're really seeing me?"

"I told him you helped me get off meds; that you were helping me get off the conservatorship."

"And?"

"'And' what?"

"Have you told him about why you started coming here? About the government and the aliens? About your previous hospitalizations?"

"No! Hell no!"

"Why not? You told him all about your trust fund! Made grandiose plans about buying a boat!"

"It... it's too...embarrassing."

"'Too embarrassing?'"

Henry now looked away and to his left, seemed deeply interested in examining the intricate weave of the carpet.

"He...he might not...like me anymore."

"But he likes knowing about your money, doesn't he?"

"It's not like that!"

"Like what?"

"My money!"

"It's not?"

"No! He loves me! And I love him!"

"And you're all prepared to just sail away into the sunset?"

Now he looked up and smashed the bottom of his fist against the chair arm.

"Yes, goddamn it! I deserve to be happy for once!"

Paul extended his hands toward the younger man, palms out, and spoke reassuringly.

"I agree. You do deserve to be happy. I just don't think that sailing away from it all is the solution."

"Why not? I'll get my money, then Ferdy and I will get as far away as we can!"

"And then what?"

"What do you mean?"

"Just what will you do? Traveling and having sex won't last forever."

"Why are you being so negative?"

"I'm not, Henry. I just don't believe that anyone can live on love."

"You're wrong! We can!"

"But Henry, you haven't known each other very long."

"Long enough to know!"

"Where have you been staying? His place?"

"Except when he's working."

"And then?"

"I go to Father's for a little while."

"What do you do there?"

"Hunt for money. Go on the Internet and manage my investments."

"'Investments?'"

"I... have a bank account and a money management account...a small one, and I trade some stocks. Day trading."

"And?"

"I'm doing pretty well. Making some money. I know I have to have my own money, my own attorney, to challenge Father in court."

"That's all well and good, Henry. But even assuming you get your trust fund, how are you going to live?"

Henry shouted at Paul.

"I DON'T KNOW! I DON'T FUCKING CARE! FUCK ALL YOUR REALITY! I JUST WANT TO GET OUT FROM UNDER THAT BASTARD'S THUMB!"

"I'm trying to help you, Henry."

"Then don't preach at me like a fucking child!"

"It's a reasonable question."

"I DON'T GIVE ONE SHIT ABOUT PRACTICALITY!"

"Part of my job is to give you some perspective."

"I fucking hate him!"

"I know there's more."

"I just wish he would fucking die!"

"Do you want to kill him, Henry?"

"Yes."

"I mean right now?"

Henry's face collapsed into a mask of shame, and consternation. He made several false starts before he looked at Paul again and then finally gained enough traction to speak.

"I am so...fucking pissed. Part of me knows you're right. I... I'm fucked up. I... wouldn't know how to live on my own. But Ferdy can help me. I love him."

"Thank you, Henry. I appreciate your honesty."

"I... I'm not exactly sure what to do now."

"Is that what you want to talk about today?"

"Can we...talk about Ferdy...some more?"

"If you want support around your relationship, I don't know how much I can help. I don't know the man."

"Oh. OK then."

"But we could explore the bond you're creating and what might lie behind it."

"What's that mean?"

"This has all been very fast"

"I've been waiting my whole life for this! I don't think it was fast at all!"

"That might be part of what I am talking about."

"What do you mean?" Henry quizzed.

"'I've been 'waiting all of my life for this.'"

"So, what? You're quoting me."

"Henry, a year ago you were adamantly trying to convince me that the government was doing business with aliens. Now today you're trying to convince me that you have met the love of your life and are competent enough to manage $500 million dollars and just sail away into the sunset!"

"So?"

"Don't you think that's a pretty big leap?"

Silence fell like a heavy theatrical curtain on the last act. Henry sat with his head and eyes downcast. Paul idly speculated about possible replies he might get from Henry.

"I still really believe that the government is in cahoots with the aliens. And I still believe Father is involved."

Paul noted how Henry failed to thought-block when he felt angry.

"And?"

"You don't really understand how lonely I've always been—until now."

"How do you think the two are related?"

Henry looked perplexed, as Paul thought he might, and decided to let Henry sit with the anxiety. Henry started fidgeting, wiping the side of his face, tugging his ear lobe, and then finally flashed a confused look at Paul.

"How am I supposed to know?"

"You mentioned both ideas. I thought maybe there was a connection."

"I don't know. Maybe."

Paul knew he was looking to be rescued, and he declined.

"Why do you think you might you have mentioned them both when you answered me?"

"I was just trying to answer your question."

"So, you don't feel there's any particular connection between what you believe about your father and your lifelong loneliness?"

"I've never been lonely for my father."

"But you've been lonely."

"Yes."

"And now you're not?"

"Not with Ferdy."

"But what about all of your other problems?"

"We'll handle them together."

"'We?'"

"Me and Ferdy."

"You and Ferdy? The two of you are going to handle all of the complex legal issues?"

"We'll get a lawyer."

"Just like that?"

"Sure."

"And where will you get the money?"

"I've got money coming in."

"How much?"

"About two thousand...a month...right now."

"That won't even make a down payment, a retainer."

"I'll get more."

"How?"

Henry replied "Maybe I can find somebody who will work...for a share...afterward."

Paul responded "Lawyers who work for contingency take at least twenty-five per cent!"

"But that would be..." Henry was incredulous.

"One hundred twenty-five million dollars!" Paul calculated for him.

"But...but..."

"And Henry, that's presupposing that you win."

"What do you mean?"

"As you yourself just said, your father has a 'great deal of money and a lot of influence.'"

Henry stood stiffly and paced before answering imperiously, "So?"

"You could very easily lose your bid for freedom. Then where would you be?"

"I...I... don't..."

"I know, Henry. I know. I just thought we should speak of possibilities. I don't want you to get hurt any worse."

"But Ferdy?!"

"You really have to concern yourself with your own needs first."

"What does that mean?"

"I know you care about Ferdy, but consider your own needs first."

"What does that mean? Really?"

"I'm just asking you to consider all of the progress you have made; how much closer you are to having what you have always wanted."

"I have it now! I have Ferdy!"

"But you're still legally bound! And you have no money!"

"OH, FUCK YOU!"

"Come on, Henry! You're off your meds, and working on getting released from your conservatorship. Once that happens, it'll be a fairly simple step to getting access to your money!"

Henry started sobbing, tears falling like a hard rain.

"I'm just so fucking tired, Paul! So, fucking tired of waiting!"

"I know Henry, but you're doing so much better now! You just gotta hang in there a little longer."

"What about Ferdy?"

"What about him?"

"I want to be with him. Openly."

"Can you do that without telling your father right now?"

"OH, FUCK HIM!"

"That's going to take some significant work, and a considerable amount of money. It will require a very good attorney, one who would be willing to work on contingency.

Henry looked up at Paul with his facial features arranged like a forlorn dog.

"My friend Shirley is one of the best criminal defense lawyers in The City. When the time is right, I will ask her to help to find the right person for you."

There was a protracted silence after which Henry finally stopped pacing and sat back down, and put his chin in his hand, seemingly pondering the imponderable. Finally, he looked up, directly into Paul's eyes.

"OK! OK! For now! But when can we have the next session with Ferdy?"

"There are legal issues involved that I need to consult about, Henry."

CHAPTER FORTY-SIX
Moving Along

San Francisco Friday July 12th, 2002

"Do you think I might have gone too far? Maybe I was being grandiose? I probably should never have consented to see Ferdy! Then I roped you in! Shit! I am so sorry!"

"I personally don't believe you did anything wrong, but the idea of seeing the two of them together again needs to be researched. The argument could be raised that you violated the treatment agreement by adding someone to the roster without prior agreement of the payee, Henry Senior (acting in Henry Junior's behalf). That would be accurate."

"Henry has a right to choose his own treatment provider, and agree or not agree to take meds. In my judgment, seeing Ferdy in session with him was in support of furthering treatment goals—goals agreed upon in the Treatment Plan."

"I can see your thinking. I'm just not sure it's strictly legal" Regina answered acerbically.

"I don't care! For me it is another aspect of my commitment to my client and his needs."

Paul took a deep breath and continued. "But what about those needs? Even if he has legal rights, does that make his decisions—potentially delusional ones, swayed by an uprush of hormones and the hope of fulfillment of longstanding desires— valid? Or does it subtract from their value?"

Regina was genuinely puzzled. "But who then ever makes decisions based on wholeness? Most of the time we all make choices based on unmet attachment and security needs!"

"It's like my old favorite saying: 'Everyone is psychotic.'"

"That may be, but not everyone has a half-billion-dollar trust fund!" said Regina.

"I could see the two of them being together, even pursuing their delusional paradise, with one small exception. He is not legally a free agent, and therefore cannot command my uninhibited fealty. It's truly a conundrum, especially because I'm not convinced that Henry is anywhere near ready to handle daily life without some assistance or supervision—much less manage the enormity of his trust fund under his own sail." Paul was genuinely concerned.

"You sound like you're speaking from experience again."

"I've been clean almost twenty years—will be Christmas Eve. I am so much less arrogant now, so much less driven. I am very, very grateful."

"You have developed a certain humility" she retorted only half-jokingly.

"I look back at my cocaine habit—both times I was strung out, actually, 1970 to '72, and then again 1979 to '82, as totally nuts! There was a point at which I actually believed that being strung out was a feature of an initiatory process. I remember thinking that it was 'evolutionarily growth-producing,' or would be when I came out the other side; came out of the ordeal and ascended. When I was immersed in it, I had a weird fantasy that it was all serving my esoteric initiation; that all of the weird rituals and antics were leading me to a greater sanity! Now the longer I'm clean, the more I realize the totality of the insanity of what I've lived!"

"It does sound pretty nutty! But you've made incredible progress since!"

"Being in recovery has led me to both become a better person and given me a lot to write about. Both in my novels and the clinical book I'm working on. I shared a few chapters of *Crucible of Shame* with you. I really have come to believe that shame underlies all the workings of the world and is generally unacknowledged."

He laughed as he related the story of how the members of his dissertation committee, especially Jeanne Achterberg, frequently reminded him that his dissertation was not, in fact, his *magnum opus*, despite the fact that he thought it might be.

"And when I argued that in 1977, A.B. Schmookler handed in a 1600-page dissertation to his committee of seven Ph.D.'s at UC Berkeley—and they approved it!"

Jeanne replied, "'This is not UC Berkeley, and you are not A.B. Schmookler!' That was the end of that."

"I had never tried to get approval for a draft that was more than 450 pages, and they turned it down flat. I complained, whined, pleaded, and argued and then Jeanne asked the most pristine question possible: 'Do you want to graduate?'"

"Obviously you listened. You graduated!"

"At the time, my dissertation felt like my supreme accomplishment. I desperately wanted it published *in toto!* I look back on that period as a dying flash of the 'me' I thought I wanted to be. I was trying so hard to find something upon which to attach my hungry-ghost needs. Amphetamines and cocaine had always amped up my pursuit, and the delusions were only starting to wear off when I quit. But it was years later until I was free enough to become Dr. Marzeky."

"Do you think it had to do with your unrequited childhood? When did you first decide that you wanted to be Dr. Marzeky?"

"I was eight years old and had a very humiliating experience at a huge family Easter dinner. Someone asked me what I wanted to do with my life, and when I talked about wanting to either go to medical school or become an astrophysicist, they laughed, all of them. And I said to myself, "Fuck you all! One day I will prove it to you! I will be Dr. Marzeky!"

"Jesus! Eight years old?"

"Yeah. I knew I was smart, and I knew I wanted an education! And I was really tired of people acting like I couldn't achieve my dreams!"

"You've always been so radical!"

"I really relate to Henry's desire to live a bigger life! I really support his desire to get away from his father. He keeps him constrained all the time; spies on him, won't let him go out by himself—even has Andrew who follows him everywhere!"

"I bet he justifies it by saying it's for Henry's 'own good!'"

"Thank you, Alice Miller!"

"Do you ever think that maybe you're too empathic with him? That there is some level, no matter how small, in which his father might be right?"

"I've had too many intrusive and demanding phone calls from him for me to feel much mercy for him."

"You sound bitter!"

"I'm just really tired right now. I think you're right about my being a tad overly empathic with Henry. His father reminds me of mine. I've worked really hard, paid a really high price, to have come as far as I have," Paul said, and felt a huge surge of emotion pass through his chest and his eyes tear up.

"I've worked," he said and then could not keep the tears from falling, chest heaving, "so hard for so long...and I still can't escape his fucking grasp! He still haunts me! I just cannot seem to let my memories go!"

He sobbed for a moment, then wiped his eyes and looked up.

"I'm sorry. This is supposed to be a consultation, not therapy for me!"

Regina came to him, and enfolded him in her arms.

"I guess this isn't conventionally appropriate either, but it feels right."

They embraced for a moment longer, then broke apart laughing.

"I think about success a lot!"

He laughed again and then told her of one of his favorite lines from Frank Herbert. "He put these words in the mouth of Paul Atreides (Maud'Dib) in *Dune*:

> *Greatness is a transitory experience. It is never consistent. It depends in part upon the myth-making imagination of humankind. The person who experiences greatness must have a feeling for the myth that he is in. He must reflect what is projected upon him. And he must have a strong sense of the sardonic. This is what uncouples him from belief in his own pretensions. The sardonic is all that allows him to move within himself. Without this quality, even occasional greatness will kill a man.*

"So, you think you're bound for glory?"

"I've always believed so."

"Why?"

"I don't know. I've just always felt that way."

"And?"

"'And' what?"

"I know there's something more. 'A feeling' couldn't have sustained you all these years."

"Actually, all of my anguish and suffering has reinforced a sort of Biblical thing—that I will be repaid for my agonies!"

"Oh God! Not that old myth!"

"What?"

"That there's some kind of cosmic balancing wheel that is going to pay you back for all that you have endured!"

"Why not?"

"It's...I'm not convinced that it's true."

"To me it makes a certain amount of sense."

"But it embraces a sort of Christianesque victim stance! That you have to 'suffer to get to heaven' kind of thing."

"You have another perspective?"

"Yes, I do as a matter of fact. Want to hear it?"

"Of course!"

"I think that suffering is a kind of passage, an initiation. It's meant to uplift the individual to a higher dimension of consciousness...perhaps by making the ordinary and usual so unbearable that one has to escape. It becomes unbearable!"

"I've experienced something like that! I've been beaten to my knees a number of times, where all I could do was throw up my hands in the air and call out, 'Please help me!'"

"That's it! So, you are acquainted with the phenomena."

"Yes. But I must admit that I have never had that amazing overall experience of transcendence!"

"But you have had a taste of that other realm where magic lives!"

"Do you really think it's possible to live that way? Depending upon 'the magical' for sustenance?"

"Personally, I believe so. But it takes lot of work. It's not like you get 'there' and you don't have to do anything ever again. It's a matter of constant work."

"As close as I can get is the unwinding PTSD that I have been doing. I have these bursts of feeling that I am done, all the shit is cleared away and then 'BAM!' I get smacked upside the head!"

"You hadn't learned your lessons yet!"

"Still really haven't!"

"But you're working on it!"

"It reminds me of a lecture I once did—*PTSD from Both Sides of the Couch*. I got the opportunity to reflect on my lessons being more universally applicable so that I can share my wisdom with other brothers, help them along their way."

Paul knew that his journey had taken him through many iterations, and he had become more relatively whole. He believed he had an expanded frame of reference, more humility and a larger (and less self-centered) sense of purpose.

He realized, too, that sharing his thoughts and fears with Regina made him feel so much better. The sharing involved something powerful, induced by not feeling totally separate and alone, just floating through the Universe fearing and guarding against everything and everybody.

He realized too how much he admired Regina's breadth of knowledge and the acuity of her reasoning. She had been an absolute lodestone throughout this past year. Even granted that it was her job to be there for him through the crashing waves and rocky shoals of this case, he knew he genuinely liked her a lot. He had even had an occasional fantasy of what it might be like to have sex with her. Though she was not typically his type—long brunette hair, small-breasted, long legs—she certainly more than made up for the differences with her wit, intelligence and grace. He knew he had to wait until this case was resolved; or they terminated their consultation arrangement, but he felt an affection for her that kept growing.

Regina suggested that he get legal advice vis a vis the situation with Henry and Ferdy.

"Good idea. I'll call Shirley Stephenson and get her to check it out."

Shirley had helped Paul navigate the legal quagmire that had resulted when a former patient had murdered his wife, and the police had very harshly interrogated Paul. That treatment had led him to having a massive flashback of being detained in a cell in restraints after which Shirley got him released with no charges and an in-house only report with Paul agreeing not to file a complaint against the notorious Sergeant Kubicek for brutality. Shirley was very much Paul's type, and they had dated briefly both before and after her timely intervention, but had just not clicked romantically. ("Chemistry," she said parenthetically). Nonetheless, they remained good friends and professional colleagues.

"I think that since Henry is your client and is not acting as a free agent vis a vis controlling his own money, you have an ethical obligation to inform the conservator about your proposed intention to include another party in your client's sessions." Regina always had the edge on him in the legal realm.

"But to do that I would have to violate Henry's confidentiality!"

"Telling his father that he wants to bring a gay man, another gay man, into his sessions?" Regina queried.

"Precisely!"

"Especially since his father does not know he's gay!"

"Amen!"

Regina named it perfectly when she said, "Sticky! I think that the ethics require you tell him, if you are going to include Henry's love interest. Conversely, you really can't without Henry's authorization and a signed Release of Information."

"But that would open the door! He's been trying to get information out of me for the last year!"

"You could make it a limited ROI."

"True. My fear is that Henry's chomping at the bit to come out of the closet!"

"Yeah, I see that. And it's his right."

"True. And if he does, I would still have to inform Senior of Junior's request, since he is conservator of Henry's money."

"Too true."

"And I believe that Henry's coming out to his father is potentially a disaster. His father is so toxically macho. He might just blow up, maybe try to get Henry hospitalized against his will."

"On what grounds?" Regina asked, probing.

"He is still manifestly delusional. If he is provoked strongly enough, he might blow up; maybe even threaten his father. Or he might just say 'Fuck it!' and run away. That would give his father grounds to call the police and have him picked up and held pending court procedures. Henry would have to show cause that he did not need to be hospitalized; was not a danger to self or others. I do not think they could prove 'gravely disabled' since he is under the ostensible care and direction of his conservator."

"Senior could claim that Henry threatened him," asserted Regina.

"And he would likely get away with it since it would be his word against Henry's."

"Exactly, especially with him testifying in his $5000 suit, and his stable of $350-an-hour attorneys by his side."

"And Henry insisting that he hadn't threatened him; that he simply told him he was gay and wanted to get out from under his control! That would blow it out of the water!"

"The attorneys would paint it as 'delusional,' and even with my testimony under oath that Henry had revealed his orientation to me confidentially, I doubt it would make very much difference—especially since it would be 'he said-he said.'"

"Exactly. I think your best recourse is to talk Henry out of having Ferdy there. Or, if it really comes to it, have Henry sign a Release and have his father come in to a session where Henry can come out with you there, if he's so convinced it's a good time to do so."

"I think it's terrible timing, but Henry has this fantasy about he and Ferdy sailing away together! Henry somehow has found a new level of strength, and now he's convinced he can win his inheritance in court! So, for him, coming out now is of paramount necessity!" Paul continued following his own course of thought.

"Jesus!"

"You betcha!"

"Considering the circumstances, I think his decision is extremely flawed—believing that by coming out, he will establish himself as a 'real' man and stand up to his father in one fell swoop."

"Feels that way to me, too. I've tried to explain to him about his father's power and influence, but he seems stuck in this fantasyland scenario that he is going to triumph."

"Have you considered talking to Ferdy privately? Maybe help him see a bigger picture?"

"It would be breaking confidentiality, unless Henry signed a Release—and I seriously doubt he will allow me to talk to Ferdy privately, even if I did it *pro bono*."

"You could broach it."

"I seriously doubt he would agree."

"So, what do you intend to do?"

"I'm gonna tell Henry 'No,' and couch it in legalities."

"He won't be happy. Do you think it'll work?"

"I don't know. I'll let you know after I do."

"Thanks."

"You up for dinner? On me?"

"Where did you have in mind?"

"Maybe the North Beach Restaurant. I like their Osso buco. They serve it over polenta with salad after."

"They make a good Veal Milanese too, don't they?'

"I've only had it there once, but it was excellent!"

"And maybe a Barolo or a good Chianti?"

"Superb choice, my friend!"

"Let's do it!"

"And no more talking business until tomorrow. Then we'll see what happens. Deal?"   (Keep the meeting tomorrow in mind when you fix the time of the initial meeting with Ferdy further back.)

"Deal!"

CHAPTER FORTY-SEVEN
Life is What Happens While
You're Making Other Plans

San Francisco O Dark Thirty, Saturday July 13th, 2002

Paul would never know what may or may not have happened if he had had another opportunity to meet with Henry again.

He was deeply immersed in an extremely sexual dream about Regina. In a fantasy he had never actually experienced, she was standing on her head while he lovingly gave her oral sex.

Then the phone rang, jolting him out of the best dream he had had, maybe ever.

Paul groped for the phone with his eyes closed and shouted harshly into the receiver.

"WHAT?"

"Doctor? It's your service."

"So?"

"I have the police on the other line. They're trying to reach you."

"WHAT?"

"They say that one of your clients has barricaded himself in a house in St. Francis Wood and won't talk to anyone else!"

Paul groaned involuntarily, his intuition immediately telling him it was Henry.

"Oh God!"

"Do you want me to put them through?"

"Yes. Of course."

"Go ahead please. Dr. Marzeky is on the line."

"Paul. Phil McLaren here."

"Phil? I thought you guys had a client of mine barricaded in his house."

"I do."

"But you're Homicide!"

"We strongly suspect his father might be dead. But he's barricaded himself in the house, and we haven't been able to determine what the situation is. He says he will only talk to you."

"Shit! What time is it?"

"0249."

"Crap!"

Paul had worked with Phil previously, and begun to develop a real friendship with the Homicide detective several years ago when one of his clients, Massimo Baldestari, had murdered his wife and his mother. It had at first looked as if he were innocent, though Phil's investigation had proven him guilty just before he committed suicide in the presence of he and Phil. It was yet another brick in the wall of the bond between them that started when they discovered they were both Vietnam vets.

"You want to send a cruiser and bring me there with lights and siren?"

"I do."

"You still in the same place in North Beach?"

"Yes. Give me ten minutes and I'll be standing out front, waiting."

Paul punched the button for his coffeemaker, brushed his teeth and washed his face before hastily dressing in an old pair of jeans, his favorite t-shirt from Hawaii and his jean jacket. Even though it was July, the wind was chilly and the overnight fog was lingering.

Almost immediately after stepping out of his house, an SFPD cruiser approached, coming up Lombard Street, lights on, but no siren. Paul flagged him from the mouth of his street and hopped in.

"Do you know The City?" Paul asked.

"Not well."

"Just go down Lombard and make a left on Van Ness. It'll be the quickest. Use the siren too."

"Then what?"

"Take Van Ness all the way to the end, then take a right onto Market. Go all the way up Market until it turns into Portola. When we get there, I'll tell you what's next."

"Thanks."

With the lights flashing and the siren screaming, the light traffic at that time of the morning simply melted. They went up the near side of Twin Peaks, and Paul directed the young officer to go left on Santa Clara and take another on San Jacinto where they immediately saw Henry's father's mansion surrounded by a large number of police vehicles flanking the layered cordons of police tape manned by uniformed officers keeping a small, but already-gathering crowd of gawkers and ever-present media vultures at bay.

Phil had given Paul's name to the outlying cordon of officers, who, after checking his licenses, held up the tape and allowed him through, pointing him to the next tape where the same procedure was repeated, and he signed another on-scene sheet denoting his presence. He was finally pointed to a small, tight clot of plain-clothes detectives standing with him and a group of technicians manning various devices: a telephone handset connected to a blue box; another tech with headphones connected to a rectangular black container; another held a portable battery connected via a long snaking flexible cord to a bullhorn; several other uniformed officers taking notes and talking on microphones and closed-circuit radios. Phil noticed him approaching as if he were a Geiger counter and Paul radioactive. He came gave a small, wry ghost of a smile and shook hands.

"Paul. Thanks."

"Glad to help. Bring me up to speed."

"We don't have the whole picture yet, but it seems that your client and his father got into some kind of row—screaming, yelling, furniture crashing, lamps broken. They both seem to have been moving through the house. They woke the next-door neighbors who called at 0228 and first uniforms arrived at 0235. They knocked on all the doors, and your client yelled at them that he would only talk to you. When the on-call supervisor heard your name, he called me. He knew we had history. Then I called you. Bingetty bangitty boom!'"

"That's it?"

"I've got a hostage situation, maybe a homicide! And the perpetrator is asking for you! OK?"

"Sorry. No coffee. Can I get some?"

Phil asked one of the uniforms to get Paul a cup. "Black, please!"

"Do you want me to talk to him? Right now?"

"Try to talk him into coming out. Giving himself up."

"'Give himself up?' For what?"

"I don't know! For all we know he killed his father!"

"You don't even know his father is in there!"

"Just talk him into coming out! OK?"

"His father has a long history of violence against my client."

"Says who?"

"Says me!"

"No police reports on that!"

"His father has him watched 24/7! Even if he wanted to, he couldn't have! He's practically a prisoner in this house!"

Phil looked up at the façade of the mansion and said, "Nice prison."

"Prison nonetheless."

"We'll try the phone first. If he doesn't answer, we can try the horn."

The phone, of course, did not answer. Then the detective tried the electronic hailer.

"Henry, Dr. Marzeky is here and wants to speak with you. Please answer the phone"

Phil tried the phone again and handed the receiver to Paul.

"Hello?"

Henry was clearly shaken when he answered, his voice both tremulous and exhausted.

"Henry. It's Paul."

No sooner had he said his name than an enormous,

ear-splitting wail bellowed out of the receiver and surrounded the group like a shroud around a cluster of mourners.

Paul listened to the raggedy breathing for the better part of a minute. Then Paul spoke to him again.

"Henry. Please listen. This is Paul, Paul Marzeky."

"You've got to help me! Please!"

"Henry! I will!"

"Paul, please! Help me!"

"I'll do whatever I can, Henry."

"I didn't kill him, Paul!"

"Who, Henry?"

"Father! I didn't kill Father!"

"Are you sure he's dead, Henry?"

"Yes! He kept beating me and yelling at me! I ran away and hid in a closet. It was quiet for a while and then he yelled once more. And then it was quiet again. I came downstairs and found him!"

"Was he dead when you found him?"

"Oh God! He had blood all over him!"

"Henry, why won't you let the police in?"

"I'm scared! They'll hurt me!"

"No, Henry. I promise. They won't hurt you."

"NO! THEY'LL KILL ME!"

"You have to trust me, Henry."

"I trust you, Paul! Not them!"

"If you're innocent, they'll prove it!"

"NO!"

"What can I do to help?"

"Help me! Please help me!"

"Will you come out, Henry? Please!"

"NO! NO FUCKING WAY!"

"I'll help you, Henry!"

"Then come in! Help me!"

"I can't do that, Henry!"

"You can! Yes, you can!"

"Hold on, Henry!" Paul said, and muted the phone.

Phil immediately said through gritted teeth, "No fucking way!"

"Phil, listen! He's my client. If you guys go barging in, you might just hurt him. He needs special handling. Let me help."

"No fucking way!"

"He's really unstable! How would you goddamn feel if he fucking killed himself?!"

"No. Fucking. Way!"

"What do you think the fucking Commissioner would think?"

"Don't try to blackmail me!"

"I'm not, Phil! I just want what's best for my client!"

"I cannot authorize you going in there!"

"Maybe you should check with the Chief of Ds or the Mayor. This has huge political ramifications!"

"You fucker!"

"Please Phil! He's really very fragile!"

"Tell him we're checking for authorization. OK?"

Paul did, and was greeted by a screeching cry for help that Paul had only previously heard when a cat was being tortured.

"Please, Phil!" Paul screamed at him.

"OK! OK! I'll call the chief of Ds!"

Phil keyed his microphone and asked to be put through to his supervisor.

"Sir? Yes sir. We've got a bit of a situation here," he said and explained the very strange circumstances to him. "Yes sir. I'll wait for you to call back."

"He's going to call the Commissioner, and he'll probably call the Mayor. In the meantime, see if your client wants anything—food, soft drink, whatever."

Henry screamed at him again, insisting he needed him immediately.

"Paul? I am so fucking scared! Please! Help me!"

Paul turned to his vet brother and shrugged his shoulders.

"I told you. We have to wait for a call back. If you try to enter, I'll arrest your ass!"

"This is unconscionable!"

McLaren answered his cell as soon as it rang. He flipped it open and turned away as he answered.

"Yes sir?"

Holding the phone to his ear, he scrunched his eyebrows intensely and continued to listen. Then he uttered a series of affirmatives.

"Yes sir!" "Yes sir!" "Yes sir!" And then, "Yes Your Honor! Yes sir, I understand! Immediately!"

When Phil turned back toward him, Paul knew immediately that he was going in, even though Phil's objection was clearly writ upon his face.

"You are fucking crazy!"

"What's that mean?"

"The fucking Mayor has consented!"

"Thank you!"

"But," he said, holding up his index finger, "there are conditions!"

"Oh, here we go!"

"You're going to have to agree or it's no go!"

"OK. Tell me."

"If you're going to go in that house, there's some paperwork we've got to do."

"OK."

"You're going to have to agree, in writing, that you are doing this voluntarily."

"Of course."

"There's more. You have to agree to not hold the City and County of San Francisco, the Police Department and any and all associated agencies or entities responsible in any form or fashion for any untoward or harmful incidents that may befall."

Paul laughed and shook his head.

"Of course! Anything else?"

"And you agree to bring your client out as quickly and expeditiously as possible, and turn him over to the police."

"Why?"

"It's a condition?"

"Why? He's not guilty of a crime!"

"Not yet! In all likelihood, he will be charged with something—perhaps murder!"

"So, you've already made up your mind about that?"

"This is a criminal justice situation. You're not a free agent here!"

Paul kept his suspicions to himself and simply asked, "OK. Where's the paperwork?"

"A cruiser is bringing it from the Mayor's office."

"How long's it going to be?"

"It's on its way."

"You already figured I'd sign it, huh?"

"I know how intense you can be, Paul."

"I guess I should say, 'Thank you!'" Paul laughed.

"Seriously though, this is a bad idea."

"He's my client! I have to!"

A black-and-white pulled up, lights flashing, and a uniformed officer rushed up with a handful of papers.

Paul scanned the paperwork by the light of a flashlight. Then he read it again slowly.

It recapitulated what Phil had told him, except that he

was not required to facilitate Henry's arrest, simply to "assist the Police Department, any and all detectives and/or officers thereof, in successfully ending the situation at 11 San Jacinto in the most peaceful and efficacious manner, eventuating with the safe resolution for all concerned." Paul didn't care. He was going in.

CHAPTER FORTY-EIGHT
A Stitch in Time

San Francisco 0404, July 13th, 2002

Paul signed it and then Phil and another detective countersigned it as witnesses. Paul asked if they had schematic diagrams; if they knew precisely where Henry was; and if there were any other people in the house.

"Henry, and by his account, his father, are in the downstairs rear, in the father's study. It's the chauffeur's day off. And his very personal assistant Martine does not seem to be available either."

"'Very personal assistant?'"

"There are rumors."

Changing tacks, Paul commented on his dislike of Andrew.

"Why?"

"I don't know. Just a bad vibe. Plus, Henry told me he's 'always around,' and that he 'reports' to his father about everything."

"Do you know his last name?"

"No, but Henry might."

"If you get his name, I'll run him on NCIC."

"Call Henry. Please. Now."

"Paul? Paul? Are you going to help me? Please?!"

"OK, Henry. I'm coming in. Alone."

"Please hurry!"

"Henry. Is the door open?"

"Come around the side to the back."

"Coming now. Alone."

The house was built in 1982, echoing a French Style Villa, on the top of a small hilltop with ocean views from two different decks, and of St. Francis Wood Upper Fountain Park. There were four fireplaces, a large library, a media room, a swimming pool and more rooms than any house Paul had ever seen, short of the Versailles Palace!

As he neared the rear door, Paul took a deep breath into his belly, and then he breathed out, shaking his hands to release the tension from his body before he opened it, and called out.

"Henry?"

"Come in. Lock the door! Put a chair under the handle! Now!"

Paul walked up the short set of stairs, past a gleaming remodeled kitchen replete with copper-bottom pots and pans hung on gleaming hooks above a granite-topped center island. He moved slowly forward over the tongue-and-groove wood floor, continued past a vast library with books on mahogany shelves to the ceiling on three sides with a library ladder sitting stationary on a side wall.

"Henry?" he called out again.

"In here, Paul."

Paul entered a hyper-masculinized room that was obviously Henry Senior's study. Paul rapidly corrected himself when he saw the inelegant remains of Henry Compton Mortenson Senior. It lay slashed from his left collar bone down to the right upper edge of his crotch, with a massive puddle of blood on the floor, with a very large spatter pattern on the back wall formed as if by an enormous polka-dot attack. Some of it was already black and congealing, the rest just beginning to achieve solidity. There was no weapon in sight, though it was immediately clear that he had exsanguinated.

Henry was sitting on the floor in the middle of a very expensive Persian rug, cradling his father's pale, ruined head in his lap. Henry's arms were covered with caked blood from fingertips to shoulders, as if someone had painted him with a wide, thick paintbrush.

Henry alternated choking sobs with gouts of tears gushing freely down his cheeks. He was rocking like an autistic child in the throes of a nuclear meltdown. Paul kept his distance and took a chair a couple of feet away from the horrible tableau and kept his back to the door through which he had entered. He sat in silence and took a deep, cupric-scented breath, sending a calming wave of energy to his client, palms open and extended.

At one point, Henry coughed and choked, then spit up a huge glob of phlegm onto the rug. Then he looked up, directly at Paul, eyes wide and sad.

"I didn't do it, Paul! I didn't kill him!"

"It's OK, Henry. Let's go slow and start at the beginning. OK?"

"OK. Please help me."

"Where did you go when you left my office?"

"I talked to Ferdy. We went for a walk in Golden Gate Park. We went to Stow Lake and the Hall of Flowers."

"Where was Andrew?"

"We ditched him."

"How?"

"In one entrance, out the other."

"Andrew took you where? Where did you two meet?"

"His SRO. Then out the back entrance to the alley and away."

"And then?"

"I had a long chat with Ferdy...about talking to my ...to Father."

"What did you say?"

"I told Ferdy I couldn't wait any longer."

"For what?"

"I told him he had inspired me!"

"'Inspired' you?"

"To come out of the closet...to Father."

"You were still going to come out to your father? Even after what we talked about?"

"I'm tired of waiting!"

"And?"

"I... I just wanted him...to be my...Dad!"

"Henry! We talked about that!"

"I know. I... just...wanted him to love me!"

"Oh Jesus!"

"I... he..."

Henry cried again, a brief squall of tears, then spoke again.

"I tried to talk to him, but he wouldn't listen. I..."

"You what?"

"I told him!"

"'Told him' what?"

"That I was gay!"

"Oh Jesus!"

"I know! I should have listened to you!"

"And?"

"He freaked out! Started yelling at me!"

"And?"

"He started hitting me! With his fucking belt!"

"And?"

"He chased me! From room to room! Wouldn't leave me alone!"

"And?"

"I finally hid...in a closet!"

"And?"

"He kept screaming! Throwing furniture!"

"And then what?"

"It got quiet. Real quiet."

"And then?"

"I just kept waiting. And then..."

"Then?'"

"I heard this scream. Really, really loud. Then it went quiet again."

"And?"

"I waited a long time. I don't know how long."

"And then?"

"I crept upstairs. Really slow."

"And?"

"I found him! Here!"

"And?"

"I... guess I... freaked out a little!"

"And?"

"I hit him!"

"You 'hit him?'"

"I... just got fucking angry! I just kept hitting him and hitting him! Yelling at him!"

"But he was dead?"

"I couldn't help it!"

"Why?"

"I've been so pissed off for so long!"

"But he was dead!"

"I just knew he would never...be the Dad I always wanted!"

"What?"

"I waited all this fucking time...and he fucking...got killed!"

"Was it his fault? Did you kill him?"

"No! He was already dead!"

"You were 'really pissed!'"

"He fucking cheated me! Again!"

"Oh, Jesus!"

When he heard Paul's words, he started crying again. Paul rebuked himself for not being more sensitive.

"He 'cheated you?'"

"By getting killed!"

"And?"

"I hit him and hit him and hit him!"

Just then the telephone rang and Paul grabbed it angrily.

"I'm just fine! Please don't call me! It doesn't help if you try to hurry me!" And turned the phone off.

"So, you kept hitting him?"

"I couldn't stop! I just kept hitting him! He was never gonna be proud of me!"

"Oh Henry!"

Henry looked up through tear-stained eyes.

"I'll never get the love I need! Never!"

Gigantic sobs erupted again, and Paul could see a glint of clarity shining in his client's eyes. He knew it might just be transitory, but at least it was a less-than-psychotic moment.

"Henry, the police think you might have killed your father!"

"I didn't! I swear I didn't!"

"Where's the weapon?"

"I don't know! This is how I found him!"

"I believe you! But we have to prove it somehow."

"What should I do?"

"You need a criminal defense attorney. If you authorize it verbally, I will call Shirley Stephenson. She'll know what to do."

Henry started to sob again and then nodded his head.

Paul pulled out his cell phone and speed-dialed Shirley Stephenson, the best criminal defense attorney in The City. Surprisingly, she answered on the third ring. He quickly and succinctly summarized the situation and said she needed to hear it from "her client."

After Henry asserted his desire to be represented by her, Paul told her that Henry had his own attorneys for the conservatorship, who oversaw the trust fund administered by his father. "I'm not sure what the contingencies are in a situation like this." Then Paul expressed another of his concerns.

"Shirley, he's on a conservatorship. And it's his father, the conservator, who's been killed. I don't know how we can work this because his money might be tied up, and it might get really funky if he is charged with murder."

"That's my department, Kemosabe."

"I'm inside the mansion here in St. Francis Woods. I doubt very much if the cops are gonna let you in."

"Just stay focused here, Paul. We need to get him a doctor. An MD, with admitting privileges somewhere secure, so he doesn't go to jail."

"He's too fragile!"

"I know. And you can support that. But you don't have admitting privileges anywhere, do you?"

"It's restricted to MDs!"

"Anybody you'd recommend?"

"The guy I use to titrate people off psych drugs. He's good. But I don't know him all that well. This might be too high profile for him, though he is a member of the International Society for Ethical Psychology and Psychiatry."

"What's that?"

"Treatment professionals who are committed to not using psych drugs or ECT, and to delivering humane treatment."

"Sounds like a good choice. Give me his name and number." Paul did.

"How are you going to manage this? I don't know if they'll let you in."

"I have friends in the DA's office. Just keep him as sane as you can! And don't come out! That's an order!"

"Yes, ma'am!"

CHAPTER FORTY-NINE
Deeper into the Fray

San Francisco 0447, July 13th, 2002

Paul had ignored the insistent buzzing of his cell phone, but then the next time—the fifth—he felt compelled to answer. Phil's voice exploded out of it before Paul could even speak a word.

"What the fuck is going on, goddamn it!"

"Hold on, Phil! You tasked me with resolving this situation and that's what I'm doing! I finally got Henry calmed down. I'm no longer fearful for his safety."

"Safety, schmaftey! What about the old man?"

"There's been...an incident."

"Incident?'"

"Henry Senior is dead."

"Dead?'"

"Yes."

"Did your client kill him?"

"He claims not. Says he found him dead."

"'Found him dead,' huh?"

"That's what he told me. Found him dead after his father beat him and chased him around the house."

"We have no report of that."

"You do now."

"Based on your client's report?"

"Absolutely!"

"And I'm supposed to buy that?"

"Phil, you know me. I don't lie."

"But I don't know your client!"

"I do! I've been working with him intensely! And I believe him!"

"I respect your opinion. We can talk about that later. When are you bringing him out?"

"He is not yet ready to transport. I need a little more time."

"What's the situation there?"

"I'm going to tell you, but please, do not jump to any conclusions. OK?"

"What? Are you playing policeman again?"

"No! I found Henry in here cradling the head of his father!"

"Oh Jesus!"

"He was covered in blood, but there was no weapon. But I didn't look."

"When are you coming out?"

"I don't mean this to insult you, but I agreed to do my best to secure my client's safety and end the 'situation' here as safely and efficaciously as possible. I fully intend to keep my word. I appreciate you keeping your word and not sending in a SWAT Team."

"When?"

"As soon as I can."

"Sooner rather than later, Paul!"

Paul immediately called the MD he used to titrate clients off psych meds, or admit someone to the hospital.

"Tommy! It's Paul Marzeky!"

Thomas Ryan O'Connell IV was a fifth generation San Franciscan who Paul had known for many years—since in the way-back-when machine when Paul had been doing his internship at Mt. Zion Crisis Clinic and Tommy had been a resident-in-training. They had formed a bond then that had endured to this day, refreshed by occasional Giants and 49ers games, shared dinners and occasional drinks at Gino and Carlo's or the Hilltop, always neighborhood hangouts usually filled with locals.

"Hey man! What is it this time?"

"Just because I call, does it mean that I need something?"

"OK. Sorry. What's up?"

"Now that you mention it, I do need something."

"You bastard! OK. What's up?"

"I have a client who needs your MD qualifications!"

"I only have a small private practice now. I'm doing research, and closing in on my Ph.D.!"

"Excellent!"

"But how may I assist you?"

Paul summarized the situation as succinctly as he could, not failing to mention the conservatorship and potential funding issues.

"Does he have an attorney? Defense, I mean?"

"Shirley Stephenson is on board. She's contacting his legal team for the trust fund. We'll get the funds released, sooner rather than later."

"I'm not all that concerned. This sounds fascinating. What do you want me to do?"

"Get him admitted somewhere immediately so he doesn't end up in police custody! He's also got some physical injuries that need looking at immediately. Mostly, I do not want him being pumped full of fucking psych meds!"

"So, that's all, huh?"

"I can give you any clinical data you need," said Paul, ignoring the sarcasm.

"Now that I've been altruistic about money, what's the compensation going to be?"

"The young man has a $500 million trust fund!"

"Wow!"

"What are your standard rates for an admission work up? You can bill for in-patient treatments, though I'll be seeing him at least once a day."

"What about me?"

"How's two thousand for the admission; and three fifty a day thereafter? I need a very private placement."

"Hillsborough? San Mateo? Belmont?"

"It'll likely have to be in The City. The cops, you know."

"I know places in Marin—Corte Madera, Fairfax, San Rafael."

"We'll have to work it out legally. Maybe rent a suite at the Palace, or a floor at the Holiday Inn."

"That'd be a trip! Whatever we can work out."

"Let me give you Shirley's number. Talk to her about strategy."

CHAPTER FIFTY
A Long Night's Journey into Day

San Francisco 0839 July 13th, 2002

Paul was so exhausted he could barely track his own thoughts. It had been a very long time since he had felt so stretched in so many directions at once. He felt like he had been channeling light and energy as if from a dozen major funnels or tunnels emanating from him, albeit all of them for worthy purposes.

Shirley had reached out through channels and had contacted Henry's lawyers at the trust fund. One of them knew the Mayor from high school and college. Another played golf with the District Attorney at the Olympic Country Club. This engendered a decidedly interesting confluence of energies that created a bit of legerdemain that could only happen in San Francisco, small town though it is with a population of 777,000!

The hardest part was getting Henry to cooperate and let go of his father's body.

Shirley had called him back and confirmed that arrangements had been made on levels far beyond his pay grade—the DA himself showed up at the scene, as well as the Mayor and Tommy O'Connell—the latter of whom, along with Paul, repeatedly assured Henry that he was going to be safe; that he was not under arrest and not going to jail; that he would be in private care with police guards; that he was not going to be medicated; that he would still be seeing Paul at least once a day, who would be on-call and available to him 24/7!

Paul longed to sleep, just to uncouple himself from the great wheel of awareness, to let go utterly, but he seemed unable to do so. Conversely, he chose to just stay awake and brew a good strong coffee—and have a Drambuie along with it!

He sat back on his leather couch, sighed deeply, and let his mind wander over the events of the day. What a whirlwind!

The part that bothered him the most was that he had broken, or at least severely damaged, his already fragile relationship with Phil McLaren. He'd been volcanically outraged when he'd had an enormous and intricate pile of orders and demands foisted on him by his superiors to stand aside and simply allow arrangements and agreements made from way upon high, to simply unfold without his interference!

"You fucker! I helped you! I went to the mat for you! And you fucked me over!"

"My first and only mandate was to protect my client. And I brought him out safely, didn't I?"

"And got him released into private psychiatric care! What a bunch of shit!"

"He's innocent until proven guilty!"

"He was covered in his father's blood!"

"No weapon! And your guys searched the entire mansion and the grounds—and found nothing!"

"I still say he's guilty!"

"And what are you proposing as a motive?" Paul asked. He felt pretty sure that Henry's coming out to his father was as yet unknown as a possible motivator, or rather his father's extreme reaction to it. Paul thought that it would likely be called justifiable homicide, even self-defense.

"I've seen the medical reports. It seems that he was beaten quite severely just prior to the victim's death!"

"And?"

"I've heard that his father beat him and emotionally abused him for years!"

"And?"

"Maybe this was one time too many!"

"Look Phil, I just couldn't in good conscience see him hauled out in cuffs and stuck away in San Bruno."

"You fucked me over!"

"I'm sorry you see it that way. When you serve me with the proper subpoenas, I will tender copies of my case notes."

"You refuse to voluntarily surrender your laptop?"

"With goddamn good reason! It's confidential material! It's protected by law!"

"We'll likely get an order for a Special Master to go through it!"

"When you do, I will comply, but not until and not voluntarily. I know this is a big case for you, Phil, but I don't have to help you convict my guy!"

There had been a gigantic wrangle about jurisdiction, access to Henry, statements, processing, and location. They had made an attempt to get Henry admitted to a private facility in Carmel, but a Circuit Court Judge issued an immediate injunction (thanks to a very ambitious DA), and so the search began for a secure facility within the 49 square mile perimeter of the City and County of San Francisco.

Shirley, supported vociferously by Paul as the treating clinician, allied with Tommy O'Connell and his admitting privileges, fought valiantly to keep Henry out of the clutches of law enforcement. Even though technically innocent, the SFPD did not want Henry housed outside of the City and County, even though arrangements could far more easily have been made in Marin County. This would have entailed a great deal of travel time for all of the attorneys, officers, administrators and many others involved, even if peripherally.

In a further ruling, the Circuit Court judge ordered that whatever facility was eventually selected would be required to be secure, to include 24/7 presence of police officers— security guards did not count! The San Francisco County Jail

Commander offered secure private facilities where Henry would not have to mingle with the other inmates and would certainly be secure, but Paul and Tommy both argued that it was all the way down in San Bruno and did not offer the kind of access necessary for Henry's continuing treatment, as well as being what Paul described as a "contaminated atmosphere," especially as Henry had not been arrested or charged.

The law firm representing Henry's trust fund had recognized the potential public relations nightmare of his not being provided with the necessary funds, and "authorized whatever monies might be adjudged necessary for the appropriate on-going mental health treatment of our client congruent with the needs of law enforcement."

Ronald Oakes Whitney, Professor Emeritus of Psychiatry at UCSF Medical Center (and close friend of the dearly departed), offered secure facilities at the world-renowned Langley-Porter Neuropsychiatric Institute, but Paul encouraged Henry to decline for several reasons—not the least of which is that he would likely be subjected to pressure (at least surreptitiously) to take meds (more pressure Henry didn't need). As well, it added the additional anxiety-provocation of the scrutiny of being on an open, though secure ward—with any number of unpredictable influences from other patients and staff. Additionally, UCSF was a teaching hospital, so there were any number of psychiatry residents, post-doc psychology interns and other staff members who would love to get a hold of his data to include in research papers or leak to the media. So, Henry's "team" politely declined.

"It's going to put a hit on your trust fund to pay for all of this, Henry," said Paul in one of his twice a day visits with Henry, who had been temporarily housed in a secure bed on the Forensic Psychiatry Unit at San Francisco General Hospital that was guarded by Sheriff's Deputies and closed-circuit cameras 24/7. It was the best and quickest arrangement they could make on short notice, and Tommy had been granted temporary admitting privileges. In a conference with the Mayor, the Sheriff had agreed, but required the guaranteed payment of an extra Deputy assigned around the clock to assure the safety and security of Henry, who would nominally not be handcuffed to his bed.

The media were, of course, clamoring for access like a bunch of hyenas after a freshly killed zebra. One damn fool reporter even went so far as to fake suicidal intention strong enough to get himself admitted to SFGH, hoping to bring "notes from the underground," only to find out that he was sent to an adjacent unit (7-A) on the same floor, but totally separate from the Forensics Unit (7-B). Even with repeated calls from his editor and the paper's attorneys threatening *habeas corpus*, it took him three days to be released (the length of the involuntary hold), at which time he was charged with an exotic stew of criminal charges like "wasting police time," "giving false information to a police officer," and "impersonating a seriously mentally ill person," the latter of which Paul had never heard before.

CHAPTER FIFTY-ONE
A Small Semblance of Normality Emerging

San Francisco 1307 July 13th, 2002

Once Henry had been safely transported to SFGH-ER, all of his clothing was carefully preserved and a full forensic examination was done—including fingernail scrapings, practically every blood, saliva, and urine test ever devised and a meticulous scan of every inch of his body with accompanying photographs. Shirley had insisted on these and Paul had managed to keep Henry relatively contained during the process, despite his frequent mutterings of innocence. Shirley had become like a super heroine figure, fending off each and every intrusion by a myriad of law enforcement officers and detectives (including Phil!), The D, and more of the media. As well, she repeatedly told Henry not to say anything to anyone (not even one Deputy Henry thought was "cute!"), especially law enforcement, without her being present. Paul reinforced this directive and made a point of putting a long, wide slab of adhesive tape across the front of Henry's metal case file holder to the effect that Henry was legally not free to act of his own accord, and any statements he made would not be allowed in court due to such a disability. And further, anyone suspected of attempting to elicit such statements would be prosecuted.

Tommy oversaw the entire admission. As admitting physician, they could not refuse or refute his presence. Too, since Henry was technically not yet under arrest, but being held as a likely suspect and a "person of interest," he did have manifest legal rights that Shirley worked assiduously to assert. The insistent pack of rapacious jackals who called themselves journalists were held at bay for the most part by security officers at the hospital plus an extra contingent of off-duty policemen hired by Henry's trustees to assure top notch safety. Even the DA was refused ingress. He was "outraged," but left muttering when he got a call from the Mayor.

Shirley and Tommy had also negotiated an access list to Henry that was kept to the very minimum. Tommy refused to prescribe any psych meds for Henry, over the strenuous objections of Ronald Oakes Whitney, who, proclaiming his title as "Professor Emeritus of Psychiatry at UCSF," even went so far as to give an interview to a San Francisco Chronicle reporter, loudly declaiming the "barbarous treatment being accorded to this fine young man, his being deprived of the most modern treatment measures possible," and praising the dubious benefits of psychopharmacology's crown jewels, brain-damaging phenothiazines.

Paul had pushed on, sustained by a huge adrenaline rush that literally drove him through the rest of the night and past the darkest hours to somewhere north of 1030, when he literally crashed on his bed fully clothed—but not before he had given his service a specific list of calls he would take and told them to reject all the rest, most especially any and all media, and the stultifying forces of law and order.

1209 July 13th, 2002

Phil had repeatedly asked, wheedled and cajoled before becoming angry and demanding about having access to Henry for an initial interview, but Shirley and Tommy were a formidable team, well-versed at turning back the barbarians at the gate and keeping Henry as protected as possible. It was inevitable, and proper, of course, that the authorities have their turn at bat, as it were, but Henry's defense team felt it best to put it off as long as possible.

1523 July 13th, 2002

Henry's mood had shifted considerably after he was examined and finally allowed to have a shower. He kept insisting that he was innocent and continued to perseverate, repeating several themes in a kind of sing-song cadence and rocking in an almost autistic manner from which he seemed to take a great deal of comfort. Henry voiced an almost unfathomable grief that was newly minted for him, as if the bulk of his life had been dammed up inside of him in titanium vaults impervious to any sort of redemption or release—and he had battered himself with self-doubts and demon delusions the entire of it. The unspeakable horrors inflicted by his fascist father's beatings and verbal berating of him had led to suffering confusion, depression, disorientation and dissociation—from which Henry had miraculously survived—were only now beginning to release in waves of varying intensity. Too, he continued to grieve the love and attention he had always wanted so badly and would now never have. When Paul later read the Progress

Notes (purposely voluminous with the awareness that they would be subpoenaed), Paul found it exciting and simultaneously disturbing that Henry was seemingly electrified with a scintillating clarity he never imagined could have existed. It poured out of him, an unexpurgated stream, a voluminous river, a never-ending infinite ocean. It was as if, for perhaps the very first time, he was safe.

If Henry had not been so experienced in handling the rigors and frustrations, the fancy flights and delusions with which he had always lived, he might have become the kind of stereotypic blithering idiot so popularized in the crass and banal media designed to reduce and marginalize any and all those who live outside the statistical "norms." He could not be restrained, could not be kept from his grief. Indeed, a private care nursing staff had been hired to sit with him 24/7 around the clock with strict orders to not interfere in any way with Henry's emerging process (of course, taking appropriate measures to keep him and themselves safe from harm), but to simply provide a presence, minimal interference, and especially, not to touch him—allowing his internal clock to direct when and what he should eat and drink.

1729 July 13th, 2002

The situation was entirely anomalous for the unit and the Sheriff's Deputies who regularly staffed it. There were those who grumbled and complained, but they were all good at following orders from above—particularly with the complex of approvals that radiated from the Sheriff and His Honor the Mayor (not to mention generous overtime allotments). It would very soon become routine for the assigned personnel to make the small extra efforts required to manage the man they began to call their "celebrity guest."

0821 Tuesday July 16th, 2002

Indeed, after three days Henry abruptly stopped what some people considered to have been his excessive immersion in the grief process, at which point he requested a shower and clean hospital pajamas (granted), Internet access (denied), a selection of gay porn magazines (officially refused, but smuggled in by a gay Deputy on the night shift), Greek food from Asimakoupoulus at 18th and Connecticut (granted, and it became a daily treat), access to a cell phone (denied, although he was allowed to use a landline with supervision), cable TV (doubtful but being considered for an extra cost of installation and maintenance) and finally to resume having regular sessions with Paul (already arranged as a Doctor's Order).

Paul had been checking on Henry intermittently both in person and on the telephone. He had also been in frequent contact with both Shirley and Tommy. Not trusting the police to do a thorough investigation, Shirley put her top investigator (who was on retainer anyway) on Henry's case exclusively. Tanya Hatathli (which name derived from her native Navajo for "singer," one of the main healing medicines of her people) was in her mid-thirties, rode a custom Harley Softail she had built herself and swung both ways sexually. She was a graduate of the Sorbonne, a crack shot with both handguns and long guns, proficient in Tae Kwon Do (brown belt), and spoke four languages in addition to her native Navajo. Her mandate was simple: find who really killed Henry Compton Mortenson Senior (presuming the complete and utter innocence of Henry Junior) and take nothing for granted, especially not the official police investigation.

When Paul was informed of Henry's sudden re-awakening, he, Tommy and Shirley had a tête-à-tête-à-tête to shape the direction of their approach as a treatment troika.

"I'm going to try to have short daily sessions with Henry," said Paul, and continued when he saw their raised eyebrows, "only I'm not going to be probing or be too deep," making it only a statement of fact and unwilling to brook any resistance.

"Where will that leave you in terms of interrogation by the police?"

"They can ask me about anything they want. I can simply refuse to answer on the grounds of confidentiality. Right, Shirley?"

"As far as your professional interactions, yes. As far as your personal information or facts unrelated to the case, you have no privilege. I've told Henry to say nothing to the police without my being present or sign anything without my approval."

"I wouldn't put it past the sneaky bastards to try!" said Tommy.

"Especially that sergeant of his! What's his name? Kubicheck? Bubbicek?" added Shirley.

"Kubicek. They call him 'Kube.' I think he used to work for the Czech Secret Police!"

"Phil McLaren figures he's got the case all sewn up, except for one small detail."

"No weapon."

"Precisely. That's why I've put Tanya on it."

"But won't she have to report it to the police if she finds it?"

"Not necessarily. Only if she knows it's the murder weapon, and only if they ask. But then again, she can't obstruct justice either."

"But back to you. Will you record the sessions? Or make daily case notes?"

"I only make summary case notes anyway. That's all I submit to the trustees for payment."

"And the police?"

"They have no right of access. And they can't prevent me from seeing my client."

"And no right to interrogate you about what transpires."

"Unless they get a court order!"

"But that will require a Special Master, won't it?"

"Absolutely! And they have to have absolutely compelling evidence!"

"Plus, I don't record anything that might have to be revealed in court!"

"I've been checking on him twice a day," Tommy spoke. "He seems to have improved."

"Has he reported any problems with the Deputies or nursing staff?"

"Other than wanting to see Ferdy!"

"That's not going to happen any time soon!"

"I do not want it to happen for a variety of reasons, and the police won't allow it anyway!"

"He's asked to have a pass out of the hospital!"

"What? That's out of the question!"

"I agree!"

"I think we should either meet or touch base at least once a day."

They all agreed, and Paul decided to go to see Henry.

CHAPTER FIFTY-TWO
Awakening

San Francisco 2021, Tuesday, July 16th, 2002

Paul went through the incredible rigmarole of entering the unit, enduring the gauntlet of crazed media vultures and multiple rings of police sawhorse barricades manned by uniformed personnel, checking identifications against a list of pre-approved and authorized individuals. He entered through the Emergency Room, nodded to two nurses he knew, then went to the bank of elevators where his ID and license were again checked before he disembarked on the seventh floor, where he encountered two Sheriff's Deputies who repeated the process before allowing him onto the unit where he was required to sign in. He shook hands with the supervising Deputy, a Lieutenant with whom he had done cocaine business many years before.

"How's my client doing?"

"Seems much better today. Two and a half days of him crying, howling, and growling was getting on everybody's nerves. Even had inmates asking to go back to San Bruno rather than stay here any longer!"

"Boy! I hear that!"

"How's yourself?"

"Overall doing really well! I'll be a lot happier once I get Henry stabilized."

"Even if it means answering police questions and going to trial?"

"He's innocent!"

"O-o-o-o-K!"

"No, I mean it!"

"If you say so!"

"It's always good to see you!"

"Yeah, thanks!"

Paul worked his way down the hall, past the first eight doors, all locked and monitored with closed-circuit televisions. Outside of the ninth and very last door on the left, Henry's private duty nurse sat reading a paperback book—one of John Sandford's *Prey* series. Hearing Paul's approach, he placed a bookmark, closed the book and looked up at Paul. He was one of the temporary hires Paul didn't know.

"I'm Henry's therapist, Dr. Paul Marzeky. And you are?"

"Thaddeus Leviton. I'm on duty until midnight."

"I'm here to see my client. How is he doing?"

"He's been pretty quiet. Ate an early dinner—bought Greek food for the whole staff, cost over a hundred bucks! He's been sleeping since about 1800."

"Cool. Thanks. Would you open the door please?"

Henry was napping on his bed, looking very peaceful indeed. Paul sat for a few minutes and observed him silently.

Shortly thereafter Henry awoke on his own and pandiculated, stretching his hands high above his head as he yawned widely. Thaddeus had conveniently left his handcuffs unlocked. Then he looked up and smiled wanly when he saw Paul.

"Paul! It is good to see you!"

"I've been checking on you at least once, usually twice, a day. But you seemed pretty involved in your process, so I didn't want to disturb you."

As they talked, a minute grew into two, into five, into ten, talking about how he was adapting to his erstwhile accommodations, his feelings of health, medical problems, even the 49ers chances (Henry was amazingly astute). Paul noted the distinct absence of what he had previously considered thought blocking (which is considered to be involuntary and driven by a psychotic process). Paul now thought he might have been impercipient, since the symptom seemed to have disappeared and might simply have been aposiopesis, the sudden breaking off in the midst of a sentence, as if from the more conscious (or voluntary) inability or unwillingness to proceed. This latter was also associated with cognitive shock, the client being too frightened or ashamed to speak.

"I must admit, Henry, you are looking a lot better."

"Thanks, I guess. The last few days have been confusing."

"No doubt."

"I kept waking up and thinking I was awake and then falling back asleep."

"Like I said, I've been checking on you."

"Then maybe you can tell me—how long have I been here? How long have I been sleeping?"

"Let's see. Tomorrow will be four days that you've been here. By my estimate, you've actually slept on and off for two and a half of those days."

"Wow! Seriously?"

"Absolutely!"

"Wow! I've never slept that long in my life!"

"Obviously you needed it!"

"It's kind of like you always say—you must have needed whatever happens because it happened!"

"Thank you, Henry! I like it when people quote me!"

"Didn't you quote Henry Miller one time? 'When you begin to quote yourself, you're becoming a literary figure?'"

"That was quite a while ago!"

"My memory seems to be getting better, somehow."

"I really need to ask: What do you remember of the night your father was killed?"

CHAPTER FIFTY-THREE
Revelation

San Francisco 0125, July 13th, 2002

The real estate agent had described the mansion as "stunning," and it certainly was. Over 14,000 square feet, it sat on a prominent hilltop from which he had panoramic Pacific Ocean views and breathtaking sunsets, but also phenomenal overlooks of the greenery in St. Francis Wood Upper Fountain Park. Of course, he owned other properties: a sweet little pied-à-terre on East 57th in New York (it only made sense, he was there so often); his hideaway villa in Zihuantanejo; and the 14th Century palace outside of Paris. But, of them all, he loved this the best. He loved The City with all of her charms and the fabulous artistic pulse.

Henry Compton Mortenson Senior paced the magnificent library on the ground floor rear of his mansion. The floor was covered with a very luxurious and very ancient Chaumont Aubusson Rug with a green, cream and gold border enclosing a cream and pale green field, and a cream oval central medallion with pale green corner cartouches, with red, cream and gold floral vines adorning the border and central medallion. Sometimes he would have a fire built and lit for him in the huge stone fireplace and just sat looking at it, contemplating all of the hours of handiwork it had taken to produce and the mystery of its history.

Some historians had speculated that tapestry weaving had been brought to France by members of the Saracen army who stayed behind in the département of Creuse in central France after their defeat at the battle of Poitiers in 732, and developed a technique of weaving rugs with depth perspective, an artistic technique so demanding in its execution that it has never been copied by the rug weavers of the East. He genuinely relished owning completely unique products. His most delicious, and private, delight was owning unique individuals, or at least bending them to his will, dominating and manipulating them. Some had even accused him of schadenfreude, and while possibly true, he did not really give a fig! It was his private delight!

The biggest problem in his life was his fucking one and only son. If he could just somehow steal the half billion, he really wouldn't think twice about eliminating the weak-willed, spineless little ass! It would be so easy to arrange an accident! He had a lot of shady information on Andrew, and he could extract payment any time! Andrew was just another minion! If anything befell Junior, there'd be a hell of an investigation, but who wouldn't kill for half a billion dollars?

As he paced, he sipped a Hors d' ge Armagnac, a superb Baron de Sigognac Platinum XO, from a balloon snifter of Czechoslovakian leaded crystal and pondered what he was to do. Junior had been doing better this past year, despite the outrageous amount of money being spent on his fucking maintenance! Twice a week for two hours at a shot! Jesus! That was $500 a week, over $60,000 a year! He could have a good weekend in Paris for that! It was genuinely fucking irritating that he could not intimidate or manipulate

Junior's therapist into divulging what he talked about in his sessions. That goddamn detective he hired to compile a dossier on him turned up almost nothing. He really was a Viet Nam vet! Shit! He should just send fucking Henry back to that resort treatment center in Arizona, but he was loathe to spend the required $30,000 a month!

Fucking Junior! He'd stopped confiding in Andrew! Fucking asshole! He knew his need to know might have verged on the obsessive (some might say "insane"), but it all helped him to better shape the course of events.

He and Martine had discussed making a baby, a healthy child to rear with the intention of his newest offspring taking over the reins of his empire—but he didn't actually trust her or her motivation (other than wealth and power) in assisting him. Besides that, he thought she might be fucking goddamn Andrew on the side! And being twenty years younger than he, any and all monies would be left in trust for their child when he died, with her as trustee! Just really didn't trust her.

"JUNIOR!! WHERE THE FUCK ARE YOU, JUNIOR?"

He always felt so driven to utterly and ruthlessly dominate the little retard! He was so fucking weak! He could barely fucking speak to him! All that mewling and shame! It was fucking sickening! The worthless fucker! The more he thought about it, the more it inflamed him! He shouted again and again as he roamed the bottom floor. And then he decided to mount the stairs to the second floor.

"JUNIOR!! YOU GET HERE RIGHT NOW, YOU WORTHLESS FUCK!!"

Henry was completely immersed in a video game, headphones on, blocking out any noise, especially his Father's intrusions. He relished the tiny glimmerings of strength he felt in Paul's office. Paul was the first person who actually listened, who tried to protect him from Father. And Father hadn't killed him yet! He must somehow be important to the High Command!

As he reached the top of the spiral staircase, Senior bellowed again.

"I WANT TO TALK TO YOU, YOU USELESS FUCKING RETARD!"

Henry had had a glimpse of a possible future, but he knew in his heart of hearts that he had not yet won through to that land of wonder where he was truly strong, magnificent in his glory, redeemed for all time—where he lived released from the curses and demons that had shackled him, contaminated him, since he could remember. But for the moment it was so excellent simply to feel alive!

He felt (more than actually heard) the door frame shudder as Father broke through the lock plate of his sealed door and bulled in like a battleship through rough and rugged seas.

"I'VE BEEN CALLING YOU!"

Henry looked up startled, goggle-eyed, aphasic, stricken.

"WHAT ARE YOU FUCKING DOING IN THERE? THOSE FUCKING GAMES AGAIN?"

Following this last outburst, the older man strode across the room, pulling his belt loose from around his waist as he approached Henry.

But instead of passively lying there, allowing himself to be beaten until Father wore out his rage, Henry shot into the air as if struck by a million volts. He pivoted, advancing upon the stunned older man, who stopped in mid-stride as Henry fronted him, nose-to-nose.

"Father," Henry said in a very calm tone that belied the ten thousand demons who were screaming inside of him, vying to get free.

The older man had been struck silent and could only stare mutely.

"I've waited my whole life to ask. Why? Why did you never love me?

A complex mélange of thoughts and feeling surged through Senior's mind, infused by a deep rage that threatened to erupt.

"You've never loved me! I'm going to go to court and get free of you!"

The older man started to defrost a little, listening to the childish prattle. He slowly lowered his hands, head filled with fog, completely uncomprehending what was transpiring in front of him as if on a cinema screen.

Misunderstanding his father's actions, and emboldened by the lack of resistance, Henry continued.

"I'm gay! And I've met a man I love!"

This last revelation galvanized the older man's ire like throwing a magnesium flare into a bucket of water. It released him from his frozen trance.

"I WILL TELL YOU WHAT YOU'RE GOING TO DO!"

Having said this, he struck Henry several times in a row before the younger man turned to run for the doorway. Senior tripped him, and alternately whipped him and kicked him both fore and aft.

Somehow Henry got to his feet, violently shoved his father back, and started down the staircase with his erstwhile parent in quick pursuit. As they reached the top step, Senior kicked Henry in the back. He tumbled several times before landing on his back with a gasp, winded but awake. The older man followed, staggering down the stairs holding tightly onto the mahogany rail.

Henry was still retrieving his breath as his father attempted to stomp on him but he twisted away, pushed to his feet, slipping slightly and then got to his feet and staggered away. His father, far more intoxicated from the delicious brandy than he had thought, managed only to lurch weakly after him. Henry headed quickly toward the rear of the house, his breath coming in short pants. He thought of several hiding places he had used previously to avoid the further reaches of his father's wrath. First a hall closet with a hidden panel (but he was sure his father was aware of it), then instead elected to follow the floor plan around, backtracked his father's path and scurried back up the staircase as Father screamed with increasing frustration.

"YOU GODDAMN BASTARD! WHERE ARE YOU?!"

The older man made a considerable commotion as he thrashed and crashed his way around the perimeter of the bottom floor, trashing vases and pulling down paintings and wall hangings. Then, following a sudden inspiration, he started back up the staircase.

"GODDAMN FUCKER! WHERE ARE YOU?"

Henry heard more smashing of picture glass, china figurines and other fragile pieces, doors thrown open, and even more screaming. He had secreted himself in an old dumbwaiter in the servants' wing, one of the last places he thought Father would deign to look. Several more doors smashed open, accompanied by basso profundo shouting and yet more stomping across the floor as Henry took advantage of the tumult to lower the dumbwaiter down to the basement, hand over hand on the hemp rope.

There immediately ensued a silence that was cliché quiet, a deafeningly profound hush.

The shattered, scattered fragments of his mind were spinning in a kaleidoscopic whirlwind as Henry settled into a round of breathing, attempting to create an internal order to buttress the terrible chaos that was enveloping him.

Just as he was assembling a sense of serenity, (perhaps just a less disturbed façade rippling across the pond of his world), the most horrifying, gut-wrenching shriek sliced through the air like a Damascus steel scimitar—a single, piercing, elongated screech that ended as abruptly as it began, leaving an even deeper lingering pool of quietude that was more alike to emptiness or a vacuum.

Henry's brain swam with multitudinous images, fractal pictures, swirls of psychedelic color accompanied by lurid smears of light, fractured rainbows splashing, intense chiaroscuro, all reflecting violent shades that only exist between thoughts, and illuminate the vast plethora of energies of the Universe not revealed unless or until an individual has experienced the uttermost boundaryless boundary, and momentarily dissolved into the Cosmic Wholeness of the Whole—and returned, in form or the formless, reinvigorated and exhilarated, alive and aware of being alive in every cell, blood thundering through veins and arteries, infusing and imbuing all that might have been previously lost, dissociated or abandoned.

He was alive within this vastness. He was an empty aloneness, with no other sound or vibration.

After a timeless time during which he simply floated, drifting as if in a transparent dream medium cast in a consistency akin to semi-hardened agar, he floated and swam effortlessly, trance-like, following a sonorous song like that of the humpbacked whales.

Then Henry was visited by an inner prompting and rose from the cramped closet where he had been confined for several small eternities. He stretched and popped most of his major muscles, tendons, and ligaments (and a couple of vertebrae). He quickly assessed the damage his father had done, which he compared to other similar incidents; and found, on the whole, that he had suffered far worse through the years. He straightened his clothing as best he could, though there was no repairing the left sleeve of his shirt, which had torn loose at the shoulder. Getting shakily to his feet, he made his way painstakingly down the hall and up the staircase where he firmly grasped the bannister and slowly made his way up.

He became increasingly more oriented as he ascended, such that by the time he got to the ground floor, he felt more-or-less functional, albeit as if patched together with super glue and duct tape. He sniffed the air like a hunting dog pinpointing a strange spoor, drawn ineluctably toward the back of the massive domicile. He was simultaneously attracted and repulsed by the impulse to return to the library, like a scent he could not ignore, as if his olfactory organs had been neutralized—though he was aware that he was breathing as rhythmically and deeply as he could.

Ears wide open, sensitive to the most miniscule sound that might vibrate his tympanic membranes, he crept cautiously down the richly appointed hallway toward the back of the house, as he had always called it, "the house." Not his house or "the mansion" or even "the palace," as he had heard Father refer to it.

The ominous silence deepened as he traveled, his every sense on alert for an ambush. Father had been known to spring from a room or crevice either to initiate or continue assaulting him, all the while screaming insults or imprecations against him. Father called these misadventures "survival training games" designed to "toughen him up." Father never for a moment considered that he might be causing harm, telling Henry that it was for "his own good." (Henry had yet to discover what Freud had called the "sadistic superego" that drove him relentlessly to believe that he deserved to endure Father's incredibly violent behaviors).

As he got to the doorway to the library, he had almost convinced himself that Father had left the house, maybe even gone to New York or San Tropez, anywhere else.

He walked through toward Father's study. As he turned the corner, he took a tentative step and stopped, stunned, branded on his feet.

Father.

He lay there unmoving; the ocean of his lifeblood spilled, saturating the dense layers of the finely wrought rug in the center of the room.

Henry thought he might be hallucinating. His feet were frozen to the roots, even though he knew his neurons were firing, the automatic and autonomic flow of his body functioning, or attempting to function, striving for efficiency without any conscious effort on his part.

Henry felt as if the room had been transposed, as if it were an abattoir scene painted by Rembrandt or Breughel the Elder.

The old man lay on his back, right arm bent acutely under him at the elbow. If it were not for the gaping bloody, still-seeping slash that ran from his left collarbone through numerous subcutaneous layers of fat and muscle down to and exposing the top of his right ilium, Henry might have otherwise believed that the man was still alive. In death, his face was serene, as it had never been in life. He had only

one thought in the pallid, disturbed emptiness: Someone must have hated Father as much as he had.

Henry staggered over to the condign figure, knees melting as he approached as if in slow motion and sank to the floor. He gingerly touched Father's face and then lifted his head into his lap, a keening moan escaping his lips.

"NOOOOOOOOOOOOOOOOOOOOOOOOOOOOOO!"

The lifetime gathering of immense losses that he had carried buried within his breast flooded through him out from under uncountable layers of leaden dross, depression and delusion that had shielded the radioactive core of his suppressed emotions, that all now exploded magma-like from the molten ocean of his consciousness.

"NOOOOOOOOOOOOOOOOOOOOOOOOOOOOOO!"

Another long ululating moan escaped his unyielding lips, all of the rage, fear, pain, shame, exhilaration, horror, disgust, joy, sorrow, misery, exultation, trust, anger, hatred, envy, indignation, surprise, suffering, enmity, benevolence and contempt he had ever carried, exploded out of him, as he repeatedly beat the condign form of his father with his tightened fists, gallons of copious tears falling untethered that changed to chest-wracking sobs and his body dissolved into a rubbery dissipation. He then bent over the fallen form, cradled the now-battered face he had so longed to touch in his arms, and embraced the eviscerated remains—saturating his arms, face, and clothing with the blood and fluids from the gaping wound that divided his father's body.

Terrible moans rolled out unrelenting from his cracked lips, broken only by the jangling of the telephone and the incessant pounding on the all of the doors. The phone rang six or seven times, before an intrusive voice through an amplified device called his name numerous times.

Finally, having had enough of the irritating, grinding, intrusive, invasive tones, he screamed without preamble.

"Paul Marzeky! Get me Paul Marzeky! NOW!"

CHAPTER FIFTY-FOUR
No Expectations, New Expectations

San Francisco Thursday, July 25th, 2002

Henry kept insisting on his innocence, as the labyrinthine, often byzantine, processes of the legal system groaned and slithered their torturous way forward, even as Henry's defense team gradually amassed more and more information, most of which seemed to validate his version of events.

Brandon Greenwood IV, heir apparent to his father's District Attorney's office, groomed his hair yet another time and then contemplated the cut of his Saville Row bespoke suit and his hand-made Italian loafers before leaving the bathroom of his private office. He had grown up well and wealthy in a large pleasant home on Lexington Street near the Dewey Traffic Circle in the West Portal District. For his entire life, he had been told that it was his destiny to follow in his father's (and his grandfather's spot before him) august footsteps. He had obediently followed the path that had been set before him. He was not an unintelligent young man, though perhaps overly programmed, and hence rigid and less imaginative, by some standards.

He was handsome and vain. After graduating from Stanford Law, he took a position in his grandfather's law firm defending *crème de la crème* criminal cases for a long enough time to establish his willingness to do whatever it took to free his clients and be a presence as a *bon vivant* on the social scene, always seen in the best clubs with socialites, torch singers and corporate bankers. After having successfully defended a number of homicide cases, his father took him onboard at the DA's office. He really didn't need the money, but he wanted to widen his support base while feeding his long-term political greed. He was especially enamored of ascending to his father's position (and the accompanying political machine) that would continue the unbroken line in the DA's office for more than fifty years.

Even though his appointment elicited cries of "Nepotism" and rumblings of recall echoed through the hallways of the Hall of Justice, "The Fourth" as he was pejoratively called, arrived at the highly sought-after position of Chief Deputy after a number of years prosecuting misdemeanors, fraud cases and other less-than-stellar cases. Nonetheless, he'd amassed a power base and connections deep within the subterranean chambers of San Francisco public life.

There were many members of the Police Department not to be numbered amongst his fans and supporters. Many of his orders, especially to his handpicked squad of investigators, were too-often seen as capricious and driven by his raw ambition. This latter was viewed with a very dim eye, issuing it seemed, as if by a regressed five-year old having a tantrum.

Brandon had badly been craving a high-profile case to really put his name and face before the voting public. So, when the murder of Henry Compton Mortenson Senior hit the media like the 1906 earthquake, he jumped at the chance to use it as his personal stairway to the stars.

Phil McLaren had been seconded to the investigation as the detective who'd originally caught the call. It didn't hurt that he (even casually) knew the suspect's therapist. Brandon envisioned that it might lead him to developing an inside line on the investigation as he put his own case together against the young killer. Other than those he considered his equals, he never, for a moment, contemplated anyone resisting his needs and demands. He utterly dismissed the possibility that anyone could have an ethical standard higher than his own and certainly not to the extent that anyone would ever deny him anything.

"Well, Lieutenant, have you managed to serve the arrest warrant yet?" he asked archly.

"No, sir."

"And why not, pray tell?"

As he had done several times previously, he reiterated the intricacies about the facts of the case, beginning with the insistence of Henry Junior's psychiatrist insisting that he be examined medically prior to his being immediately admitted to a secure unit as "Gravely Disabled" under the auspices of the Welfare and Institutions Code Section 5150. Henry was, therefore, exempt from questioning of any sort prior to his attorney and psychiatrist approving it. He was most certainly "incompetent," as described by the tenets of the law. This latter fact was affirmed by a psychiatrist approved by the DA's office, who essentially listened to the man's raving in the locked room on the Forensic Psychiatry Unit and agreed that the man was in no condition to give a statement. It was further deemed that any such statement would be objected to strenuously by both psychiatric and legal authorities; and, in any case, would be deemed inadmissible in any court in the land.

"And you have a man on duty there?"

"Of course, sir."

"And when do you anticipate being able to question him?"

"I'm told he has apparently come out of whatever state he was in—they have called it "a coma," and a "reverie." Whatever it was, by all accounts, it was pretty severe. And then he slept for two and a half days. Apparently, he's able to converse with both Shirley Stephenson and his therapist now."

"So, soon then?"

"One can only hope."

"I want the man in a cell by the end of the day!"

While Phil McLaren rolled his eyes and continued negotiating the often-arbitrary demands and ambition-driven moods of the Chief Deputy, Paul was having a palaver of a totally different sort with his client who was experiencing an ebullience that verged on the voluble.

"Paul! Paul. I feel so much better!"

"Henry, I'm really glad! A lot of people have been very concerned about you."

"But, what do I do now?"

"You're going to have to talk to the police, make a statement."

"But I didn't kill him!"

"I believe you. But Shirley and I have to prove it."

"How can you do that? I remember...the blood all over me."

"And you got it when you were holding him. Right?"

"He was dead when I came upstairs!"

"You never saw a knife of any sort?"

"No! I swear!"

Paul contemplated asking the next question, hesitating to be the proximal cause of his client regressing, but plunged ahead anyway.

"You didn't by any chance see a machete?"

His client jumped as if hit by a bolt of lightning.

"FUCK YOU! YOU DON'T BELIEVE ME EITHER!"

"Henry, I'm sorry I had to ask. The police most certainly will, especially when they subpoena my case notes."

"They're going to get to see your case notes?"

"Relax. Remember, I have told you before that I only put down the minimum information in my notes. There's nothing incriminating. Besides that, they haven't served the subpoena yet. When they do, there'll be a Special Master who will determine what parts of my notes they are allowed to see."

"Are they going to question me? Will you be there?"

"Shirley will be. She'll actually be better for you than me," he said, and paused before going on, "But I'll be observing, Henry. I want you to know that I totally believe you."

"Do you really?"

"I do. I know you could not have done this, even though you mentioned it as a fantasy."

"I didn't do it! I really didn't!"

"I know, Henry. I know. We're all doing the best we can to protect you. But they have a right to question you. We can't stop them."

Behind the scenes, there were, of course, all kinds of wrangling. The entire process around the police interrogation (Paul refused to couch it as an "interview"), involved the most extreme of these negotiations. Between what the police wanted (practicing power politics) with input from the DA's office (ditto, ditto) and what Shirley and Tommy, with input from Paul, would allow (exercising compassion for their client), was a huge gap.

The police wanted Henry "escorted" in handcuffs to the Hall of Justice (denied, he was still very fragile and had not yet been discharged from intensive medical and psychiatric care). They wanted Shirley and Tommy excluded from the "interview" (obviously denied, Henry had a right to be represented by both, especially in the hospital setting). They wanted to send in eight men working in pairs for continuous "interviewing" with no cap to how long they could be employed (denied, limited to four men total and only for as long as Henry could tolerate it without further injuring his health as adjudged by Tommy). They wanted to tape record the entire proceeding (granted, with the proviso that Shirley would be doing so independently of the police). They wanted to have their own psychiatrist as an observer (decision still up in the air as both Tommy and Shirley objected to him even as an observer). They wanted Henry transported to a "secure treatment facility where he could be observed 24/7 and assessed there" (again denied, as he was only a "person of interest," and he was still under intense psychiatric care and too fragile to move—thank God for San Francisco judges—though this latter might become a possibility depending on the interview and the insistence of the DA pulling his Draconian political strings).

The prospect of cramming two detectives, Henry's psychiatrist and attorney, plus recording equipment into a room built for a single patient and his bed seemed so overwhelmingly ridiculous that the Sheriff agreed to allow them to meet in the Staff Room (with a guard, of course). It also meant that Paul would be allowed to sit in, though not ask questions or talk to Henry in any manner (even if Henry were to address him directly). Any comments or information he might have to contribute would have to go through either Tommy or Shirley.

An interesting development had come about just two hours before they were all due to convene. Tanya called Paul and said that she had been "poking around" (one of her favorite phrases) Henry's life a little.

"And?"

"Well, your client was not very cooperative when it came to his boyfriend."

"And?"

"So, like I said, I did a little poking around."

"And?

"So, I started poking around some of the clubs South of Market. I do know a few people there." She was actually almost a cult figure amongst those who lived in the dark underworld of "alternative lifestyles."

"And?"

"It didn't take me too long to find the little sucker."

"'Little sucker?'"

"I mean Ferdinand Okisaki."

"And?"

"Henry did tell us at least part of the truth. Ferdy does work in a bunch of clubs."

"And?"

"Well, it seems, since all of this hullabaloo started, he hasn't been living in his SRO, though he has been paying his rent."

"Interesting. Where has he been living then?"

"I staked out his hotel, and, when he came to pay his rent (every Monday), I followed him to his uncle's house on 36th Avenue in the Sunset."

"Very good!"

"Thank you most kindly."

"And then?"

"He was hostile. Didn't want to talk to me. Tried to make a deal so he could talk to Henry."

"Oh really?"

"Yes. It seems he had tried it on with the DA's investigators already."

"Oh, really?"

"And they told him he didn't have to talk to us."

"Did he have anything to say?"

"After sorting through his bullshit, he kept insisting that he was 'in love' with Henry, even though he seems to know little or nothing about his psych history."

"OK. Anything else?"

"He talked about he and Henry 'hanging out' a lot, going to clubs, dancing, 'having fun.'"

"How is that helping us?"

"It's just an intuition, but it's what he's not telling us that might be most interesting."

"OK."

"He's very sketchy about where he was the night of the murder, though he told me that the police and the DA have talked to him extensively."

"And?"

"He claims he was waiting for Henry at his SRO, by himself, until he had to go to work around 0300."

"Just around the time of the murder."

"Yes! I thought you might find that interesting."

"Anything else of substance?"

"Not right now, but I'm convinced the little worm is hiding something. I'm just not quite sure what, yet. I'll stay on it."

"Thanks, Tanya! Good job."

"How much pressure should I put on him?'

"Keep it loose, but stay on it. I think you're right about him. Something sneaky."

"Yeah, but I gotta tell you—I think he really cares

about Henry."

"I'm glad he's not the sleaze bag I originally thought he might be."

"Me too."

"He kept asking all kinds of questions about your client," she said, "wanting to know where he is and such. I'm going to keep working him. Do we have a budget if I offer him some money to open up?"

Shirley assured her there'd be a budget and immediately thanked her for her diligence.

When she conveyed this information to Paul, he had similar questions as she, but, at that point, they were ushered into the Staff Room. Paul had been rather rudely reminded that he was there only by sufferance and that he would be the proverbial fly on the wall. Paul had quickly agreed and took a seat at the back of the room against the wall.

Shirley's persona shifted as soon as the proceedings became official. She became more rigid and warrior-like, projecting a very protective aura around Henry as she took her place to his right side. Paul could feel it from the back of the room

After adjusting all of the instruments, doing sound checks and announcing their own names and ranks, Henry was again read his rights and agreed, nodding to Shirley.

"Will you please state your name and date of birth for the record?"

Henry complied. When asked what had happened the night of his father's death, he told his story in a very straightforward fashion, only flinching once when asked to describe the beating he had taken. He then went on to talk about the tremendous fear that had driven him to hide and subsequently re-emerge to investigate.

"And what did you do when you allege that you found your father's body?"

Shirley spoke up loud and clearly at this point.

"Detective, you asked my client to tell you his version of events. Now you're casting aspersions as to whether he's telling the truth or not!"

"Merely asking what he did when he found his father's body!"

"Then ask that, not 'allege!'"

Henry then recounted his remembrance of finding his father and then, quite volubly and with much feeling, talked about the tremendous emotional upheaval he had felt.

"Henry, I don't think the detectives are interested."

"As a matter of fact, ma'am, we're very interested in anything your client has to say about the murder."

"HE WAS FUCKING DEAD WHEN I FOUND HIM!"

"Sir, I'm asking you to keep your voice down!"

"I DIDN'T FUCKING KILL HIM!"

"Sir, you're going to have to calm down! Please!"

Shirley said, "Henry, just calm down. It's OK."

"Where's Doctor Paul? I want Dr. Paul!"

"Henry! You need to talk to the detective."

"I DON'T CARE!"

"Sir, we really need to get your statement!"

Tommy tried. "Henry! Please help us!"

"I WANT DOCTOR PAUL!"

Shirley said, "Dr. Marzeky is right here. Would you answer the detective's questions if he were sitting here with us?"

"Ma'am, I don't think..."

"Yes, I don't doubt it!"

"Ma'am..."

"Do you want this interview to go forward or not?"

"Ma'am..."

"Paul, can you come over and assist us? Please."

Paul came over, held out his hand to Henry, shook it and sat down.

"I'm right here, Henry. I told you this was going to happen. Can you please try to answer the detectives' questions?"

Very reluctantly Henry muttered, "OK."

Paul turned to the detective, Groshilde was his name, and said, "It might be better if you just ask straight

questions. Henry is very sensitive to people trying to manipulate or lie to him."

"It's my job to get the truth!"

"We're all interested in the truth. Why can't you operate from the premise of 'innocent until proven guilty?'"

"The DA thinks he's guilty!"

"The DA doesn't have a clue!"

"He thinks this case is a slam dunk!"

"What a fucking joke! All he wants is a conviction by any means!"

And then Paul continued, irritated. "Can we just get on with this, please?"

The interrogation of Henry continued fruitlessly for the better part of an hour before Tommy insisted they have half an hour break.

Paul took a moment to have a private aside with his client.

"Henry, is there anything you're not telling us? Anything you left out?"

"No! Nothing!"

"If you are ever going to be released from custody, and have any kind of life, we have to find out who really killed your father!"

"SEE? I KNEW YOU DIDN'T BELIEVE ME!"

CHAPTER FIFTY-FIVE
The Ineluctable Force of Law

San Francisco August 8th, 2002

The usual focus of an interrogation was designed around the idea that the "suspect" was guilty, not innocent; and that, given enough time and repeatedly asking the same, often inane, questions, he or she would eventually "break," proving him or her guilty. It was very similar with the entire concept of torture, but usually it was just mental and emotional, not physical (at least in the presence of witnesses).

The next two weeks, Henry was questioned in the "textbook" manner, according to police standards. Paul was convinced that, if it weren't for the presence of "Henry's Defense Team," the rotating teams of detectives would—given their methods and absolute belief that Henry was guilty—very quickly have broken down the fragile walls of his mind and elicited a confession as a result of this great duress. Paul was convinced that the DA was delighted, generating enormous waves of attention and utilizing his sadistic power to manipulate both the press and the police. Paul believed he was gleefully wallowing in the schadenfreude, like a bloated spider sitting in the middle of his web absorbing the remains of a very rich insect.

The detectives did hammer, kept in check only by the presence of one or the other of Henry's defenders. They seemed especially aware that everything was being recorded for posterity and review. Over and over, almost the same exact set of questions; they were always deeply immersed in the self-righteousness of their convictions, the dubious impeccability of their methods, and the staunch belief in the pristine nature of their being uniquely positioned to bring a miscreant to justice. They were all so alike, so almost robotic, so similar in training and disposition as any State-sponsored entity that had ever existed—all super-patriots who extended the mandate of killing for God and Country to breaking any and all laws, driven by their own vituperativity to achieve their "divine" purpose and uphold the delusional unassailability of the State (as they conceived it), and the twisted sense of power that was in turn reflected on them as agents, dissolving them of all doubt and buttressing their small, damaged selves against the ravages of unmet needs.

Paul kept supporting Henry in the face of this withering harangue. Clearly the stress and exhaustion were wearing on him.

"I don't know how much more of this I can take! Every single fucking day! Can't I get a day off from this shit?"

"I'll talk to Tommy..."

"NO! IT'S NOT ENOUGH! YOU'VE GOT TO STOP THIS!"

"Henry, I don't know if we can. The police have a right to question you."

"But I've told them, over and over, I did not kill him!"

"We all believe you, Henry."

"Then why don't they stop?"

"They're convinced you're guilty!"

"But I didn't kill him!"

"You have to admit that it looks pretty bad, Henry! They found you covered in his blood, holding him!"

"I miss him! He'll never be my Dad!" and his sonorous moaning turned into short hiccoughing sobs, and then, finally, into great choking sobs. Paul felt completely conflicted; wanting to reach out and take him into his arms, pretty much violating the ethical constraints while honoring his human ones.

Paul elected to put a hand on the young man's shoulder as he cried.

"I'll never get to have a real Dad, Paul! Never!"

Paul realized that Henry kept mentioning this, but it had never really impacted him as it did in that particular moment. It struck him like a physical blow. Of course! Of course! It was like the first ray of dawn coming through the open windows of his bedroom. Of course! How could he have been so dense! Henry had long ago shut down emotionally to protect the fragility of his never-nurtured-or-loved little heart. He had mostly lived and spoken from his fear that the forces of law and order would obviate this tremendous possibility. There was no way that he could ever convey this to the police, but he absolutely had to have a conversation with Tommy and Shirley as quickly as possible.

CHAPTER FIFTY-SIX
Illumination?

San Francisco 1534, Thursday, August 8th, 2002

Paul told Henry three times not to speak to anyone at all until he returned, then hastily called both Tommy and Shirley. Of course, he was unable to reach either of them but left a brief urgent message for both of them. Then he called Regina.

The last two weeks had played hob with his schedule, spending so much time with Henry. They really had not had a consultation session in that time and he was really feeling the need, especially with his newest insight in his pocket. It seemed so simple, but he had to tell someone!

Regina's didn't answer either, but she called him back in two minutes and they connected, agreeing to meet in two hours. It would give Paul enough time to get home, eat, shower and change clothes before he went. He had to get away from the oppressive atmosphere of hanging out with law enforcement so many hours every day and the intense overwhelm that had developed from seeing so much, far too much, of Henry. He knew Henry was still hiding something, or at least not telling him something. Whether it was out of fear or truly something he had dissociated, Paul was unsure, but he hoped to flesh it out more with Regina.

When he arrived, they hugged briefly.

"It's good to see you," they said simultaneously.

Even though he admired her greatly and appreciated her skills, Paul was anxious to get beyond their official relationship. He had seriously come to appreciate her slightly off-kilter looks and her kind of kooky sense of humor. She bade him to sit, and then went to the kitchen for a minute and returned with two hot steaming mugs of coffee. They both shared a love of strong black coffee. He sipped and smiled, then thanked her.

"So, what's this new insight you want to share?"

Paul outlined his conversation with Henry and the context of his thinking that had piggybacked on it.

"It made so much sense and was simultaneously was such a 'Duh!' moment for me! It might be the key to his entire pattern of psychopathology! If I can pull a few bricks loose from his delusional system; if I can start working more deeply with those feelings of abandonment and isolation, I might be able to really make significant progress! I am excited!"

"Not to rain on your parade, Batman, but remember that dentist in St. Louis, Dr. Sell, the 'mentally ill' one? Or rather, the one the courts judged to be 'mentally ill'? They sent him to the federal prison hospital and insisted that he take psychotropic meds with the aim of getting a judgment that he was no longer 'mentally ill' and therefore could be executed?"

"Yeah. I remember him. The fucking APA sent in a neutral *amicus curiae* brief, not supporting either side, but The International Society for Ethical Psychiatry and Psychology supported his right to not take psych meds, especially since the state's intention was to artificially 'make him sane' so they could execute him. Dr. Sell also complained about emotional and physical abuse at the federal prison hospital in Springfield, Missouri."

"Was it true?"

"I don't know. Prison psychiatrists thought Sell was delusional because he believed the government engaged in a conspiracy around the fire at the Branch Davidian settlement in Waco, Texas that killed 81 people. Dr. Sell produced Army records proving that he had indeed been sent to Waco in the days leading up to the fire to help identify charred remains."

"I had no idea."

"For a delusional man, he had a lot of resources. His attorneys cited Washington v. Harper 494 U.S. 210. The Supremes had clearly stated in 1990 that forcing medication on mentally disordered inmates could only be ordered 'when the inmate was a danger to self or others and when the medication was in the inmate's own best interests.' It also warned that they must first consider 'alternative, less intrusive means' before forcing meds."

"Are you anticipating a situation like that with Henry?"

"Maybe. I don't know. I'm going to share this info with Shirley too. Then there was Riggins v. Nevada 504 U.S. 127 in 1992 that asserted that the client 'had a right to decide what was in his or her own best interest.' So, I am kind of relying on that."

"How did it get resolved?"

"Just this year, in Sell v. United States, 539 U.S. 166, the US Supreme Court chastised the lower courts, imposing stringent limits on their right to order forcing meds on a criminal defendant who had been determined to be incompetent to stand trial, for the sole purpose of making such a one competent and able to be tried. Since the lower court had failed to determine that all the appropriate criteria for court-ordered forcible treatment had been met, the order to forcibly medicate him was reversed."

"Wow! Great research!"

"If this process keeps up, Henry might be adjudged 'unfit for trial,' and I anticipate that the judge might try that same ploy!"

"It sounds like you're prepared."

Paul mused "Do you think I, or Tommy, for that matter, should mention the concept and get it introduced in court? Or do you think I'm being too psychoanalytic?"

Regina, always on top of the legal aspects, replied immediately. "I don't know that the court would grant us legal status to prevent Henry being drugged against his will unless we had some very big guns behind us. Plus, the DA will likely oppose our using the argument against forced drugging as being essentially irrelevant. It doesn't have much to do directly with guilt or innocence."

"Forcing the brain to ignore traumatic material through obliterating the pathways to the forebrain is just brutal, simply vicious."

"Henry may be motivated to stay delusional because it protects him from having to feel his rage and the deeper loss and damage he carries."

"What's next? Are you planning to have some more sessions with him?"

"I'd like to, but given his current state, I don't think it would be workable."

"It might actually make him worse. He might regress or relive old traumas."

"I agree. I may have just taken this case as far as I can, at least for the present."

"You're going to keep supporting him, aren't you?"

"Of course. It's just that I don't feel like I'm doing very much for him right now."

"It probably means a lot to him even though."

"I'm sure it does, but I just can't escape the feeling that he's holding out."

"But why?"

"I can't decide. It may be purposeful, or it may just be dissociative."

"Do you have any idea what it might be?"

"I suspect he may know exactly who killed his father."

CHAPTER FIFTY-SEVEN
A Further Unravelling

San Francisco 2118, Thursday, August 8th, 2002

Paul had messages from both Shirley and Tommy by the time he was ready to leave Regina's. Regina demurred when he invited her to join them as she had too much paperwork to complete. Paul suggested to them that they share a communal dinner—and they decided they would go to Zihuantanejo at 30th and Mission. They specialized in high quality Mexican seafood dishes. Paul decided on prawns (camarones) with homemade mole, with rice, beans and salad. Shirley ordered the combo plate with chili rellenos and chicken fajitas while Tommy opted for Cheesy Beef Quesadillas. They shared several baskets of real tortilla chips and two orders of exquisite guacamole, accompanied by two rounds of cold Dos Equis.

"God, this feels good!"

"It certainly does," said Tommy as they clinked bottles.

The food was quickly served and almost as quickly consumed. As they were sitting back and having after dinner drinks—a Mexican coffee, a Kahlua on the rocks, and a Drambuie—conversation turned back to their client, and a discussion of strategy.

Paul shared his latest insight with the others, and it was enthusiastically received, though the legal relevance was questionable. They, too, agreed that it was clinically intriguing.

"Have you talked to Tanya lately? Anything new?"

"She had another conversation with Ferdy. She feels like he's holding out; that he knows something that he's not telling us. She's gonna keep tracking him."

"Do you think he might have been there the night the old man died?"

"I don't see how he could have been. According to Henry, the old bastard practically searched the entire house looking for him."

"What if Henry actually killed him and Ferdy secreted away the weapon?"

"Now you're reaching!"

"But Henry and Ferdy are both hiding something!"

"But that doesn't mean they're in it together!"

"No. I guess not. Just adding one and one together and getting three."

"So, Paul, do you think you might be doing any sessions with Henry soon?"

"He's too unstable. And if the goddamn cops keep on the way they have been, he may get sent to Vacaville!"

"Oh, Jesus no!"

"Oh, Jesus yes!"

"Is there anything we can do to subvert that, if they try it?"

"It really depends on whether he keeps refusing to divulge what he knows. I think we're all agreed that he's withholding something. Paul, have you decided if it's voluntary or dissociative?"

"I believe he knows far more than he is telling us. Mostly his silence is purposeful, and I think there is information emerging that he does not yet understand, and that may be causing him deep anguish because he cannot fully express his emotions." Paul paused a moment, then went on. "It's part of what happened when I opened him up. He's had a lifetime of being suppressed, not 'allowed' to express himself. And on the heels of this 'awakening,' he's discovered his sexuality."

"That would give strength to the State's argument for medicating him against his will to 'make him sane and competent.'"

"He's still unstable. He has periods when he is clinically dissociated. I know the police and courts like nice crisp answers with sharp corners, but in my clinical experience, he is experiencing the classic pattern of waxing and waning of symptoms."

"It may be too esoteric of an argument for that sanctimonious prick at the DA's office!"

"Well, I guess we can just embarrass him in court!"

"So, what do we do next?"

"I hate to say this," said Tommy, "but we don't have a lot of choice here. The inherently twisted logic of the DA's office is working against us. I do not know how much longer they'll wait before they decide Henry is constituted enough to go to trial."

CHAPTER FIFTY-EIGHT
Time has Come Today

San Francisco Saturday, August 10th, 2002

Henry stiffened involuntarily when he heard the key turn in the lock, and then relaxed when he saw that it was Paul.

"Oh God, Dr. Paul! Please! Please! Can't you stop these police? They're here every day! Every day!"

"Henry, they believe you're withholding information!"

"But I've told the truth!"

"Are you sure there was nobody else in the house that night?"

"Yes! Yes! Yes!"

"Do you have any idea where the weapon might be?"

"No! No! No!"

"I'm sorry, Henry, I'm getting battered by the police, too."

"Can't you get me out of here?"

"Where would you go, Henry?"

"I'd probably go be with Ferdy."

"And how would you support yourself?"

"I want my trust fund! We could live on that!"

"You have to petition the court! It could take years!"

Henry seemed to shrink visibly in front of Paul's eyes, as if becoming a smaller size of himself, like a Russian matryoshka doll being revealed within another, larger one.

Then he jumped up, threw his arms wide and started screaming.

"NO! NO! NO!"

Paul stood and approached, whispering calming words, but Henry was beyond hearing.

"I CANNOT TAKE THIS SHIT ANY LONGER!"

Paul tried again as he edged toward the door and the Panic Button.

"LET ME THE FUCK OUT OF HERE!"

Unable to reach Henry, and fearing for his safety, Paul pushed the button summoning extra staff.

Henry continued to scream at the top of his lungs, tugging at the wrist handcuffed to the bed frame.

"LET ME THE FUCK OUT OF HERE! NOW!"

Henry's private duty nurse and a bunch of Sheriff's deputies swarmed into the room quickly subduing him and pinning him to the bed. He was quickly wreathed with leather restraints, and positioned face down. Paul went to the Nursing Station and quickly called Tommy, who answered on the first ring.

"What's up, Paul?"

"Henry went over the edge! Started screaming and I couldn't calm him. The deputies put him in four-points. I think a milligram of Ativan IM STAT might be a good idea."

"You got it! Can you take a VO (verbal order)?"

"Not any more. Let me get a nurse."

He did so. The order was written and noted. The nurse went to the med room, secured a pre-loaded syringe, and then went to Henry's room to administer it.

Paul shook his head in despair and called Shirley to give her the latest news before he went back to check on Henry.

CHAPTER FIFTY-NINE
Yet Another Twist

San Francisco Monday, August 12, 2002

Henry slept solidly for about two hours, then started thrashing around, murmuring denials in his sleep.

"I didn't kill him! I didn't kill him!"

When he first fluttered his eyes, yawned, and seemed ready to embrace that which is usually called "reality," he seemed fine, that perhaps he was going to reconstitute. Very soon thereafter though, he began to look manifestly anxious, preoccupied and started to perseverate.

No amount of Paul's intercessions seemed to but briefly puncture the bubble of distance that Henry seemed to quickly and effectively project around himself as protection.

"I didn't kill him! I didn't fucking kill him!"

Each iteration kept getting louder—until the consensus of everyone within hearing range was that Paul should call Tommy to order another milligram of Ativan for the good of all and himself.

Then, at 0410 Paul called Tommy with the latest lack-of-progress report.

"How's our guy?"

"Somewhere between the same and worse."

"I know you hate psych meds..."

"Are you really going to go there?"

"If he weren't your client, what course of treatment would you prescribe?"

"In this acutely exacerbated state, with him so agitated and perseverating, I think something stronger than Ativan is indicated."

"Like what?"

"Well, he was on 10 of Stelazine BID PO initially. But with him in the hospital, I would be inclined to go old school—5 of Haldol IM. Then see how he does in two hours, and then, depending, maybe 5 more. Maybe it will knock back this agitation."

"Get me a nurse and I'll order it. Then come back. I want to talk some more, since you got me awake already!"

Henry calmed almost instantly and Paul told Tommy so.

"Even in his sleep, he's been yelling about his innocence"

"What do you make of that?"

"I still feel he's hiding something or shielding someone."

"Maybe all this pressure pushed him over the edge. Maybe he's become truly psychotic!"

"When the fucking asshole CDDA showed up, he proclaimed he was going to 'talk to the chief suspect' in person!"

"He was going to try to talk to Henry without Shirley being present!"

"What'd you do?"

"I called Shirley as soon as I heard he was in the building. She doesn't live too far away. I stayed as calm as I could, but I was fucking seething!"

"I bet!"

"I reiterated to him Henry's right to counsel, and he would just have to wait until she arrived."

"Excellent!"

"The motherfucker tried to have me arrested for 'interfering with a law enforcement officer!'"

"Jesus! What a butt-head!"

"Shirley got there just in time to subvert him!"

"Then what?"

"He saw how freaked out Henry was, but I still think he might try some sneaky ass move. If he could somehow get him into custody, he could try to move him to Vacaville—dope him up against his will, get him to confess!"

"Maybe a little regular Haldol is a good idea. If he responds to the IM, we could put him on a low dose, like 2 milligrams PO BID."

"I'm worried about Henry. He freaked out as soon as I mentioned it."

"This might be Posttraumatic Stress Disorder. If we can secure long-term private treatment for him, it would be a much better choice. Protect him from the police."

"PTSD sounds like a good addition to his diagnosis, even as a rule out. But they do have a right to 'interview' him! How do we end this?"

"Let's see if he responds to the Haldol. It can't be easy for him to be stuck in some kind of existential hell."

"I agree. It seems like cruel and unusual punishment. We should get Shirley to argue that with a judge. Put a stop to the harassment."

"I just wish we could get through to Henry. If he would just tell us what he's been hiding."

"It really makes him look guilty."

CHAPTER SIXTY
Rust Never Sleeps

San Francisco 1128, Monday August 12, 2002

Brandon Greenwood IV pranced and prowled in full-throated roar through the offices of the District Attorney located in the Hall of Justice at 850 Bryant. He was in full sway, strutting like a bastard peacock, with his most arrogant and vituperative colors fanned. His paid informant at SFGH had just delivered the latest information about developments with the pesky Henry Compton Mortenson Junior, the little murdering bastard who had, to this point, successfully escaped the clutches of both him and the law. (He personally resonated with Louis XIV's comment, "I am the State"). It had been an excruciating gauntlet for him to have 'walked' these past weeks. He longed, just really ached in his gut, to eviscerate the young man in the press and send him to Death Row at San Quentin—after, of course, a suitably gruesome court drama played out with himself as the valiant crusading DA (like an old Pat O'Brien film). He had to work to maintain as calm and super-professional appearance before the press and the public as he could.

"Goddamn sons-of-bitches! How fucking dare they oppose me?"

Anyone within hearing range, who could, retreated as far and fast as they could. It didn't matter what the cause, the source was too well known to be mistaken. The sound of his voice was as distinct as a klaxon-horn.

The Chief Deputy District Attorney was well insulated inside the walls of his own demesne. He felt no constraint. Everyone who worked there had signed a confidentiality form that he bragged made the Official Secrets Act seem like a kindergartener's first assignment. He had incorporated the most solid, boilerplate terms possible, under the most severe of penalties. It had been challenged all the way up to the California Supreme Court and found to be legal, but barely so.

Yelling was grating, irritating, but the least of his many punishing personal qualities. The City and County had paid out enormous sums, barely ameliorating the damage of his violent outbursts. If he were not his father's son and part of an unbroken line in "The Office" as he insisted it be called (reminiscent of J. Edgar Hoover's calling his office "The Seat of Government"), he would have been permanently banned to the hinterlands long ago.

He was known, even occasionally anonymously mocked, for his volcanic rages and the tumultuous tsunamis he created whenever he felt his not-so-tender feelings injured in any way public or private; or if he felt impugned or pictured in any way that varied from his grandiose self-image, he reacted as if he were a raging five-year old in a 250# body. Some wags had compared him to the *ronin*, a master-less samurai, who wandered into a village inn in feudal Japan. Everyone notices a flea on his shoulder, but no one speaks of it, feeling it to be disrespectful. Finally, the innkeeper, having served him his drink, and feeling it to be his responsibility, plucks it from his cloak. The samurai immediately draws his sword and cuts off the hand that touched him. To the samurai, it was an insult to even insinuate that he might have had a flea on his august personage!

The more psychologically minded of the inmates of The Office would have said (if they dared) that he was deeply narcissistic, and possibly bipolar, given the nature of his incessant mood swings and vast irritability. Given his longstanding presence and the tremendous power he wielded, not to discount the breadth of the family influence and money. There had been more than one "dustup" in which either or both had kept public exposure neatly sealed and settled, kept from the ever-ready grasp of the press, the always hungry-for-the-next-spectacle San Francisco public who usually looked with favor upon the disgrace, humiliation, or the defrocking of public officials. In the old days, when The City was still considered a small town (777,000 people within its 49-square miles), "Mr. San Francisco" Herb Caen often delighted in exposing such scandals in his daily columns in the Chronicle.

So, it was not at all unexpected that, after weeks of impatiently haranguing his staff and investigators, today's rampage began with his sleeves rolled to the elbows, tie loose, collar sweat-stained, eyes wide and energy amped up beyond frenetic.

"Goddamn it! Let's get that little fucker!"

"Why now, sir?"

"I just got some confidential information—never mind how—that Henry fucking Mortenson Junior, might have completely blown his stack this time! They sedated and restrained him early this morning! Word has it that he's gotten no better by now either!"

He induced a fear-based loyalty and sycophancy. His loyal retinue would not have seemed out of place in a medieval Medici's court. He nonetheless regularly kept them in line with crude carrot-or-stick tactics that ranged from simple compliments and small pay raises to outright bullying, verbal abuse, and far beyond. He had torn ties and shirts and blouses, even thrown shoes, pens, and on one memorable occasion, a laptop computer, at anyone who he considered miscreants for not obeying his tyrannical orders quickly or exactly enough.

"I want to roll on this as soon as possible!"

"What do you want me to do?"

"Get a hold of the Investigators! Now! I want an update! Now! Goddamn it!"

Underlings and staffers hurried and scurried to do the master's bidding, fearing above all to incur even greater intrusions of his wrath and fury. The nepotistic Chief Deputy could be mean, insensitive, even sadistic, especially in the courtroom. He'd been known to have no compassion or empathy for those less endowed with power or education. Though he would vehemently deny it, his disgust with and diminishment of women generally was very rudimentary. There was a memorable case in which he had verbally shredded a teenaged defense witness on the stand without a moment's hesitation, as if he were doing battle with the most hardened pathologically lying criminal who had ever stepped on his most tender memories and defamed his lineage. The young woman had to be psychiatrically hospitalized afterward.

The District Attorney's Bureau of Investigations (DAI) is composed of sworn peace officers who work under the direction of the prosecutors in order to fully develop documentary, physical and testimonial evidence for trial. Toward this end they had been following the same leads and individuals that Tanya Hatathli had been unearthing, though with a completely different orientation and agenda. They were also far less interested in pleasing the erratic Chief Deputy's often vagrant whim and follies and so were much clearer in focus and likely to produce actual, factual and unabashed results.

Their offices were located just down the hall on the third floor from the DA's office, making it easier for disparate staff to communicate. These agents worked closely with the Bureau of Investigation of the California Department of Justice on cases that extended beyond the limits of the City and County and had tentacles in multiple jurisdictions. They also worked extensively with Federal Bureau of Investigation, the National Guard, U.S. Marshals, U.S. Postal Inspection Service, California Department of Insurance, California Department of Justice, University of California Police, San Francisco Sheriff's Department, United States Secret Service, as well as the San Francisco Police Department.

Their routine investigative efforts had yielded an unsubstantiated complaint that the victim had been complicit in the death of his wife many years earlier, but there had been no witnesses, and the complaint had been dismissed. Since then, he had grown in status and political power, and incurred nothing more extraordinary than parking tickets. He was rumored to have been a ruthless international businessman, for which of course, he was praised. Junior appeared to have lived a relatively unblemished life with the exception of a possession of marijuana complaint when he was fourteen and a pair of arrests by the San Francisco Psych Police Unit resulting in his being confined on 5150 holds and subsequently hospitalized. There also seemed to be a history of other private psychiatric hospitalizations that was blocked from their access.

They had also looked further into the legal history of Ferdinand Ferdy Okisaki. He had never been arrested, but his very traditional Japanese parents had reportedly tried twice to have him civilly committed as "morally intransigent" because he was gay and refused to cease being so.

Andrew Shaun Murdock had been another focus. He was the majordomo of the San Jacinto Avenue household and chauffeur/bodyguard of young Henry. He had a speckled background—also known as Shaun Kelly, Shamus Murdock, Anthony Andrews, and Earl Tontine. He had served in the Army Special Forces in Lebanon in the early '80's and been separated administratively after ten years' service. He had worked variously as a firearms instructor, bodyguard and international courier. He'd had several felony arrests for carrying firearms without a permit, but the charges had always been mysteriously dismissed on "orders from above."

They had applied to the FBI who grimaced, and grudgingly spoke to the CIA to get unredacted copies of his paperwork, but this request had seemed to have been buried at the bottom of an endless pile—strongly hinting that Andrew had deep and twisted ties to the "spook" community.

But Brandon IV was completely, even obsessively, focused on Henry. He had not for a moment wavered in his belief as if he were in pursuit of the Holy Grail.

"We'll get the little bastard this time!" chortled Brandon IV. "Let's rustle up a good team to go over and get him into custody! NOW!"

"But sir," intoned one of the newly hired (and hence more intrepid) baby-lawyers, doing her internship, "that just does not seem right. He's still hospitalized. We can't just arrest him!"

He turned his brooding dark eyes on the young woman, and asked, "And you are?"

"Cynthia Morse, sir. I'm interning here."

"You were, now, you're fired! Get out immediately!"

Her face imploded as she burst into tears and fled in terror.

"Now, where were we?"

He continued machinating, his vile and despicable plans grinding ahead, driven by the incessant desire to win, no matter the cost, which was in turn driven by infuriatingly unforgettable memories of a childhood that had never been enriched by even a modicum of nurturing.

"Let's see if we can get a court order to take him into custody, and move him up to Vacaville."

The California Medical Facility (formerly State Hospital for the Criminally Insane) in Vacaville is one of five forensic facilities in California that have hosted any number of mentally unstable and criminal types, including Timothy Leary and Charles Manson.

It would be an extremely illegal, or at the least, a highly extra-legal maneuver, that would result in Henry being moved, but such a maneuver was consistent with the bull-headed arrogance of "The Fourth" as he further contemplated his scheme to swipe the young man from his current and rightful legal residence.

But he had not been at all prepared for encountering a very outraged Shirley Stephenson. She growled at him and seemed ready to attack like an enraged mama bear guarding her endangered cub.

"And what the fuck, exactly, do you think you're doing here?" she demanded.

Brandon IV followed by his entourage—two Assistant DAs, two DA Investigators and inexplicably two uniformed SFPD officers—had bulled his way onto the unit by flashing his credentials. The officers looked perplexed, being confronted by a fiery, good looking young woman who completely ignored their badges and credentials, and immediately got in the face of the CDDA. They had thought they were going to be on a heroic expedition fronted by a bully strongman. Instead, they suddenly found themselves shamed and turned into ludicrous comic figures.

"I, madam, am awaiting notification of a court order remanding your client into my custody for immediate transport to the Medical Facility at Vacaville."

Shirley screwed up her face, and said, "Are you fucking insane?"

"You madam, are flirting with being arrested for interfering with a law enforcement officer in the performance of his duties!"

"Are you on drugs? That is the most ridiculous thing I have ever heard! You and your circus clowns showing up here is illegal. I'm going to call the circuit court judge on call and have the whole lot of you thrown out of here!"

"Arrest this woman!" he screamed as half a dozen Sheriff's Deputies arrived in response to a call for backup.

Paul and Tommy arrived immediately behind them accompanied by Medical Director Troy Ames MD, and the Hospital Attorney Horace Thomas, rumored, but not ever proven to be, a distant relative of Associate Justice of the Supreme Court Clarence Thomas. Troy and Horace now simultaneously raised their voices above the din and ordered everyone out of the room. "The Chief," as he styled himself, immediately started sputtering and tried to raise his voice (and restore his truly questionable authority). When he admitted that he had no legal authority to do what he proposed, he and his entourage were immediately escorted out of the room. He, too, went down the hall and into a large conference room.

Chaos was reigning, each and every one present having opinions vaingloriously attempting to attain whatever upper hand might be had. Finally, Troy stood on a chair, raised his undeniable *basso profundo* voice almost to the edge of distortion and shouted: "SHUT THE FUCK UP! EVERYBODY!"

Having said this, he turned to the extra deputies who had arrived as backup, and said, "Thank you, gentlemen. You may return to your duty stations."

When everyone had, at least minimally, obeyed instructions, Troy Ames asked everyone to sit down and remain quiet, before he spoke.

"We have a very complex situation here. This is not a court of law, so there is not going to be a presentation of evidence. I represent the City and County on this property. I, therefore, will not brook any bullshit from any one of you," he said and glared at Brandon Greenwood IV. "I have ultimate responsibility here," and he said, "and notwithstanding any extra-Constitutional issues that may be involved, Horace here is my legal expert and will speak to any and all such issues that are raised."

"The Fourth" started to rise from his chair, and Troy gestured to him, scything him like a field of wheat.

"No, Brandon, here I am the dictator! I'm running this meeting! And I do not care what the repercussions of that decision may be. I have the authority of the president of the Board of Regents of the University." He paused for a moment and then said, in a very quiet voice, "By the way,

I've also spoken to the Mayor, who has completely disowned this preemptive attempt of yours."

The Chief Deputy started to rise again, but the Administrator swept his hand toward him and silenced him.

"Your father is highly displeased."

That seemed to settle the man's hash, and he sat back down.

"First of all, Henry Compton Mortenson Junior is decidedly not going anywhere!"

"Thank you," uttered Paul and Tommy simultaneously. Shirley showed a Cheshire-like grin and made a point of shining it on the Chief Deputy.

He then dismissed all of people from the DA's office, leaving just Brandon, Tommy, Paul and Shirley alone with himself and Horace. Then Shirley spoke.

"I want everyone to know that I have spoken to the presiding judge. She informed me that she was definitely not going to issue a court order releasing custody of my client in order to move him to Vacaville. I believe she used 'extremely irresponsible' and mentioned 'endangering the mental health of a fragile client.' You will hear more about this from both your father in his official capacity, and from the California Bar Association."

Even this less-than-official censure wasn't enough to silence the volcanic arrogance of the CDDA.

"Troy, I absolutely object. That man should be

incarcerated!"

Shirley shot right back and screamed at him.

"You have no evidence, you jackass! Just a self-righteous desire to punish him!"

"He's clearly guilty, even though I can't prove it yet!"

"And you call yourself an attorney? You have no right to interfere with his authorized treatment!"

"SHUT UP!" Troy shouted.

The silence that descended was glacial, and put an end to any and all possibility of retort from any quarter. Paul excused himself, as did Tommy, with the intention of seeing to Henry, leaving the two main adversaries to stew in the aftermath of the confrontation. Before either of them could brook any further opposition, Troy and Horace, shaking their heads, dismissed them.

CHAPTER SIXTY-ONE
This Could be Heaven, This Could be Hell

San Francisco Minutes Later, on the Unit

Paul and Tommy renewed their utter distaste for the malicious presence of the CDDA and vowed to keep Henry safe from him and his entire ilk. They both knew it was too soon to tell, but also hoped that—despite their shared distaste for the use of psych meds—the low dose of Haldol might have the desired effect of stanching his runaway emotions and agitation.

Henry, for his part, was finally resting comfortably, drifting in a half-dream/half-reverie state punctuated occasionally by a small scream or shout. He jerked once in a while as his consciousness lifted, moaned groggily and fell back listlessly. His entire world was awash in a gray fog as if the building had osmotic walls that were allowing the outside in.

He recognized Paul when he stepped into the room, then attempted a small grin that came out more as if an admixture of rictus and moue.

"Paul."

The sound escaping his lips was so quiet as to almost

escape detection. Paul more felt than heard him.

"Feeling any better?"

"Are they...are the coming back?"

"The police?"

"Yes."

"No. I doubt it very much?"

"Thank God! I am <u>so</u> tired."

"We're gonna make sure that nothing like that ever happens again!"

Henry laughed weakly, then responded. "Some reporter tried to get in!"

"How did he do that?"

"She...acted...sexy."

"That must have been a good laugh, huh?"

They all laughed, and then Tommy asked, "Are you feeling any better?"

"'Better?'"

"You know, your thoughts, your ideas."

"I don't know. Maybe."

"We'll check with you in the next couple of days."

"I.... want to thank you, both."

"No problem."

Then Paul said, "I will see you tomorrow."

"No, Paul, can you, will you stay for a little bit? Talk?"

"You sure?"

"Yes, please."

"OK."

Paul sat down as Tommy left.

"Do they still really think I killed Father?"

"They have a lot of circumstantial evidence."

"But I didn't do it!"

"I believe you. But is there anything, anything at all, you haven't told us?"

Henry closed his eyes and stayed quiet for several long moments.

"I remember...there... that it felt like somebody else was in the house."

"When?"

"After I woke up. Before I found Father."

"But not after?"

"No. I don't remember much after I found him."

"Do you remember when I came in?"

"I asked for you. I remember."

"And after that?"

"Not much until I woke up here."

Tommy thought Henry's memory loss might be attributable to the concussion he had suffered. Paul, of course, countered that it might be trauma-induced retrograde amnesia and added that, from both his long personal and professional acquaintance with dissociative behavior, he was convinced that some of it seemed clinically dissociative, and Henry might spontaneously recover with more treatment.

"The major issue here, Tommy, is that I believe it will be treatment, methodical, steady treatment, that will help him recover core elements that his basic personality needs and might never have had, all related in many ways to chronic lack of nurturing."

"You really believe he might one day function more fully, even 'normally?'"

"Browne talked about trauma-related somatic phenomena, such as emotional numbing, psychogenic amnesia, and flashbacks—and said they may act as an "Incomplete or partial experiencing of the traumatic material... [as if] a piece of the external world now lives in the person but is not part of that person [and] becomes a continuing focus of stress acting from within...[that] now exists outside of time in an unstable state, and unless and until it is fully experienced, it will continue to exert its effect indefinitely.'"

"Jesus! How do you remember that kind of quote?"

"I don't know. Certain things just stick in my mind."

"You amaze me! You should have gone to med school."

"I wanted to, way back when."

"So, you think it's possible to recover function; that it's not organic brain damage?"

"I'm paraphrasing here, but Van der Kolk spoke to this. He said dissociation is a 'state of physical hyper arousal that is so intense that one's ability to reason and remember is radically decreased, and the brain simply cannot comprehend, or make sense of the experiences.' Cognitive shock, right? Then these memories get split off from conscious awareness and stored as fragments, or they are suppressed."

"Again, do you think this very deep and very ancient level of awareness is recoverable?"

"Only with a lot of deep personal work over a long period of time."

"Why?"

"I can only cite my own experience. I have always sought out my earliest memories because I believed they were the source of my dysfunction."

"And?"

"I have had some pretty solid success but only after more than a quarter of a century of therapy and personal growth work—plus, of course, lots of drugs!"

"But why don't traumatized people recover or even seek to recover?"

"There's a lot of discussion in the literature about 'addiction' to trauma, and replication of trauma in individuals who become so inured of trauma that they accept it as 'normal.' Some such people may even seed or recreate traumatic situations because it feels comfortable, what Bradshaw called 'the terrible familiar.'"

"That kind of sucks!"

"I addressed the whole topic in my Master's thesis: *Addiction and Dissociation as Autohypnotic Phenomena.*"

"What do you mean?"

"Autohypnotic dissociation might become entrenched, or generalize to situations related to the original traumas; and again, Van der Kolk, I believe, said it may become an 'established method of coping.'"

"OK. I can see that. Somebody gets used to dissociating, when that person is 'prestressed,' let's call it."

"Exactly! That's part of why I love you, man. Quick mind!"

"Thank you."

"And it may spread to all forms of defensive posturing or protection simply from use, or maybe as a weird kind of neuroplasticity."

"Wasn't it Lifton who talked about what he called the 'dissociative field?' A person becomes a kind of magnetic attractor for trauma that reinforces his or her already diminished capacity to feel. And, that undermines any effort somebody puts forth to seek a healthier adaptation, by invalidating or self-sabotaging their ability to mobilize inner power and make better decisions. I could even argue that it sounds a little like pre-frontal cortex injury."

All of these thoughts led Paul into a better, more compassionate understanding of Henry's obsessive, even maniacal, beliefs about aliens and the government. It was conceivable that Henry's contaminated field had been created and maintained by his massive isolation and the frequent violence of his father and created the immense shame he undoubtedly felt.

But what did any of it matter when Henry was still under suspicion of murder and effectively in custody?

CHAPTER SIXTY-TWO
Relentless and Methodical

San Francisco 0930, Tuesday, August 13th, 2002

Shirley Stephenson paced the length of what she called her gallery—a long, narrow hallway with windows that overlooked the Embarcadero with a view of Alcatraz and the Bay Bridge in the further distance—that led from her home office to the conference room. The walls opposite were lined with some of her favorite art works. One was an original poster from the Vorpal Gallery opening for MC Escher's first US exhibition in 1970, a long narrow print of his 1943 lithograph of *Reptiles*. Another was an original oil painting by George Durkee of a North Beach street scene she had purchased in 1985 from the artist himself on Columbus Avenue (near Vallejo) when he was painting it *en plein air*.

Tanya had just called and told Paul that she had been surveilling the elusive Ferdy and had managed to corner him again as he was just finishing one of his jobs cleaning a SOMA gay nightclub. Though it was open 24/7, he "cleaned up around the edges," as he called it, from 0300-0800 every day at Bootie, a club that featured hallmarks such as the Midnight Mashup Show (that often consisted of aerial act performers or drag queens), a regular show at 2300 that rotated throughout the month between the live mashup rock band Smash-Up Derby, a burlesque show called The Hubba Revue and a drag revue, The Monster Show.

463

When Ferdy came off shift, tired, dirty and exhausted, she was waiting. But using a combination of intimidation and bribery (news about Henry), convinced him to have a meal with her at The Grubstake on Pine Street, built from converted railroad cars. She gave him a ride on the back of her Harley to make sure he didn't get lost.

"He had a lot of questions about Henry and was very concerned because he hasn't heard from him in over two weeks."

"He doesn't know he's been hospitalized?"

"No. He only knows what he's read in the newspapers. Apparently, Henry was not out of the closet and had very few friends in the gay community. Ferdy is much better connected. Check this out. The last time he talked to him, Henry told him he was going to come out to his father. Told Ferdy that he wanted 'the Daddy he had never had.'"

"Oh Jesus! That seems consistent with what Henry told Paul."

"I'm hip. But I brought him here and told him we'd be willing to bring him up to speed about Henry, but he had to talk to the three of us—you, me, and Paul."

"Is he good with that?"

"Seems OK. I just fed him. I'm his 'buddy' now!"

"OK. Good for you."

"Where should we meet?"

"I'll call Paul and get him on board. Let's use my conference room."

"An hour?"

"Sounds good."

Paul was less than enthusiastic initially, having been awakened from a deep sleep during which he had been dreaming of Shirley, so he wasn't as grumbly as he might have been under other circumstances.

"Hey!"

"Hey yourself. I know it's really early for you, but Tanya cornered him, and bought him a meal and got him talking. It seems that he has lots of questions and concerns about Henry."

"Oh really?"

"Yes. Really."

"And? I presume this is related to your phone call?"

"Yes. They'll be at my home office in an hour. Wanna come?"

Paul laughed. "I could read that question several different ways!'

"No, dummy. I meant to the meeting!"

"Oh. That's too bad!"

"Paul!"

"OK. OK. I'll make some coffee and grab a shower! See you there!"

He was the last to arrive and found the rest of them gathered around an old walnut table Shirley had refinished herself that held pride of place in her home office.

He helped himself to a cup of Shirley's fresh brew (she and Paul bought the same blend at Graffeo's). She had also provided a fresh carrot cake from Just Deserts.

Ferdy looked worn out and was obviously in post-work mode, with smudges of dirt on both his right shoulder and left knee. His collar was damp with perspiration and the sleeves were rolled to the elbows. He looked up, his face mirroring both his weariness and his concern.

"Why are all of you here? Where's Henry?"

"We're his defense team, the only ones standing between him and Vacaville right now."

"What do you mean?"

Having signed a Release for Ferdy, Paul did not hesitate to share information.

"Henry's in the hospital; has been for two weeks."

"But why? Was he injured?"

"No, It's a psych unit."

"But why a psych unit?"

"You obviously don't know him very well."

"Not very well, I guess. We only met maybe two months ago. We've been having a lot of fun. Going to clubs, dancing."

"And you haven't seen him being, let's say, a bit odd?"

"'Odd?' In what way?"

"Did you know he had been hospitalized several times? For psychiatric reasons?"

"No! It can't be! He's a little strange sometimes. He used to laugh about what he called his 'rants' about the government and aliens and stuff. But I just thought it was part of his personality."

"And he never mentioned his previous psych history?"

"No! Never! I don't believe you!"

"Unfortunately, it's all true!"

"No!"

"I'm afraid so."

Hearing this, it seemed to register as real for the first time, and he started crying.

Through his trembling lips, he struggled to speak, even as tears continued to roll down his cheeks.

"Where is he? Can I see him?"

"He's on the Forensic Psychiatry Unit at SFGH. He's

loosely in police custody right now. The three of us, and of

course Tanya, have been working our collective asses off to keep him out of the clutches of the legal system."

"But why? Oh my God, why?"

"The police suspect he killed his father."

"What? No!"

"I'm afraid so."

"No! Oh Jesus!"

"Have you been lovers?"

Ferdinand looked nonplussed, then his face twisted into an angry grimace.

"Why does that have anything to do with you?"

"Henry is our client. Anything to do with him, especially concerning his current hospitalization and possible incarceration, concerns us."

Ferdinand looked crestfallen, tried to manage a smile through his dwindling tears, and asked, "Do I have confidentiality?"

"It would be a conflict of interest since we represent Henry."

"Oh. OK."

"So?"

"Yes."

"And?"

"And what?"

"Being intimate with Henry, did you ever experience anything unusual with him?"

"Sexually?"

"No! I meant emotionally. Did he ever act particularly strange in your presence?"

"I told you about his 'rants!'"

"Yes. I mean other than that?"

"No. Well, once in a while, he would get a little spacey looking...after we smoked weed."

"You smoked weed with Henry?"

"Once or twice."

"And did he get manifestly stranger after that?"

"No. I just thought he was stoned."

"Did he ever tell you he was hearing voices?"

"No! Never! He wasn't like that!"

"He has a long psych history."

"I don't care! Henry's a sweet man!"

"Did you know his father was beating him?"

"He...he told me. It started when he was a kid."

"Did he tell you about anything recent?"

There was a long silence during which Ferdy's face twisted before he turned back into a semblance of himself and he answered.

"He told me his father had been getting more and more angry with him, but he didn't tell me he'd been hitting him recently."

"Do you have any idea who might have killed Henry's father?"

"No. I don't. I really don't."

"Where were you the night he was murdered?"

"I don't know. What night was that?"

"Two weeks ago, yesterday."

"What time?"

"Somewhere between 10 PM and 2 AM."

"Most likely sleeping. I almost always sleep until 0200 and then go to work."

"Are you quite sure?"

"Yes! Absolutely"

"I go to work at 0300."

"Every day?"

"Yes. Every day."

"Did you kill Henry's father?"

"No! Of course not!"

"You were deeply involved with Henry. It would make a kind of logical sense."

"What? Are you crazy?"

"No, sir, and we are quite serious."

"This... This is crazy! Why are you persecuting me?"

"'Persecuting' you? Wait until the police find out about you!"

"Why the police? I haven't done anything! Besides, I've already talked to them!"

"Shirley is required to turn over any relevant information we uncover."

"But I didn't do anything!"

"Still required. It's the law!"

Now he stated crying again, in even greater earnest.

CHAPTER SIXTY-THREE
That Fateful Night

San Francisco 0125, July 13th, 2002

Ferdy had followed Henry when he left his room at the SRO. They had had the best lovemaking session ever, even though this was only the fifth time they had gotten together, always in his small, shoddy but neatly kept room. He had asked Henry several times if he could come home with him, but Henry had adamantly refused.

"I can't take you there. My father spies on me! Even when he's gone, the house staff tells him everything that goes on! I never have any fucking privacy!"

Ferdy thought that his new lover must surely be exaggerating and resolved to look more deeply into what he was hiding. It wasn't all that important really, but his curiosity was piqued. When Henry left this time, ostensibly to make his way home—Ferdy had no idea exactly how, cab or bus—and was totally surprised to see him walk two blocks down Eddy Street, turn the corner on Geary and get into the back seat of a limousine! He'd had some suspicions that Henry might come from money—he always had clean, high-quality clothing and paid for all their meals and entertainment with cash. Since he was on his 360 cc Honda, he decided to simply follow him discretely.

Staying two to three vehicles back and following the long white stretch limo was easy. Through the Tenderloin traffic and out to Geary Street and past Cathedral Hill they kept going. He stayed in close proximity. Passing St. Mary's, Ferdy thought that perhaps they were headed for the Richmond District. They passed Arguello Boulevard and kept going, finally turning on Park Presidio and following it through Golden Gate Park where it became 19th Avenue/Highway 1. He began to think Sunset district but feared, too, that they might be heading out of The City. He had a moment of panic, because he only had half a tank of gas. They passed through the Parkside District and kept going. Approaching Sloat Boulevard, he thought perhaps they were headed to Lake Merced. As they approached Stern Grove, the limousine slowed and moved into the left turn lane onto St. Francis Boulevard. Holy shit! This is a really nice neighborhood!

When they came to a gorgeous fountain, they made a right onto Monterrey Boulevard and a left onto San Jacinto and pulled into the courtyard of an enormous French style villa. It was absolutely gorgeous!

He watched, goggle-eyed as Henry, his Henry, emerged from the back seat and entered the house. Holy shit!

He surreptitiously hid his bike in a thick shrub hedge that grew alongside the property, and, after checking the eaves for security cameras, scooted around the side of the massive building to the rear entrances. One was an old oak door, heavily banded with iron and seemed to lead downstairs. The other was a solid-looking door set in a steel frame with two sturdy deadbolt locks that were securely closed. He hid himself between the outside wall and another hedge that branched off the one that separated the property from the one next door. He was simultaneously excited and frightened as he snuggled down to listen.

He did not have a clue what he was doing or was going to do next. He just knew he needed to know more. His intuition was insisting.

Then the shouting started.

"JUNIOR!! WHERE THE FUCK ARE YOU, JUNIOR?"

Henry Senior had always felt driven to dominate the little retard ruthlessly! He was so fucking weak! He could barely stand to fucking speak to him! All that mewling and shame crap! It was fucking sickening! The worthless little fucker! The more he thought about it, the more it inflamed him! He shouted again and again as he roamed the bottom floor. And then he decided to mount the stairs to the second floor.

"JUNIOR!! YOU GET HERE RIGHT NOW, YOU WORTHLESS FUCK!!"

Henry was completely immersed in a video game, headphones on, blocking out any noise, especially his Father's intrusions. He relished the tiny glimmerings of strength he felt in Paul's office. Paul. The first person who actually listened, who tried to protect him from Father. And Father hadn't killed him yet! He must be important to the High Command!

As he reached the top of the spiral staircase, Senior bellowed again.

"I WANT TO TALK TO YOU, YOU USELESS FUCKING RETARD!"

Henry had had a glimpse of a possible future, but he knew in his heart of hearts that he hadn't yet won a place in that land of wonder where he was truly strong, magnificent in his glory, redeemed for all time—where he lived released from the curses and demons that had shackled him, contaminated him, since he could remember. But for the moment it was so excellent simply to feel alive!

He felt (more than actually heard) the door frame shudder as Father broke through the lock plate of his sealed door and bulled in like a battleship through rough and rugged seas.

"I'VE BEEN CALLING YOU!"

Henry looked up startled, goggle-eyed, aphasic, stricken.

"WHAT ARE YOU FUCKING DOING IN THERE? THOSE FUCKING GAMES AGAIN?"

Following this last outburst, the older man strode across the room, pulling his belt loose from around his waist as he approached Henry.

But instead of passively lying there, allowing himself to be beaten until Father wore out his rage, Henry shot into the air as if struck by a million volts. He pivoted, advancing upon the stunned older man who stopped in mid-stride as Henry fronted him, nose-to-nose.

"Father," Henry said in a very calm tone that belied the ten thousand demons who were screaming inside of him, vying to get free.

The older man had been struck silent and could only stare mutely.

"I've waited my whole life to ask, Why? Why did you never love me?"

A complex mélange of thoughts and feeling surged through Senior's mind, infused by a deep rage that threatened to erupt.

"You've never loved me! I'm going to go to court and get free of you!"

The older man started to defrost a little, listening to the childish prattle. He slowly lowered his hands, head filled with fog, completely uncomprehending what was transpiring in front of him as if on a cinema screen.

Misunderstanding his father's actions and emboldened by the lack of resistance, Henry continued.

"I'm gay! And I've met a man I love!"

This last revelation galvanized the older man's ire like throwing a magnesium flare into a bucket of water. It released him from his frozen trance.

"I WILL TELL YOU WHAT YOU'RE GOING TO DO!"

Having said this, he struck Henry several times in a row before the younger man turned to run for the doorway.

Senior tripped him, and alternately whipped him and kicked him both fore and aft.

Somehow Henry got to his feet, violently shoved his father back, and started down the staircase with his erstwhile parent in quick pursuit. As they reached the top step, Senior kicked Henry in the back. He tumbled several times before landing on his back with a gasp, winded but awake. The older man followed, staggering down the stairs holding tightly onto the mahogany rail.

Henry was still retrieving his breath as his father attempted to stomp on him, but he twisted away, pushed to his feet, slipping slightly and then got to his feet and staggered away. His father, far more intoxicated from the delicious brandy than he had thought, managed only to lurch weakly after him. Henry headed quickly toward the rear of the house, his breath coming in short pants. He thought of several hiding places he had used previously to avoid the further reaches of his father's wrath. First a hall closet with a hidden panel (but he was sure his father was aware of it), then instead elected to follow the floor plan around, backtracked his father's path and scurried back up the staircase as Father screamed with increasing frustration.

"YOU GODDAMN BASTARD! WHERE ARE YOU?!"

The older man made a considerable commotion as he thrashed and crashed his way around the perimeter of the bottom floor, trashing vases and pulling down paintings and wall hangings. Then, following a sudden inspiration, he started back up the staircase.

"GODDAMN FUCKER! WHERE ARE YOU?"

Henry heard more smashing of picture glass, china figurines and other fragile pieces, doors thrown open and even more screaming. He had secreted himself in an old dumbwaiter in the servants' wing, one of the last places he thought Father would deign to look. Several more doors smashed open, accompanied by basso profundo shouting and yet more stomping across the floor as Henry took advantage of the tumult to lower the dumbwaiter down to the basement, hand over hand on the hemp rope.

The ensuing silence was cliché quiet, a deafeningly profound hush.

The shattered, scattered fragments of his mind swirled in a kaleidoscopic whirlwind as Henry did a round of the breathing exercise that Paul had taught him, then another, attempting to gather some kind of internal order to combat the terrible chaos that was enveloping him.

Ferdy heard the incredible din resonating through the house, the screaming and shouting, Henry crying out in agony. He surreptitiously let himself into the lower level of the mansion using a set of lock picks his uncle had given him. Listening to the scurrying trail of Henry's feet across the floor above approaching the basement, he felt a surge of the purest rage he had ever felt. He stopped briefly at a pegboard wall, looked up at the collection of gardening tools racked there, outlined in marking pen, and secured a machete from its place.

He kept expecting that he might hear Henry's voice when the door above the stairs swung open, but the silence of the building was deafening. He hid himself in a small alcove as he caught sight of Henry crawling into what appeared to be a disused dumbwaiter. Henry did not see him, had no idea that he was there, though Ferdy smiled at the sight of him and shook again with rage at the sight of his obvious injuries. Again, and again his body shook with rage as he crept quietly toward the staircase. He stepped gently onto it and made his way up, acutely aware of the lack of sounds in the house.

Having grown up in a rather plain tract house in Kansas, Ferdy was unprepared for the vast sweeping ceilings and the grand furnishings of the mansion. After granting himself a few moments to stare in awe, he continued purposefully. He felt like an erstwhile Crusader on a misbegotten mission.

Further and further he crept into what he had started calling the "Cave of Darkness," for surely anyone who could inflict the kinds of shameless damage that Henry's father had, had to be a very dark figure indeed, perhaps, he convinced himself, even Satanic.

Along finely woven runner carpets, past expensive, assuredly authentic, antique furniture and a vast plethora of china and plaster and porcelain art figures; gliding past walls that had been carefully hung with art masterpieces created by artists he did not recognize, he moved silently forward, room after room filled with marvels it would take him a lifetime to catalogue.

Having started his search on one side and in the back of the enormous space, following on a side hallway, he continued his route all the way around to the other side, seeking his prey. He had decided to punish dear Henry's perpetrator, the man who had harmed his man; punish him, warn him to never contemplate such actions ever again.

He entered a room that was decorated in a hyper-masculine manner—unread, matched leather-bound books, stuffed animal heads, leather furniture—that was obviously Henry's father's study. And just like that, he came face-to-face with the older man who fronted him as if he were but a scruffy intruder, perhaps even a burglar. Then, his forehead rose when he realized that Ferdy must be one of Henry's vagrant friends that he had picked up on a jaunt to the nether regions of The City, his city, where he ruled and held sway by the might of his personality.

"Who in the fuck are you? And what are you doing here?"

Snarling, he set down his snifter of Armagnac, intending to beat the intruder severely with the same belt he had used on Henry.

He never got a chance.

CHAPTER SIXTY-FOUR
That Fateful Night   Part II

San Francisco 0212, July 13ᵗʰ, 2002

The shattered, scattered fragments of his mind were spinning in a kaleidoscopic whirlwind as Henry settled into a round of breathing, attempting to create an internal order to buttress the terrible chaos that was enveloping him.

Just as he was assembling a sense of serenity, (perhaps just a less disturbed façade rippling across the pond of his world), the most horrifying, gut-wrenching shriek sliced through the air like a Damascus steel scimitar—a single, piercing, elongated screech that ended as abruptly as it began, leaving an even deeper lingering pool of quietude that was more alike to emptiness or a vacuum.

Henry's brain swam with multitudinous images, fractal pictures, swirls of psychedelic color accompanied by lurid smears of light, fractured rainbows splashing, intense chiaroscuro, all reflecting violent shades that only exist between thoughts, and illuminate the vast plethora of energies of the Universe not revealed unless or until an individual has experienced the uttermost boundaryless boundary, and momentarily dissolved into the Cosmic Wholeness of the Whole—and returned, in form or the formless, reinvigorated and exhilarated, alive and aware of being alive in every cell, blood thundering through veins and arteries, infusing and imbuing all that might have been previously lost, dissociated, or abandoned.

He was alive within this vastness. He was an empty aloneness, with no other sound or vibration.

After a timeless time during which he simply floated, he drifted as if in a transparent dream medium cast in a consistency akin to semi-hardened agar. He floated and swam effortlessly, trance-like, following a sonorous song like that of the humpbacked whales.

Ferdy had so convinced himself that his rage had passed—and that he would be able to have a simple conversation with the older man—that he was well and truly surprised when he saw the older man snarl, his whole face creasing with disgust. He immediately intuited exactly what he was intending. As a massive tsunami of wrath and volcanic lava blasted through the top of his head, pushing aside all remnants of reason, he rushed the sneering, imperious older man, whose façade of superiority melted into sheer and abject terror.

Blinded by the red sheen of the flashback of all of the hatred he had experienced—the bigotry and beatings, taunts and curses, the deprecations of so many small-minded individuals, the pastors and ministers, his own father and uncles, all aimed at "beating the Devil out of him," forcing him to recant his "evil ways" and the desire for sex and the companionship of men that he had had since he was four— exploded out of him with a silent shriek and he slashed the old man with all of the gathered force in his body, slit him open from the clavicle to the testicles as some of the pressurized blood splashed on him, sloshed over him as if with a wide, thick paint brush.

The old man screamed once, the most horrifying, gut-wrenching shriek Ferdy had ever heard, far worse than the many animals he had sacrificed for the table. It sliced through the air like a Damascus steel scimitar, a piercing, elongated expurgation that ended as abruptly as it began, leaving him behind in an even deeper silence that was more alike to a vacuum. He collapsed to the floor and lay immobile.

At the urging of an inner prompting, Henry rose from the cramped enclosure in which he had confined himself for several small eternities, then stretched and popped most of his major muscles, tendons, and ligaments (and a couple of vertebrae too). He assessed the damage his father had done, made a quick comparison against other earlier similar incidents, and found, on the whole, that he had suffered far worse previously through the years. He straightened his clothing as best he could, though there was no repairing the left sleeve of his shirt, which had torn loose at the shoulder or the huge gap that had opened in his right pant leg. Getting shakily to his feet, he made his way painstakingly to the staircase, where he firmly grasped the bannister and slowly made his way up.

He seemed to become increasingly oriented as he ascended, such that by the time he got to the ground floor, he felt that his more-or-less functional body had been patched back together with duct tape. He sniffed the air like a hunting dog pinpointing a strange spoor, ineluctably drawn toward and simultaneously repulsed by an impulse to return to the library, as if he were avoiding a scent he couldn't yet smell—as if his olfactory organs had temporarily been shut down, perhaps secondary to a broken nose, though he was breathing miraculously well, rhythmically and deeply.

Ears wide open, sensitive to the most miniscule sound that might vibrate his tympanic membranes, he crept cautiously down the richly appointed hallway around the back of the house, never even the "palace," as Father referred to it.

The ominous silence deepened the further he traveled, all senses on the alert for a possible ambush. It wouldn't have been the first time Father had sprung from a room or crevice to initiate or continue an assault, screaming insults or imprecations against him, calling the "survival training games" designed to "toughen him up." It was always for "his own good." (Henry ate the large piles of emotional shit as if it were his birthright. It would be many years before he discovered what Freud had called "a sadistic superego" that drove Henry relentlessly to believe that he deserved the incredible violence of Father).

As he got to the doorway to the library, Henry had almost convinced himself he was alone, Father having fled to New York or San Tropez. As he turned the corner and took a tentative step, he stopped, stunned, frozen to his roots, branded on his feet.

Father lay unmoving, an impossible amount of his lifeblood having leaked out and saturated the dense layers of a finely wrought rug. Completely unable to move, he was frozen from the infusion of adrenaline, noradrenaline, glucocorticoids, gamma-aminobutyric acid (GABA), dopamine, and serotonin, as his sympathetic and parasympathetic nervous systems fired simultaneously. He felt as if he had been transported to an abattoir scene painted by Rembrandt or Breughel the Elder.

The old man lay on his back, right arm bent acutely under him at the elbow. He looked like a glassine page from an anatomy textbook neatly opened from collarbone to crotch. The wound was still seeping, though some of the blood was darkening and congealing like viscous polka dots, and the wall behind his body was splattered in a perfect outline where he had been standing when he was attacked.

Henry staggered over to the condign figure, knees melting as he approached, as if in slow motion, and sank to the floor. He gingerly touched Father's face and then lifted his head into his lap, a keening moan escaping his lips.

Ferdy observed his lover, watched as his face and body shifted through a variety of small movements before collapsing into a waxy mask. Then he made a silent retreat down the staircase and out the back door, pushing the door bar with his elbow. He swiftly retreated, then secured a windbreaker from the saddlebag on one side of his bike and placed the bloody machete in the other. He rolled down the hill, and popped the clutch at the bottom to start the engine as he stealthily fled the scene.

"NOOOOOOOOOOOOOOOOOOOOOOOOOOOOOOO!"

The lifetime gathering of immense losses that he had carried buried within his breast flooded through him out from under uncountable layers of leaden dross, depression and delusion that had shielded the radioactive core of his suppressed emotions, that all now exploded magma-like from the molten ocean of his consciousness.

"NOOOOOOOOOOOOOOOOOOOOOOOOOOOOOOOOO!"

Another long ululating moan escaped his unyielding lips. All of the rage, fear, pain, shame, exhilaration, horror, disgust, joy, sorrow, misery, exultation, trust, anger, hatred, envy, indignation, surprise, suffering, enmity, benevolence and contempt he had ever carried exploded out of him, as he repeatedly beat the condign form of his father with his tightened fists, gallons of copious tears falling untethered that changed to chest-wracking sobs as his body dissolved into a rubbery dissipation. He then bent over the fallen form cradling the now-battered face he had so longed to touch in his arms and embraced the eviscerated remains—saturating his arms, face, and clothing with the blood and fluids from the gaping wound that divided his father's body.

Henry was struck again by the immense loss he would never be able to release. All that he had carried, buried, under uncountable layers of leaden dross that had shielded him from the hidden radioactivity, his suppressed emotions simmering now burst forth magma-like from the molten ocean of his consciousness, in a long keening, ululating moan that embodied all of the encapsulated rage, fear, pain, shame, exhilaration, horror, disgust, joy, sorrow, misery, exultation, trust, anger, hatred, envy, indignation, surprise, suffering, enmity, benevolence and contempt.

"NOOOOOOOOOOOOOOOOOOOOOOOOOOOOOOOO!"

Chest-wracking sobs cracked his body, his faithful servant that had turned to rubber as he bent over the fallen form and buried his face in the neck that he had so longed to touch. At long last, he now embraced the eviscerated remains, immediately saturating his arms, face, and clothing with Father's lifeblood.

Terrible moans kept echoing out of him, broken only by the jangling of the telephone and pounding on the doors. The phone rang and rang and rang and then an intrusive voice on a bullhorn started calling his name like a droning mantra.

When he could no longer stand the intrusion, he screamed into the phone without preamble and yelled, *"Paul Marzeky! Get me Paul Marzeky! NOW!"*

CHAPTER SIXTY-FIVE
An Epilogue for Henry

San Francisco 1230, September 8th, 2002

It seemed the best for all involved (even Henry agreed) that he remain on 7-B temporarily, albeit without the handcuffs and 15-minute checks around the clock. Everyone involved, including his law firm acting as temporary conservator, agreed that it was the best idea to get him transferred to an upscale "psychological health recovery unit" as soon as possible, while he worked his way through the legal system to free himself of the restraints of being conserved. He was very expressive about his desire to be released and "live his own life." To this end, the temporary conservators wanted something close by, and found two possibilities: one in Los Altos Hills off San Antonio Road, the other in Mill Valley on Summit Road. The latter was a seven-bed residential treatment facility run by a psychiatrist and his wife, a psych nurse, who were friends of Tommy's, called Mount Tamalpias Treatment and Recovery Center. At $500 a day, it was only half as expensive as what the California Pacific Medical Center Psych Unit charged daily.

In the interim, Henry had continued improving. Paul was privately grateful, even though he was taking a low dose of Haldol twice a day.

Having been granted "grounds privileges," Henry, decked out in hospital pajamas and robe, asked Paul if they could have a session outside. Paul warned him about confidentiality and the possibility of his getting too stimulated and distracted to manage it comfortably. Henry agreed, and relented to having a session indoors, but only after a refreshing walk around the grounds of the hospital in the Potrero District. He hinted too that he would love some Greek food—"it's just a few blocks away, nobody will know"—but Paul demurred, citing that he would know.

When they returned, Paul was directed to an unused conference room where he was assured that they would not be interrupted. Henry seemed far more upbeat, far less preoccupied too, and no mention of aliens, not even once. Paul decided to take it upon himself to broach the topic of his father's demise. The net result was an extremely powerful session, a summary session, the last he would have with Henry, and one of the most meaningful.

"So, Henry, it's been quite a journey."

"Yes Paul, it certainly has."

"I'm very glad that you're going to get the chance to get off the conservatorship."

"Now that Father is dead, there is no reason ...there's nothing keeping me from being freed...from Father."

"Why do you think he hated you so much?"

"I don't know. I always thought...he always said I was inept, useless, stupid."

"He never gave you credit for anything, did he?"

"No. I never had a chance. The only one who ever really listened to me was Ferdy. I mean, other than you!"

"I believe you."

"Where is he? I want to see him. Nobody will tell me anything."

"I imagine no one wants to upset you."

"'Upset me?'"

"Henry, I don't know exactly how to tell you this, but Ferdy's in jail."

"'In jail?'"

"Henry, Ferdy...was...the one who...killed your father."

"No! Not 'Ferdy'! He's the sweetest man I have ever known!"

"I'd never lie to you, Henry!"

"NO! NO! NO! NO!" he screamed as he pounded the table with his fists.

Paul sat quietly as Henry poured out his denials.

"No! It can't be! I refuse to believe it!"

Paul sat silently, waiting.

"NO! NO! NO!"

It was only then that Henry allowed himself to feel the import of what he had been told, and started crying—a few tears at first, then chest heaving, deep sobs followed by chest-wracking, heaving waves of massive sorrow and shame denied validation. And now, to have the only person he ever really loved taken away from him forever! Forever! It was all just too much! He couldn't take any more!

"I want to die! I just want to die!"

"You're just starting to get to have your own life now, Henry!"

"I don't care! I don't care!"

"You may not now, Henry, but you will."

"No! I love him!"

"I know, Henry. I know."

"I want to get him out of jail!"

"You can't, Henry."

"Why not? I've got money!"

"No, you don't, Henry. Not yet."

"But it's mine!"

"Not until the courts release it."

"I've got to do something! Can I see him?"

"They won't allow that either, I'm afraid."

"But Paul I ..." was as far as he got before he started sobbing again.

"Why, Paul? Why?"

"Henry, I do not have all of the details yet. But it seems that Ferdy followed you home after you met with him on the day of your father's' murder."

"What? Why?"

"He was attracted to you. Curious about you."

"Oh my God!"

"He was outside the house when he heard your father beating you."

"No!"

"I'm afraid so. He snuck in the basement door."

"Oh my God!"

"He confessed."

"But why?

"Seems that he thought you needed a champion."

"But why kill him?"

"Apparently, he wasn't planning to kill him. He wanted to talk to him. But your father started to come after him, like he was going to start beating him too!"

"Oh my God! I didn't know!"

"I know, Henry. I believe you."

"I wouldn't have wanted him to do that!"

"What's even more important, Henry, is that the police believe you."

"Finally! Bloody finally!"

"I know this has been a real ordeal for you."

It seemed as if the validation from Paul gave Henry permission to have a second round of deep emotional expurgation. He slumped over, then fell to the floor sobbing, and repeating Ferdy's name over and over like an arcane mantra, as if the repetition could somehow revive the past and erase the terrible consequences that had ensued thereto.

Paul sat, breathing deeply into his belly, and extended his hands, palms out toward Henry. He allowed all of the compassion he was feeling to flow to him, feeling that there was no other way possible for him to extend any comfort to the man in the moment.

Paul feared to speak at that point. Serious tears wanted to breech his own most staunch defenses, as he was acutely feeling so related with Henry personally, and anticipating the loss of their therapeutic relationship as well.

Paul felt the depth of Henry's sorrow, felt it arise and slam into his own solar plexus with a palpable force. He had known such losses and the sense of an empty future. He had also experienced the intricate, intimate process of unwinding his ancient sorrow, especially when compounded of years of longing and desire thwarted him like a pristine golden apple hanging beyond his fingertips. He decided he would share this with Henry.

As Henry continued his heartfelt release, Paul could not help but reflect on the twisted path that had led him to the current moment. If only Henry had been able to notify someone, anyone of the horrors he had experienced, or had had someone who would have really listened and acted in his favor. This was the very crux of the matter. Given the money and power Henry's father had controlled, there had been, and indeed even now seemed, very little he could have done. No one would have believed him. His claims would have been dismissed out of hand, especially given Henry's status as a "mentally ill person," and even more, as the subject of a conservatorship with his father in the driver's seat.

It seemed quite typical of contemporary society. Children were, for the most part, commodities. An abusive society routinely allowed for the abuse of children as yet another profit-making scheme in the great wheel of consumption. The blood rites of the Catholic Church, and its countenancing sexual abuse by the clergy was yet another outrage. It allowed the initiation of generation after generation of children into the abusive rituals and diminished possibilities that ensured that assured reduced consciousness, and hence, profit on every level to continue unabated. The drama of the world-at-large needed slave citizens to continue unbroken, guaranteeing that no one would ever look too deeply into their own personal matrices and uncover the awful shame therein.

Though the rise of the World Corporate State dated to approximately four hundred years ago, there had always been brutal, tyrannical regimes through most of what was called "recorded history," recidivisticly rewritten by the victors, which quote has been variously attributed to Winston Churchill, Joseph Goebbels, and George Orwell.

"Paul, whatever am I going to do?" asked Henry, which shook him out of his reverie.

Paul took one last deep breath before he spoke.

"I don't think there's anything I can say that might be of comfort to you right now. All I can tell you is that I have suffered great loss in my life, too, loss that took me years in more than one case to recover. But I did recover. And I have gone on, often never believing that there could be anything in my future that could compensate for what I lost."

Henry was sitting up now, watching him closely.

"I'm not trying to be your cheerleader right now. You know me better than that. I'm sharing this very personal information with you for a very good reason. I want to give you something to hold onto through the next years of your life unfolding, something to remember when you hit rough patches, as you undoubtedly will."

"You sound like you're terminating our therapy."

"Oh, hell no, Henry! But things are about to shift in your life. And I wanted to give you a little gift, something from me to you."

"What's that mean?" Henry asked, immediately suspicious.

"Very shortly you're going to be discharged from here—after all, you are now a free man—but the lawyers want you to stay close by so they can see you when they need to. There's a lot of paperwork to get sorted out. In the meantime, you're going to need really strong support."

"What does that mean?"

"You're going to be living in a very small, very exclusive facility in Mill Valley."

"No! I want to go home!"

"Henry, that's just not possible. Your father's home is being held in trust for you, of course. But your treatment has been very expensive to this point, what with all of the extra staff and the overtime, and it will likely need to be sold. And it will continue to be expensive, perhaps for years, until this whole thing is sorted out."

"I just want to get free of all of this bullshit!"

"You will be. But it won't be until everything is sorted out and you can get your day in court. In the meantime, you're going to need some supervision. You've got to admit that you can't manage very well right now on your own."

"I don't...I can't...Goddamn it, Paul, I fucking need you!"

"Clinically, I have to agree with Tommy. We both feel you need a situation in which you can continue to heal, to thrive while you do. You've had a very abusive life, Henry. It's going to take a lot more work to clean it all up."

"Paul, you saved my life. You can't just walk away!"

"I'm not walking away from you, Henry. I am still committed to helping you sort out your life. It's just that you will be in residential treatment with a new primary therapist. I will still see you for sessions twice a week, same days, same times. And I will be consulting with your new therapist. I know him. We went to graduate school together. His name is George Gnossospopolous. I will, actually, be supervising him as well, building up his hours for Ph.D. licensure. So, you will be seeing lots of me. And you have all of my numbers. You can call me any time."

"He sounds Greek."

"Yes, he is. I'm quite sure you can ask him about getting a pass to get some Greek food together sometime."

"You said 'Mill Valley.' That's only ten miles away."

"True. You'll have the opportunity to see a bit of the town, too. It's really lovely."

"Thanks, I guess. Are you sure you're gonna come see me?"

"Four afternoons a week. We'll work out a schedule."

Henry hesitated; face scrunched up in concentration and then spoke.

"Do we still have confidentiality? I have something to tell you, but I don't want anybody else to know yet."

"OK. Sure. Please tell me."

"You know how you and the police and everybody else kept saying that I was 'hiding' something."

"Yes."

"And I kept saying I wasn't."

"Yes."

"I remembered..."

"What, Henry?"

"When I was sitting there, holding my father's head..."

"Yes."

"I remembered what everybody thought I was hiding."

"OK."

"I remembered Father...he killed my mother. I saw him push her down the stairs!"

———————

As he was leaving the hospital, Paul rang Regina and told her there was some new material he wanted to share with her in person. They decided to meet at another restaurant that had become a favorite of theirs. He really wanted to have breakfast again. They arrived almost simultaneously, she on foot, at "Dish," on the corner of Haight and Masonic. After relating to her that it was called the "Family Pharmacy" in the late '60's, they had a long meandering chat about the weather (always a topic in San Francisco), the 49ers upcoming season, and new possibilities for them. The he told her about Henry's revelation. Of course, she understood they still had confidentiality, and congratulated him on the successful outcome.

"So, are we still officially in a confidentiality agreement with Henry?"

"If you wish to continue to be. Lord knows I need consultation!"

"Do you think that would prevent us...I mean I really like your company. I'd like to explore going beyond the professional."

"I've been feeling that too. I would really like to see if we can be more."

"I guess that means now we can have a real dinner date."

Paul immediately reflected on the beauty of something Jung had long held: There are gilded edges to every shadow.

www.ingramcontent.com/pod-product-compliance
Lightning Source LLC
Chambersburg PA
CBHW030539020726
47494CB00005B/1431